THE NEMESIS EQUATION

KENNETH TAM

FOX MAGNUS

FIRST SPACE LORD, EARTHER NAVY

THE NEMESIS EQUATION

THE SEVENTH EQUATIONS NOVEL

KENNETH TAM

Published in Canada by Iceberg Publishing, Waterloo

Library and Archives Canada Cataloguing in Publication
Tam, Kenneth, 1984-
The nemesis equation : the seventh equations novel / Kenneth Tam.
ISBN 978-0-9865017-7-7
I. Title.
PS8589.A7676N44 2010 C813'.6 C2010-900089-7

Iceberg Publishing
55 Northfield Drive East, Suite 171
Waterloo ON N2K 3T6
contact@icebergpublishing.com
www.icebergpublishing.com

First pocket paperback printing: July 2008
Special international edition: January 2010

Cover Artwork: Wesley Prewer
Cover Design: Kenneth Tam

For Jacqui, my mother.

Thanks for figuring
out the solution!

LAROSIAN GALAXY MAP
NOT TO SCALE · VIEW FROM 'ABOVE'
LAROS
(UNDER DEFENSIVE BLOCKADE)
FALLEN LAROSIAN EMPIRE
(INFECTED WITH OMEGA TYPE 1)
DERELICT
LAROSIAN
FLEET
HYPERSPACE
CORRIDOR
TO KROGG 'A'
CARNARVON
HYPERSPACE CORRIDOR
TO NEW HALIFAX
DESTROYED HYPERSPACE
CORRIDOR TO GENESIS

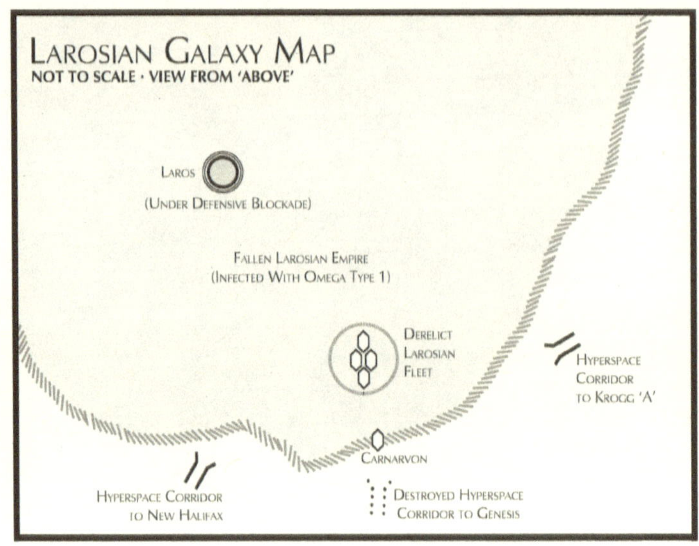

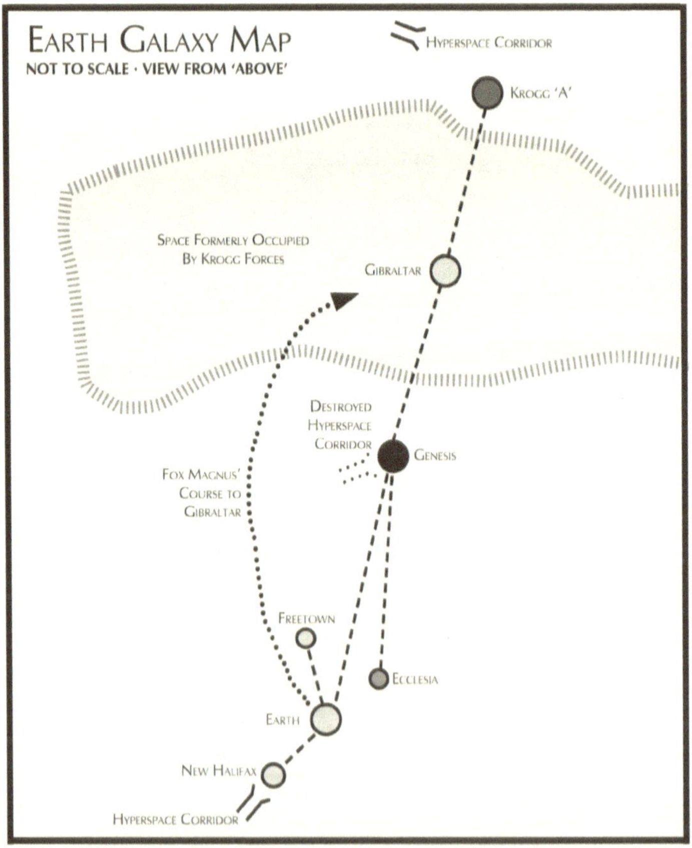

EARTH GALAXY MAP
NOT TO SCALE · VIEW FROM 'ABOVE'
HYPERSPACE CORRIDOR
KROGG 'A'
SPACE FORMERLY OCCUPIED
BY KROGG FORCES
GIBRALTAR
DESTROYED
HYPERSPACE
CORRIDOR
GENESIS
FOX MAGNUS'
COURSE TO
GIBRALTAR
FREETOWN
ECCLESIA
EARTH
NEW HALIFAX
HYPERSPACE CORRIDOR

FOREWORD

So the rules of the game have changed.

This was, I must say, to be expected. It's often said that militaries prepare for the war they fought last time, and if your new enemy happened to have front row seats for that war, and has the ability to adapt, then you can expect him to school you when he gets you into action.

Ironically, the same thing the Earthers did to the Kroggs, Omega is now doing to the Earthers. Nothing Lab Forepaw or any of their elite officers throws at the plague is a surprise to him. He knows what they think, how they fight, and how their instinct works.

He calls himself their God, and for all intents and purposes, he does seem awfully omnipotent.

So this is the real test, I suppose. A young and idealistic race, with a philosophy forged in the midst of a victorious war, is now facing defeat for the first time. How will the Earthers bounce back... and will Omega let them bounce back? What about humanity, now down to precious few specimens because of the destruction of the refugee fleet just short of Earth?

There doesn't seem to be a lot of hope.

I imagine it's quite clear by now that the plague has a sadistic streak that really does make the Marquis de Sade seem pale. He's toying with his prey in a cruel fashion, because he knows there's nothing the Earthers can do to stop him. The Larosians are struggling to get themselves back into the fight, to help their old allies, but what can a burnt-out and plague-infested Empire really do at a time like this? Omega has all the momentum, and all the cards.

And then there are the Kroggs, who have plans all their own. The Earthers refused to let the Larosians destroy that old enemy because Setter Caine and his fellows believed such an action would be wrong — that murdering a race out of fear of future fighting was simply unacceptable. Setter wouldn't return to Elandra and Phealan as a murderer... but now how much will that righteousness cost his people, and the humans?

So a past decision based on what seemed to be very clear principles is now looking like a rather poor choice. The Earthers are running out of friends, and they have nowhere to hide. The only question remaining seems to be whether their scientists can come up with a solution to the problem.

But Omega threw a wrench into that process too, didn't he? Elandra Caine and all her research, gone in a flash — along with Admiralty House and millions of Earthers. Will Celia Lazarus and her captured Omega specimen be able to cope with the problem, and find a cure?

The light is dimming for the Earthers. Their ideals are being ground down under the weight of Omega's terror, and as things turn for the worse, it seems inevitable that their vaunted confidence and innocent idealism are going to collapse. What does the plague have in store for them in the pages to come?

Nothing good, I can assure you.

But before we move on to that, you know the drill: time to renew thanks, to those who've helped get the series to this crucial penultimate point.

After two books in the background, both the Kroggs and the Larosians are beginning to re-emerge in *The Nemesis Equation*. Cody Herauf's input into this process was very useful, and his discussions about how the Kroggs would come back to the forefront — their anger and their abilities — was absolutely indispensable to the plotting of this book. The old nemesis is thus returning, but on the flip side, the venerable Larosians are coming back into the fold as well. Cody must be thanked for his contribution to both of these developments, and for the essential part his two races continue to play in this series.

Ami (Cairn) Dune watched the Genesis refugee fleet burn at the end of *The Vengeance Equation*, and now she and a number of other veterans from the 141st Flying Squadron will be taking part in the next battles against the plague fleet. All of these characters owe their existence to my good friend Wes Prewer, who led them through Krogg War adventures in *Retaliation*.

As ever, the image you see on the cover of this book is also a product of Wes' skill and determination. I say it every time: we owe a lot to Wes for his continued dedication to these books. His attention to detail, his patience, and his understanding of the Earther mindset are exceptional, and I've benefited greatly from his continued enthusiasm. Many thanks to him, once again.

I think after the events of *The Vengeance Equation*, you'll have a good idea of what I meant when I praised my fine friend Peter Caron for his strategic brilliance. Omega had to break down the Earther way of war, as demonstrated in the Krogg War, and develop a strategy that would defy the very best in officers in the new navy. Lab Forepaw at their head, the Earthers made the best decisions they could... and then were blindsided. This blindsiding was, I fear, beyond me alone — I don't think I could have unravelled Earther defenses nearly so well as Peter did.

And, I should say, there's more to come. Peter doesn't possess any excess meanness, so Omega's nasty streak can't be blamed on him, but the plague's continued efforts against the Earthers and their remaining allies are all the more effective because Peter was involved in plotting them. The question now is how quickly the Earthers can identify what's happening, and how effectively they can adapt to counter the plague. Or if adaptation would make any difference at all, which is a fair question. Anyway, once again, big — huge — thanks to Peter. Wouldn't be here without his help...

And while I have to acknowledge that 'here' is arguably a place we don't really want to be, it's still good to be here.

Moving into the home stretch of the thank yous, I must again name my parents, Jacqui and Peter, who are awesome. Just that simple, they're awesome.

Atlas is, was, awesome too.

So now let's get into the penultimate battle against Omega. It'll be a bloody affair, but perhaps there'll be hope in the end...

PROLOGUE

It was somber in Sol space.

Ships floated out of the recommission yards and joined their new squadrons, then began taking on crews. Gunboats based on the Earth orbital stations flew patrols or sat on the deck receiving tune-ups. Picket ships on the Pluto Orbital Plane kept their scans directed outwards, ready to sight and report any incursions.

Lunar refugee camps which had been ready to receive hundreds of thousands of Genesis survivors — all of whom were now dead — stood empty. Search and rescue teams flew relentlessly over the waters where the British Isles had once proudly stood, scanning for any sign of survivors. None were expected there, of course — not only had the blast been utterly devastating, it had occurred over a week ago — but it never hurt to check.

Recovery operations were underway in Europe and everywhere else hit by the wave generated by the destruction wrought on the British Isles, and those efforts were yielding survivors. Many Earthers were being healed at hospitals across the planet.

Two days ago, Setter Caine had made a planet-wide address, once again rallying the Earther people in the face of Omega's seemingly incomparable strength. And, as true Earthers always did, the inhabitants of this planet continued to stand fast.

They mourned now, and felt an incomparably great sadness because so many of their fellows had died — some three million at last count — but they didn't stop working, they didn't stop living, and they remained as determined as before to stop Omega.

Or to die trying.

It was a very Earther state of mind, and it was one that Setter Caine had compelled himself to adopt. His mind and body continued to function, even though every night since the blast he'd slept in his home, with no one lying in the bed next to him.

Decades prior, he'd slept alone for countless days of campaigning during the Krogg War, and since then he'd spent many more nights alone when either he or Elandra had been at work.

But on every one of those occasions, he'd known that Elandra was out there, and that he'd see her again.

That was no longer the case.

She was gone... his beloved wife. She... who had always been able to help him deal with the great, crushing burden he took upon himself. Over the course of the past century, Setter had come to rely on Elandra, as she had relied on him. Now he was truly alone, and even his Earther philosophy was quaking before that reality...

But quaking only slightly. His personal resolve remained. It had to.

He couldn't allow himself to surrender to Omega in *any* way.

So as he stood on the deck of his house and admired an entirely unremarkable Newfoundland evening, he reminded himself yet again that he needed to persevere, do his duty, and give all the support he could to the mission to stop Omega.

And he had to do all that without Elandra's support.

But not on your own. As alone as you feel, you're not by yourself.

That was the great contradiction he was coping with: he felt alone, and yet he wasn't. There were still two billion Earthers on the planet with him, ready to fight to protect their homes. And more importantly for him, there was one great young Earther.

Phealan had begun to take up the mantle of leadership, and the more Setter reflected on this, the more he consciously understood its importance. As a proud father, he'd always known his son would have a fine future, but Phealan now seemed to bring with him so much natural wisdom... along with an energy that came with youth.

That, more than anything else, bolstered Setter's confidence during these difficult days. The elder Caine was determined to fight Omega, and die if necessary... but Phealan had such energy. Perhaps the key to victory lay with the young wolf who'd never fought a war... who hadn't learned lessons against the Kroggs that Omega could use against him.

I'm not alone. But it's not the same... I mustn't think like this...

"Don't beat yourself up for missing mom," Phealan appeared next to his father on the deck, folding his arms as he did.

He had virtually read his father's mind — Earther instincts, as ever, were quite helpful in shortening conversations.

Setter managed to laugh softly, "When the job is to lead, you shouldn't get tied up by the past... I try not to... but you know how it is."

Phealan smiled, "I don't actually know... I'm new to the Deputy Supreme Consul thing, after all. But I don't see much point in denying that we're hurting."

"It's tempting to try, though; to ignore all pain would be nice," Setter nodded in agreement. "But it makes no sense."

The Caines shared a silent moment after those words, and Phealan looked up at the gray sky as drizzle started to fall.

"It's a fine day," his observation came with no mirth or sarcasm. "I love this."

Setter nodded, "A fine drizzle, certainly."

For just a moment, the elder Caine allowed himself to enjoy the simple pleasure of the environment around him. He closed his eyes and breathed deeply. The damp air was a comfort to his lungs, and it did refresh him.

"Omega's not coming here again for a while," Phealan's next statement seemed sudden, and his father frowned.

"I'd agree, but then he's defied our expectations so far."

Phealan looked down from the sky and his ears twitched as the drizzle tickled them, "He has. But he's not coming here next. The next moves in this battle are going to be out of your hands... and mine. It'll be up to Andra and Fox... we have to wait and get ready."

The certainty in those words drew another frown from Setter, and he looked at his son, "You seem quite sure of that."

Phealan met his father's gaze and his eyes narrowed slightly, "It's what your instincts are telling you. I'm just saying what you already know."

"Yes, but he used our instincts against us," Setter shook his head.

He immediately realized he was already shying away from the promise he'd recently made himself — not to let Omega change the way the Earthers fought — but he couldn't help it. Even for an Earther, becoming mired in self-doubt was tempting...

"You see what he's doing," Phealan shrugged. "I think his last move... the raid here and the attack at New Halifax... was designed specifically to make us second-guess our instincts. We can't let him shake us. We just have to get ready."

Setter's answer was a slow nod, "Yes."

Phealan let out a long breath with that acknowledgment. His own mind felt like a spiral: he didn't know anything about fighting wars, let alone recovering from the huge losses they'd suffered.

But he knew his father. And his father knew those things. So there was only one strategy that seemed right to the young Caine: make certain Setter Caine had the support he needed so he could continue to trust his instincts. It was up to Phealan to fight Omega's mind games, while Setter fought Omega.

For now that meant counseling his father... in the future it might mean a great deal more.

But that was for later. Phealan was certain, as his father was, that the next fights would be at Freetown or Gibraltar... or both. Gallant officers at each of those bases would have to make the front-line decisions. Setter and Phealan would deal with the fallout.

The drizzle continued to fall, and the Caines stood together on the deck to enjoy it. The war was outside their grasp... for now.

CHAPTER 1

Despite all the activity that filled it, the Gibraltar system had a tomb-like atmosphere.

Sitting next to a window in his pinnace as it flew from his flagship *Chimera* to the massive *Gibraltar One* station, First Space Lord Fox Magnus watched the hurried comings and goings of Earther ships. What he saw told the story clearly enough: the Earther Navy was scrambling to ready itself to face a mighty, evil enemy.

Literally hundreds of vessels were in this system, many of them Earther Navy warships, and many more representing the Earther Survey Service, a scientific fleet that had been carrying out exploration missions in the space once occupied by the Kroggs. Those explorers weren't safe traveling alone any longer — all civilian ships had been called in to port, so they would be able to combine their defenses.

Gibraltar was becoming the collection point for everyone seeking refuge from Omega in this part of the galaxy, because the base was the most unassailable position on this side of Genesis. Between its powerful squadron and the epic armaments of its stations, it seemed somehow impossible to break.

But no one would find out how well it could hold back the Omega plague fleets, because it was soon to be abandoned.

Omega knew this place would be impossible to take. He didn't want to fight here, and now he's forcing us to abandon it.

Heaving a sigh, Fox looked away from the window and let his head loll back against his headrest; Gibraltar *had* to be given up, after all the construction and work to fortify it, because basing all these ships here left the Krogg homeworld open to an end-run attack. Planners in the forty years since the Krogg War had never conceived of such an attack being attempted.

Well we didn't foresee Omega's return either...

Omega had shredded the rulebooks the Earthers had carefully compiled from their hard-fighting experiences during the Krogg War. He'd outsmarted them.

The intelligent plague that had driven humanity from Earth to Genesis over 700 years ago, and then had been neutralized by the Earthers he'd created, was now infesting Larosians and using Krogg biology to turn humans into vicious, mindless minions. Genesis was lost, with over ninety-nine percent of its population dead or infected. Only Earth, Freetown, and the remnants of a ravaged Larosian Empire were left to thwart the rising tide of Omega.

If the plague got control of Krogg 'A', and was able to absorb into himself all the Krogg biomatter on that planet, he'd be unstoppable... if he wasn't already unstoppable, which was a point that could be argued.

Fox didn't indulge in that debate, though. The wily First Space Lord wasn't about to concede defeat just because Omega had defied Earther plans so far. There was no point becoming morose: the Earthers had to do everything they could to stop this sentient disease, and being over-awed by his abilities wouldn't help that at all.

To beat him, they had to change their tactics... and that meant in Gibraltar's case, they had to abandon their strongest port aside from Earth, in order to defend Krogg 'A'. Omega had sent a wave of ships through the Larosian galaxy, so they could appear on the alien homeworld's flank at any time. Forces holding station at Gibraltar, theoretically blocking the direct route between Genesis and Krogg 'A', would be of no use if that happened.

And if Krogg 'A' fell...

It doesn't bear thinking about unless it happens.

Fox halted his ponderings. The plan was in place: over the coming week, he would oversee the redeployment of everything in Gibraltar space to protect Krogg 'A'. He'd get his ships, his crews, all of the civilian survey ships, the orbital stations, and anything else that wasn't nailed down ready for a seven-day run from this system to the alien world.

Once there, he'd link up with his old friend, Vice Admiral Chronos Claw, and mount a defense. Fox and Chronos had been through plenty of scrapes together in the old days — hopefully they could weather this one too.

Though this feels less like a 'scrape' and more like a dismemberment...

Fox actually almost smiled as that grim thought crossed his mind. Whatever words he chose, the challenge was immense. There seemed to be no certainty when one was fighting Omega.

"Landing in about three minutes, sir."

Fox blinked abruptly and looked up at the pinnace ceiling, nodding in reply to the pilot's report, "Thanks."

Once he landed, he'd be meeting with Admiral Garvin Jardaw and Vice Admiral Karl Kandam — the two head officers in Gibraltar who were working around the clock to get the fortifications ready to move.

Soon, too, Rear Admiral Lang Sandpelt — another of Fox's oldest friends from their days aboard *Flame* — would be probing Genesis space, trying to determine just what ships Omega had ready there. Once they had that information, they might be able to figure out where the plague was headed next — here to Gibraltar, or perhaps out towards Earth, and Freetown...

Or both, since he's actually able to be in many places at once...

Fox let out a sigh and shook his head. Omega had used a hefty curtain of confusion to outmaneuver Lab Forepaw, the First Lord of the Admiralty... and now he was managing to use it against Fox too. The plague was forcing confident, experienced Earthers to massively second-guess themselves.

Fox had to stay focused, and he knew it.

"Let's see what you can manage, Omega..." he said softly to himself. "Let's see what you've got."

His pinnace landed a few moments later.

CHAPTER 2

"It's not looking so bad, Audrey... it doesn't appear that he has too much sitting in Ecclesia right now..." Admiral Andra Ursla (recently unretired) tried to make her words as reassuring as possible, and Governor Audrey DeBrooke, erstwhile leader of the Freetown colony, nodded in reply.

The Freetowners had seen signs that led them to expect an attack a week ago, but now they knew Omega had only been posturing and drawing attention away from his strike against Earth and the New Halifax corridor. Some on the Freetown colony were feeling as though they'd dodged a bullet — that Omega wouldn't bother with the sandy, warm, tropical colony now that he'd demonstrated an ability to strike at the Earther heartland.

Audrey didn't agree. Not by a long shot.

Omega had vaporized much of the British Isles on Earth, killing millions, but it was quite clear that he was still only toying with the Earthers. He was demonstrating his immense cruelty, and trying to wrong-foot them. When it came to the serious fighting, she had to assume that Freetown, her colony and her people, were going to be targets.

And if this bastard could destroy Genesis civilization, and then attack Earth with such success, how could little Freetown possibly resist?

At least help was at hand: orbiting the planet now were the remains of the Genesis Fleet, under Sarah Manchester, as well as a massive fleet of Earther recommissioned ships under the leadership of veteran officers like Andra Ursla, Jax Furgus, and Barty Stowt. That was a total of close to 400 vessels, all in position to protect Freetown from attack — nothing to shake a stick at...

But it was hard to be confident, even with all the reassurances.

Realizing this, Andra Ursla was trying to comfort the Governor.

Freetown wouldn't fall the way Genesis had. All the citizens of the small colony had been inoculated against Omega. It was surrounded by warships. It was as safe as it could be...

"You'll forgive me if I'm a bit hard to convince right now, Andra," Audrey said after a few moments' pause.

For her part, Ursla didn't blame the human. The great bear had been a scourge to the Kroggs in the last war, and yet now she was starting to fear that all she'd learned back then was going to count for nothing... as though she really did have to learn an entirely new way of fighting to stop the plague. It was a daunting prospect, given the circumstances.

Bloody terrifying prospect, let's not mince words.

Ursla contained a sigh, and decided again that if reinvention of everything she knew was necessary, then that was just what she'd do. Simple.

Simple.

Right now, the challenge she had to deal with was the defense of Freetown, and while she wasn't as personally anxious as Audrey, she could certainly see the difficulties. The colony was essentially made up of a single city that occupied half an island on the lush, tropical paradise. That containment was a blessing and a curse — defending forces wouldn't be wildly spread out, but then Omega's attacking forces would be able to concentrate.

As Omega had proved in the destruction of the British Isles, it was quite possible for one ship to break through orbital defenses, and for an island to virtually cease to exist.

Even failing that dramatic end, though, there was so much that could go wrong for Freetown. A landing by Omega minions would be incredibly difficult to control, for one. Based on reports that had come from Varnia Broadpaw's *Renown* back at Earth, Omega-infected creatures, be they human or Larosian, were remarkable combatants.

More seeds of doubt. Seeds Omega was good at planting—

"Folks, this is a meeting, not pondering time," Jax Furgus, the crotchety old lion Admiral, leaned forward and rapped his knuckles on the table in *Orion's* main briefing room.

Ursla's ear twitched and Audrey looked up at the Earther, almost surprised that she and Andra weren't alone. They'd both been lulled into deep, dark thoughts, and had managed to forget they were in a planning session. The fallout from Omega's attack was proving quite persistent.

"Sorry," Audrey's apology was both soft and unnecessary.

Ursla shook her head, "We'll find a way to stop ourselves from doing this."

Vice Admiral Barty Stowt, the other bear sitting some ways down the table, half-smiled, "Maybe if we start talking to ourselves…"

"Hardly necessary."

The chilled interdiction to Stowt's attempt at a light comment came from Sarah Manchester. If Ursla and Audrey were being trapped by distressed thoughts, Sarah had resigned herself to living in a genuine psychological hell. She'd literally lost a world — she'd been the leader of it and she'd lost it — so now all she could do was settle into a cold rhythm, avoiding emotions in order to do what remained of her job.

She had a fleet, and that was all. So by Gods she'd try to hurt Omega with that fleet before she died.

It was all she could think about, and so as she looked from the Earthers to Audrey and back, she leaned forward, "We are well established, but I wouldn't suggest that we predict Omega's next step. I'll feel more comfortable once I see Lang Sandpelt's report from Genesis."

Impressively enough, Sarah's tone didn't shift when she spoke the name of her now-infested home system.

Ursla nodded in even reply — the Allies knew that Omega had few ships sitting in his freshly infected system of Ecclesia, past home to the Genesis Church's Commonwealth of the Faithful, but he could have a powerful fleet at Genesis, waiting to move against Freetown, Gibraltar, or both.

"In the meantime, civil defense is fine, I think," Patrick Conroy was the speaker this time, and all eyes turned to him. He was still a civilian, as no service had reinstated him to a military rank. His experience was much appreciated by Audrey and the Earthers at hand, though it seemed to him that Sarah wasn't terribly glad to have him around..

Despite being married to the ArcGeneral and being the most renowned human cruiser officer of all time, Pat had been given very little access to matters of the Genesis Fleet during the past week. While Sarah froze him out, he'd made it his business to go down to the colony and to help the Freetowners prepare for a fight. Planetside combat was something he knew far more about than he'd have liked to, both from his experience in the last war, and from some of the things he'd seen shortly after its end.

"I'd just ask for some marines if I were you, Audrey. Your fencibles are still having a hell of a time policing the city, they won't be free to guard a frontier," the Irishman's calm words caused Ursla's eyes to narrow thoughtfully.

Sarah stared at Pat. As a civilian, he technically didn't belong at this meeting... yet here he was, making strategic recommendations.

Ursla didn't care what rank Pat did or didn't hold: his advice was good, so she looked to Barty Stowt, "How many marines did we bring along?"

The bear cocked an eyebrow, "The entire Light Division, under General Brawn. Just about 10,000 troops in five brigades."

Jax grunted in surprise, "You took the time to load up with marines? My squadrons shipped without any."

Ursla shrugged to her old comrade, "We figured this sort of thing might come up. That's 10,000 marines I'm more than happy to send down if you need them, Audrey. I can get General Brawn to meet with you..."

Audrey had barely started to digest what Pat had said, so she felt very rushed when the suggestion was made. Marines? Did she... need marines? Despite all her efforts, Audrey still wasn't feeling at all comfortable in the role of Governor. That had been James' job. She'd commanded the fleet. But now over half her fleet, what there had been of it, was gone. And so was her husband...

"I'd certainly recommend that, Audrey," Sarah interceded in her cool, rational tone. "The Earthers could secure the capital in case of a landing by Omega minions."

Audrey heard the words through cotton — the way she heard everything these days — and then nodded, "Indeed. Yes. Yes, Andra, I'll definitely take you up on that."

With a kind smile, Ursla nodded, "Alright, Barty you've got the General with you, right?"

Stowt bobbed his head in confirmation, "I'll have him meet you at your Government House this afternoon, Audrey. That alright?"

Nodding, the Governor looked from Earther to Earther. There was no question of who at this table was going to be most instrumental in defending Freetown, and to her shame, Audrey wasn't even in the top five.

She was struggling just to do the easy job of government... what the hell would she have done if the Earthers weren't here to help? She was racked with doubts she hadn't felt for decades... probably since before the Quest that brought the Genesis Fleet to Earth...

But she wasn't alone now. She had to remember that. She had old friends to rely on.

Maybe, with their help, she could avoid becoming the next Sarah Manchester — the next leader to sit at a briefing table with the Earthers, knowing she'd failed to protect all those people who'd put their faith in her.

Then again, if they failed here, there probably would be no tables to sit at in a month's time. Avoiding a glance at Sarah, Audrey contained a sigh.

"So, that's civil defense. How are the pickets looking, Jax? Tom still out there...?"

Ursla moved the meeting forward, and the commanders at Freetown continued to prepare.

CHAPTER 3

The planet Laros was... well, altogether... *weird.*

It was nice enough, certainly, but it was quite different than any planet Christine Schaeffer had ever been on... which was to say it wasn't like Genesis.

Yes, come to think of it, Christine had never set foot on a planet other than Genesis, so she probably wasn't qualified to label the austere, green-skied world 'weird' or anything else.

And now that she thought of it, this was a planet full of telepathic aliens who were undoubtedly reading her thoughts right now, because she wasn't too good at lowering the mental volume...

Don't worry about it, the last human to set foot on this world told us it was freakishly upside down, or something like that.

Christine blinked and looked sideways at Captain-Elite Tovarrin of the Larosian Stealth Guard, her escort during her time on the surface. The Captain-Elite was a skilled swordsman and warrior, like the great Torallis had been, but he was of a new generation — a generation of Larosians who had matured on their homeworld, trapped there by the plague that was spreading through the Empire.

These aliens hadn't realized that the plague was actually Omega until the Earthers had provided them with that information just last week, but now that they knew, the Larosians were preparing to make war on the great enemy of the universe. After forty years of waiting for a chance to fight back, the Larosian people were ready.

And young Tovarrin, a highly skilled warrior in the Guard, was to be one of the new war leaders. For some reason, Christine smiled at the Larosian as she thought that, and the young Captain-Elite bow-nodded in return.

Thank you for your compliments, ArcLieutenant Schaeffer.

"But of course," she replied verbally, feeling unusually playful. Strange though this planet might seem, it was also impressive. The Larosians had been trapped here for decades, but theirs was still a remarkable civilization.

For the first time since she'd left Genesis, Christine was witnessing a functioning, powerful planet in action, and the sight of it made her dare to think — perhaps even to believe — that Omega could be stopped.

Looking away from Tovarrin, Christine let her eyes travel over the rows of

Larosian civilians she was standing between.

As soon as *Carnarvon* had arrived over Laros, inoculations had begun, and she and Graham had been invited down to the surface to witness the last day of the process. The population of the planet was being systematically dosed with Earther UDRC to fortify their blood against Omega's infection. No Larosian would be taken over by the plague ever again — they would at last be able to fight their foe.

It was a momentous development, so Christine, Graham Manchester and Captain Joyce Furgus of the second battalion, 54th Regiment of Foot (2/54th) Earther Marine Corps, had been invited down to honor the occasion.

These inoculations would free the remains of the Larosian Fleet — just about forty ships — for cruising operations; soon they would go out after the Omega ships that had escaped into this galaxy and were heading for the Krogg corridor. *Carnarvon*, with Christine and Graham aboard, would cruise out with that fleet, and she would again be back to the strange, silver living spaces that she'd still failed to become accustomed to.

Though somehow, she was coping. Had someone asked her a year prior if she'd be able to tolerate living aboard a totally alien ship, trapped in a skin suit that kept her nerve endings from feeling like they were ablaze whenever they were touched by open air, and with no human companionship, she wouldn't have known what to say.

She'd probably have asked the questioner if he or she was intoxicated.

She certainly wouldn't have jumped at the chance to have such a strange experience, though.

Now it was different. The Earther regen treatment that had misfired and made her skin hyper-sensitive was definitely manifesting itself in other ways… it was continuing to influence her mind, and change her ways of thinking. She was feeling less and less like her old human self, and more like what she could only assume was an Earther.

Everything about her, from cell structure through personality, seemed to be in flux… and somehow that was helping her stay surprisingly balanced.

Hopefully that balance would allow her to keep Graham alive, because the junior Manchester sibling was by no means balanced… far, far from it. His wife had been taken by Omega, and the plague had used their unborn child as the Trojan horse to allow him to absorb her.

Now the man was out for blood revenge — one human against a plague that had the ability to be consciously present wherever just one of his cells existed, across at least *two* galaxies.

Even her new Earther blood couldn't make her think that was an even fight.

You seem to be a bit conflicted.

Tovarrin drew her attention again, and she stopped staring at the ranks of people in line for their inoculation shot, breathed in some of the air of this open square, and cocked an eyebrow at the Larosian.

"I'm still a little surprised at myself, I suppose."

Tovarrin approximated a smile, the light of the midday Larosian sun reflecting off his shining armor and making Christine wince for a moment, "Why are you surprised?"

His words were almost as smooth as his thought transmissions. Christine's hand fell instinctively to the hilt of the saber on her hip, and she shrugged, "It takes getting used to. I didn't used to be anywhere near this calm. I was a lot... *flightier*, is probably the best word for it. But now everything about me feels different, from the way I think to my fighting ability."

Tovarrin's head tilted slightly, his mind reaching out to touch the surface memories that Christine quickly offered to explain her past to him.

She'd been given Earther regen treatments to save her life after a fluke accident. The concentration of the treatment had caused overactivity in some of the regenerative processes, and one of the side effects was seemingly a shift in perspective...

Not unlike the shift that Admiral-of-a-Fleet Narosh had experienced after his accident on the deck of *Orion* forty years earlier.

The Earthers were certainly wise beings — and much of their wisdom seemed to be carried in their blood...

Aha, and the flux in her DNA had caused a complication: Tovarrin's eyes drifted down from Christine's face, again re-examining the plain green jumpsuit that fell loosely over her slim frame. It hid a white form-fitting shell of clothing.

"Sorry, I hadn't actually explained that," Christine noticed his interest in her attire. She offered up more thoughts to the Stealth Guard Captain.

Her nerve endings had been hyper-sensitized — the very sensation of air against her bare skin was equivalent to a second-degree burn. Doctor Celia Lazarus had laced the human's skinsuit with stasis field filaments. It allowed her to function so long as she wore it with gloves and boots, and kept a stasis patch on the back of her neck to protect her head.

They'd hopefully be able to reverse the damage when she got back to Earth... if Earth still existed and if they got back... but in the meantime, the arduous, over-sensitive life continued. Her quarters on *Carnarvon* had been specially modified so she could exist outside the suit for sleeping and bathing, but the highly specialized cocktail of atmospheric anesthetics and strobing stasis fields was by no means comfortable. It simply kept life from being agonizing.

And for working outside her cabin, she was in this suit all the time. She'd tried to make the Earther auto-tailor she'd brought with her from *Renown* produce some agreeable garments to put over it, but she was no fashion designer. Her jumpsuits all looked quite bland, and rather too big... as though she was wearing the clothes of an Earther wolf (which, she guessed, was the sizing preset on the auto-tailor, that she couldn't figure out how to change).

Christine wasn't nearly as concerned now about what she wore as she had been when she was an active young woman prone to intermittent (and largely unsuccessful) dating back on Genesis, but she still did feel odd in the overclothes...

I think we might be able to help you with that.

Christine blinked against her own thoughts and frowned, "Pardon?"

Tovarrin bow-nodded, "Allow me to take some measurements. Then I will show you. It is tradition among our people, and my Guards in particular, that all great sword-wielders should be given proper protection..."

Raising an eyebrow again, Christine opened her mouth to speak, but a hand landed on her shoulder first. Turning in surprise, her eyes met those of Captain Joyce Furgus (daughter of Jax), and the lioness nodded, "Graham's heading back up to *Carnarvon* to meet with Narosh. Said you could come now or meet him up there later."

"Ah... um. How long would this take, Tovarrin?" Christine looked back to the Captain-Elite, but the Larosian shook his head slightly.

"As you turned I recorded your body shape from a number of angles. I will send your armor up to *Carnarvon* when it is complete."

Joyce frowned, "Armor?"

Christine looked from Tovarrin to Joyce and shrugged at the Earther, "Anything to improve on my failed fashion attempts. I look like I borrowed a jumpsuit from a bear."

"Ah," a smile crept onto Joyce's face. "Well, I can help you fix the auto-tailer, but armor sounds like a sharp addition to your wardrobe too. I'm sure Graham will agree."

Christine paused at that, but pushed on, "Yes, I'll come up. I look forward to the armor, Tovarrin. Thank you."

The Larosian bow-nodded, "Glad to be of help."

With that, Christine and Joyce turned and went to find Graham.

CHAPTER 4

The Krogg home system felt empty as Earth's Naval ship *Formidable* floated silently over its red planet. Aboard that ship, Vice Admiral Chronos Claw released a long, deep sigh as the numbers scrolled across his screen again.

Omega seemed to be everywhere: he had Freetown on its knees, Earth's defenses off balance, and the population of Genesis absorbed...

It seemed likely to Chronos that Krogg 'A' would be one of his next targets, and that, of course, was not good news.

The Earther squadron in Krogg space was composed of thirty-two ships, sixteen of them being ships of the line, and only half of those the massively powerful *Venerable*-class ships. That force had long been thought sufficient to control the Kroggs, but against Omega, it seemed terribly inadequate.

Somehow Chronos had to protect this system with those ships, because the Kroggs themselves were entirely disarmed. The living ships that had once formed the mighty Krogg Navy had been set free, and were now scattered throughout nearby space living as pack animals. The Krogg soldiers who'd once numbered in the millions were now living non-military lives, with only a handful serving as part of a small 'security force'. Disarmament had been a condition of peace forty years ago, because back then, the Kroggs couldn't be trusted.

These days, Chronos did trust his former enemies, but given the current climate, allowing them to rearm was simply too much of a risk. While Chronos' instincts told him the aliens were friendly, Omega had proved that instincts could be fooled. The Kroggs would have to be passive during the fight for their world, lest they return to their old ways.

So the defense would fall to the Earthers. And it would not be easy.

Omega had ships in the Larosian galaxy, giving him access to abandoned Larosian vessels that he could seize and add to his fleet. He could also attack Krogg 'A' from the flank, through the hyperspace corridor. *And* he could have a massive fleet in Genesis space, that could come this way through Gibraltar. Protecting against either one would leave the planet open to defeat from the other, so the only defense against both was to move everything here, and fight both when they converged.

Chronos shook his head silently at that thought. Once Gibraltar was abandoned, all the strength from that base would move to this system. That meant four squadrons of older *Chimera*-class ships of the line under Chronos' friend Fox Magnus, and two more squadrons of *Venerables* under Lang Sandpelt. A sizable infusion of strength, but enough?

Those numbers would be combined with all the packed ships — disassembled vessels that had fought the Krogg War and been stored in case they were ever needed again — that Fox had hauled out with him. Those would have to be assembled once they reached Krogg 'A', but they would pad the defense force's numbers.

The *Gibraltar* stations would be moved out here as well, and together with all that mobile firepower, perhaps it would be enough to keep Krogg 'A' free of the plague.

But what if Omega hit with the same sort of tactics that he'd used against Earth... there'd be no stopping him with so few ships...

"Ahem."

Chronos blinked at the noise and shifted his mind out of its pondering. He was sitting in the main briefing room in *Formidable*, and his guest was noticing his preoccupation...

Turning away from the holo screens he'd been studying, Chronos nodded to the second figure in the room, "Sorry Krag, lost in thought."

Peacelord Kragran tilted his shiny, black alien head and smiled with some understanding, "Circumstances do seem to warrant deep thoughts, Chronos. I understand."

Kragran, of course, was a Peacelord of the 'reformed' Krogg people, and his race's official liaison to Chronos. Without their Queen to guide them, the Kroggs had begun to mimic the Earthers — as victors over the Queen in the last war, the Earthers were considered the strongest and most appropriate examples for the Krogg race to emulate.

But now, Kragran noticed with some interest, the Earthers were facing defeat on a scale previously unimagined... which, from the Krogg perspective, was a definite opportunity. There was a new force in the cosmos, one from whom they could learn...

"Thanks," Chronos interrupted Kragran's musings as he turned to the Krogg. "Anyway, the reason I brought you up was to show you what we have in mind for our defenses. We're pretty sure that Omega will be coming after your planet... all your biomatter pools in particular... so First Space Lord Magnus is bringing a strong reinforcement force from Earth, and Admiral Jardaw is going to move the Gibraltar facilities here. It should become a powerful position."

Kragran's head tilted as he considered that statement. The Omega plague had already used a small sample of Krogg biomatter (provided to him by the Larosians in a misguided attempt to kill him) to augment both Larosians and humans, turning them into warriors. It was thus likely that the disease would seek to control Krogg 'A' itself, and the raw supplies of biomatter that lay in great breeding pools on the planet's surface.

The Kroggs themselves were safe — Krag's scientists had confirmed with the Earthers that the immune systems in living Kroggs could resist the plague — but raw or embryonic biomatter, of which there was so much on Krogg 'A', would provide Omega with unparalleled abilities to upgrade and design.

Decades before, the Queen had relied on those great lakes of biomatter to fashion her armies. Omega would wish to do the same...

Of course, the Earthers would not allow this, and Krag certainly would not. The future of the Krogg people as a power in this galaxy was not going to be turned over to another maniacal leader with poor reasoning. No, the Kroggs had learned much from the Earthers: when they next reached out of their home system, it would be with much more wisdom.

Thanks to the Earthers, we will exceed the Queen's understanding of power...

"Did you get the scans of Omega biological characteristics I sent down?" again Chronos interrupted Kragran's thoughts, but without pause the Peacelord offered an even nod.

"We believe our natural defenses make us immune to infection. Remember, my friend, that it is because of the natural defenses of Krogg immune systems that your drugs cannot simply crush Omega... the same defenses will be too much for him to overcome in our bodies. But should Omega gain a foothold it is still possible that he can use our raw, defenseless bio material, as he did in his infection of the Larosian Natosh and the Genesis humans. I imagine that is his goal..." Kragran spoke the words without the hiss that, forty years earlier, would have tainted all his verbal communications.

Chronos was already nodding, "Indeed. Now, we'll be setting up a strong perimeter out here. I'll need your security forces watching the planet and ready to respond in case of a landing. Is that possible?"

Kragran straightened slightly, wondering for a moment if Chronos was asking for Krogg military aid — a request that would have saved much of the secrecy behind which his military leaders were even now shrouding their rearmament efforts.

He decided to test his counterpart with the question, "If you need our support, I shall call forth the legions of old, Chronos. We may rejoin our ships, make ready our warriors."

Staring at Krag in surprise, Chronos said nothing. The Peacelord had somehow seemed eager to make that offer... but no, the cat didn't get a sense the Krogg leader had anything sinister in mind. He was probably just eager to help, which was awfully good of him.

"Sorry, Krag, but it's not your time to get back into the fight yet. I'll send down the Fourth Division from my squadron, and I know when Lang arrives here he'll have the rest of Third Division with him. That's 20,000 Earther marines we can put around the biomatter pools. And we'll handle orbital defense ourselves."

Kragran understood Chronos' caution, and was quite alright with the Earther's reluctance. It was perhaps very apt of them, as Kragran knew what his planners and military leaders were telling him at every secret meeting: the new Krogg Fleet, with its mighty Hyper Motherships and its newly-evolved philosophies and tactics, were easily equal to the might of the Earther Navy. Some dared suggest the Kroggs might even exceed their teachers, though Krag himself was not so optimistic... yet.

A bright future for the Krogg military, and the Earthers did not — and could not — be allowed to realize it was coming.

But with Omega on the way, Krag was beginning to see that the moment to reveal the new power of the Kroggs was close at hand. The arrival of the plague would undoubtedly overwhelm the weak Earther position here, and thus give the Kroggs their chance to step out from beneath the Earthers' *guidance*. With Krag and his Peacelords at their head, they would reclaim and redefine the greatness the Queen had once sought, but had failed to find...

"Krag?"

Kragran blinked his one eye in surprise — he'd become lost in thought yet again.

"We would be glad to host your divisions. I will consult with my Peacelords and we will begin deployment. You'll keep me informed as word comes in about Omega's successes?"

Claw cocked an eyebrow at the last part of Kragran's question, "I hope he won't have any more successes, my friend."

Kragran paused, then offered a Larosian-style bow-nod, "True. Very well, I'll return to the planet."

Chronos came to his feet, "Have a good flight. I'll get hold of someone in the marines to talk to you once we get things settled."

Kragran nodded again, then turned and left *Formidable's* briefing room.

As he traveled the *Venerable*-class ship's long corridors on his way back to the flight deck, the Peacelord decided that he would soon again be a *Warlord*. The Earthers would learn just what sort of fighters they'd helped create — all that was needed now was time, and the arrival of Omega.

CHAPTER 5

"Christine's apparently having some armor made. Joyce told me."

ArcGeneral Graham Manchester looked up with his now-standard blank expression at Admiral-of-a-Fleet Narosh, who stood opposite him in one of *Carnarvon's* meeting rooms.

Christine… armor?

"Fascinating. Will it be of practical use?"

Graham's tone and expression did not change — not even a little — as he asked the question. His emotions simply didn't seem to exist anymore, his body and soul having been thoroughly consumed by his vendetta. That was why Graham was in this galaxy — why he couldn't go home and lead his Genesis Fleet.

Omega was Graham's enemy. Nothing — no responsibility, not even to the men and women of his Navy — would stand between him and his revenge.

Narosh had made it clear that the Larosian people would understand and appreciate this hunger for revenge, as they had themselves entertained it after the death of their great leader, the Son of Praaxus. Now they would help the junior Manchester satisfy his own need for destruction.

But Graham remained puzzled about the reason his young aide had stayed with him on *Carnarvon*. Christine had left a sister behind, and her body had been damaged by the complications of regen. By rights she should be around other humans… but instead she'd elected to stay with him. That made no sense to Graham, but he accepted Christine's presence and was politely grateful for her assistance.

In the end, she was a secondary concern. The annihilation of Omega was all that really mattered…

"The armor? All our armor is functional, though I believe she wanted it to serve as fashion accessory for her jumpsuits. She's been getting increasingly modest about the plain design of her auto-tailored overclothing."

Graham looked back to the pad of reports he was going through, "Yes, well she has nothing to be embarrassed about. She can't wear anything else, after all. But whatever she pleases. Have you seen this report from *Cervenzon*?"

An involuntary telepathic ripple reached Narosh's senses, and he paused to study it. Graham might have appeared indifferent about his aide… but when he remarked on Christine, there was almost a tremor of feeling in his otherwise still mind. Subconsciously, Graham was hurrying to drive those thoughts away — to keep out all emotion — but there had been *something*...

"Well, did you or not?"

Narosh blinked and returned his focus to the conversation, "Which report from *Cervenzon*?"

"This," Graham turned his chair and raised the pad towards Narosh. The Admiral-of-a-Fleet took it and began to scan the English writing. He couldn't read that language on the page, but the telepathic report laced into a sublayer of the screen came through and drove pictures into his mind.

"So they will not be able to ready their hyper drives. Unfortunate... that leaves us with only six Battleships?"

"Indeed, including *Carnarvon*. I believe a modest rethinking of our order of battle might be necessary, Narosh," Graham's remark caused his counterpart to look up from the pad.

"You don't believe the Battleships should lead the way?"

Leaning back in his chair, Graham shook his head, "I don't believe the Battleships should even join the Warcruiser column. We should cruise on our own."

Narosh's head tilted slightly and he lowered the pad, "*We*? You still wish to command the Battleships, Graham? They do not handle like the ships you are accustomed to — I'd advise you operate from a Warcruiser. Its maneuverability will mean it will garner less hostile attention..."

Permission to enter, sir?

Narosh stopped speaking as the request entered his mind, and he immediately recognized the telepathic voice.

By all means. Narosh replied telepathically, then verbally added, "Novash is coming in."

Just as Narosh spoke, the meeting room door slid open, and Admiral-of-a-Division Novash — the first Larosian to meet an Earther at Genesis over forty years earlier — stepped into the room, trading nods with its occupants.

"Any good news?" Narosh could have instantly scanned Novash's brain for that information, but it was more courteous to make Graham privy to those communications.

Novash tilted his head, "*Lysandris* and *Sarnkauer* will both be able to join the fleet, at over eighty percent effectiveness."

"Good," Graham offered his approval tersely.

"Indeed. We should be ready to leave Laros space in approximately ten hours. Then we just need to find out where Omega is going and we'll be able to give him a very nasty surprise..." Narosh's words carried a certain enthusiasm with them.

When they'd restored *Carnarvon* to working order, the crew of *Renown* had managed to keep the ship's revival a secret from Omega. If all was as they expected, that meant the plague believed this galaxy to be entirely defenseless, having been ravaged and destroyed by an earlier version of himself — one with which he evidently could not communicate.

Omega couldn't know that a Larosian fleet would be cruising to do battle with his force of ships that had rammed through Artemis Tigar's blockade at New Halifax. If they could just find him, they could surprise him... and with surprise on their side, Narosh knew the Larosians would be victorious.

But finding the plague's ships, in itself, was not a simple matter. The one place they knew he would head towards was the homeworld of their old adversary...

"I maintain we can probably stop him at the Krogg corridor. We can reach it ahead of him, if we leave immediately..." Novash had lifted the line of thinking directly from Narosh's mind, and shared it verbally.

Narosh nodded in reply, "Yes, it would be a perfect site. And now with thirty-nine Warcruisers and six Battleships, we will have enough force to stop his advance. We may even go through that corridor to help the Earthers defend Krogg 'A'... and help make certain that our old nemesis and our new one remain separated."

"He's not going straight for that corridor with only eight ships," Graham's cool words dampened some of the Larosians' enthusiasm. "You have a floating park of just about six thousand ships sitting between the New Halifax corridor and the Krogg one; he's going to start re-infecting them, you can count on that."

Now Novash looked to Graham, "Yes, but that 'park' is massive, we could never police it all, and he might slip by us. And by that reasoning, couldn't he be infecting all the planets along his route to strengthen his force anyway?"

Graham shook his head, maintaining his blank expression, "No. No, he's moving without leaving a trail. Even if he took over every world he passed, he doesn't have the hulls he'd need to move their populations. No, he expects the Earthers to have ships after him, so he's trying not to leave them a trail by infecting planets. He can pick up ships from that dead fleet of yours, though, because the Earthers don't know how many ships were there in the first place — they couldn't tell if he removed any. Then he heads for the corridor with a massive force of infected Larosian vessels. More than a match for us, or for the defenses at Krogg 'A'."

Novash and Narosh looked at each other briefly, rather surprised by the ease with which Graham seemed to be climbing into the mind of this beastly plague.

"So we need to stop him short of those derelict ships, gentlemen," Graham's smooth words carried some finality with them. "We take everything we have and hide it amongst the derelicts, then we pounce on him. And while we're going, we might as well bring every extra crew member we can — stuff them into every extra space, bring as many transports online as you can. We'll restore as many infected ships as possible, and then we'll move them to aid Krogg 'A'. Agreed?"

Narosh tilted his head, and Novash blinked.

"Very well," the Larosians said in unison, and Graham nodded without changing his expression.

Rear Admiral Minnie Maximane settled into her seat as *ENS Galahad* exited the New Halifax hyperspace corridor. With fellow *Champion*-class *Hector*, seven 74s, and eleven frigates in tow, *Galahad* was the flagship of the Earther force sent to chase down Omega's eight-ship unit in the Larosian galaxy.

Minnie didn't have a particularly strong force for this mission, but given the need to strengthen the home defenses it was all that could be afforded. And it would be enough. All her ships were survivors of the action at the mouth of the New Halifax corridor, so they knew what they were facing. Theirs was a simple plan: they'd head straight for the Krogg corridor — try to beat Omega there — and hope that in the meantime, Graham Manchester somehow slowed the plague's progress.

"All ships clear and free to navigate, ma'am," *Galahad's* Master reported from the far side of the battle plot.

Minnie nodded, "Get us moving. Signal Officer, squadron to follow in close order. Stand by action stations."

The Allies were ready to chase down Omega, and as *Galahad* accelerated into energy drive, Minnie Maximane was mildly confident that the plague would be destroyed in this galaxy, one way or the other…

CHAPTER 6

Varnon Broadpaw and Varnia Broadpaw were still basking in the happiness of their reunion. Varnon was beyond elated that his daughter had survived the destruction of Genesis, and Varnia was just as happy to be home. And their joy was actually about to be further buoyed: both the intrepid wolves were pacing the corridors of Fengate Hospital in Sydney, Australia, along with their good friends Labrador Forepaw and Dran Nightclaw.

"I'm sure it's this way," Varnon pointed down one of the corridors as the lost group shuffled past it. Lab stopped at the rear, frowning down the hall and shaking his head.

"I really don't think so."

"We might as well *check*," Varnia glanced at Lab, and the canine shrugged.

"Might as well, sure."

Dran Nightclaw cocked an eyebrow and looked from the Broadpaws to Forepaw, "Are you certain of that?"

The quartet stopped and stood in the busy hospital intersection, closing together to give room for patrons and medical staff to get around them. As the three male Earthers looked curiously to each other, Varnia let out a sigh.

"You know this is ridiculous. Really..." she looked first to her father, "You're the First Consul of Earth..." then to Lab Forepaw, "...and you're the First Lord of the Admiralty..." and finally to Nightclaw, "...and you're Comptroller of the Navy. And you can't decide whether you want to go down a corridor together?"

The three Earther leaders exchanged rather sheepish glances, except for Dran Nightclaw who looked his normal, reserved panther self... if perhaps a little wrong-footed.

Varnon then puffed himself up with mock defensiveness, "Well, daughter dearest, when you get to our age you start choosing the most important moments to agree, and the rest you leave for disagreements because they add amusing banter and levity to otherwise boring situations. Believe me, when they start writing books about us, they'll be thankful."

"Shut up and get in here Varnon, or by the Earth I'll bleed on you!"

The voice came rather loudly from one of the rooms on a nearby corner, and the four Earthers standing in the middle of the intersection all craned their necks to get a peek in.

"I think that's our room," Lab said after a moment, and with a smile Varnon nodded and led the way to the door.

As the four Earthers filed into the room, Admiral — now *full* Admiral — Artemis Tigar shifted himself upright in his bed, "Well look at this, it's all the Flag Captains from the old days, and Dran and Varnon too!"

The tiger's smile was genuine, as he'd fought the Krogg War alongside each of these people — they were dear friends of his, and for the most part, his museum had been looking after their ships... until recently, that was.

"So... um, how's it going?"

Varnon's question was hopelessly inadequate. As Artie shifted again on his cot, he looked down with a thoughtful frown and began counting his major limbs.

He stopped after zero, "Well, losing both arms and both legs all at once is rather... confusing."

"Yeah, just about all you could do now *is* bleed on us," Varnia smiled, and Tigar chuckled.

"Stole that line from a human movie. But the docs say I can have my new right leg and left arm back on Friday, then my other leg on the following Wednesday, and then the last arm that Friday. So I'll be out of it for a while."

Forepaw raised an eyebrow, "I saw the pod they picked you up in, I'm amazed you're not missing more."

Tigar tried to shrug, but it didn't work quite as well as it would have if he'd had arms, "Yeah, I must have listened to Jax's advice on getting off ships in the nick of time. I'm sure not complaining."

The guests all nodded at the comment — at one time or the other, they'd all lost limbs in the line of duty. Earthers seemed to have a propensity for that, and perhaps they risked it more freely because they knew it would be pretty straightforward to get new ones attached. The importance of not having one's arm torn off lessened when the perfectly compatible new limb was only a two-week hospital visit away.

"Well, *Agamemnon* will be back in fighting trim before you are. We actually had to manufacture a new bridge module, but all things considered it was one of the lighter repair jobs my yards had to handle this week," Nightclaw's comments were smooth, and Tigar smiled.

"The old ship fought well. Any idea who'll get it next, Lab?"

The First Lord shrugged, "I'm still trying to scrape all our working ships together in one place. Ami Dune might move her flag across eventually, but she's in an 80 right now and pretty happy. You heard Kylie Peregrine went down?"

Smile fading, Artie nodded again, "Indeed. And I obviously heard about London... how's Setter doing?"

Varnon's eyebrows furrowed, "He's still with us, still leading the way. And it helps that Phealan has stepped forward."

"We'll all do our parts," Lab added quietly. "And I think we're going to give Omega a bit of a surprise soon."

Artie's eyebrow rose abruptly again, "Really? We have ships moving in on Genesis?"

Nodding in reply, Lab tilted his head, "Lang Sandpelt took all the *Venerables* out of Gibraltar, fifteen ships for a reconnoiter in force. He'll cause some damage and tell us exactly what Omega has sitting there."

"Aha," Artie settled back in his bed again with a small smile, "That'll ring the bastard's bell a little bit."

That much enthusiasm coming from a limbless Admiral drew smiles to the faces of his friends.

Varnon added a raised eyebrow to his smirk, "Careful, you'll really turn into Jax if you keep up the irreverence."

Artie groaned in protest, "Excuse me, who had all his limbs shot off, exactly? Was it you, I'm forgetting... oh wait, no, let me count mine..."

The laughter stopped his complaints, and the five old friends continued to commiserate about the coming struggle.

With London's facilities gone, Fengate Hospital had by necessity become the headquarters for the new efforts to unravel Omega's genetics. Looking for a weakness in his biology might well be the Earthers' only chance to defeat him, and possibly to undo the carnage he had wrought. There were still billions of Genesis humans who might be saved...

So, freshly detached from *Renown*, and bringing a relative wealth of experience from her interactions with both old and new Omega, Doctor Celia Lazarus walked through the front door of the hospital with a box of equipment in her arms.

"We'll move the infected human down to containment in the basement, if that's alright with you ma'am," Ernile Cuttar, the head of Beckett Lupus' old Recon Squad, came up beside her.

Given the trouble that single infected Omega-human had almost caused when it had been captured by *Renown*, Beckett and Lieutenant Colonel Howler had elected to assign the elite squad to transport it to the hospital.

"Sounds good. Talk to the marines down there, too. Let them know what we're dealing with," Celia Lazarus looked to the Sergeant, and he nodded.

With that they parted company, Doctor Lazarus checking with the front desk for the location of her new office, and the squad walking cautiously alongside a stasis tube as it was floated on a hover-cart to the nearest lift.

Omega was in Fengate, but it was on Earther terms.

"Well, we best get back up to the orbital," Lab glanced from Artie to the nearest chrono. "Lang should be hitting Genesis any time now, and I should see the news live. Want me to get them to patch you directly into the feed?"

Artie smiled, "See, I knew I wouldn't even have to ask."

The old warhorses all chuckled, and with brief waves and nods, the Earther leaders departed.

Artie flopped back in his bed rather awkwardly, then frowned.

"Medic! Medic! Itchy nose, get in here!"

He waited for word of Lang Sandpelt.

CHAPTER 7

Rear Admiral Lang Sandpelt stood silently at *Audacious'* plot. The *Venerable*-class ship of the line was sitting just beyond Genesis space with its energy drive activated and its field stretched to 300 percent. Fourteen other *Venerables* sat in a line abreast off its starboard broadside: the two Battle Squadrons from the Gibraltar fleet, known as the Fifth and Sixth squadrons of the Earther Battle Fleet. This was a formation of the most powerful ships in the known history of the galaxy, and Lang meant to make full use of their abilities.

Omega couldn't be expecting an Earther counterstroke — that much Lang was certain of — so now it was just a matter of getting close enough to have a look at Genesis. They'd see what the plague had cooking for them, and then get out and return to Gibraltar with the news.

No heroics, no unnecessary risks. Get in, see what's there, shoot some of it, and then run.

The mission was actually reminding Lang of a similar reconnaissance patrol he'd been part of while in *Flame* back at the beginning of the Krogg War. Of course that time he'd been in an 18-gun sloop with no support; now he had fifteen ships of the line with 250 guns each, over 1,500 boats between them, and the better part of a division of marines for good measure.

On the whole, he was in better shape this time.

"Alright, we'll go in on the quiet vector. With all the jamming he's doing, we won't be able to get a solid reading on what's waiting for us until we're around the star, so I'm going to move ahead with Fifth Batron and take a look. Sixth will stay right here in reserve, ready to ride to the rescue if we get in deep..." Lang looked from his Flag Captain to the holo of the Commodore of the Sixth Battle Squadron in the battle plot, and both officers nodded. Sandpelt had been with this ship and these squadrons for almost a decade now — the relationship he had with his officers was even more intuitive than the normal Earther instinctive connection.

This would be doable. Lang didn't want to assume things would run like clockwork, because as soon as he claimed something would be easy — even to himself — it'd be lights out. But he had a good shot at not getting annihilated...

"Let's get a move on," he said after a pause. "Captain, lead the way. Signal Officer, Batron Five to follow us into the system."

As the orders went out, the eight ships of Lang's leading group slipped into line ahead behind *Audacious* and began to make their way in-system at about 350 pls. The system's star was between them and the Genesis planet, so hopefully they'd be masked from Omega's eyes. Despite Fox Magnus' concern that Omega might have posted pickets, there seemed to be none around... which could mean the plague was staging an operation somewhere else...

One way to find out.

Returning to his chair, Lang kept his eyes fixed on the large bridge plot.

"We'll reach the sun in just about forty seconds, sir," the Master reported.

"Stand by to interface our scans with the ships of the Sixth, just in case we find something messy. And prep pods as well — word has to get out if there's a problem here," Lang didn't like preparing for the worst, but given Omega's exploits to date, prudence seemed necessary.

"Twenty seconds."

Settling himself a little further back in his seat, Lang steepled his fingers before him. As that sun got closer, a list of the potentially horrible things he could find was running through the back of his mind. There could be a thousand Omega ships here, all covered in bits of Krogg biomatter, just waiting for him to be so audacious as to stick his nose in for a look...

Good plan coming in a ship called Audacious.

"Ten seconds."

Lang took a deep breath and watched as the sun filling the forward plot began to fall aside of the steadily advancing squadron.

"Here we go."

Everyone on *Audacious'* bridge held his or her breath as they passed the sun and the shorter-range sensors cleared. Not even the jamming fields Omega had been using would be able to blind them at this range.

"Receiving close-range scans, sir," the Sensor Officer confirmed, pacing behind the line of consoles that made up the sensor section on *Audacious'* bridge.

Lang felt his breath catching as he waited for something to appear on the plot... it seemed like a very long few seconds, and as he waited visions of thousands Omega ships clouded his mind.

Then the sensor data came in, and he didn't have to imagine thousands of Omega ships anymore. They were right there, clear as day in his battle plot. And about 200 of them were within spitting distance of his squadron.

It was as though they'd been waiting for Lang to arrive...

"They're turning right for us... they must be able to see us!" the Sensor Officer barked immediately.

Ships in energy drive with their fields stretched that far should have been impossible to detect, but the Omega vessels were definitely coming right for them. And if one them managed to ram one of the *Venerables* with its energy drive field spread so thin, the result would be disastrous. The Earther ship would either crash-reintegrate and be forced to fight, or it simply would never reintegrate from energy into matter...

"By the Earth — all hands stand by for action!" *Audacious'* Captain roared.

"Master, take us around 180 degrees and get us out of here, 500 pls," the First Lieutenant was already following the orders of his Captain, and Lang managed to breathe once.

"Transmit telemetry to the Sixth and tell them to get out of here, maximum speed," he looked to the Signal Officer as he spoke, but then the plot started beeping and he looked back.

Audacious was already turning away, but—

"By the Earth..."

More than 100 ships fell on the Sixth Battle Squadron. The seven *Venerables*, presumed safe, were knocked into normal space as explosions began to go off within their stretched energy drive fields... *hyperspace* explosions, that bubbled up from a lower level of subspace and were incredibly destructive.

The ships of Batron Six hadn't even beat to quarters, so they were defenseless as they were pushed into normal space by the hyper charges. Four were destroyed immediately by *spines*. The Omega ships had *Krogg spines* on them, and as Lang watched the flagship of the Sixth vanish in a hailstorm, his heart seemed to skip several beats.

The three surviving ships of the squadron flared their drives and scattered, but only two escaped the storm. One launched boats and message pods at the same time, the other tried to cover it with an outpouring of energy shot from carronades and guns.

By launching boats, though, those ships had made their statement — they were going to stand and try to buy time while Fifth Batron ran for it...

"We've been had..." Lang said softly to himself, then he came out of his chair and marched quickly to the plot. His ships were still in energy drive. "We've got no choice, we must make a straight run for it. They're going to buy us time to—"

Hyper charges started going off in the layer of subspace 'beneath' Batron Five.

"Sir! *Tremendous* and *Thunderor* have both fallen out of energy drive — reading large hyperspace explosions all through our area... it's a *minefield...*"

A hyperspace minefield. How bloody clever.

One of the original human Battleships called *Audacious* had been sunk by a mine on the first day of the First World War. Lang had read about it in Garnan's History, and thought nothing of it at the time...

"Starboard six points — reverse port engines."

The Master roared those orders, but it was too late. *Audacious* was snatched from energy drive as a high-powered hyper charge knocked it back into a material state and sent it cartwheeling for just a moment back towards the sun.

"Energy drives are cycling — we need a minute to be ready to run."

Lang held onto the edges of the plot to keep himself upright as he watched the Omega ships close in. There was no minute to be had.

"Signal Officer, order the squadron to scatter. Everyone try to get out if they can. *Audacious* will stand here. Launch boats."

Audacious came under full control of its normal-space drives, then turned its great bow towards the oncoming horde of over 200 Omega ships. For the first time Lang got a good look at those monstrous vessels: they were Genesis ships from the last war... old mothball ships, as the humans called them. But growing over them were bands of Krogg flesh. How had Omega gotten so much Krogg biomatter so quickly? Had he grown it?

If he'd grown that much this quickly on his own, then he'd be unstoppable if he reached Krogg 'A'...

"Range in nineteen seconds."

It didn't matter how the plague had gotten that biomatter — he had it. Lang swallowed hard against the promise of destruction that fact carried — not just for him, but for Gibraltar, and for Krogg 'A'.

The last two ships of the Sixth died. And four more of his ships from the Fifth were blasted into normal space by hyper charges. Two of these mighty *Venerable*-class ships came up alongside *Audacious*, and together the three great warriors launched their 330 boats into space.

Lang watched as his Flag Captain turned *Audacious* to port and ran out the broadsides. In the plot, he saw two more squadron mates fall out of energy drive, then pair off and join their third, isolated squadron mate, sitting in space well away from *Audacious*.

"What a perfect trap this has been..." Lang glanced at his Flag Captain as he said it, and the coyote nodded in reply. Then Lang looked to his Signal Officer, "Send out the pods at the last possible second, we need to record as much information as we can."

The Lieutenant nodded evenly.

None of the Earthers on this bridge, or on this ship, or in its boats, or in the ships that stood alongside it seemed terrified by their impending doom. They were ready to die — that was part of their duty — and while they might not have wanted such a wasteful end, this was all they had.

Two Battle Squadrons of *Venerables*, the toughest ships in space, lost to a trap that Lang Sandpelt shouldn't have walked into.

Hopefully what was learned would make up for what was lost.

"In range."

"Fire as you bear."

Lang listened in silence as *Audacious'* Captain fired his guns in anger for the last time. In the plot, boats in claw formations lunged at the Omega ships, and were cut to pieces by mixed maelstroms of lasers, spines and missiles. They died bravely, making their last stab at the enemy.

One more ship from the squadron was knocked from energy drive near the edge of the system, and the ships that had overwhelmed the Sixth crushed it instantly.

And then the last ship, *Conqueror*, escaped the perimeter of the system and hurtled towards Gibraltar at over 3,000 pls.

Hopefully not a total annihilation, then...

The spines started slashing in, and as the first broadsides were sent out, *Audacious* and its compatriots rolled for a second firing. While about a half dozen Omega ships were crushed by the weight of energy shot, two dove right in to ram.

One hit the ship ahead of *Audacious*, one the ship behind, and both *Venerables* toppled sideways at the impact. Trying to haul themselves around to fire again, both were systematically shredded by spines.

They launched their message pods in a last act of defiance, then died.

The story repeated itself with the other group of three ships well away from *Audacious*, and Lang Sandpelt watched with sad eyes as his fine crews died.

He swallowed once more, took his hands off the edges of the plot and held them at his sides, straightened his shoulders, and listened as the Signal Officer ordered his ratings to fire off the energy-hyper pods.

Audacious' Captain came to stand next to his Admiral, and as he did a cluster of Omega ships slammed into the flagship of Batron Five. The great *Venerable*-class ship of the line writhed, and then a laser shot tore through its already buckling hull.

A piece of shrapnel cut Lang Sandpelt in half.

Audacious exploded.

Such was the end of the Fifth and Sixth Battle Squadrons of the Earther Navy.

On Genesis, Omega-Natosh laughed and clapped his hands with almost child-like glee.

CHAPTER 8

Carnarvon sat in orbit around Laros, its main systems temporarily running on standby power plants as engineering crews from the Larosian homeworld finished overhauling its main reactors.

As a great old Larosian Battleship, *Carnarvon* was formidable. It took a lot of punishment to stop a battlewagon, as these ships were designed to draw fire and enemies into close action, so smaller, faster Warcruisers and fighters could have the opportunity to use their maneuverability to the fullest extent. That being the case, it wasn't proving too difficult at all to put the ship to rights — even after it had spent forty years adrift in deep space.

Of course, that fact wasn't foremost on Christine Schaeffer's mind right now.

Her attention was being occupied by the matte-silver breastplate sitting on her bed.

She'd just gotten back to her quarters after discussions with Graham and a number of Larosians, and she was rather tired. All she had wanted was a restful evening and a good sleep — after she got out of her bloody skin suit and into a somewhat numbing bath, thanks to the stasis field generators and atmospheric cocktail in her room.

But when she'd returned to her quarters she'd found a pleasant distraction — one that would be worn over her poor attempts at auto-tailored fashion, and that would offer her some protection.

Who knew they could manufacture armor this quickly.

It wasn't shiny or fancy... it looked purposefully subdued, perhaps having been made of a different ore than was usual for Larosian armor. She wondered about that, but then she realized she mightn't have to: there was a note on the breastplate. Raising an eyebrow at the piece of paper as she saw it, Christine took three steps to her cot and picked it up with her still-gloved hand.

The typed script revealed that the message had come out of a computer translator, but that was no matter, "Here is your armor as promised. And I took the liberty of having some Genesis ore mixed into the alloy, so it will shield you from telepathic probing. After our conversations, I thought that might suit you, and it could also prove useful in future encounters with Omega. Honorable death to you, Christine!"

Signed by Tovarrin, the note answered the question about this breastplate's dull finish — Genesis ore was the mineral found in the Genesis asteroid belt that blocked conventional telepathy. The Larosian Stealth Guard had used it at Krogg 'A' to penetrate the Queen's Hive without having their heads popped by the great telepath, but from what Christine understood, it was so detrimental to general Larosian communication that it was kept out of regular use.

"Nice of them to think of me," Christine dropped the note to her bed and bent over to study the gift more closely. It looked thin. It *was* thin. The plate was only about three millimeters thick.

Sheesh, is that supposed to stop anything?

Almost without thinking, Christine hauled her saber from its sheath at her hip, swung it quickly up over her head and carried it down against the plate with as much force as she could muster.

The blade glanced off, and a rather unpleasant shock drove up through her arm.

Oh. Alright, it's tougher than it looks...

Sheathing her sword, Christine lifted the armor in one hand. It was remarkably light — less than a kilo, even. She had heavier raincoats. And it almost seemed able to flex...

Larosian forging was most impressive, it seemed — a similar piece of armor coming out of a Genesis foundry would probably be four times as heavy. But then all Larosians wore armor, so they clearly had perfected the process.

There were old-fashioned clasps on either side, right at hip-level. She keyed one and then the other, splitting the armor into front and back halves joined by a ring at the collar. Moving to her mirror, Christine lifted the light alloy over her head, held her arms up to the arm holes, and let it drop slowly down over her.

After shifting around within the breastplate for a couple of moments, she managed to settle everything into its appropriate place, then she locked the clasps on either hip and stood back slightly to examine herself in the mirror.

Not too bad at all.

The armor was fitted, but not too tightly... it wore like a vest, leaving the ends of her shoulders exposed to give her full use of her arms, and ringing her suit's collar precisely with its perfectly-machined... or perhaps perfectly-*forged* neck hole. The seams that allowed it to split when she put it on vanished when it was clasped shut, and the front and back plates were sculpted in just such a way to match the form of her body, maximizing her mobility.

All in all, *very* nice — not clunky at all. She could wear this all the time, and it'd keep Larosians out of her head.

This was actually verging on exciting... a *change* in wardrobe! Maybe it would give her a new lease on...

Life?

Right, there was no way she could finish that sentence while remaining at all in touch with reality. She was wearing new armor, and that was wonderful, but the situation she was in was no better. No point trying to fool herself.

Examining her reflection in the mirror for a while longer, Christine started to think of different colors of her poorly-fitting jumpsuits that would go with the gray metal. She did this not so much because it'd change any of the hardships to come... but because she wanted to.

It was as human as she'd felt in a while.

"I understand Christine's armor contains some Genesis ore for privacy's sake."

Graham turned from the front of *Carnarvon's* bridge as Narosh addressed him verbally, impassively examining his Larosian counterpart, "Is that so?"

Narosh nodded with something of an alien smile, "It is indeed so, my friend."

The casual quality of Narosh's words perhaps betrayed the copious amount of Earther DNA that had been pumped into his blood over the years past — the DNA that had saved him from Omega's grasp in the first place. Now the Admiral-of-a-Fleet crossed the silver bridge and stopped next to his human comrade, "Would you like some too?"

Graham turned back to the front of the ship as Narosh came to a halt, then tilted his head at the question, "I have a box of Earther shields, remember. I've no need for armor, and I've no need to hide my thoughts."

Narosh tilted his head as well, wondering as his eyes crossed the front of *Carnarvon's* bridge just what the human was staring at. Larosian ship control was a purely telepathic affair, so there were no detailed control surfaces or displays like those found on an Earther or human ship. Crew members saw everything in their minds.

But Graham was staring at the front of the bridge as though it wasn't just a silver wall.

Curious...

"Indeed, you've no reason to hide your thoughts from us, Graham. But as I recall, you told me about having problems with Omega last time you were near his Natosh avatar."

The comment took seconds to pierce Graham's impassive outer shell, but then it struck home with dark immediacy. The human's head turned quickly, and his eyes narrowed, "That was a *difficult* day."

Graham's defensiveness should have surprised Narosh, but somehow he'd almost expected it.

"Fair enough. But the armor would still be useful for you, based on Omega's telepathic skill. I can put the armorers to work right now, you could have something fitted by the morning."

After a few seconds' pause, Graham looked back to the front wall of the bridge, and let his eyes return to their normal size. Narosh could just detect the small voice in Graham's head that told him to hold fast.

"You'd also be showing some solidarity with Christine. She could probably use a bit of that, if you're willing," Narosh elected to try a different tack, recalling the brief flash of almost-emotion he'd seen earlier.

"Aha," the ArcGeneral was again thoroughly impassive, and for the most part his mind seemed equally uncommitted... but the word was more of a response than Narosh would have gotten from any other approach.

Interesting.

"I'll have the armorers get to work, then," Narosh turned without waiting for Graham to verbalize his decision, and the human didn't contradict.

As the Admiral-of-a-Fleet left the bridge, Graham stared at a point on the silver wall, waiting however long was necessary for the fleet to get moving.

CHAPTER 9

"What's the news, then?"

Fox Magnus arrived on *Gibraltar One's* bridge at a quick step, having just come across from *Chimera* in expectation of Lang Sandpelt's report from Genesis. It seemed Lang's sense of humor was active even across a week's travel of space, though, since the first two pods sent back from Genesis both arrived while Fox was on the pinnace ride over — the one place where he couldn't get the update immediately.

Good old Lang, making me wait...

Fox stopped.

His eyes fell on the main battle plot — the massive glowing holo projection that dominated the center of the C&C deck. He found himself unable to move.

By the Earth...

This was literally impossible. Unthinkable.

Horrifying.

At least 1,000 Omega ships... not like the ones Artie Tigar had fought, but Genesis Navy ships with *Krogg biomatter* grafted to them. All displayed for Fox in huge holo projections that cycled through various windows in the plot — numbers and scan analyses, estimates of speed and fire capability based on detected maneuvers...

A thousand Omega ships.

How had the plague mobilized such a force in so short a time? How had he managed to get that much Krogg biomatter? Was he growing his own stocks? If he was, what could he do if he actually took Krogg 'A', and its small *seas* of the stuff...

Fox found that his mouth was trying to work — trying to say something that would make sense of all this. Or even make light of it. *Something* to make it appear that he was ready for and expecting the appearance of such a force at Genesis.

But words weren't coming.

Trying with only moderate success to blink himself out of his shock, Fox took a few steps forward and neared the shoulder of Garvin Jardaw, his voice only seeming to return to him as he noticed Karl Kandam's grim expression on the far side of the plot.

"So how did Lang manage to get himself out of that?" Fox asked the question, attempting to inject some of his typical bravado. Surely his assumption that Lang had escaped would hold up — Lang was a damned fine commander, and an Earther to boot. The last war had proved that good Earthers could get themselves out of impossible situations...

Jardaw's ear twitched and he glanced down at the small-statured First Space Lord.

Fox looked up at the polar bear Admiral, then took a deep breath and returned his gaze to the plot. A new window popped up near him, providing a direct answer to his question.

Conqueror was the sole survivor of the squadron, and the last feed sent in a pod from that ship had shown long-range scans of the Genesis system... scans that included the battle plot marker of *ENS Audacious*, and the pennant of Lang Sandpelt, winking out of existence.

Fox Magnus stood in silence.

Varnon Broadpaw's mood was grim.

So was everyone else's in the C&C chamber of Antarctic Base — Ami Dune, Dran Nightclaw, Lab Forepaw, Varnia... a cloud of dread fell over all of them... again.

A third of the Earther Navy's front-line battle fleet had been eliminated in ten minutes. *Five* minutes, actually. Mighty *Venerables* under an outstanding officer, and they were all gone. Outsmarted by Omega, then crushed.

And the loss of those fourteen ships was only half of this equation; their nemesis had amassed 1,000 new, more powerful ships at Genesis. Ready to reach out and strike at will.

Where would that strike come? Freetown, Earth, New Halifax, Gibraltar, Krogg 'A'? How could they know — their record for guesses wasn't looking particularly good just now.

"He's going after Krogg."

The voice was from the only Earther who could likely see such footage and still quickly overcome shock.

Setter Caine turned from the main battle plot and looked to his assembled colleagues — those who now ran his Navy, and helped him govern. He was Supreme Consul, and he needed to be confident for them, even though he didn't really know where Omega was going.

"Why do you think so?" Varnon looked from the plot with some reservation. "I mean, no offense or anything, but he hasn't exactly been predictable lately..."

Setter raised an eyebrow, "I'm aware."

Varnon's ear twitched and he glanced back to the plot, "Get all that together for Krogg 'A'? Why not just come straight for us, take us when he's got that much marked superiority?"

"If he just prepared a thousand ships in a few weeks, we'll never out-build him, Varnon," Dran Nightclaw offered quietly. "He can come for us whenever he pleases."

"And he wants the Kroggs with him... or gone for good," Lab added quietly. "He can use their biomatter, that much is obvious... and since he seemed so keen on getting into Larosian space, I'd guess he wants as many alien soldiers as he can create before he comes to crush us."

Setter nodded at both points — his friends were still thinking, and that was crucial. They just needed something positive to rally to...

Hell, something 'not too bad' would serve rallying purposes at a moment like this.

"If he's going for Krogg 'A', his forces in the Larosian galaxy will be heading there too, then," Ami Dune was the junior officer among those assembled, but Setter nodded slowly as she spoke.

"That'd be my guess."

There were several nods of agreement, then eyes shifted back to the plot for a moment.

"So the sooner Fox gets out of Gibraltar, the better," Varnon said after a moment.

Setter sighed in agreement, and turned back to the plot, "Being there does us no good."

"Gods wept."

Pat almost wished he hadn't been invited up to *Orion* for this briefing.

Who could blame him?

Ursla nodded slowly and then keyed off the main briefing room's holo tank. They didn't need those sensor feeds playing over and over in the plot for their entire meeting...

"They're weeping alright," Jax Furgus growled the words at Pat's comment, then slowly shook his head. "That bastard... Lang was too good a kid to have to go out that way."

"He died fighting hard," Barty Stowt said in low tones, and Jax nodded harshly.

"A lot of you seem to be following that path lately."

The Earthers at the table all blinked at Sarah's cold words, then turned their gazes on her. Staring at the table top, she didn't even notice the eyes that fell on her.

Pat glanced somewhat nervously from the Earthers to his wife and back, but as the Earthers looked away again he let out a short breath. Tensions were higher than they ought to have been... but then how could they not be high?

"Setter's certain they'll be going for Krogg 'A'... those ships, I mean," Ursla began slowly. "He doesn't think a major fleet strike will be headed this way yet. Omega wants to play with us for a bit, and he needs to get the Kroggs under his control. We think his force in the other galaxy is heading for the Krogg corridor, so Fox and Garvin Jardaw are pulling out of Gibraltar with *everything*. They'll be reinforcing Chronos at Krogg."

There were a few nods with that explanation — no one was certain that Omega wouldn't be coming for them at Freetown, but even if he was coming this way, there wasn't anything more they could do to stop him.

"So we're as ready as we can be up here," Ursla said after a moment's pause, then looked to Pat. "Now we just need to worry about the city below."

The Irishman frowned, "I'm their representative, am I?"

Jax leaned forward in his seat, "Audrey isn't here, so you're the best we've got. Serves you right for all the time you're spending in a tropical paradise."

It was supposed to be a good-natured jest, but it took everyone a moment to realize the rough old lion wasn't actually scolding Pat.

The Irishman again tried to ignore the evident tension, "Aye. Well, we need troops, probably. They've got the population forted up behind the shields of the capital, but if Omega gets to ground, I don't know what they'll be in for. So whenever you can, get General Brawn down there for a look."

"On his way this afternoon," Barty Stowt interjected quietly, and Pat bobbed his head.

"Aye, that's good then. We'll be better off that way... though 1,000 ships..."

"They're not coming after us, Pat," Sarah cut her husband off with a cool tone. "We're not potential raw materials, the Kroggs are. So he's going that way. And back to the point at hand, I'll send Commandant Plummer down too. I have 30,000 marines left in this fleet, they might as well be put to good use."

"If they're not coming this way, why bother?" Pat surprised himself with his immediate counter, and Sarah's eyes lunged up from the table to meet his cool gaze.

"Because Omega seems to be everywhere," Ursla inserted herself into the exchange. "And better to be safe than sorry."

Orion's intercom chirped to life just in that instant, as if to prove her right.

"Beat to quarters — hands to stations! Omega squadron inbound!"

The room cleared fast.

CHAPTER 10

The Earther Survey Ship *Grimbold*, formerly a 64-gun ship of the line, emerged smoothly from energy drive in Gibraltar space. As the familiar planetoid and stations appeared in the ship's main battle plot, Group Captain (formerly ArcGeneral and President) Elizabeth Hastings released a somewhat relieved sigh.

They'd made it here, thank Gods.

Word of Omega's return had been carried out to *Grimbold* by one of Gibraltar's sloops, along with orders for the survey vessel and the dozens of other ships like it to return immediately to the safety of the Earther base.

As the skipper of *Grimbold*, and the senior civilian master in her survey group, Liz had immediately joined her other two ships — two more ex-64s — and set off for Gibraltar at maximum speed.

Evidently, they'd gotten in before Omega had been able to arrive to cause harm… though they hadn't heard any news of just what the plague was up to for the past two weeks. There was no telling what damage it had reaped now… or, perhaps more accurately, what the Earthers had done to *it* so far.

But they were about to find out.

"Captain Forbes for you, ma'am," the Earther Signal Chief of *Grimbold* reported after a moment of examining local comm traffic.

Liz nodded, "In the tank."

Jessica Forbes was the most junior civilian Captain in the survey group, though with a CV that included service as Pat's Flag ArcColonel in *Harbinger Bishop*, she could hardly be mistaken for a novice ship handler.

Now, the woman appeared in the Earther plot on *Grimbold's* bridge, "Do we know anything yet, Liz?"

Shrugging, the former ArcGeneral glanced at her First Lieutenant, and he in turn cast a glance at the Signal Chief, but it seemed evident that there was no immediate message coming in from *Gibraltar One*.

"Seems they're a bit preoccupied…" another image appeared in the plot as Liz was speaking, that of the third civilian Captain in her squadron, Farley Carr. A Carrier skipper during the war, he'd been with the Earther Survey Service for almost twenty years, but he'd been kind enough to award Liz command of their survey group even though she had only a decade of time in explorer ships.

"Looks like they're getting the *Gibraltars* broken down to *move*," he said almost as soon as his feed into the conversation stabilized. "And I see a lot more warships here than normal... that's *Chimera* out there, and it's wearing Fox Magnus' pennant."

Leave it to the Earther to notice details — that was one of the reasons Liz had very much wanted a veteran Earther Captain in her survey group... or perhaps more precisely, why she'd joined Farley Carr's. She'd come to the Survey Service after her term as President of Genesis, seeking peace and a return to the life she knew best — the one of a spacefarer. The Survey Service was full of like-minded people; it was a mixed-race force, with both humans and Earthers crewing its ships as they went out from Gibraltar and studied the planets that had been overrun by the Kroggs.

The remains of many destroyed civilizations had been found by the Surveyors so far — with no survivors — and though the missions of the survey ships were often quiet, they let veterans of the Krogg War stay in space and explore the unknown. With old 28-gun frigates and 64-gun ships of the line rigged up *en flute* (with most of their gun batteries taken out and put into storage at Gibraltar), the Service crossed the entire breadth of the old frontier.

And at the young age of ninety-eight, Liz was one of its Captains. She'd received regen, of course, though because she'd taken it later in life she'd been confined to the body of a fifty-three year old... albeit a youthful one, with no aches or pains thanks to Earther medicine. The Earthers couldn't turn back the clock, but they certainly could make fifty the new thirty.

Jessica Forbes had left Freetown to hitch up with her former ArcGeneral several years after Liz had joined, having been driven from the colony by its incessant politicking with Genesis...

Liz's thoughts halted sharply.

Genesis was gone.

Her home, that she'd poured so much blood, sweat and tears into... that she and Harvey Bingham had together wrestled into a new society... that saga of effort had been for nothing.

"Signal coming in now... coming to all of us," Jessica's comment from the plot brought Liz's mind back to the present.

Beside the holos of the two civilian service Captains, a red canine glowed to life in *Grimbold's* plot. It was none other than the intrepid fox himself...

"Liz, it's Fox Magnus here..."

Hastings' first instinct was to reply to the letter, not the spirit of that greeting — *of course* it was Fox Magnus, that seemed quite evident and had she felt playful she might have called him on it... but Fox's tone was too grim.

"What's going on, Fox?" her question drew a blink from the First Space Lord.

"Farley, glad to see you. Jessica, you look well," Fox nodded politely to each of the other two Captains, certain he'd met them both at some point in time but not remembering specifically when. He then looked back to Liz, his gaze darker than she'd have thought possible.

This was *Fox Magnus* — he didn't get discouraged.

"Omega has 1,000 ships in Genesis. Krogg War ships from your mothball fleet, and he's grafted Krogg biomatter and weapons to them. We think he's coming after Krogg 'A', so we have to pull back there to protect the planet."

Fox's words pushed Liz's mind into a spin; she'd been enjoying the peace of the Survey Service for too long... what was this?

"I should add that he has ships moving through the Larosian galaxy, we think heading for the Krogg corridor. They'll flank us if we don't pull back. Omega hit the refugee fleet out of Genesis and didn't leave any survivors that we know of. He also hit Earth space, wiped out most of a fleet of recommissioned ships and killed Kylie Peregrine in the process. And then he attacked New Halifax and shredded Artie Tigar's blockade fleet... Artie's in hospital but that's how some of Omega's ships got through. And he hit Earth itself. Vaporized London with a Superdreadnought. Destroyed Admiralty House. Lab wasn't there at the time, neither was Varnon or Dran. But Elandra Caine was, and she's dead. Along with about three million Earthers."

It all spilled from the First Space Lord, with no ceremony and a haggard cadence. Liz's horror — literal, deep-seeded, bone-chilling horror — grew with each sentence.

Genesis population gone... the Earthers getting torn to bits... *Elandra dead with London...*

The refugees gone.

Not only had all the work she and Harvey had done come to nothing, and fallen to a coup and then Omega... no one had escaped? No one outside the Genesis Fleet, perhaps? How many humans were left in this galaxy? Or did that even matter... even if there were survivors, could they withstand the coming of Omega?

Liz tried to open her mouth to say something, but nothing came out.

Fox nodded slowly in the plot, "That'd be about the size of it. Get formed up with the rest of the Survey Service ships. I'm recommissioning all of them. Your guns are being unpacked from *Gibraltar Four* for rapid refitting, you'll be battle-fit in about thirty-six hours. Liz, I'd like to commission you an Earther Admiral for now, give you authority to command the Survey Fleet in action. We're going to need solid commanders at Krogg 'A', and Lang Sandpelt just lost fourteen of our *Venerables*, and himself, getting intel from Genesis."

Liz's mouth continued to move without sound, and Fox nodded again.

"Good, we'll talk soon. Farley, Jessica, if you could get your ships into line for refitting. You're regular service Captains again. Thanks all, I've got to get back to it."

Fox disappeared. No one bothered to point out that Forbes had never been a Captain, only an ArcColonel, or that Liz hadn't agreed to anything, or that this was all too much...

But then, judging by the abrupt way the information had all spilled from Fox, he wasn't quite over his own shock just yet either.

While Liz's mind continued to struggle with the enormity of what she had just heard, *Grimbold's* First Lieutenant, an Earther veteran of the Krogg War, quietly nodded to the ship's human Cruising Master, who turned the ship towards *Gibraltar Four*.

Liz remained silent and stunned. Not only was Genesis gone, but the Earthers were staggering, and the plague sounded... unstoppable...

She had to lead... but how?

Answers weren't forthcoming, but she couldn't help but continue to ask herself the questions. As she did, *Grimbold* and its consorts cruised into the Gibraltar system.

CHAPTER 11

Pinnaces flew off *Orion's* flight deck in a blur, and as Ursla dropped into her seat on the bridge, Esther Arbear, the First Rate's new Flag Captain, nodded to the plot, "Forty-one ships, we can't get a solid read on any of them."

Grinding her jaw, Ursla watched the scene as it was set in the main battle plot; the Omega ships were heading straight for Freetown, cruising fast from the hyper limit in a rather haphazard formation.

Forty-one ships theoretically shouldn't be much of a problem for the defense fleet — the Earthers alone had over a hundred vessels sitting in-system, all of them in a position to intercept, and the Genesis Fleet was sitting directly between the Omega ships and Freetown.

"They could have chosen any vector to come in on... why did they position themselves to go through the Genesis Fleet?" Esther Arbear's remark was apt, and indeed, it was the same question Ursla was asking herself.

Omega didn't do anything without a reason, it seemed. Even if the reason was to create sheer terror.

"He might be looking to infect them... he can't know they've been inoculated. But he also has a good track record against Genesis ships — he got Peltier and Lutjens..." Ursla's quiet answer was verbalized as soon as the thoughts started crossing her mind.

It seemed that he was picking the weak part of the defensive ring, hoping it was the easiest route to Freetown.

And dammit, Sarah was in a pinnace flying back to *Unity Genesis* — there was no reliable human officer aboard one of the Genesis ships to lead a counter-attack.

"Genesis Fleet's drives are coming online, they're beginning targeting sweeps," *Orion's* Sensor Officer's report interrupted Ursla's thoughts.

There are kids commanding those ships... they don't know what they're getting into...

ArcLieutenant-Generals Togo and Rozhestveski still held the second and third in command positions for the Genesis Fleet, and it looked as though at least one of them was moving to act on his or her own initiative.

"Send to acting commander of Genesis Fleet, do *not* engage. Shift fleet tack by 112 degrees on the zee axis and avoid contact," Ursla turned to the Signal Chief with the order, and the Lieutenant nodded as one of his ratings keyed the message in and sent it.

After another pause, Ursla glanced towards *Orion's* sensor controls, "Range on the Omega ships?"

The Sensor Officer quickly checked relative velocities, "Three minutes to the Genesis Fleet, eight minutes to Freetown."

Nodding, Ursla looked back to the Signal Officer, "My squadrons to stand by to advance. Barty and Jax's squadrons should hold positions until they recover their flag officers, then join at their discretion. Genesis Fleet to the reserve… now where's Ed?"

"The Freetown Fleet is in orbit of the planet. They shifted while you were in the briefing," Esther Arbear answered the question, pointing at the position of the handful of ships in the plot, and Ursla nodded quickly in thanks.

The Admiral was about to deliver more orders through her Signal Officer, but just as she turned he held up his hand. Two of his Ratings' screens had begun to flash, "Incoming, both Rozhestveski and Togo."

Ursla nodded to the plot in front of her, "In the main tank. Esther, get us ready to move."

As *Orion* set about preparing to deploy with the other First Rates of its squadron, two humans appeared in the battle plot, stabilizing just as Ursla came to a stop next to the large holographic display.

Both looked furious.

"*You can't order us around dammit!*" that was a woman's voice, so it was Rozhestveski.

"*We'll stop them and then you'll see who's bloody useless around here!*" Togo joined in.

Ursla had to take a second to absorb the spite carried in those words. These young Genesis officers were under a huge amount of stress, and the great bear Admiral could understand that… but whether or not they had an excuse for their behavior, she couldn't allow their fury to jeopardize the security of this system.

"I'll put a warning broadside across your bow if you don't get out of the way. And I mean that — you're not doing any fighting without Sarah at your head," Ursla's dry words drew silence from both ArcLieutenant-Generals, and before either of them could protest, the bear's eyes narrowed. "I know we're all stressed, but I've fought a war before and you haven't. Now sidestep and let my ships get into action first, we'll need you to watch in case this is a trap. Keep an eye on the other vectors, don't let anything through."

With that, Ursla looked away, and the Signal Officer killed the feed.

With a short breath, Ursla shrugged at Arbear, then nodded to the Signal Officer, "Get us to energy drive. They'll either move aside or we'll have to push them out of the way. Contact Ed."

•••

Audrey DeBrooke barely slid to a halt short of slamming into the table in Freetown Government House's war room. The holo display on the plot table showed a chaotic orbital situation, with the Genesis Fleet lumbering to get out of the way of Ursla's smooth-maneuvering First Fleet.

Sarah must have been in that briefing on Orion... *yes, there's her pennant moving on a pinnace. Damn, caught in a meeting...*

"All personnel reported within the city limits. Guns are coming online and city shield is standing by."

The report drew Audrey's attention immediately — the adrenalin flooding her system seemed to be clearing her head, at least for the moment. She'd take advantage of that...

"Raise the city shield. All planetside gun crews coordinate fire with the stations. All civilians to lock down bunkers, Home Guard to alert. We might have to face Omega landing forces," Audrey's quick orders sent various persons around the war room to their consoles, and the Freetown capital city prepared to receive the plague.

"Shit... sorry, ma'am. A bus of *surfers* are still out on the far point. ETA twenty minutes for them — they're coming in on the old path, they just called in."

Audrey frowned. Surfing was an interesting enough pastime, but the only place to do it on the capital island was out on the southeast point, almost forty kilometers beyond the city shield. The capital literally filled one half of this lovely tropical island, and it was growing, but for now they hadn't shielded that outer sector. Only gun batteries sat out there — protected compounds holding three Earther guns each, all pointing skyward to stop landing attacks.

"Tell them to head for a gun position, we're not opening the city shield," Audrey's conclusion came quickly, but the war room staffer with the headset frowned.

"Ma'am, the gun positions don't have gates..."

Right, no ground access. Only way in and out is by dropship, and a bus is still a low-flying hover vehicle. Dammit.

"Alright, they come home then. Get on the horn with Commissioner Clyde, get at least fifty constables to the city gate in case Omega gets here before the bus does... actually, make that all his front-line constables..."

There wasn't much of a ground defense system in Freetown's capital — the Freetown Constabulary was a full-time police organization with about 1,600 trained officers, and the Home Guard was a part-time militia force of weekend soldiers who, when called up, could muster about 18,000 men and women in decent fighting condition. They were meant to fend off landing attacks by Templars from Ecclesia, not trained to handle Omega's minions...

But they were all she had.

I really need to bring the marines down. Soon. If I get the chance...

The city's defensive shield did form an impenetrable barrier on the ground, but it was weakened by four 'gates' — smaller sections with special field conditions that allowed them to be opened and closed. There was a gate each on the highways that headed out to the unpopulated half of the island (highways which dropped quickly into rough-cut roads after leaving the city), and two more for the major rivers that drained through the capital out into the sea.

If they opened a gate to let this bus of surfers in, Omega could send minions to lunge through behind them. Presuming, of course, he somehow got minions on the ground in time.

It's Omega. Just assume he can.

"Commissioner Clyde reports he's emptying the Constabulary offices right now. The militia's been called up to take over civil security... and as a reserve..." the report drew another nod from Audrey.

Damn all, she wished the Earther Light Division was here right now. Hell, she'd even take the Genesis marines at a time like this...

"Omega ships ETA six minutes."

As the clumsily-handled Genesis Fleet got out of the way, the Earther recommissioned fleet took its place, and with only a minute to spare before the Omega ships reached weapons range, the Earthers came out of energy drive and presented their broadsides.

Andra Ursla dropped into her chair, frowning for a second at what she thought was a blip in the battle plot. Deciding it was nothing, she turned to the Signal Chief, "All squadrons to independent fire."

The gunners of all the Earther ships in Freetown space quickly ran out their cannon. These weapons, the same guns that had defeated the Kroggs forty years earlier, now glared at a still mysterious Omega force.

"Looks now like some of the refugee fleet is in there with them, ma'am," the Sensor Officer reported in quiet tones, and Ursla ground her jaw. Omega had no decency... he was using some of the ships full of refugees he'd captured just short of Earth to do his dirty work here.

"Range in thirty seconds."

Then came the twist.

"Contact in *Freetown orbit!*"

Ursla didn't quite process that report at first, but she managed to digest the words within a few seconds, and again she was out of her chair. There was a new Omega contact in the holo plot... right over the Freetown planet.

It must have come in under the sights of the Genesis Fleet, because one of the rearguard Destroyers for that formation had just stumbled into lidar range of it. It appeared to be one of the larger transports from the Genesis refugee fleet... but it wasn't carrying refugees anymore.

They must be minions now.

"Three small craft just launched from it — heading for the city..." the report was confirmed by the rushing icons in the plot, and Ursla ground her jaw again. They were landing infected refugees as troops.

He was, that is. Not *they*. This was all *him*. In his unsettling way, Omega was with all his minions at once.

"Twenty seconds to range on us ma'am... for the Omega ships, that is."

Ursla nodded, saying nothing as she watched boats from Freetown's orbital platforms chase the three landing craft. Those landing ships were of Genesis manufacture... big-model thousand-person carriers designed for commercial transport work. But whatever Omega had done to them was allowing them to outrun the small craft of Freetown — no mean feat considering those boats were powered by Earther power plants...

The Genesis Fleet rapidly turned on the Omega ship in orbit, their missiles smashing its hull so it came apart and plunged into the atmosphere. Just as they did that, two of Ed Jeffries' Freetown advanced Battlecruisers descended quickly after the small craft. *Savanna Felix* and, ironically enough, *Andra Ursla* both leveled their long carronades at the three dropships.

Two blossomed out of existence, then one dropped with unbelievable speed — right out of range of the Battlecruisers' lasers.

Ursla watched in silence. One of those things could carry a thousand Omega troops... a sizable enough enemy force, even if she was going to land the Light Division soon. Colin Brawn would have his hands full.

The massive burst of speed the last craft had used to escape the Freetown ships' long carronades had accelerated it past the velocity that even its Omega-altered spaceframe could handle. It started to buckle, and then it crashed into the ocean and sank, a subsurface explosion coming seconds later.

That it?

"Life signs on the planet... the Omega troops must have *jumped out* of the lander when it was over the island, ma'am!" *Orion's* excellent sensors delivered the grim news, and Ursla barely suppressed a growl.

"Warn Freetown that there are minions on the unshielded side of their city island. We'll deal with them after the ships are destroyed.

The message was sent, and Ursla took a deep breath. It could have been much worse... but many minions had jumped from that speeding craft... and somehow survived... well Colin Brawn could stop them later. For now, there were more pressing matters.

"Tell the Genesis Fleet to scour orbital space for more stealth landing ships," she then glanced at the range counter in her plot just in time to see it tick to zero; the Earthers could engage.

"Fire as you bear!" Esther Arbear's order was sharp, and *Orion's* great broadside roared silently in the vacuum, hurling shot into the oncoming Omega ships.

Along with the flagship, the rest of the recommissioned force loosed its energy shot, and then all ships rolled and fired again.

Missiles began to slash back from Omega's vessels — by some small favor to the defense fleet here, these ships lacked the spines that Lang Sandpelt had found on the Omega vessels at Genesis. The Earthers didn't even bother with canister — breaking by squadron, they avoided the clumsy attack and surged forward.

As Ursla returned to her chair, it seemed quite evident that this space attack had been a diversion, trying to give that landing time to do its job. Now the Allies had thwarted the landing attempt, but they couldn't take chances. They'd clean this up and make sure there was no subterfuge left.

In the plot, the number of Omega ships dropped almost instantly from forty-one to thirty, and no Earther ships had suffered much damage. It wouldn't take long to deal with—

"Down 144, full ahead emergency — all hands brace!" the Master whirled from the helm consoles with that warning for the ship's personnel to hold tight…

Ursla saw it in the holo plot and her eyes widened: a *Dreadnought* was coming in to ram, and while the Omega-controlled ship had only about sixty percent of *Orion's* mass, it was moving with tremendous speed.

The tip of the Dreadnought's nose hit *Orion's* shields before the Master could move the First Rate out of danger. Anyone who hadn't braced for impact was thrown raggedly through the ship.

It took Commissioner Jason Clyde almost ten minutes to get 1,500 of his Constables out of their barracks and into riot gear at the gate for the main highway. That was actually brilliant response time, considering some of his teams had to come from as far as forty kilometers away, and it was all made possible by the high-speed highway that they were now defending.

Modeled on a Genesis main transit artery, the highway moved regular hover vehicles at four or five times normal speed. Its thirty-meter width and its tall, silver, angled walls turned it into a veritable bridge across the city. Now this part of the highway was blocked by landed hover cars, his Constabulary men and women sheltering behind them as they waited to receive a tourist bus.

Clyde stood in the center of the highway, watching his Constables lay down Earther shield generators when the call came in, "Commissioner Clyde, this is Barracks. Reading?"

"I hear you," Clyde turned from the developing defenses, and as he spoke he grabbed an energy rifle offered to him by a passing Constable.

"Omega dropship just got past orbital blockade — we didn't even see him coming, apparently. The Earthers are stopping the main body, but indications are we've got some Omega soldiers outside the shield on this island right now."

Clyde frowned, "It landed here?"

"Got right past our guns too, sir... hang on... no, apparently the Omega soldiers *jumped out* when it made a low pass, and it was shot down by battery twelve. But you've got incoming."

Great.

Clyde lifted the energy rifle he'd just taken and checked its charge, continuing his orders as he did, "Alright, get on the horn with that damned bus and tell them to move faster. Once the militia's turned out I want another thousand Guards here, the rest in the Constable stations as a reserve."

"Yes sir. If that's all."

"Yeah, out."

Clyde had been a Private in the Genesis Marines during the Krogg War, and he wasn't one for much ceremony. He had with him 1,500 Constables, but as the name implied, they weren't *marines*. A number... maybe even half were ex-marines, but for many the energy rifles they were being handed right now were very foreign weapons, used only in training...

"Sir!"

Clyde blinked and looked up from his rifle as one of the senior Constables sprinted up the highway to him, "Sir!"

"Heard you the first time, *what*?"

The Constable was pointing, and as Clyde took a couple of steps forward he realized at what: here came the bus, and there were three Omega soldiers running alongside it... running like animals.

"Take cover!" Clyde roared. "Pulsar car forward. We drop those three as soon as they're within a kilometer!"

The bus was weaving from side to side and was clearly redlining its engines, trying to get past these new chasing enemies... but they were damned fast.

"They're close!" someone called from further up.

The thick mass of Constables nearest the gate shook itself into a rough line — the sort that they'd been trained to use for riot control — and raised their weapons. Clyde moved a bit closer to the front, but seeing one of the Constabulary cars nearby, he elected to climb up on that instead. With a good view of the bus rushing up the highway from beyond the shield, and with the gate and the gatekeeper's kiosk all in sight, he squared his shoulders and nodded to himself.

Only three of the Omega bastards, they could handle that.

"Alright, open the gate," Clyde ordered into his headset, gauging the distance to the bus. Then he roared his next order, "Kill them!"

The Constables in line opened up with their Earther-made energy rifles, and instantly the trio of Omega chasers was snatched away from the bus.

But as the big hover vehicle hurtled to the gate, a *mob* of the Omega soldiers suddenly appeared from the jungle beyond, jumping over the high sloped edges of the highway... *hundreds* of them were only meters behind the bus!

"*Shit*!" Clyde whirled and started waving more Constables forward. This was such an unmilitary outfit... "Get ready to close the gate on my word."

The line of Constables and now the pulsar car opened up on the rushing Omega soldiers, the energy fire instantly driving back whichever of them it hit.

But more came forward...

And then the bus was through.

"Close it up!" Clyde jumped off the car as the line of Constables parted to let the bus rush through it.

The large vehicle came to a sharp stop on the highway.

The gate slammed shut behind it.

And two Omega soldiers had made it through.

Though his Constables weren't soldiers proper, they were disciplined nonetheless. They didn't panic, holding their ground as the two seething once-human creatures sprinted towards their line.

Then the pulsar car lined up on the plague beasts, and cut them both in half.

Collapsing into a pair of heaps, the bodies flailed and hissed, and Clyde nodded to the pulsar car driver, then ordered into his headset, "Ashes of them both. Set everything to maximum output and burn the bastards."

The rest of the Omega soldiers threw themselves pathetically against the shields, and Clyde let go a sigh of relief. Turning to the bus, he decided to find out just what bunch of idiots had gone surfing at a time like this.

Then it occurred to him that they could be Omega soldiers themselves, using the bus as a Trojan horse...

He cursed his stupidity and waved a dozen Constables to join him in advancing on the large vehicle with his rifle leveled.

This Omega was a crafty bastard...

The bus door opened.

Clyde stopped abruptly, bringing his rifle to his shoulder and laying his sights squarely in the middle of the doorway...

A rather good looking brunette in surfing gear descended from the bus, then stifled a scream as she realized there were rifles pointing at her. Slowly the bus emptied — mostly a load of scared surfer girls. Typical.

"Shit. Women..." Clyde turned from the spectacle and waved some of his Constables forward, "Get these *ladies* to the Garrison. We'll check for infection and send them home from there. And burn any Omega soldier that comes close to the shield."

Omega was on Freetown, but at least Jason Clyde had saved a busload of surfer girls.

Rubbing her head, Ursla slowly stood up on *Orion's* bridge.

The battle plot was still glowing, and in it the last of the Omega ships were being shattered. But Orion had a four-deck-tall, fourteen-section-long gash in its starboard side. Thanks to the efforts of the Master, the gash missed all of the First Rate's gun decks, but it was still a sizable problem for structural integrity.

"Dammit, I told Setter I'd bring it back without a scratch..." Ursla turned to Esther Arbear, who was also rubbing her head and standing.

"Search and rescue pinnaces just launched," the First Lieutenant interrupted before either bear could speak again. "Everyone was wearing their shield, though, and sensors have accounted for forty-two personnel in space — alive."

The report was aptly timed and the news, for once, was good.

"Alright. I'll take that," Ursla's eyebrows bobbed and Esther smiled.

"Call from Government House, ma'am... they think as many as 1,000 Omega troops got down... they tried to rush the main highway gate when a busload of surfers went through, but the Constabulary held them back and killed the two who got inside."

The Signal Officer's report raised the eyebrows of every Earther on the bridge, even as they dusted themselves off and rubbed bruises.

"Busload of *surfers*?" Esther Arbear could barely contain her disbelief. Actually, she didn't contain it.

Shrugging, the Signal Officer reread the passage, "...'when a busload of surfers'... yes ma'am..."

Ursla shook her head slowly, "Well, I think this is one gift horse we don't look in the mouth. Let's just hope our luck holds, and Fox has this easy a time out at Gibraltar."

CHAPTER 12

Liz Hastings had never seen an Earther installation in such a seeming state of chaos. As she strode away from the ramp of her pinnace she had to stop twice to avoid having Earthers bang into her as they rushed across the deck with toolkits. On the far side of *Gibraltar One's* main bay a crew of engineers was unbolting a grav tractor assembly, presumably to pack it for shipping...

They really were pulling up sticks. The Gibraltar system was going to be abandoned, and the Earthers were rushing to get it packed as quickly as possible.

"Gods damned, I've never seen an Earther crew this worked up..."

Liz hadn't even seen Jessica Forbes close with her, and now as the two humans stopped again in the middle of the hectic deck, the former ArcGeneral and President of Genesis shook her head slowly.

"Omega... damn all. He's not only killed us, he's got under their skin..." Liz let the words hang as more Earthers rushed onto the deck with crates, then started loading them into a pinnace.

There was almost an air of panic here... not quite, but as close as Earthers ever got. And with Earthers, anything approaching panic qualified as *very* unsettling.

"Don't worry about this... looks worse than it is..." Farley Karr's comment signaled his arrival behind both Liz and Jessica, and the two humans now turned to face him.

"You've seen it this bad before?" Jessica's question came first, and Karr shrugged.

"Once had all four reactors in *Diadem* nearly overload at the same time. Saw plenty of this then... though I'll grant you, it's not pleasant to see this sort of reaction over a threat that's a week away," the Earther Captain's tone didn't inspire too much confidence, and both humans sighed as the comparison was made.

"Losing Lang was a cold bucket of water. Actually I'm inclined to say *acid*, because the shock's not going to wear off for me for a while..." the voice was from a fourth party, albeit a familiar one.

Karr looked past the two human Captains, and both women turned again to see that Fox Magnus had appeared in front of them on the deck. He must have arrived in amongst the crowd of Earthers who'd been lugging those boxes...

Actually, Karl Kandam and Garvin Jardaw, both coming up behind the First Space Lord, *were* the Earthers who'd been carrying the boxes...

"We're getting our personal kit onto our ships. All crew are being scheduled pinnaces for that — we'll be breaking up *Gibraltar One* last, but if Omega gets here early and we have to evacuate, we might as well have our stuff," Fox seemed to be trying to revive some of his dashing character — that confidence he'd shown so well when he commanded *Flame* and *Atlas*.

But even Liz could sense his underlying discomfort, and his grief. He and Lang Sandpelt had been friends for something like fifty years.

"Shipping out personal effects instead of equipment?" Jessica's question was prudent enough, though somehow it seemed cold when it reached Liz's ear.

Fox shrugged and forced a dapper smile to his face, "We're miserable enough as it is. A few extra portable manufacturing plants will produce more gunboat parts, but I expect the touches of home will help our crews' state of mind more than having six extra gunboats."

Liz raised an eyebrow — the Earthers were worried about *morale*... this was definitely bad. There was no other word broad enough for it, just 'bad'.

"Indeed," she concurred almost immediately, hoping to get off the subject before more about the Earther state of mind was revealed. She didn't want the heroes to be demoralized in any way... because she knew damned well that they were the only ones who could salvage this whole giant mess.

Tilting her head, Liz caught Fox's eye, "You said you were going to need to commission us back into the service?"

The change of subject was welcome, and the First Lord's reply was a little bit lighter, "Indeed. We're going to be reloading the Survey Service ships with their guns immediately. I'm going to have to draw some of your Earther officers and ratings to augment the crews of the packed ships I brought along, but for the most part it'll be a coherent fleet of the ships that used to be Surveyors... and I want you in command."

Karl Kandam and Garvin Jardaw were now both standing behind Fox, nodding to the new arrivals with the most pleasant expressions they could muster.

"Chronos, Garvin, Thena and I will be splitting the recommissions and the regular ships once we get to Krogg, and Karl's going to take over the *Gibraltars* once they're rebuilt out there... it's a tall order for reconstruction, too, but we've kept enough tender ships out here to work everything through... we hope. That said, your survey ships will mostly be armed before we leave for Krogg, and most of our recommissions won't be ready until we've been there for a while. You're my big right hand on this one."

Liz was nodding as she listened intently; she wasn't accustomed to beating a hasty retreat, and the Earthers certainly weren't, but Fox seemed to have a good grasp of the finer points here. Somehow that didn't surprise her.

"Alright then... how many ships are we looking at... and when are we leaving Gibraltar space?" Liz countered thoughtfully.

"No final numbers yet. The yards think they can rearm about eighty ships from the Survey Service before they all pack it in for departure... and I'm sending them out in three days. Everything else is going as soon as it can — *Gibraltars Six* and *Five* are shipping out in two days, with a squadron of *Chimeras* going along to look after them," Fox's eyes drifted to the pinnace he'd placed his box aboard. "We're actually hoping you could join that convoy... help protect our personal items, and such."

Liz managed a grin at the lame attempt at humor, "Fair enough... get *Grimbold* in for arming asap, and the rest of my ships, and tell me who the skippers are. I'll call a meeting first thing tomorrow and we can start trying to pull together a coherent unit. Probably won't be easy, but we'll take a run at it..."

"You'll do well, I know you will. Nobody knows how to handle chaotic circumstances the way you do, Liz," Fox again offered a dashing smile. "You'll have veteran officers and crews under your command. I'm pretty sure Dudley Redvers will be coming in tomorrow, so you can have him as a division flag officer... basically you just need to remind everyone how to fight."

Liz felt a chill at those words, "Last time we all fought, it wasn't against Omega."

Fox's ear twitched, then he tilted his head, "True."

Waiting for a moment, Liz expected the Earther to produce a platitude or anecdote to give her more confidence... but Fox could do no more than look at her.

The time for confidence was over... or nearly so. Desperation was going to take hold soon at this rate, Liz realized. It was going to be a hard fight, and there was nothing Fox could say to change that.

So instead, and surprisingly for the first time, Fox extended his hand to her, "It's really good to see you again, Liz."

Managing to approximate a smile, Liz nodded in reply and took his hand, "You too, Fox."

They'd be partners in war yet again.

CHAPTER 13

Lieutenant General Colin Brawn frowned slightly as he stepped off the bottom of the pinnace ramp, his eyes sweeping across the main landing field that dominated one of the flanks of the Freetown capital city. It was much like Antarctic Base — a giant, flat, open space with no defensible features save for buildings. This wouldn't be a place he'd set up a perimeter — not if he could help it anyway.

"General!"

Brawn blinked at the hail, turning to face an approaching human. He immediately recognized the man and his uniform: Commandant James Plummer was the commander of what remained of the Genesis Marine Corps, and he'd been a good compatriot over the past days of discussions.

They had a tall order on their hands. With Omega clearly showing an interest in landing on the planet, it seemed evident that a ground defense would be necessary... but with millions of people crammed into the perimeter of a single main shield, the Allied troops would face two problems: first, the area was too compact to allow for much maneuvering, and second, the area was too big to hold in its entirety if simultaneously attacked from two or more sides.

In other words, this island was *not* easy to defend, particularly since half of it was unshielded and only guarded by the small gun battery stations that dotted the coast.

And Omega was already out there...

But Colin Brawn had been a marine for a century now, and he knew his trade well. Since his days as a Major commanding the marines in *Atlas* — and after rather famously saving Pat Conroy's camp from the Kroggs around the time of the Battle of Gibraltar — he'd come to command brigades, then divisions, and now no less than the Light Division, one of the most elite mobile combat units in the Earther Marine Corps.

If anyone could meet Omega's challenge in this place, it was him.

Well, hopefully...

Squaring his shoulders slightly, Colin nodded to Plummer as he came to a stop. The human replied in kind, deep creases in his otherwise youngish-looking face seeming to reflect the strain he was under... the fact that the Marine Corps force he commanded probably represented at least one percent of the surviving human population of Genesis couldn't help.

Plummer looked up at the taller bear General, "This place is indefensible."

Mildly surprised by the frankness, Brawn glanced away from the city, noting the glow of the perimeter shield that kept the Omega soldiers away from the land approaches.

"The shields are doing their job," the bear observed after a moment. "That's a start."

Plummer didn't sound enthused as he replied, "How many marines can you bring down here exactly? Somebody told me you've got the Light Division, so that means about 10,000. That it?"

Shrugging, Brawn returned his gaze to the Commandant, "That's what we've got. What about your troops? You've got at least 25,000, don't you?"

"Yes... but as you might guess, mine aren't exactly feeling tip-top just now. They need a break after all that's happened to them... I don't know how much use they'll be garrisoning a tropical *paradise*."

Brawn opened his mouth to disagree, but he was cut off by the arrival of newcomers behind him: Commissioner Clyde and Brigadier Mustafa Bengal, the panther commanding the Guards Brigade of the Light Division. Of the 10,000 troops under Brawn's command, the 2,000 Guards headed by Bengal were the very best, easily on par with the Guards Brigade of the Heavy Division — the vaunted formation that had assaulted the Queen's palace at the end of the Krogg War.

Bengal came to a stop alongside his General, and with him, Commissioner Clyde of the Constabulary decided to reply to Plummer's concern, "My troops will keep your marines in line if they get too relaxed, Commandant."

Brawn's ear twitched at the sharp words, and he glanced to Bengal. The Brigadier had gained a great deal of experience in dealing with humans after the Krogg War, and now he merely tilted his head and gave an instinctive sign of his displeasure at the candor.

The humans were already going at each other. *Already*.

"Gentlemen, this isn't the time for rivalries," Brawn wasn't subtle in dissuading this sort of talk, especially given the circumstances. "Based on what we know, we need every pair of boots we can get on the ground. If your marines need rest, Jim, we'll rotate them through central zones for breaks, but I need them on the ground with the Light Division."

Both men looked up at the bear as he spoke, their eyes narrowing in turn. Technically speaking, at least by the terms of the Krogg War, Brawn was the junior force commander here; Plummer was the Commandant of half the Genesis Marine Corps... under normal circumstances, that would have matched him to General Kudlee or General Lupus. As the head of planetary security for Freetown, Clyde was at least the same. Brawn was *only* a Lieutenant General — the senior officer not of the entire Earther Marine Corps, but just one of its (admittedly elite) divisions.

However, he also happened to have earned plenty of battle experience in the Krogg War, as had Mustafa Bengal. And then Bengal's Guards had helped quell some of the strife on Genesis after the war. These Earthers were much more experienced than their human counterparts: rank was immaterial. The humans had to know that the Earthers on the ground were their best chance at stopping Omega's minions, and as such, were in charge.

"We'll start landing as soon as I have guaranteed billets for us. We've been through enough not to have to suffer discomfort while we're out here..." Plummer's tone remained sharp, and again Brawn sighed. Concern for the well-being of one's troops was commendable... but when a mission was as vital as this, there had to be limits to creature comforts.

Time to lay down the law.

"Gentlemen, bickering aggravates me. Do you really want to aggravate a bear of my size?"

Those words drew glances from both humans, and Bengal then tilted his head, "I second that, though I am a panther. Perhaps we should tour the defenses."

The flatbed hover truck slid slowly to a stop beside one of Freetown's winding rivers, then lowered itself to ground on the bank. Brawn, Bengal and Plummer hopped off the back as the vehicle settled, then Clyde stepped out of the passenger compartment and waved them up to the point in the shield that might offer Omega a breach.

"This is one of our river gates," Clyde turned to the three marine officers. "It's a one-way shield, stopping anything from the outside coming in. Problem is, the water flows from outside into town on its way out to sea, so in the gate area here, the shield drops every three seconds for about half a second, and relieves the water pressure. If they're going to break through our shield, I get the sense it'll be at this gate or at the other one like it up the road."

Brawn frowned at the shield as it hummed unevenly, the field dropping and restoring at abrupt but regular intervals. This was definitely a weakness... but if they closed the gate the water pressure from the river would build, and the weight might eventually collapse the shield entirely.

"How far up the road is the other one?" Plummer frowned at his human counterpart, and Clyde looked in the direction of the other gate.

"About twelve kilometers up the highway. It's the same size as this one."

Brawn glanced at Bengal, the panther meeting his eyes. There was no question; these two points would have to be given particular protection against incursions by the minions. If Omega was able to breach either of them, the rivers flowing from the outside through Freetown's capital could become conduits for hundreds of his troops. More, if the plague managed another drop.

"Alright, we'll put a brigade on each one of these," the General's words were heavy. "We'll set up a perimeter with two battalions lined up to hold the gates themselves, and then two battalions in reserve in case anything breaks through..."

Plummer slowly nodded, "Good plan, keep a couple of flying battalions ready to set up a broad cordon if anything slips in."

"Exactly," Brawn nodded to the Commandant, then looked back to the energy barrier. "We can't hope to put troops along every meter of this shield line, so we're going to have to deal with any penetrations by rapid response — defense in depth. Commissioner Clyde, I think your Constables would probably do best in that role. Your people know this island much better than we do, so when it comes to containing a breakthrough I'd say that'd be your job."

Clyde's eyes narrowed slightly, but he said nothing. After a few seconds he offered a jerked nod.

"What about the rest of the division?" Bengal drew Brawn's attention again, and the latter bear's ear twitched once more. What indeed.

"Well... hm. You and the Guards should stay at the spaceport, Mustafa. If the perimeter breaks, that'll be our fall-back position. We'll be aiming to evacuate in that case, so we'll need to hold it, a lot like 2/54th held Darymanis spaceport. The other brigades..."

Brawn paused thoughtfully. This city was not small, by any means. There were the highway entry points to watch, he supposed... though if the entire division went on line to protect the gates at the perimeter, he'd have nothing left in reserve to respond to serious breakthroughs... But he had the entire Freetown Constabulary to respond to those breakthroughs, and the Genesis troops...

"How many reliable marines do you think you can really count on, Jim? How many can you bring down here?" Brawn turned back to the Commandant, and the weathered man shrugged.

"That I can count on? Maybe 5,000, but I'd feel safer saying 2,000 or so. I can trust 1st and 2nd Marine Regiments to do their jobs, even now. The rest... well, not top form."

"Not top form to fight for the last planet of human settlement?" Clyde's words made no attempt to hide his bitterness. "We're trying to save our homes and you're too sad to help? That's great. You know we'd have helped you out if you'd just–"

"Irritated *bear*!" Brawn's roar scared some birds out of a nearby tree. Bengal rounded him to glare at Clyde, while Brawn kept his stare fixed as civilly as possible on Plummer. "Two regiments is fine for now. We'll put them at the two highway gates, dig them in solidly. The Light Division's last two brigades will stay mobile, but they'll be stationed near each of those gates in case you need backup. Fair?"

Plummer nodded evenly, and Clyde was silent behind Brawn.

With a single short nod, Brawn dismissed the meeting, “Good. Let’s head for the spaceport. We’ll get back into orbit and get things organized.”

By the look of things so far, Colin wasn’t going to enjoy this job... but hopefully they’d save Freetown anyway.

Hopefully...

CHAPTER 14

Liz Hastings settled slowly into the old chair at the head of the conference table in *Grimbold*'s main briefing room. The Captains that had been assigned to her command from the Survey Service were finding seats throughout the room, and the clustering of so many uniforms suddenly reminded the former President and ArcGeneral of what she'd missed from her Naval days.

So many fine officers were here — people who'd been determined to stay in space because they felt that it was where they belonged. She recognized many of the names of those assembled as noted fighters from the last war — Earthers like her own Farley Karr, and others including Calis Landry and Rayn Felner from Ami Dune's old 141st Flying Squadron. These officers had forged brilliant reputations against the Kroggs. There were human officers too, Jessica Forbes not least among them. Many veterans of the last war who'd taken regen were present, and then there were also some sons and daughters of officers she'd fought with back in the old days.

Sarah's old Flag ArcColonel, Rodney Evan-Thomas, nodded to Liz as he sat at the far end of the table, and her lips twitched slightly in a smile to acknowledge the familiar face.

These were the best sort of people she could have asked for in putting together a scratch command to fight against Omega. They would do their duty, fight fiercely, and use every trick in the book. And Liz was absolutely certain that they wouldn't have a hope of stopping the plague.

Not that it was good to think such a thing — she knew there'd be no chance of victory if she didn't believe in it first — but she didn't have that confidence, no one did. All she could hope was that they'd put up a good fight when the tired 64s and 28s rearmed from the Survey Service made a stand against Omega.

She didn't want to tell anyone in this room just how slim their chances of survival were… and she expected that no one needed to be informed. They were all fairly certain death was coming. Lang Sandpelt — no mediocre officer — and his *Venerables* had already demonstrated the odds against them.

Liz blinked before she got too lost in that line of thought. It was time to start explaining things to her people, "So, we're all commanding ships of First Gibraltar Provisional Battle Group. I'm calling us the Surveyors Provisional Battle Group, I figure it's closer to what we're used to."

There were a few nods — a name didn't seem terribly important just now.

"And I was talking to Fox about half an hour ago. He's sending a squadron of *Chimeras* out in two days to escort *Gibraltar Five* and *Six* on the run to Krogg. He wants us with them as escort, and then to help stiffen the Krogg defenses, in case Omega is able to catch the rest of the fleet before it can retreat from here."

Liz's dispassionate words drew shallow frowns from many in the room, but no one was surprised or shocked.

"The good news is that Freetown seems to be holding out well enough for now. Andra has stopped one attempted landing already, and they're in the process of putting the Light Division on the ground under Colin Brawn. Everyone's best guess is that Gibraltar is next, then Krogg 'A'. One big push to get Krogg biomatter. If he gets that stuff, it'd just about end the war, based on what he was able to do with it on those black Omega ships."

Again there were nods, and glances shared between Captains who were old comrades. Calis Landry and Rayn Felner looked knowingly at each other. Evan-Thomas and Jessica Forbes exchanged 'this is going to be fun'-type glances.

"So your ships have all been lined up for yard time. I have the schedule here now, I'll send copies around. Everyone's getting re-gunned, full upgrades. Human officers who haven't yet, get time in the war-gaming sims to get used to fighting with guns instead of missiles. I'm thinking we should break this Battle Group into five squadrons, and I'd like to take one. If you all want to start forming groups based on who you're most comfortable fighting with, it'd be a good idea. We'll make sure to group any teams together in the same squadrons. Any questions?"

Liz felt as though she was doing all the talking… and she was. It was a briefing, after all — it was just strange how unused to giving briefings she'd become. Decades before, when she was the matriarch of the Genesis Fleet, they'd been second nature… but once she'd become President, things had started to change. She felt rusty.

"I'm guessing our survival chances in a standup fight aren't so good," Farley Karr was sitting at Liz's right hand.

She shrugged and nodded at his observation, "All you have to do is ask Jax Furgus how well 64s did against the Kroggs. And then think much worse."

There were soft chuckles from some of the Earthers who knew Jax. No one could even remember how many 64s the Kroggs had shot out from under him…

"We can't hurt the black ships, so we need to figure out how to keep them off the backs of our real capital ships," Evan-Thomas piped up, already reverting to the mind of a fleet Flag ArcColonel. He wasn't thinking about surviving the upcoming fight, he was trying to figure out how to help Fox Magnus' ships win it.

Of course, his words were an open death sentence for the Captains of the Battle Group... and none of these hardened old spacers blinked at that implication. After all, they were fighting for the salvation of their respective peoples; this was the job that they had all been forged for.

"My thoughts exactly," Liz nodded to her old colleague. "So, once we get squadrons sorted out I want us thinking tactics. Go over the logs we have from Earth, Freetown, New Halifax, the other galaxy... *everywhere.* Look at how Omega is handling his ships, go over the after-actions from our survivors. And look at how Lang lost at Genesis. We need viable ways to wreck Omega's fun when he comes calling. We get in his way and Fox and Garvin and Chronos might have a shot at beating him."

Again there were nods, and the Captains began now to turn away from her, talking amongst themselves and forming squadrons in ways that would take advantage of their past experience, current dispositions, and respective strengths.

Liz realized all the talking she'd done had amounted to perhaps five minutes, and yet it had seemed much longer. She took a deep breath and then glanced at Karr and Jessica Forbes, "We sticking together in a squadron?"

Jessica smiled at her comrade, "Don't see why we should break up a winning team. You'll need a new Flag Captain, *Admiral.*"

Karr gave a giant grin, "And I need you two to look out for me."

"I'll join, if it's alright."

Liz's eyes shifted up and discovered that Captain Evan-Thomas had come down the table.

"Sure you don't want to take a squadron of your own, Rod?" she asked quickly, but he shook his head.

"I fight best for great commanders. And that's you."

A somewhat surprised blink was Liz's answer to that, and then those fine Earther Captains she'd noticed before, Calis Landry and Rayn Felner, arrived at Evan-Thomas' shoulder.

"This is going to be one hell of a squadron," Liz said quietly after a moment.

The Earthers and the humans smiled at each other — sad but meaningful smiles. Their fates hadn't changed, that much they knew. But to die in good company was, surprisingly enough, a significant thing just now.

The First Gibraltar Provisional Battle Group — the Surveyors — had been formed.

CHAPTER 15

In all her years, Audrey DeBrooke had never seen anything quite like the landing of the Light Division. Altogether, 10,000 Earther marines were coming to the Freetown capital city — more than had been concentrated on any one planet for combat operations since the Battle of the Antarctic Plain.

And what marines they were.

Audrey knew what good marines looked like — Freetown was home to numerous veterans of the Genesis Corps, many very fine soldiers who had killed Kroggs and fought on distant worlds.

But they were toddlers compared to the sharp veterans of the Light Division.

It was just something about the way these Earthers handled themselves... how they moved as she watched them come off their landers. Columns of khaki would descend ramps, walking in step with arms swinging in unison, shoulders held in perfect position. It was as though they were a single entity.

They stopped in crisp columns on the field before her, standing like towering statues of strength while they waited for their companies and battalions to disembark from the landers. Because this was a parade-ground exercise, they'd even ordered themselves by height so that the tallest bears were on the flanks and a smooth curve of head height joined one side to the other.

It's like art.

As soon as Audrey thought that, she had to mentally shake herself: these were probably the deadliest troops in the universe, including the Kroggs. But Omega's minions were like the extensions of a single great mind — a force very tough to reckon with, and quite probably a match for them.

But these Earthers were so finely tuned to each other that their parade motions could appear all as one. That had to mean they could fight as a single great force. The reputation of the Light Division, the *First* Division of the Earther Marine Corps, was legendary. Just as renowned as the Second, Heavy Division. She couldn't ask for fiercer defenders.

Indeed, the very sight of them gave her some confidence again — no mean achievement, because she was still being swallowed by so much angst and depression at the plight faced by her world. Maybe with the Earthers here...

"They're a sight for sore bloody eyes. My eyes were actually aching while I was waiting to see them, dammit."

Pat Conroy appeared next to Audrey, his presence startling her even though it shouldn't have — he'd come out of the control tower with her to watch as the Guards Brigade of the division formed its ranks.

For his part, Pat was still determined to be positive. There'd be no more bickering between the Genesis Marines and the Freetown Constabulary with the Earthers on the ground... and if anyone could handle Omega, it would be these wolves, cats and bears.

Audrey seemed to have come to the same conclusion, and Pat was glad to see a tiny spark of relief on her face as she watched the disembarkation spectacle. The poor woman had been through enough, and after seeing what had happened to Sarah, Pat knew all too well what could become of the acting Governor of Freetown.

The events of the last weeks were killing Sarah, and Pat again felt like he could do nothing for his wife. She was completely shutting him out... the way she always seemed to when she actually needed him most, but wouldn't admit it to herself. The same had happened during the last war, and between the wars when she'd finally come to terms with her past... it was as though he wasn't part of her inner circle. If he let it, that fact could depress him greatly.

So instead of dwelling, he was keeping busy...

"Pat Conroy, is that you?"

Pat blinked out of his pondering as a vaguely familiar voice reached his ears, and then he noticed a feline was approaching, "Tom Katt, you bastard!"

The khaki-clad tiger who had been striding over to Audrey and Pat halted with a surprised smile on his face, then closed the last few meters between them with his hand extended, "Good to see you too, Pat."

Pat shook the Earther's hand enthusiastically and grinned, "Been *decades*, hasn't it?"

"It has. I see you've decided to come down to the ground for more trouble?" the tiger's smile broadened. "I suppose if Beckett Lupus couldn't convince you to behave back in the Krogg War days, then I was never going to."

Pat laughed, but then caught Audrey's confused expression out of the corner of his eye, so he stepped back to introduce them, "Audrey DeBrooke, this is Lieutenant Colonel Tom Katt, of the Third Foot Guards. Just after the last war, he helped us sort out our special ops teams, and he helped us out of some trouble with the Churchers."

"Actually it's full *Colonel* now, Pat. And I've moved on to the First Guards," Katt grinned.

Pat laughed, "Listen to mister ego."

Audrey shook Katt's hand with a nod, "Colonel Katt... pleased to meet you. Great name."

Katt chuckled, "Everyone says that. I must admit, I'm proud of it."

With a brief laugh that surprised her, Audrey nodded, "I would be too."

Just as Pat was about to continue with Katt, Brigadier General Mustafa Bengal approached the trio.

"Reunions and introductions?" the panther asked with a smile.

"Had to say hello to this old troublemaker," Katt's hand waved towards Pat.

Grinning, the Irishman shrugged, "Might as well."

Mustafa agreed, "Certainly. Good to see you again, Pat. Been a few decades!"

"That's what I said," Pat shook the General's hand, then stood aside to allow Audrey to do the same.

She met Bengal's eyes as her grip tightened around his, then offered soft but certain words, "Looking as brilliant as expected, Brigadier. Our thanks for showing off, it's boosting morale around here."

That was certainly true. Even forgetting their post-war history on Genesis, these marines had been famed fighters in the last war. When it came to looking sharp and fighting like devils, none could compare to the Guards.

"It's our pleasure to be here. Colin thought you might like to see us come off parade style like that. It's not much good in the field, but parade surely does make for a gallant show," the panther's deep voice was almost as soothing as the appearance of his marines. "We were wondering if the Guards might march through the streets, perhaps generate some confidence in the people here."

Pat thought carefully about the offer... for all of a second, "I think that'd be a damned good idea."

Bengal smiled at the Irishman and nodded, "Then we'll set off immediately. The rest of the brigades will move to their areas of operation, but we'll take a tour before returning here."

"Good good, go to it."

The Brigadier didn't waste any time: he smiled and glanced sideways at Tom Katt, "You'll be heading up the line, so best get to your unit."

Katt clicked his heels together, "Certainly. See you later Pat, Governor."

With nods from the two humans, Katt set off in a blur, and then Bengal turned to face his command, snapping his own heels together, "Guards Brigade, in column of fours to the left. Colonels, we are to parade through the civilian district. By regiment and battalion, march out your marines!"

The orders flew across the field. Audrey and Pat didn't even bother to try to keep up as the Guards arranged themselves into a column four wide and 500 long. The entire 2,000-marine brigade became a long snake across the landing zone.

Led by the first battalion of the First Foot Guards — with Tom Katt at their head — and then followed in succession by the second battalion of the First Guards, the first of the Third and the second of the Third, the brigade began a steady march, with Bengal slipping smoothly into place at Katt's shoulder.

It was a sight to see.

The long column of khaki marched in time — its marines' cadence as perfectly coordinated as if it was being guided by a drum — and it headed straight out of the spaceport, then turned into the streets of the residential district.

Audrey and Pat took deep breaths and tried to soak in the brief comfort, then went back to the control tower. More landers were coming in — many marines were still on their way down.

Jason Clyde heard about the commotion of the Guards Brigade parade, and decided to see the spectacle for himself. Having grabbed a hover car from the Constabulary lot, he was able to head off the quick-marching Earthers, arriving at an intersection just as they began to pass.

Halting his car and climbing out, he left the hover field running and stood with his arms draped over the door and roof as the smart khaki marines walked on by. The Earthers were so damned good at this. They looked incredibly crisp, and yet they fought like brilliant beasts...

He was glad he was on their side.

"Um... excuse me. It's Commissioner Clyde right?"

Clyde nodded slowly to the sweet voice, not really paying attention as his eyes fixated on the Earthers. But then something in the back of his mind suggested he look at the speaker.

Turning then, he nodded, "How may I help you..."

He stopped.

It was the brunette who'd been on the surfers' bus that had nearly let Omega into the city. She wasn't wearing all that much, and what she *was* wearing was damn near painted on.

Surfer girls, damn me...

Clyde had been under a lot of stress lately, no question about it. As the brunette smiled sheepishly and stepped closer to him, he started thinking it was a good time for a break. No one would miss him with all these Earthers marching around. They'd deal with any problems for the next hour... his Constables could do without him that long...

"I just wanted to *thank* you for saving us," the brunette shrugged. "And I wanted to ask if this means we're going to be alright. I'm a bit freaked out by all of this, you know..."

Smiling with confidence that he shouldn't have felt, he nodded, "Between the Earthers and us, we'll be alright. In fact, things are so good I was just about to go off duty for a while."

The girl seemed to brighten a bit, "Really?"

The Commissioner nodded, no longer even thinking about his duty, "Yes indeed. How about I take you wherever you're going, and I'll reassure you again."

With a nervous but agreeable shrug, the pretty girl nodded, "Alright. I'm Carmine, by the way."

"Call me Jason," Clyde let the girl climb into the hover car.

And so while the Earther Guards were parading through the streets and rallying the people, Jason Clyde, the head of the Constabulary and the man who would coordinate their response to any breaches of the shield, was getting a morale boost of his own.

Some might say it seemed like a good idea at the time.

But even that would be tough... *impossible* to argue.

CHAPTER 16

"Graham has decided he doesn't want to wear his. Apparently he isn't worried about having the Larosians in his head... and I can't say I'm surprised. Seems like they'd get nothing more than an icy reception in there, just like we're getting out here."

Christine nodded.

Then she realized she had no idea who was talking or what they were talking about...

Uhm... whom... right, Joyce Furgus. About Graham's armor...

Joyce had come to Christine's quarters to help her figure out how to improve the cut of the clothes coming out of her auto-tailor, but Christine's heart and mind had only been half into that process. The importance of fashion was... well, it was gone. Christine had rather suddenly stopped caring about the cut of her clothes.

That, in itself, was no problem — she was quite certain that worrying about how she looked would be ridiculous under these circumstances. What was distracting her was the new and growing sense of certainty she felt. She was still coming to terms with the fact that her personality was seemingly in flux — little changes were continuing to surface, and it was becoming increasingly difficult to keep up.

When did I stop caring about how I looked?

Obviously, Christine had never been as obsessed with appearance as had some of the socialite types on Genesis, but she had always liked to look good. Now she found that she genuinely didn't care. The starkness of that realization hadn't fully registered with her until Joyce had helped her create a much neater jumpsuit, with pant legs and sleeves that weren't absurdly baggy... and she'd felt nothing when she tried it on.

It was a strange development, in a series of strange developments...

"Christine, you alright?"

The young human blinked twice and realized the lioness was standing just behind her, looking at her in the mirror.

"Uhm... fine. So... sorry, I really didn't process what you were saying."

Joyce smiled and half-shrugged, "I was saying Graham is cold as a fish and doesn't care if the Larosians know it. So he told me he wouldn't be wearing his armor until he needs it for action."

Christine raised an eyebrow at the Earther marine, "So I'm the only human wearing this... well I really... actually... you know I don't much care. I think."

Joyce put a hand on the young human's shoulder and grinned, "I thought as much. But if you cared, I'd say it makes you look distinguished... thanks to my fine fashion assistance, of course. I'm almost jealous."

That drew a chuckle from Christine — as if the fine-haired cat in the sharp khaki uniform of the Earther Marine Corps gave a damn how she looked. And *as if* Earthers got jealous...

Wow, that was the most 'my age' thought I've had in a while.

Joyce had become Christine's friend and confidant — the only one Christine regularly talked to aboard this ship, maybe with the exception of Tovarrin and Narosh. Graham was too absorbed in his mission. She worked with him for hours every day, either helping him with his sword technique, or looking at tactical scenarios, or just sitting on the bridge with him... but he wasn't focused on anything but Omega.

So Christine went to Joyce when she wanted to talk, because talking to Earthers really did seem to suit her now. And Joyce was more than happy to be the best friend (or mom or big sister) whenever Christine needed that — and to accept the changes the young human was experiencing without judgment.

Earthers were good at that sort of thing, obviously. Hopefully Claire was getting the same kind of help back on Earth...

The thought of her sister came as a surprise to Christine. Claire hadn't been on her mind much, and even now she wasn't able to dwell on her. Glancing back over her shoulder she nodded to Joyce, then let her smile fade as she sighed.

"Alright, so what were we supposed to be doing now?"

With all her preoccupations, ArcLieutenant Schaeffer wasn't really on top of the schedules she was supposed to be keeping — not a good thing since she was the senior aide to an ArcGeneral...

Joyce shrugged slightly, "Graham and Tovarrin should be meeting us in the sparring chamber in about ten minutes."

Christine nodded, "Right."

"I understand we are only four days from the main concentration of the derelict fleet," Tovarrin looked sideways at Graham as the two proceeded through the newly-gleaming corridors of *Carnarvon*.

A single nod was Graham's response, but as the Captain-Elite of the Stealth Guard watched the gesture, he also peered discreetly into the human's mind. He was about to spar with this man, and he wanted to be certain the ArcGeneral was in form to meet attacks...

Look around as you please, Tovarrin. If you're worried that you'll hurt me, don't concern yourself.

Tovarrin nearly stopped as he read the newly-rising surface thoughts from

Graham's mind. How had the ArcGeneral known what he was doing? Humans weren't telepathic...

"If you're wondering, no I'm not telepathic. But the number of times you've glanced at me in the last five minutes rather tipped your hand."

Graham's words were dispassionate, and as Tovarrin peered into the junior Manchester's mind, he recognized yet again the intensity of the cold that had grasped it.

"Is it healthy for you to be so withdrawn and dispassionate, Graham?" Tovarrin's question was quiet, but Graham heard it across the abyss that he kept between himself and everyone around him.

"No, it isn't. But it's the way of things."

Tovarrin inclined his head slightly at the reply, "You may change your behavior if you wish. You clearly have the self-discipline, you may be able to accomplish your quest without repressing so much of yourself. You may find shards of inner peace in other ways..."

"No peace. This is the way it is. Don't press the question, my friend. I don't expect you to understand."

Tovarrin didn't understand, nor did anyone else who saw Graham — Larosian, Earther *or* human.

But as the sparring chamber appeared before the pair, Tovarrin put that feeling aside. Later today he was due to train with Joyce Furgus again, and whatever the state of Graham Manchester, the Captain-Elite was certain of the lioness' ability. It would be a good afternoon.

Christine had always found that sparring cleared her head... though since she'd been confined to her suit it had become even more important. Fencing had been the purpose for the original skin suit, after all — wearing it made her feel as though she should be swinging her saber all the time.

Christine winced as she watched Joyce Furgus somehow slide back out of range when Tovarrin opened their sparring duel with a draw cut that would have caught someone slower. Then the young human blinked and thus missed the counterattack, as the Earther Captain surged forward with carefully controlled bursts of explosive motion... and then Tovarrin countered...

They went back and forth, neither one managing any success for long minutes. The clash of fighting styles was incredible. The juxtaposition of the crisp khaki of Joyce's uniform and the shining silver of Tovarrin's armor was striking...

Aha, thinking about clothing. Perhaps you haven't lost all your human qualities after all.

Christine sighed at that thought, then spared a look at Graham, who was standing and watching impassively as well.

"Well, should we get started again?" she asked evenly.

Graham nodded, drawing his sword as he did. The straight blade of the mortuary-hilted weapon glinted in the bright light of the chamber, and as he keyed on his shield he turned to her. Her own saber was already in hand, so she re-keyed her shield and turned…

Just in time to meet his attack.

She parried and fell back across the floor, gaining distance between them, and then met his eyes. By now she was immune to the chill that was at the core of his grim gaze, so she lunged forward.

Her short cut from the right was parried, but she recovered and drove for his stomach in a fast blur. Her blood was hot and her instincts — fueled by the Earther DNA now flowing through her — guided her attack.

And despite that, she landed *hard* on her back.

What the hell?

She rolled and was immediately on her feet, but Graham came forward again, his blade missing the shield around her midriff by a hair. His feet then shifted easily across the floor, bringing him inside the arc of her saber and denying her riposte. His free hand caught her wrist, and then his sword came alongside her neck.

Christine froze.

What the hell?

Joyce and Tovarrin had stopped their own sparring to watch the two humans — Christine was overbalancing backwards because Graham had come so far forward… how had he gotten inside her guard?

Her eyes had darted down to the sword at her throat, then they shifted back up to his eyes… and she saw a glimmer of anger in the stare. Anger, an emotion which was clearly not in keeping with his cold façade.

And then the anger was gone.

Graham stepped back and sheathed his sword in a smooth motion, allowing Christine a moment to straighten up and take a deep breath.

"Thank you for the exercise, Christine," Graham nodded to her.

Then he turned and walked out.

Christine sheathed her saber and frowned at his back as he exited the chamber. His control might be starting to slip… if he didn't get a shot at Omega soon, he might let loose some of his anger…

They'd find the derelict Larosian Fleet in four days. Perhaps he'd have his chance then. In the meantime, she'd have to be more attentive.

Shaking her head, Christine went back to her sword work. She found a Larosian to spar with, and he didn't replicate Graham's success.

CHAPTER 17

Elsewhere in the Larosian galaxy, *ENS Galahad* led a wary column of Earther ships through dead space.

On the bridge of the *Champion*-class ship of the line, Rear Admiral Minnie Maximane frowned at her holo plot and tried to figure just what her prey was up to. Omega was out here somewhere, and so were Graham Manchester and the Larosians.

But communication with Graham had been nonexistent... and obviously Omega wasn't going to leave a trail of bread crumbs to follow. Not that *Galahad's* beaten-up sensors would necessarily be able to detect actual bread crumbs out there...

"Updates just came in from the squadron, everyone's holding together fine. *Jupiter's* engineer even managed to correct that field variance without shutting down the reactor..." Mel Ramsay, Minnie's fox Flag Captain, came to a stop at the plot.

The two stood side by side for a moment, staring at the icons in the holo chart, and the black line that suggested Omega's expected course through the galaxy — a direct run to the Krogg corridor.

If only Omega had stopped to take over some old Larosian colonies on his way, it would have given Minnie a path to follow. Not that she could wish absorption by Omega onto any Larosians... damn, she just wish she knew where his ships were.

Only a few weeks before, she was certain her instincts might have answered the question for her... but now, after all the losses the Earthers had suffered after trusting instinct, she couldn't help but doubt whatever popped into her head.

She knew she shouldn't, but she did.

"If you want, I can get the crystal ball out of storage," Mel Ramsay said after a moment. "Might show us where he is."

Minnie allowed a smile at the remark, "I'd rather play catch with it. Damn me, Mel, I just don't know... and Graham's out here with the Larosians looking too..."

Her words drifted off as her eyes swept through the plot again. They were passing through the outermost sphere of worlds that had been part of the Larosian Empire, following a vector that took them straight at the Krogg corridor. Their only hope was to get there before Omega did, so they could stop him.

But would Omega be going where they expected, or would he do something more clever… or something more necessary?

That question came to mind as Minnie's eyes fell upon the horde of plague-ridden, derelict Larosian ships, sitting where they had been infected on the former front lines of the Krogg War. Thousands upon thousands of Larosian ships, all dead in space, overrun by Omega Type 1.

They weren't quite on the direct route to the Krogg corridor, but if Omega could get hold of them, he could infect them with his current version, and perhaps add thousands of ships to his battle line.

Aha.

Well that's what Minnie would try, but of course Minnie Maximane — ever her late-father's daughter — was not a megalomaniac sadistic plague bent on annihilation of all free life…

But it was what she'd do.

"I think we need to adjust course, Mel. I think he's heading for those plague ships."

Captain Ramsay frowned briefly, her own eyes shifting through the blue light of the plot and settling on the cloud of black-trimmed silver icons representing the old Larosian Fleet. Yes, that would make sense.

"It makes sense. If you're comfortable with it, I say we try."

The gravity of this decision was immense, despite its simplicity. If they were wrong and Omega got through the corridor ahead of them, he'd be free to fall on Krogg 'A' from the rear.

But if Minnie's instinct was right, then they had no choice: if Omega reclaimed thousands of Larosian ships, there'd be no way the entire Earther Navy — let alone her battered little squadron — could stop him. They had to head him off at those derelicts, not let him take any.

Minnie nodded to her Flag Captain, "Let's do it."

"Cruising Master," Ramsay called instantly through the tank, "adjust course, port eleven, down six. Signal Officer, pass the adjustment on to the squadron."

Minnie scratched her neck, "Hopefully this isn't a mistake."

Mel Ramsay's ear twitched and she nodded, "Hopefully."

The squadron followed *Galahad*.

Basking in his ability to simultaneously be everywhere one of his minions was, Omega contemplated just how completely he was about to crush the first line of Earther defenses.

He loved his work, he *really* did. This was what he'd been craving for what seemed an eternity, and he was doing it so very well. All the joys of torturing humans were just a distraction: he was going to dismantle the Earther spirit before they faced him in the climactic showdown — and of course, there would indeed be a *climactic* showdown, just later.

For now he watched the remaining ships from his first wave cross through Larosian space at high speed, headed where the Earthers would never expect them to go.

So predictable, the Earthers. Do-gooders were always easy to figure out.

Hell, they even wanted to save the Kroggs. What a joke! First the weepy cattle race hadn't had the balls to wipe out the Kroggs, and now they wanted to protect all the black-carapace types from him?

Come on. They knew by now that he was using Krogg biomatter to great effect. The smartest thing they could have done was blow up the fucking planet. But no, they had to be noble. And they were going to pay for their naïve optimism. Each of Omega's major avatars — Omega-Gillian, Omega-Paine, and Omega-Natosh — smiled at that prospect.

Well, Omega-Gillian moaned more than smiled, but that was just due to circumstance.

Ah, it was good to be evil.

Speaking of which, on Genesis, Omega-Natosh watched as a gang of teenagers fought to the death with sticks. It was pretty tame, but he was tiring of sadistic rape and torture for the present. Not that he wouldn't get back into it — perish the thought — it was just time for a bit of a break.

He'd do some skinning later, though. He loved that — it never got old. There was nothing like peeling away the skin in strips just an inch wide, and then feeding them to children or whatnot… ah, grand memories…

Fresh memories, he realized — that particular escapade had been just this morning. He really was living the high life.

Ooh, one of the teens from the pack fighting to the death had just torn off the arm of another and was using it as a club against the rest! How very poetic…

Alright, enough play time.

Focusing for a moment, Omega reached out from each of his avatars to his many billions of minions, and carefully checked his status everywhere.

The Earthers were about to be hit in many places, and in ways that they hadn't even thought possible. Freetown, Gibraltar, and Krogg were all going to fall, and then he'd have his chance to move against the real prize.

Earth would be his again.

And when it was, he'd have to force himself to keep the Earthers alive for as long as possible — he couldn't get carried away. Torture in groups no larger than family units… he'd have to figure out a way to get Earthers to feast on human children, perhaps. That'd be a nice way to destroy their do-goodish bullshit.

One way or another, those beasts would learn the gravity of their failure.

He was their God, after all.

And just as he thought that lovely fact, Omega-Gillian was pierced by a burst of sheer primal pleasure — the sort that was packaged with lust.

Excellent, the pieces were all just about in place.

"About time I get this show on the road," his avatars said that at once.

Lying in the surfing girl's bed, Commissioner Jason Clyde grinned at the lovely brunette Carmine, then laughed, "*Again*, Carmine? Why not..."

Carmine smiled, and then kissed him.

Clyde let out a long breath against her lips, sure someone was looking after the deployment of the marines throughout Freetown's capital city. The Earthers were seeing to things, and Omega was nowhere to be found.

So if a sweet young woman wanted to get 'on the road again', he'd be glad to oblige.

He opened his eyes to stare at Carmine and to marvel at just how lucky he was. He met her sweet gaze.

And then he watched her eyes cloud, and turn from beautiful blue to inky black as she pulled away from him.

That's when his skin began to crawl.

"My name's Gillian, actually. Gillian Hodge... but I think we'll both agree I'm *sweet...*"

Jason Clyde tried to reach for his gun on the night table, but already his mind was not his own.

So he kissed Gillian Hodge, and renewed their passion far more viciously.

Omega laughed and made sure he got a recording to send to Graham.

Freetown was about to fall.

CHAPTER 18

Ursla sat quietly in her cabin on *Orion*, trying not to think too much about the fate of the planet below her ship.

Freetown couldn't be allowed to fall… but the unfortunate reality was that there wasn't anything she could do to guarantee it *wouldn't*. They'd stopped one attack already, but she knew Omega had a great deal more in store for this system. He wasn't going to quit it just because he'd faced a single setback…

Somehow she felt as though this problem of how to beat Omega was one she should discuss with Artie Tigar, her great old Flag Captain from the Krogg War, but of course he was lying limbless in Fengate Hospital, having already discovered that decisive victory wasn't a foregone conclusion against the plague.

Closing her eyes for a moment, Ursla endeavored to shut out the more negative possibilities of what might come.

And fortunately, the comm chimed at just the right moment to halt her musings.

"Bridge to Admiral Ursla, it's Esther here, Andra," it was the voice of Captain Arbear.

Ursla paused as she heard the summons, took a quick, centering breath and looked up at the ceiling speakers, "Hello Esther, what's up?"

"Strange readings from one of the currents in the ocean below. Near the wreckage of that transport we shot down."

Ursla blinked and then her eyes narrowed. She was tempted to ask just what qualified as 'strange', but she realized she already knew as much as she needed to. It wouldn't be good.

"Alright, I'm coming up. Have the Signal Officer order the nearest squadron of 44s to get into synchronous orbit over that current and to have boats standing by."

"Aye, aye," Esther Arbear closed the link.

Standing slowly, Ursla turned and made her way out of her cabin.

The Light Division's Fifth Brigade had just finished disembarking when Pat and Audrey decided to leave the tarmac and head to Government House. The arrival of 10,000 Earther marines might put the people at ease, but much still needed to be planned to deal with the possibilities of further landings.

"Last I heard from Clyde, he'd ordered the distribution of the last of our riot gear to the Guard depots. We have plenty of energy rifles and pulsars for ourselves thanks to the Earthers, but if the people get panicked I'm more worried about civil unrest..." Audrey was explaining the ground situation in even tones.

Paying little attention to the path she was taking across the landing field, she went nose-first into the chest of Colin Brawn. The General looked down at her with an amused expression, "Sorry to interrupt..."

Audrey stepped back quickly, shaking her head as she realized what she'd done, "No no, my fault entirely..."

"Aye, he is rather big. Can't understand how you didn't see him," Pat managed a light smile, and Audrey laughed shortly despite herself.

"Not sure how to take that, Pat," Brawn smiled with his own reply, and Pat shrugged.

"Only in the best ways that don't lead to you crushing me, you big old beast..."

Brawn chuckled, "Good thing I have news requiring your attention then, isn't it?"

The bear's expression slowly sobered, and Pat and Audrey looked at each other.

"What's the news then?" the Governor asked in low tones.

"Something in the currents out there," Brawn pointed towards the eastern shore of the island that held Freetown's capital city. "Andra's moving ships into position to have a look at it, but I think we should get to the war room to figure out just what's going on."

The two humans nodded slowly, and they followed the General to a waiting hover truck.

Esther Arbear nodded to Ursla as the latter emerged on *Orion's* bridge. As the two bears stepped to the side of the First Rate's plot, Ursla found herself frowning at her Flag Captain.

"Those signatures are *almost* a reading..." she wasn't sure just what she was looking at.

Arbear nodded, "Almost a clear indication of Omega life forms... but not quite, I know. Jax sent *Ceylon* and *Singapore* in for a closer look... they should be in range to scan properly in about two more minutes."

"Have we let Government House know?" Ursla's gaze remained fixed on the flashing black cloud strung through the Freetown ocean.

"Government House and General Brawn as well," Arbear confirmed. "The division is deploying to look after the weak points along the shield perimeter — the highway and the river gates. Commandant Plummer's about to insert the 1st and 2nd Marine Regiments, and the Guards Brigade is parading through civilian sectors to boost morale."

Ursla nodded slowly as the situation was made clear to her, pausing for a moment to tap up a new screen in the holo plot. The deployments of troops in Freetown's capital came up in the light blue holo projection, and Ursla watched as each Earther brigade snaked its way through the city to its designated defensive position.

They didn't seem like nearly enough troops to hold a city… and yet this landing marked the single largest marine ground operation since the Battle of the Antarctic Plain.

They'd have to be enough, because the only place the Earthers could concentrate a greater force on the ground would probably be Earth itself.

And if Omega was hitting Earth directly, Ursla didn't want to think about the ramifications.

"Alright, send to Sarah that she needs to get Plummer's troops on the ground soon. Let her know that we'll network *Ceylon's* scans as soon as we have them."

Arbear nodded at the orders, repeating them to the Signal Officer who passed them on to the tech sitting at the signals keyboards. Orders sprang from *Orion's* comms, and the Allied fleet over Freetown paid close attention to the currents that rolled through the planet's great ocean.

Omega was there, waiting for them to see him...

CHAPTER 19

Fox Magnus stood silently in *Chimera's* observation lounge, watching the last *Gibraltar* stations packing up and preparing for the flight out to Krogg. Soon they'd have to leave; *Conqueror* was nearing the veteran Earther base, and close on that ship's heels was a formation of those new Omega ships.

The First Space Lord swallowed at that thought, and again remembered the face of Lang Sandpelt, his once-midshipman aboard intrepid little *Flame*. How times had changed… In the days when Fox and *Flame* had plied the stars, nothing could do this to the Earthers. Earther timing was impeccable, Earther instinct always on the right track.

And now… well, not so much.

Letting out a long, steadying breath, Fox closed his eyes for a moment, and then his ear twitched as he heard the door open behind him.

"Hi Liz," he greeted his visitor before he turned, and Liz Hastings managed not to halt in surprise. She had been recognized by sound alone enough times over the years — the Earthers had big ears after all — but somehow it was still surprising... and a little unnerving.

"I sound that obvious?"

Fox managed a smile as his eyes met those of his human comrade, "Not really… I just knew it was you. So, your Surveyors are ready to head out with this convoy?"

She nodded in reply as she paced forward to face Fox across the broad table in the room, "We're all set. I hear *Conqueror* sent a drone forward?"

The First Space Lord matched her nod in reply, "They caught sight of a tailing force of those black ships and took a big risk dropping out of energy drive to send word ahead. We can't be sure Omega's *really* coming… but I get the feeling he is."

"We can't be sure… but he is?" Liz tilted her head slightly, and Fox shrugged.

"I know, he led Tom Locke on a wild-goose chase when he hit Earth… but he's coming. And he wants this place and Krogg 'A' and everything out here… I just *know* it. So we've accelerated the breakdown schedule as much as we could… we're sending you out to Krogg in about six hours with most of the stations, the regular garrison and your Surveyor group… but not that squadron of *Chimeras* I'd promised before. I'm going to keep the main force here."

Liz frowned now, "You're not going to try to engage those ships, I take it?"

Shaking his head, Fox turned back to look out through the glass, "We'll wait for *Conqueror*, hopefully, and then we'll all make the run together. I want to give the last survey ships out there the best possible chance to get to safety before we cut and run."

"Yes, but that'll mean you won't be in the Krogg system while we're preparing the defenses, Fox. We need you there to run the show..."

Fox blinked twice and sighed.

"He killed Lang, Liz. I don't feel right running from him after that."

The answer felt odd as he delivered it, and Liz stepped around the table and slowly approached the dapper fox from behind, "Yes, he did. But if he kills *you* here... well, we're not going to be in good shape at all."

Fox stared out at *Gibraltar One* as she spoke, and contemplated her words. He wanted to stay. He wanted to fight. He was tired of ducking and running... which was odd, considering that was what he did best — what he'd always done best.

But today things felt so much different than they had in the past, and for all Fox's experience, and for all the pride he took in his ships and crews, he just wanted to draw a line in the sand and hold it until he fell.

"Omega's got you jumpy, Fox. You need to think about what you're doing here. No point drawing your line in the sand until we get to Krogg. And then it'll be you and Chronos and me and Garvin... that'll be a hell of a line to cross. So wait 'til then."

Liz Hastings was a veteran of fleet command and political leadership... and here she was, right again. He wasn't thinking as he should have been, and now he needed to fix that.

Grinding his jaw, the First Space Lord nodded slowly, "Yes. Yes that does make more sense."

"Good. We can still leave some ships behind, if you like..."

He shook his head, "No. I'll call Karl and see if he can get *Gibraltar One* packed up in time to bring with us. We abandon the system entirely, leave a pod telling anyone who arrives late to scatter and stay out of sight."

Liz nodded, "Alright. So how much of a head start will we have?"

Fox's eyes settled on *Gibraltar One* and he blinked a few times to fire up his memory, "About fifty hours based on what *Conqueror's* telling us. You go on out ahead in six hours like I said. We'll probably wait for *Gibraltar One* and get moving right after it's ready... or leave it if it'll take too long."

That was it, then. They really were going to leave Gibraltar behind. What a strange feeling.

"I'll head back to *Grimbold*," Liz nodded after a moment.

Fox glanced at his old comrade, "I should have asked... did you want something? You came here, after all..."

"This is actually what I was looking for," Liz managed a smile, and Fox tilted his head.

"Alright then. Talk to you in a bit."

Liz nodded again, turned, and walked out of the room.

Fox Magnus took a deep breath. Gibraltar was soon to be gone...

Garvin Jardaw felt an awful sense of finality as he walked past the now-deactivated main battle plot on the command deck of *Gibraltar One*. It was as though this long-serving station was being broken up for the last time, when in fact it was just moving systems again... something not uncommon for Earther-built bases of its type.

No, the finality was just a sign of the times, Jardaw decided. It was hard not to be grim as the black ships of Omega swept towards this place...

"Garvin, you sticking around much longer?"

Karl Kandam had been talking to a group of engineers about what to do with the gun deck, but when they left to set about their work, the panda turned to the polar bear.

Jardaw shook his head as he came to a stop before Kandam, "I'm heading over to *Medusa* in a few minutes. Fox just signaled that he wants us boosting in nine hours, so your engineers need to get a move on."

Kandam nodded, his words smooth, "We'll see what we can manage."

"Excellent. I'll see you when you're finished loading... which ship are you flying your flag from?"

Kandam smiled, "There's the new *Namur* out there."

Garvin smiled with a simple nod in reply — the old *Namur*, 74, had been Kandam's ship during the early stages of the Krogg War, before Gibraltar had been built up. Perhaps history was repeating itself for the best.

"Well, I'll talk to you when you get out there then," Garvin said finally, and with a last nod to Kandam, turned and left the command deck.

"Word from Gibraltar is that everything is coming our way as fast as it can. So nothing to worry about, Krag. We'll have this system forted up tight."

Peacelord Kragran offered a typically ponderous nod in response to Claw's assurance, and the cat looked past the Krogg out to the red world they were orbiting. *Formidable* and the squadron remained in close orbit, on full alert now as no one quite knew where Omega might be.

In this galaxy, in the Larosian galaxy... he could be coming from anywhere at any time...

"You remain sure you don't want us to help in the defense."

It didn't quite sound like a question, and Claw nodded, "We'll look after it. It's not your time yet. We don't want you to lose all the progress you've made."

Kragran's head tilted slightly and he looked at his Earther counterpart, "So your marines will land to protect our biomatter pools. And we will conceal ourselves?"

Claw sighed and nodded again, "I'm sorry Krag, that's just the way it needs to go. You trust me, right?"

"Yes, but do you trust *us*?"

Claw blinked at the pointed question and looked at the Peacelord for a moment before turning away. He didn't quite know how to answer that one... he wasn't asking the Kroggs to stand with them, but should he be? Was this just anxiety from decades before manifesting in the present... not allowing him to accept help? The Kroggs were certainly cooperating, doing everything the Earthers asked of them...

No, it's too soon. We can't risk it. It hasn't been long enough.

Claw remained silent, with no polite answer to give.

Kragran contained a smile, and as he looked at his planet through the glass of *Formidable's* conference room, a Telepath from the surface beamed a coded low-intensity thought into his head.

Secret search missions launched by his hidden Krogg Fleet had located another great herd of Superdreadnought-beasts that were even now being drafted into military service, further reinforcing the already-powerful ranks of the new Navy. And the Earthers remained entirely unaware.

"You *can* trust us," Kragran said, and then he approximated a smile.

Claw took a deep breath and nodded, "Well I trust *you*, Krag."

The Peacelord bobbed his head. That was good.

It would serve the Kroggs well to be trusted.

CHAPTER 20

Audrey felt someone pushing on her shoulder. She didn't respond at first because everything was dark… then she realized she needed to open her eyes.

"Audrey… Audrey some news…"

Governor Audrey DeBrooke had been sleeping. She realized it in that instant, and swung her legs off the couch as though she could pretend she hadn't been.

"When did I go to sleep? I can't sleep now…"

Pat's hand stayed at rest on her shoulder for a moment, "About half an hour ago, and you needed it."

She blinked a couple of times, "So… so is something happening?"

"You could say that," Pat waved his hand towards the door to her ready room — a small office with a desk and a couch off the Freetown C&C room.

Tugging at her jacket to try to make herself look presentable, she stepped ahead of Pat and made her way into the colony's nerve center.

"That's another half dozen, sir. Really not sure what's getting into them…"

Colin Brawn nodded evenly in reply to the comm call from one of his Brigadiers, then spoke as he realized the reporting wolf was thirty kilometers across the city — not in range to see the gesture, "Thanks Kath, send them back with a detail. I'm going to get Plummer to put his troops into riot gear, you keep an eye on that lock."

"Don't worry, we're watching. Out for now."

The link cut, and Colin glanced up at the Commandant standing across from him in the mobile command center they'd set up at the spaceport, "More looting it seems. The Guards' parade is getting the people who can be inspired out into the streets… and apparently the *very* confident have decided to take advantage of the distraction for monetary gain."

Plummer frowned in disgust, "Great. World is about to get hit hard by Omega… so I'm going to loot the home theatre store?"

Colin bobbed his eyebrows and shrugged, "I can't shed any light onto it… not too good with the whole capitalist system."

"Lucky you," Plummer shook his head slowly and then looked to his staff. "So we break out the riot gear. Simon, arrange transport to get us to the affected areas. Joanne, you stay here and oversee deployment. Everybody else, tell our boys and girls to play nice with the locals. Crowd control, not suppression. Yet."

There was a rushed barrage of movement and the staff of the Genesis Naval Marine Corps' 1st and 2nd Marine Regiments began to make the preparations to deploy their 2,000 troops out of the spaceport.

Omega was prowling, and in the meantime *greed* was setting in.

Turning away from the human officers, Colin Brawn keyed his comm again, "Mustafa, just a heads up for you: we're seeing looting out there. Seems to be escalating."

There was a pause on the line, then the smooth voice of Brigadier Bengal replied, "You sending out the Constables?"

"Can't get a hold of Clyde, but Government House knows. Meantime Commandant Plummer's going to put his troops out there in riot gear. Be ready in case you see any activity on your parade."

On the other end of the line, Bengal began to nod before replying verbally, "Indeed... just a moment..."

The Guards Brigade's march through the capital was nearing the apogee of its loop — soon the column would make a turn that would carry it back to the spaceport, having crossed through much of the city's residential area.

But now, as he led his column over the crest of a blind hill, Bengal's eyes fell upon what could best be described as a street fight, with about twenty participants on each side.

"We have a bit of a street fight right here, Colin. I'm going to break it up, but Clyde will need to send patrols out to get everyone into their homes again."

"I hear you. Go to work, I'll track him down."

The link cut and Mustafa Bengal glanced over his shoulder at the Colonel of 1/First Guards, "Your Light Company I think, Tom."

With a nod, Tom Katt waved his free hand, and fifty Earthers from the column abruptly raced down the slope of the hill at an even pace, shields glowing to life as they did. Their Brigadier quickly joined them.

The Earthers were paid no heed as they stormed in with inhuman speed, and as Mustafa led the Earthers towards the fray, he began to see the viciousness of the battling on the street.

This was a mess.

There was a great deal of blood. At least a dozen humans were down, some clearly *dead*, and the rest were fighting with whatever blunt objects they had. Clubs, fence posts, canes, *anything*. One or two even had swords...

It was a melee. As surely as if the Guards were storming into a medieval battle that had come to grips.

"Careful everyone, looks like there are dead here. Don't take chances, just put everyone who resists on the ground," that was Tom Katt, and Bengal approved of the direction.

As he approached the first grappling pair of humans, he found a slight woman trying to ward off a large man using only a stick. The man, wielding a knife and a pipe, lunged at the woman again as Bengal slid to a stop next to her.

The cat caught the wrist of the attacking fellow and frowned, "Not very polite of you, sir."

The woman rammed her stick into Bengal's side.

Frowning in surprise, Bengal looked down at the piece of wood as it hit his shield and glanced away. Then, without releasing the man's hand, he swung his hips around and took the woman's legs out from under her with a sliding foot.

She dropped to the ground, then grabbed a dagger from her boot and tried to stab the Brigadier. A passing marine of the First Guards shot her in the back of the neck, dropping her into a coma.

Shaking his head slowly, Bengal looked back to the man whose wrist he still held, "Sorry for the misunderstanding."

The man shrugged, "Just as well if you ask me. Bitch had it coming. Now let's go break some more of these bastards..."

Bengal managed to contain a sigh as he released the man's wrist, then drew his own sidearm and shot the human in the back.

These people were seriously self-destructive...

"We'll need med teams down here as quickly as possible," the Brigadier said into his headset, and the specialist medics from within each squad of First Guards came racing down the hill ahead of the column.

There'd be a lot of regen to do on this group...

The rest of the Guards column was almost upon the mess now, and as One Company of First Guards finished cleaning up the brawl, Bengal waved the marching Earthers to pass by without stopping. Everyone else in Freetown who wanted to see the brigade march would have a chance.

Activating his comm again, Bengal turned away from the street, pausing to wave at a smiling toddler in the window of a nearby house, "Colin, seriously, this is a mess."

"Still nothing from Clyde, but Audrey's going straight to the station houses now. They're calling in everyone and getting riot gear on. Plummer just sent out his first company to the commercial district, so we're doing alright."

"Should we stay out here and help?" Bengal turned back to the street, only to have a human lunge straight into his chest, and bounce off. The Brigadier shot the man before he could get up. "They might need us."

There was a pause on the line, and Bengal could almost sense the General shaking his head, "Come back in directly, I think. I don't like the way this is looking... if Omega hits hard and we're out dealing with looters, we won't be able to counter. So rally here at the spaceport, asap."

Bengal nodded, shooting another charging human, "Understood. We'll wait with the prisoners until some constables arrive to collect them, then we'll come in."

Mustafa Bengal shot another screaming human.

This was going to be one hell of a day.

CHAPTER 21

Pat didn't particularly appreciate the display of human nature that was playing out on the screens in Freetown Government House's war room.

"I don't know why, but somehow I got it into my head that everyone would be just fine so long as they were inoculated against Omega's infection," he grated the words out as he stared at the city maps up on the screens. Silent alarms all over the capital were being triggered now, as looting verged on rioting. "Forgot that it was a coup that let the bastard into Genesis to begin with, I suppose."

Audrey was barely listening — she was having a tough time realizing that her people were doing this. Hours ago they'd been turning out in droves to see hope march through the streets with the Earther Guards... now they were fighting in those streets.

Brawls were starting up all over the city, as if all the pent-up fear and frustration brought on by Omega was being released in this one instant...

"Where the *hell* is Clyde?"

Audrey's question forced some panicked glances among her staff, then one delivered the unpleasant answer, "No answer on his lines, ma'am... but the last station house just reported ready to deal with civil unrest. Everyone's geared up."

Riot gear. Audrey and James had almost elected to get rid of that old Genesis surplus kit, but they'd decided to keep it all for a rainy day — even though Earther shields effectively replaced the padded Genesis-ore equipment.

Now the helmets and protective vests would see good use.

"The Guards are almost back to the spaceport," Pat observed quietly from Audrey's shoulder, and she nodded.

"Yes they are... is that a company of 2nd Marine Regiment looking after those prisoners Bengal took?" her finger pointed to the icon of a unit in the vicinity of the fight the Guards had broken up.

Pausing with a frown, Pat nodded, "Indeed. So let's just go with the martial law enforcement plan — scour the city, lock it down. We still have to worry about that Omega ghost in the waters out east. We don't need to deal with recriminations until we figure out what the bastard's up to."

"Indeed," Audrey's word was quiet as she stared again at the city map. Why were her people causing unrest now? They'd stood fast through so much...

Well, evidently the hay bale had finally severed the camel's spine... or however that antiquated saying went.

"Order the Constabulary to put itself under General Plummer's command, and tell Plummer to restore order in the city."

The commands were transmitted.

From his C&C at the spaceport, James Plummer saw the orders scroll up on one of the mobile display screens.

Alright, so at least that idiot Clyde won't be stepping all over this...

"Order the Constables in the station houses to stay put until we tell them to do otherwise. I don't want them sending out squad cars to every call so they can get wiped out piecemeal."

It probably sounded as though he feared an organized enemy, not gangs of frightened looters, but he was determined not to underestimate the mobs. He'd seen what had happened during the coup, and while he hadn't been on the ground for it, he knew better than to repeat mistakes made by the Naval Marines while trying to stabilize the Genesis capital.

Omega would probably *love* it if a second human planet was too wrapped up in its own chaos to notice his arrival...

But then, Omega wasn't strictly Plummer's problem.

"Guards Brigade is arriving here now, sir."

Colin Brawn had been standing silently on the opposite side of the post from Plummer, watching the screens as he listened to the Commandant's deployment orders. Now he looked away from the monitors and thought about his own marines' dispositions.

Nodding to the Lieutenant who'd brought the message to him, Brawn ducked out of the post and looked across the landing fields in time to see Mustafa Bengal order his column to halt on the far side of the port.

Tapping his comm to life, Brawn began walking towards the long line of elite marines, "Mustafa, set up a perimeter, shields securing the landing field... and a secondary line, too. Just to be sure."

"Very good. Brigade, let's get to it."

For some reason Brawn had the feeling the spaceport was going to need to be well fortified...

But things were under control here, surely.

Yeah, that's a good thing to be thinking at a time like this...

Tapping his comm again, Brawn locked onto *Orion's* signal frequency, "*Orion* here, Signal Chief."

"Chief, is Admiral Ursla on deck?"

"Just a moment..."

There was a pause, then Ursla's voice came into Brawn's ear, "Problems, Colin?"

The Lieutenant General contained a sigh, "Plummer's troops are securing the city against looting right now, and the division is deployed... I'm just starting to get a bit of a bad feeling. How are those strange readings looking?"

On the bridge of *Orion*, Ursla looked at Esther Arbear and arched her eyebrows at the question, "Um... still *strange*, Colin. Sorry, I have nothing more specific than that for you."

There was a slight harrumph on the line, and Ursla managed to smile at Brawn's reaction.

"Yeah believe me, I'm wondering too. I'd keep your reserves on alert though — those gates you're watching might be the least of our problems if minions start rolling in on the tides."

There was a pause, then, "Thanks for *that* lovely image. Alright, keep me up to speed."

As the line cut, Ursla took a deep breath and shrugged at Arbear, "I suppose that was overly-dramatic imagery."

Arbear cocked an eyebrow, "Let's hope that's all it was."

"Well, honestly, I don't know that there's a whole lot more we can do to prepare."

Audrey blinked and nodded once.

Pat chose to ignore the seeming apathy of her reply. He was feeling altogether too comfortable with the situation — well, no, *comfortable* wasn't the word, or at least not the best word. He couldn't think of the best word, actually... stupid inner narrator on the fritz, and him a *writer too*.

Writers, what a pack of phonies...

Pat stopped his mind's witty kick, wondering why it would start up now of all times.

Because you're comfortable, remember Pat?

The thoughts didn't quite seem like his own, but he ignored that and focused again on the city maps. Plummer had put half his troops into the field already, and the Guards Brigade was fortifying the spaceport. Earther brigades sat watching the weak points in the city shields...

Yes, everything was as ready as it could be.

"The next move is Omega's then, Audrey. Nothing we can do but wait."

Audrey nodded just once again, and Pat looked back to the screens.

Won't have to wait long, thank you kindly.

Pat frowned at the thought.

Above his head, a mob began collecting near Government House.

CHAPTER 22

"Whoa hang on a minute... where the *hell* did they come from?"

Plummer turned from the screen he was looking at to a panel being monitored by one of his Captains. About sixty people were congregating barely a block from Government House.

Taking a couple of steps towards the screen, the Commandant was stopped by the surprised exclamation of another of his Captains.

"Another group forming near the hospital, sir."

"Where are the people coming from?" Plummer looked to the master city map.

No one had an answer to that, and the silence did little to improve the Commandant's darkening mood.

"Find out where they're coming from. And tell the Constabulary stations in those areas to deploy everyone they've got to protect Government House. Let's not allow this to get out of hand."

Plummer knew all too well that people were remarkably susceptible to being carried away by a mob mentality... but he hadn't expected it to be *this* bad here on Freetown. On Genesis during the coup it had made some sense — a deeply divided and bitter society had been itching to unleash its repressed rage — but on the unified colony that had stood against the Church for over forty years? That just didn't track.

Every one of the people on this colony was from a Naval background... surely they couldn't have the same sort of deep-seated rage that had existed on Genesis...

But here were two mobs, growing fast.

"Alright, send a company to Government House... those numbers are getting too big."

Crowd control was suddenly becoming Plummer's primary occupation, and he didn't like it at all.

Pat had been coming out of the bathroom when he'd seen a handful of the Government House security detail rush past him with riot gear kits in their arms.

They were heading upstairs — they'd clearly left the guard room in the underground level of the House's structure, and were presumably going up to deal with an immediate threat...

Casting a glance down the hall towards the door to the command room, Pat ground his jaw thoughtfully, swore under his breath, and then turned and followed the detail up the stairs. He'd rather see what was going on outside for himself.

As he reached the top of the stairs he found himself in the midst of a small sea of commotion. Just about every one of the fifty Guards assigned to Government House were hurriedly suiting up in riot gear, and none seemed to notice him as he paced through their irregular throngs towards the window.

What the hell is all this about?

He stopped at the nearest window.

No mob out there.

"Um, sir?"

Pat turned away from the window and found himself face to face with the House security head. She nodded to him, "Kathleen O'Shea, sir, this is my detail. And you were looking at the wrong end of the street, actually."

Pat frowned at her words — they *almost* had an Irish accent like his own — but his brain clicked away from wondering about that to registering her words. He turned back to the window and looked again to where he had just been looking — up the street to the left.

Then he dutifully turned his head to the right... and consciously had to stop himself from taking a step back in surprise.

"How'd they light up that cruiser?" he asked after a moment.

"Motolov cocktail, I think they call it," O'Shea said matter-of-factly.

"*Molotov*, that is," Pat said quietly.

Like it mattered.

A Constabulary hover cruiser that had been parked across the road to act as a barrier was burning to high heaven. The two dozen Constables in riot gear in the street behind the burning car were falling back in a disordered gaggle as a stampede of people forced their way around it.

"There must be a hundred people out there... where the hell are Plummer's troops?"

Pat really hadn't meant to ask the question out loud, but O'Shea answered him anyway, "Last I heard, the company that's coming down from the spaceport is getting attacked on every street. It's like the city is going mad."

Pat blinked.

Surely not mad *mad. Not Omega mad. No. No that couldn't happen. They're all inoculated.*

No, this is just bad timing.

"Well, that's it then. I'm telling Audrey to declare martial law. You have energy rifles, correct?"

O'Shea nodded.

Pat looked away from the window, "Use them. Put every damned one of them into a coma if it comes to it."

"Yes sir," O'Shea seemed pleased with the latitude, and for some reason neither she nor Pat wondered if the Irishman actually had the authority to give such an order.

No matter.

"Good luck out there," Pat patted O'Shea on the shoulder once, then turned and stepped through the mass of House Guards as he made his way to the basement stairs.

This was insane...

"Look at *this*..."

Colin Brawn turned from the window at the spaceport's control tower and took a few steps towards one of the sensor panels being crewed by his marines. They'd patched the control tower's consoles into the same domestic security grid that Government House and Plummer's provisional C&C were using to keep an eye on the mobs, and to look for any signs of Omega at the same time.

Well, Omega wasn't the problem right now, sadly enough.

The mobile column that Plummer had sent out to support Government House had been stopped by almost 500 people. The Genesis marines had gotten nowhere *near* the House before they'd been stampeded, and now their hover trucks were stopped in the middle of one of the larger roads while the marines tried to beat the mob back with batons. Some of them were literally bogged down with people climbing on top of them, so the column couldn't raise its altitude for an escape without leaving vehicles behind.

They had to break up that mob, but Plummer's troops didn't have energy rifles, and their live rounds would almost certainly prove lethal...

Brawn sighed again — he was doing that rather a lot today.

Tapping his comm, he let his eyes drift over the map to the nearest concentration of Earther troops. One of the battalions being held in reserve from Third Brigade was just five minutes up the highway from this little debacle.

"Brawn to Colonel Sarsaw, I need one of your companies to help a Genesis marine relief column and then to secure Government House. Things are getting pretty dicey out there."

Pat watched the crowd grow in the street above from the relative safety of the war room. The House security guards were just about to go out to meet the oncoming horde of people. Two dozen constables from the street, and another dozen who'd managed to arrive just ahead of a rush of even more people, joined the guards on the steps of the building.

"What the hell is causing all this?" Audrey asked quietly. "I never thought our people were so... so..."

"You never think they are," Pat's answer came with an air of finality. He'd seen a society unravel before, and he was disturbed by how familiar this felt. "But don't worry about it. We're about to put this to rights, and then we can deal with Omega."

Audrey nodded, and then they were both silent again as they watched the House detail emerge onto their screen, having exited the building for the first time.

Pat watched O'Shea shake her men and women into a skirmishing line, and then saw the Constables integrate, bringing the entire force up to just about eighty-five riot-geared officers.

They'd end this foolishness.

They began to advance.

They stopped.

Pat blinked twice and waited… yelled orders that the crowd must disperse were heard over the war room speakers. Those warnings were given twice more, but the mob pushed forward all the same.

So the order to fire was given.

The map screen Audrey was staring at glowed as lines representing energy pulses lashed out at the mob.

Pat breathed a sigh of relief at the barrage.

And then he stopped breathing when he realized the mob was *still* pushing forward.

Should've seen this one coming, eh Pat?

There was another volley… and nothing.

They kept pressing forward.

"Gods wept…"

Government House was in danger.

CHAPTER 23

"They're not stopping… they're taking direct energy fire but the crowd isn't scattering."

Colin Brawn shook his head as the report came over the speakers of the control tower. What the *hell* was making these people so insane — advancing over the comatose bodies of their comrades? They weren't infected, they simply couldn't be. For them to be infected, Omega would have had to find a way around Earther biological defenses, which meant his marines would also be infected…

And they weren't.

One of the Lieutenants at the panel to Brawn's left looked up at him, "We've lost all contact with the column Commandant Plummer sent out to Government House."

"What about Colonel Sarsaw's company?"

The Lieutenant looked back to his panel for a moment, consulted quickly with the Sergeant in the seat next to him, and then looked back up, "They're about five minutes down the road from Government House, meeting extremely heavy resistance. It'll take them a while to fight their way over."

Colin stared at the Lieutenant for a moment, then looked at the panel again before glancing up and out the window. The city lay before the control tower, and at this distance it didn't seem to be in an uproar…

"Relief by ground isn't going to work. Damn. Alright…" Colin tapped his comm, "Mustafa, get a company together and prep one of our dropships. We're going out to Government House to pull out Pat and Audrey and the rest."

Looking to his nearby Chief of Staff, Colin bobbed his head once, "Look after things here. I'll be back."

He left the tower.

"Pull back to Government House, get ready to put up the perimeter shield," Pat looked up from the displays in the situation room as he delivered those orders.

"What the *hell* is going on out there…" was all that Audrey could manage to say for a moment. Then she blinked and looked to one of her Signal Officers, "Request reinforcements from General Brawn. We're going to need an air-drop at this rate."

The speakers in the room crackled on cue, "Audrey, Pat, this is Colin. I'm coming out of the spaceport in a dropship. We're going to pick you up, see if you can clear a landing spot for us just outside the main gate."

Audrey let out a breath with some noticeable relief and glanced at Pat, "I love Earther timing."

The Irishman nodded but frowned at the map on the screen, "Colin, we're being mobbed out there, why not land on the roof?"

"We're in a battalion dropship Pat, I want you and all your staff and guards out. So unless you want us crushing your building, we'll need a piece of road."

Aha.

"Well that does make sense... see you in a minute then. And thanks!"

Pat was already turned around and heading for the door as the link cut, and Audrey frowned and followed him, "What are you doing?"

"We all better get into riot gear, Audrey. We're not going to be safe for long..."

The pilot hadn't bothered to close the ramp of the dropship as he skimmed the tops of the buildings, and so Colin Brawn did what he hadn't done since his days on the Avalon campaign during the Krogg War: he stood at the open door, holding the railing and smelling the air.

Freetown's air didn't smell nearly as sweet as Avalon's had. Especially not with this much chaos going on below.

Mustafa Bengal came carefully up beside his General, "It's madness out here."

Colin nodded as he sighted Government House ahead in the distance. A sea of people was flooding through the streets towards the building, and the sounds of a near-rabid mob were loud and clear over the quiet Earther turbines that powered the dropship along.

"At this stage they're not even stopping when we stun some of them... tell the company we're going to have to force them back the old-fashioned way."

Mustafa nodded, "We'll do that. You get into the House and get everyone out."

The dropship dipped lower, slowing its pace and cruising down one of the streets towards Government House barely four meters above the ground.

"Nowhere to set down, sir," the pilot's voice came through Brawn's comm, and he nodded to Mustafa.

"That's alright, we'll make room at the front gate. You get the humans out of Government House and then get back to the spaceport straight away. We'll head back on foot," Colin's reply was directed to the pilot, and as he spoke he turned to look over Bengal's shoulder at the Guards assembled behind him. It'd be a long and rough afternoon for them.

Turning back to the open door, Colin allowed himself a deep breath, swung his rifle into his hand from its shoulder-slung position, keyed his shield, and then flung himself out the hatch.

The drop was only four meters — less than twice his height — and he landed on his feet, his rifle humming immediately as he crouched and sidestepped against the force of the drop.

He'd come down in a crowd of about fifty rioting Freetowners, and he was firing fast.

Mustafa and a half dozen Guards landed in the same clump of rioters, and as their rifle fire knocked the mob into a coma, their little section of street became quiet for a moment.

"I'm heading for the House. You know what to do, Mustafa!" Colin began a sprint towards the government structure.

All around him, energy rifles sung.

Pat stepped out the front door and adjusted his helmet one more time. It was a snug enough thing, uncomfortably machined out of Genesis ore but quite able to stop some idiot from clubbing him to death with a rock. Granted, the Earther shield on his wrist would help stop any such attempt, but if the mob closed in and overwhelmed that shield, the helmet might buy him more time.

"Why are we bothering with this kit when we've got our shields, Pat?"

Audrey finished tugging on her riot vest as she stepped out the door, and for a moment Pat stood and frowned at the mob beyond the gate.

"You think a shield is going to last forever against *that*?" he stabbed his finger at the rioters.

"Yes... well. I should still show my face. People might respond to their leader..." she sounded slightly desperate as she said that, and Pat managed to stop himself from shaking his head.

It was her decision to make, even if he was certain there was going to be no reasoning with a mob this fierce, "Suit yourself."

"So. Now what?" Audrey looked at Pat, and for a moment the Irishman didn't answer.

The rest of the war room staff was coming out of the building behind the pair, most of them in riot gear as well.

What to do...

The whine of the dropship drew his attention for a moment, and he watched with some relief as Guards threw themselves from the low-flying personnel carrier into the mob and began shrinking it.

"We help clear a place for that thing to land, and we get aboard. Come on..."

Pat wasn't in a patient mood, so he stepped quickly down the steps at the front of the building, passed the monuments that decorated the lawn, and headed straight for the gate.

One of the guards at the entrance looked back just in time to see the big Irishman rush past, and then with Audrey and a few of the other officers from the war room close by, Pat rushed to assist O'Shea's rapidly collapsing string of security officers.

"O'Shea, we must clear space for the lander to pick us up! Push them back!"

He yelled that twice before she heard it over the comm, but when she did her response was immediate.

"Maybe you hadn't noticed sir, but I'm *trying*..."

Pat's finger was clamped down on his trigger, and his rifle was spraying the crowd, but new attackers seemed to keep coming. It was amazing that O'Shea hadn't been completely overrun with them pressing forward like this.

Oh dammit, I just thought *that...*

Of course the mob started to push in too close. And as the security officer next to Pat drained the last shots out of his rifle's cell, the Irishman realized the mob might just have been staying back to absorb the fire of the Constables and the House Guards.

Because now — when almost two dozen defenders would soon need to swap power cells for their weapons — a surge came.

Pat didn't wait for it. He wasn't sure what possessed him to lunge forward *into* it, but he did. For a moment he kept firing, cutting a gap in the front ranks of the horde of people, but then he stopped shooting and slid his hands away from the trigger and to the stock and barrel of the rifle.

As the first mobbing person screamed at him and reached out to grab him, he brushed her arms aside and drove the butt of the gun into her nose, drawing a crack and a splatter of blood. She screamed and collapsed back. Broken bones could be set later.

Pat continued hitting people, and as he led by example, O'Shea and a handful of others followed him... to try to get him out before the mob killed him. He pushed further in, though, part of him trying to figure out if his decision to attack was going to qualify as one of Sarah's 'charge the guns' moments — because it was pretty much him against 500 Freetowners... or more. And he only had one shield.

Swinging his rifle around again, he connected with a jaw, which crunched, and then he whirled on the nearest man.

And came face to face with Jason Clyde.

The Commissioner stared at him with a smile on his face.

"*Clyde*? What the fu–"

"Now now, language," Clyde said serenely.

Pat glared.

"Come *on*, Pat, you're having fun, admit it."

What the hell was he saying? Well, he obviously wasn't helping the situation...

"You're traitorous scum, I'd take you in but we need the room for people who deserve to live," Pat spat the words, then quickly swung his rifle over to point squarely at the Commissioner's chest.

Now he just had to decide whether to take the safety off...

Someone swatted his rifle down, and he took a step back as the forceful blow seemed to imply a threat to his person. His head whipped around, and he almost expected to see an Earther — few could muster the strength to wrench a gun from his hands...

Instead he saw a surfer girl in skimpy clothes.

Pat scowled and began to bring his weapon up towards her, then he froze.

He knew this girl.

"Oh Gods wept no. It can't be."

Gillian Hodge — really Omega-Gillian — smiled at her once brother-in-law, "It's me, Pat. How about a kiss?"

He took two more steps back.

The mob seemed to freeze all around them — she had ordered their silence.

"You can't have infected them. Every one of them is inoculated," Pat stammered.

Her eyes blackened and she shrugged, "Oh come on, Pat, you're supposed to be smarter than that. A *writer*, remember. A *comfortable* writer."

What? Wait... his thoughts from earlier, those thoughts that hadn't felt like his own...

"They *weren't* your own," Omega-Gillian pointed out happily. "Now wait for it, the revelation... I'm..."

"Telepathic," Pat breathed the word.

Omega didn't actually need to infect humans. He could seize control of their minds with his own... if they weren't shielded by the telepathic-bouncing properties of Genesis ore.

The ore in the riot-gear helmet Pat was wearing at this moment...

"There you go!" Omega-Gillian clapped absurdly, like a child. "I don't need to infect anyone, I just need to take that Genesis ore off your head."

Pat didn't move fast enough to escape that threat... he felt hands closing around his head shield. Hands from behind... oh *Gods* no. *No*...

The hands were ripped away, and Pat staggered forward, sweeping his rifle around behind him.

Colin Brawn stopped his whirl with a steadying hand.

The General's eyes were narrow as they settled on Gillian Hodge, "Been a long time since I've seen that body. Different owner back then."

His cool words drew a smile from Omega-Gillian, "Want to see more of it, big bear? Clyde did, and I can only imagine what Graham would think when he saw the recordings of you and me. Bet I'd be sore..."

Brawn leveled his rifle and shot her in the head.

The energy seemed to do nothing.

Omega-Gillian cackled, and then the mob started moving again, "Not so fast big bear. This planet's mine."

Pat couldn't look away from Gillian as she said it, so Colin picked him up and handed him to Bengal, who'd emerged in the crowd. The General then dropped his rifle and drew his sword.

"Mustafa, finish the evacuation and hold the spaceport. Get as much ore together as you can and start evacuating anyone she hasn't gotten control of."

The cat nodded, "Will do... good luck."

Literally holding Pat a few centimeters off the ground, Bengal shouldered his way back through the crowd, then began delivering orders into his headset, "Round up the Government House staff and get them into the dropship, quickly!"

Pat didn't even notice as Bengal hauled him past Audrey. Audrey certainly didn't notice him: she still hadn't put on her helmet. Human hands closed around her and yanked her away.

As Earthers rushed into the crowd, escorting people wearing helmets away from the action, Omega-Gillian gazed up at Colin Brawn with a smile.

"This should be interesting," the plague said.

CHAPTER 24

"You *can't* be serious..." Plummer whirled on his Captains as the audio from Colin Brawn's comm came into the command post.

No one actually replied to his words — and that was probably for the best. What could they say to Omega-Gillian's revelation?

"Alright, we need to get as much Genesis ore as we can together... line trucks with it or something. And we need to start evacuating people immediately."

"Sir..."

Plummer glared at the Captain who'd first opened her mouth, "*Omega* is here. Helmets on, everyone. And let's save people!"

There was silence, and no one moved. Plummer's eyes grew wild, "Get *moving*."

"But... how, sir? We don't even know what the range of her control is. Or why we haven't been affected here..."

Plummer's mouth started working to spit back an angry response, but his mind slowly started turning over the problem.

Problems.

What could they really do?

He hadn't realized how determined he'd actually been to save these people... now his determination was consuming him.

And he couldn't do anything to satisfy it. Humans seemed to be no match for Omega.

Andra Ursla stood at her plot on *Orion*'s bridge and stared into the blue holo.

Omega had gotten past them all. Again.

Walked right in... or probably *drove* in, on that damned busload of surfers.

"But how'd he beat the med tests Audrey had run on those people from the bus?" Esther Arbear looked through the plot at her Admiral, and Andra's head fell forward.

"He's powerful enough to round up a mob telepathically, I'm guessing he convinced the examining doctor that he wasn't infected..."

Arbear shook her head slowly and sighed, "Our doctors need to do all the examinations from now on. Meantime, thoughts on how to control this?"

Ursla closed her eyes for a moment. *Control* this?

She shouldn't be doubting herself. She shouldn't be doubting their ability to do something about this mess... but she was. If only for a moment, she was allowing herself to wonder just how the hell anyone *anywhere* could stop a plague that thought and fought as cleverly and spitefully as Omega.

Bastard... how does he keep finding the gaps we leave... the Kroggs never seemed to...

Not now. Not now.

"We can't isolate them from Omega's mind down there — not without handing out Genesis riot gear to everybody. But..."

Ursla paused in thought, and something occurred to her.

"Get me Colin."

The Signal Officer nodded immediately, but after a moment of trying, the Lieutenant looked up, "Sorry ma'am, sounds like his comm is being jammed. I can get Brigadier Bengal though."

Ursla nodded, "Alright, patch him in."

There was another pause, then a soft thud as the comm was patched into *Orion's* bridge speakers, "Bengal here, Admiral."

"Is Colin alright, Mustafa?" Ursla hadn't intended to begin by asking after the Lieutenant General, but the question was born of her concern.

"Afraid I can't say, we just pulled out with everyone we could grab from Government House. Most of the Guards are with me pushing down on foot towards the spaceport."

Ursla nodded, more to herself than in answer to the question. She hoped Colin Brawn was alright... "Listen, I'm guessing the reason the whole city didn't just bubble up around you has something to do with the telepathic range of Omega's avatars down there. That original busload that came through the shield at the beginning of the siege *must* be controlling the mobs."

Must nothing. Ursla had no idea if her assumptions were anything near the truth, but she had to try something.

"So you think if we get to the core of the mobs and kill the avatars, the crowd will return to normal?" Mustafa's question came back in uncertain tones.

Containing a shrug, Ursla looked up at the ceiling speakers, "One way to find out. Controlling that many humans without actually infecting them must take a lot of telepathic power... if you can break his grip we might be able to secure the city."

It was ambitious, to say the least. But she was right, there was one way to test the theory.

Silence dominated the line for a long second, and Ursla could swear she heard the sound of running boots.

"I'll tell you in a minute, Admiral. I'll go off comm 'til then — the mob is rather loud."

The audio cut, and Ursla took a deep breath and looked through the plot at Arbear.

She hoped they could salvage this...

Colin Brawn was stepping forward with sword in hand while Omega-Gillian offered a playful wave and slid back into the crowd behind her. His mind set, the Lieutenant General gave chase.

As Omega-Gillian slid between people, Brawn rammed them aside, and his instincts kept him on her trail. She was running away from the mob, and he wasn't going to let her go...

Behind Brawn, the crowd began to erupt in anger again, being directed by one within its ranks.

The arrival of Mustafa Bengal in the mob's midst was marked by the parting of two of the people in the clearing where Brawn had just been. Jason Clyde was still standing there, but it couldn't be him — he was inoculated, and the avatar would have to be infected.

A dozen other Guards appeared in the crowd, and anyone who turned on them was summarily beaten unconscious. There was no room for niceties right now — physical damage could be fixed later.

Who was the avatar?

Bengal's eyes swept the crowd in all directions. Even as Clyde charged him and he broke the man's legs, he didn't stop searching for the human who wasn't *quite* human...

Black eyes.

He stopped in mid-turn and saw a male dressed in the same sort of surfing garb Omega-Gillian had been wearing... and yes, he had black eyes.

"I see him," Bengal spoke very quietly into his microphone, but the avatar clearly knew he'd been noticed.

The Omega minion started to back into the crowd... only to connect with the chest of one of the panthers of the Guards Brigade. Whirling fast, he drove his fist into the cat's chest, and the marine staggered in surprise at the inhuman strength of the strike. But as the avatar turned back towards the Brigadier, it discovered it had no legs.

Bengal was in the last motion of a powerful sword strike as this minion's eyes fell on his figure again. Slightly crouched and holding his sword at the end of its smooth stroke, the cat drew himself back up to full height and waved his marines in.

"Well played," the avatar grinned as its torso fell forward at Bengal's feet. "But takes more than that to stop me. I infect every cell of this body, you have to destroy it all to stop me..."

Bengal held up a hand to the fallen avatar, "Let me finish, please."

A half dozen marines were gathered around him now, and he looked up at them, "Take him to the lawn of Government House and use an energy charge. Quick as you can."

Omega's avatar frowned, "Shit, hate it when you get thorough..."

The marines collected his pieces and carried him through the crowd.

For another minute, the riot around Government House continued. Then an energy charge flashed on the building's lawn, and every human in the road collapsed.

Mustafa Bengal heaved a deep breath and sheathed his sword. This would take a while to clean up...

CHAPTER 25

"Why wasn't I informed immediately?"

Sarah's question was harsh as she emerged onto the bridge of *Unity Genesis*, and her Flag ArcColonel turned to her with a shocked expression on his face.

"It all happened so fast, ma'am... just mobs of looters one minute, and then General Brawn said it was Omega..."

Sarah bit back her condemning comments and moved immediately to her chair, "So the Earthers have secured Government House?"

"We think so... looks like the mob attacking there was decapitated when the Omega avatar was blown up. Brigadier Bengal is ordering units from all around the city to attack the mob concentrations..."

Sarah offered a single jerked nod, and then the question that she'd been trying not to think about escaped her lips.

"What about Pat? Is he okay?"

She had to ask it, even if she felt that asking about only one man, only her *husband,* was selfish in all this chaos...

"Evacuated with most of the Government House staff in a dropship. They're still trying to make sure they got everyone, but they know for sure that he's in the spaceport now, ma'am. Safe."

Sarah nodded once, trying to make sure she didn't look too relieved. It wouldn't do for her to seem overly sentimental about her own affairs at this moment.

"So the situation is under control?" she asked unevenly, immediately feeling frustrated by the lack of command in her tone.

"Seems so, ma'am."

Sarah had missed a major movement... but at least it hadn't been the deciding one.

Brigadier Bengal stood in the control tower at the spaceport and stared for a moment at the screen before him, then nodded to himself and continued his words to one of the Colonels of Second Brigade, "We'll need two companies at least... probably from your reserve. The concentration is rolling down the commercial district."

He was referring to one of the mobs that almost certainly had an avatar of Omega at its head. There were a dozen such mobs already moving through different parts of the city, and another ten seemed to be forming... Omega was throwing down the gauntlet.

And Mustafa Bengal was taking it up, with the power of the Light Division.

"We're on it, Mustafa. Need more to clear bodies at the Industrial Park?"

Bengal's eyes darted from point to point on the screen — a company from the Fifth Brigade had cut down an avatar in the center of an 800-strong mob in the Industrial Park, and now all the bodies of the fallen needed to be collected and brought down to the spaceport for medical treatment.

"If you have hands to spare, but only if you do."

The voice of the Colonel was cool over the comm, "I'll send another company that way. We've still got a pretty good reserve if you need more."

Bengal nodded, "Alright, thanks Ned. I'll call if they're required."

"Sounds good. Talk to you soon."

The link cut and Bengal watched on the panel as 150 marines from Second Brigade left their stations in reserve and started making their way to different parts of the city.

He was being forced to weaken the perimeter to clean up the mess in town, but so far there was no sign of a strong force of Omega minions on the island, so he wasn't too worried. There were still full battalions watching each gate, their reserves had just been weakened a bit...

"New mob forming near the spaceport, sir. Looks like we've been singled out."

Bengal turned from the panel he'd been staring at to the one in front of the Lieutenant who'd spoken. About 200 humans had gathered down the road from the spaceport entrance, and more seemed to be on their way...

Well, that was more than a little futile. Just about 2,000 Guards were ready to stop their advance, and the entire port had been ringed by a double layer of shields.

"Warn the picket battalion that they're coming in."

Pat hadn't stayed long in the control tower. Several field triage centers had been set up around the spaceport, where people who'd been injured in the evacuation were now quickly being treated, so he'd started going through those posts to look for Audrey. She had to be around somewhere, and her leadership would be needed again soon...

Then his comm picked up the warning to the marines of 1/First Guards that Omega had a new mob approaching. For some reason he felt determined to stand with the Earthers as they faced their attackers, and began walking across the field toward the gate as the mob came into earshot down the road.

He'd search for Audrey later...

"Let's have a line to the left..." Pat heard the order in his earpiece and noted a Major waving troops from the first battalion of the First Guards into a line of two ranks along the shield perimeter facing the road.

"We'll start knocking them down as soon as they get into range," Tom Katt's orders followed quickly. "When they get close enough, Number One Company will come out with me and we'll get the avatar."

Sounded very organized, very calm, just as Pat would expect from the venerable old Katt. Just shy of forty years prior, Tom had helped the Genesis Marine Corps set up its dedicated special forces. He was a cool customer, and they'd need that today...

Pat arrived at one flank of the 250-Earther line, nodding to the officers around him as he swung his rifle out of its slung position and held it ready across his chest.

"Should you be out here, Pat?" Katt arrived beside the Irishman almost immediately, and Pat shrugged.

"All the times you've seen me shooting at things I really shouldn't be shooting at, you think this is unusual?"

The tiger Colonel grinned, despite the dire situation, "Remind me not to hang out with you more often."

Pat laughed, "I rarely give such good advice."

"Sir, they're coming up."

The report drew Tom Katt's eyes back to the shield and he nodded, "Alright everybody, let's drop them evenly. One Company, keep your swords handy."

Pat smiled. He hadn't had the chance to stand alongside Earther marines in forty years. It was quite reassuring to again witness their smooth confidence up close. If you gave the Earthers an inch on the ground, you'd be hard-pressed to get it back from them...

They did this with style.

"Battalion, make ready," Katt's words were easy, and Pat brought his rifle up in time with the rest of the Guards in the line.

For some reason, he hadn't actually looked down range until this order came — he hadn't watched the angry mob of about 1,000 appear from around a corner down the road leading into the spaceport.

A chill ran through him for a moment, but then he cast his eyes sideways again. The Earthers weren't just calm, they were in pleasant spirits. Some were smiling, others cracking jokes. They had an easy day, by their standards; they were about to unleash hellish volleys onto a mob of civilians, but they'd actually be killing only one or two living things in that group — Omega avatars. The rest would wake up from their comas, free of the plague's telepathic tendrils.

Nothing weighty on the conscience, no real threat, and so a bunch of relaxed Earthers ready to meet an unimpressive foe.

Letting out a deep breath, Pat felt better. Of course the situation was still bad, but it wasn't Omega-on-Genesis bad. It reminded him more of the feeling of being trapped on a planet with Beckett Lupus' squad around him... it could have been *much* worse.

He didn't even wonder about Audrey...

Pat stopped thinking as the order to fire came. He clamped down on the trigger of his rifle and the front ranks of the mob caved.

CHAPTER 26

Colin Brawn slowly entered the warehouse, checking all the angles he could as quickly as possible. His sword stayed ready in his hand, hanging down by his right hip but in a position that would allow him to come on guard quite easily.

He'd chased Gillian... Omega... whoever... for about an hour now, and she was leading him right across the city.

She couldn't be allowed to escape, Brawn was sure enough of that. On his own he was fairly certain he could deal with her... but why take the chance?

"Clear on the east entrance, sir."

The report came over his comm, and alerted him to the presence of six marines of 1/49th from Fourth Brigade in the building with him. It was very much like the old Krogg War days now. Colin had fought alongside 1/49th during the Avalon and Amaratsu campaigns, before transferring out to the Guards Brigade, and now the regiment had sent marines to aid his hunt here.

Hopefully it was a sign that their luck would be good.

"You're still coming close but *missing*, Colin."

The voice echoed sweetly through the warehouse and Colin froze, his sword immediately swinging forward to a ready position.

"This is too much, I have to play..."

Brawn tensed, eyes darting around. He was surrounded by huge squared mountains of boxes, all marked as being full of housewares.

Alright, where is she...?

Shifting his weight slowly, Colin slid forward, watching closely for any signs of movement.

Then he heard a clatter and a thud.

"She's engaging over here, sir!"

The six marines of 1/49th had found her. Moving smooth and low, Colin sprinted for the noise.

"By the Earth she's fas—"

Colin rounded a corner and watched one of the cats from the small assisting squad fly right past him.

Gillian was standing at an intersection between boxes, unarmed and presumably unshielded, but as the squad made runs at her, nothing they threw seemed to connect. And her hands found everything.

The Sergeant of the squad surged forward as Colin watched, but the experienced cat's lunge was almost a foot wide of Gillian — she'd moved faster than the Sergeant had. And her hand was down on top of the cat's skull so quickly that he collapsed to the hard floor with a thud, saved from having his head crushed only by his shield.

Colin's eyes narrowed.

As the squad struggled to peel itself off the floor around Gillian, she turned to him and smiled, "Big bear, there you are. Guess you don't want to cuddle?"

"You're good. Better than I expected," his words were cool.

Gillian flashed a brilliant smile, "Aw gee, thanks. You're not so bad yourself, I figured you wouldn't even keep up."

Colin swallowed once, his stare fixed on the slender woman dressed like an unimposing surfer girl. Omega was a devilish enemy...

But he'd finish this now.

Sliding his right foot forward, Colin drew his sword forward before him and prepared to meet his foe.

Gillian's smile broadened, "Oooh, this'll be fun!"

She began to advance across the floor towards him.

"We'll see, won't we..." he held his ground, and then threw himself forward in a blurring advance.

His sword, a saber styled much like Setter Caine's, came quickly from its high position down in a driving strike against Gillian's skull...

And she wasn't there.

He knew it as soon as he got into range — her speed was astounding, her technique of avoidance well suited to getting out of the way of the usual Earther sword-handling style that had grown from a mix of ancient Japanese and modern Larosian schools, and that had proven quite effective against the Kroggs.

Colin was proficient enough in that type of sword work, but he preferred the quickness of the one-handed saber, and he had strength enough to make up for not using both hands to strike a target.

His style made him faster, and maybe — just *maybe* — it'd allow him to catch her unawares...

She was behind him.

He began to turn, rolling his saber fast as he traversed left and ducked.

She flew right over him — clearly having intended to knock him down by throwing herself into his head. He rolled the saber back and lunged again in a fluid motion, and Gillian was only centimeters from his blade when it passed her.

He'd missed, but not by much.

"Nice," she smiled again, then threw herself to the left as his sword moved to catch her.

Colin lost sight of her again as she slid just away from the point of his sword, and he ground his jaw, letting his instincts track her... left... above...

and dropping fast…

He slipped sideways again, and his sword came up to guard his head in a smooth motion…

"This'll hurt!" she yelled as she fell on him… and then his sword sliced through her stomach as she dropped.

Nearly cut in two, she sprayed the room with her blood as she fell heavily on the floor.

Colin blinked as his shield deflected the mess, then sheathed his sword in a smooth motion.

Well, that had been a bit more work than he'd have liked, but Gillian was taken care of.

The marines were beginning to pick themselves up with difficulty, and Colin went over to the Sergeant and offered him a hand, "Thanks for cornering her."

The experienced marine smiled, "Thanks for keeping her from killing us."

Colin shrugged, "You looked down, not out. But either way, let's get her outside and vaporize her. Don't want to take the chance that she can somehow survive nearly being cut in two."

The Sergeant nodded, "Yes sir. Let's collect her, everybody."

There was a pause, and then the squad Corporal looked to the General and the Sergeant, "Sir… she's gone."

Brawn stiffened and then turned to the pool of blood that had surrounded the fallen body…

How was that possible?

"Damn. Damn damn damn, we have to track her," Colin turned back to the Sergeant. "Get outside, see if she left a blood trail. I'm calling backup, though. She's too dangerous to leave out on her own."

There were sounds of commotion coming from one of the warehouses up the row, so the squad of Constables decided to check it out. They'd been breaking up rioters in the industrial sector when the Earthers had sent in 150 marines and subdued the situation. Now, the dozen officers in riot gear were looking for victims of violence — anyone needing emergency medical assistance…

A girl came stumbling out of one of the warehouses, bloody and crying.

"Help me! Help me please, they're trying to kill me…"

The lead Constable hurried forward to catch the girl as she tripped and nearly went face first into the road.

"Call in an EMS truck — *hurry!*"

The Constable was no doctor, but that gash across her stomach looked bad. Two more officers came forward and helped him hold her up, and then in a timely fashion an EMS hover truck hummed up the street and stopped. The big vehicle was designed to serve as a mobile surgery, and now its hull had been hastily augmented with raw sheets of Genesis ore from a hardware store. Those would keep Omega out of the minds of its doctors and patients as they worked inside.

The Constables hefted her up to the guards on the back of the vehicle, and then backed away as they let her in. As quickly as it had arrived, the truck then sped off.

"Alright, let's see who's in these warehouses who'd do something like that," the leading Constable ordered through gritted teeth.

Innocent, pretty girl, and somebody had cleaved her open...

"She came out of that one!" another Constable pointed to the building.

Leveling their rifles, the twelve Freetown officers made their way quietly towards the structure, fanning out as they neared the entrance.

One of them neared the door and pulled a heat sensor from her tactical vest, "Seven readings... looks like they're heading this way."

"Get ready for them," the lead Constable nodded, and the squad fell back to the cover of a couple of picnic tables and grounded hover cars on the road.

Hands tightened on the grips of weapons as the door swung open. The lead Constable's eyes narrowed, "This is the Freetown Constabulary, hands on your head. We *will* open fire."

Someone tapped him on the shoulder, and he whirled and found himself abruptly face-to-face with a cat Sergeant, "Good to hear. We're hunting the head Omega avatar and we thought she came out this door. Looks like Gillian Hodge, dressed like a surfer girl... the General there nearly cut her in half..."

The Constable blinked and looked back to the warehouse. Colin Brawn was exiting the building, sword once again in hand.

"We... she... she was in one piece but split open across the stomach... we put her in an EMS truck... wait... *you* were in *there*? How'd you get out here without me seeing...?"

The Sergeant blinked, "We're good, but that's not important." The cat looked up at Brawn, "She's got a hover truck, General! EMS truck. Please tell me one of you got the number on its plate..."

The head Constable nodded, "Sure."

Brawn was abruptly in front of them both, "Call it in, Sergeant. I'm going to get your battalion into trucks and we're going after her."

Colin Brawn sheathed his sword again. The hunt was still on...

CHAPTER 27

Pat nodded to a nearby marine as he hurried back through the open port in the perimeter shield, wishing he could take off his helmet to wipe his brow. But there was no way he was taking that chance.

Behind him, the marines of Tom Katt's 1/First Guards were collecting the comatose victims of the mob that had been attacking the spaceport, bringing them inside the shield and handing them off to medical staff from the Freetown Emergency Services who then brought them to a shielded area to recover.

It hadn't actually been that hard to find and kill the avatar, at least not that hard by Pat's reckoning. He'd honestly expected it to be much worse, but evidently Omega wasn't so tough when all he had were telepathically-controlled minions.

A very minor consolation.

"I think we might want to suggest evacuating these people to orbit for treatment," Katt was suddenly beside Pat, and the Irishman blinked once and nodded.

"I do believe we've got transport enough in orbit to take some of them. Maybe all of them. I'll try to find Audrey and talk to Sarah to see if we can set it up."

Tom Katt nodded and then turned back to the shield. Watching the well-named cat leave, Pat sighed, turned in the direction of Plummer's mobile HQ, and started walking.

Now, where's Audrey?

Pat stared at the maps for a long moment and then glanced at Plummer, "You've been able to get most of your people back in safely?"

The Commandant was still extremely angry, but he found it difficult to direct that anger against Pat. Clyde was... or had been... a complete idiot, as far as Plummer was concerned, but Pat was very well known and respected. He was a war hero, and as was evidenced by the gear he was wearing, he'd been in the thick of things already today.

So the marine nodded, "Minor casualties, and some joined the mob, but Colin's marines have got them controlled. They're starting to bring casualties in here for treatment."

Pat turned from the screens to look out one of the nearby windows. A long file of marines from 1/First Guards was bringing in the remnants of a riot — each Earther had one or two rioters on his or her shoulder, and was carrying them carefully to the waiting gurneys of the Freetown Emergency Medical Service.

"We need to start getting them up into orbit, away from this mess, so they can recover. Can you get Sarah on the line for me here?" Pat glanced back at Plummer, and the Commandant nodded, snapping his fingers and pointing at one of his staff officers.

"And can you get some people out there looking for Audrey? I couldn't find her but I'm sure the Earthers wouldn't have left her behind. I probably shouldn't be making decisions outright, being a civilian," he added, and Plummer snorted a laugh.

"You're the best human leader we have," he said without thinking, and he didn't bother to qualify the remark as he ordered two more of his staffers to go looking for the wayward Governor of the colony.

Pat didn't visibly respond to the vote of confidence. He stared at maps and waited to talk to his wife.

Ursla sat in her chair and stared at the holo tank with something approaching relief. The map of the Freetown capital showed that Brawn had dispersed half his division into the city in order to control the mobs, and now all of the concentrations of Omega-influenced humans had been broken up.

Saved by the skin of their teeth... again. Better than not being saved, of course, but Ursla didn't like cutting it close against Omega.

"Signal coming in from *Unity Genesis*, ma'am."

Ursla blinked, for half a second not recalling just what ship that was. Her mind had somehow defaulted to thinking that Sarah was back on *Joseph Barron*.

"In the tank," Ursla slowly got to her feet and moved forward to the side of *Orion's* holo plot. Sarah glowed to life in the display, and the elder Manchester's blank expression greeted her old friend.

"Pat's saying we best evacuate the civilians from the city... do we have the ships for that?"

Ursla's brow furrowed, "That'd be quite a tall order. We have a bunch of Freetown haulers that we can supply with survival kit — maybe turn their cargo bays into mass population rooms... but I doubt we can get more than a couple of hundred thousand into them. And there are millions of people down there, right?"

Sarah frowned, "Still, we spread the rest between our ships if need be."

"Of course," Ursla agreed. "Alright, well we can start sending pinnaces down now to collect their wounded. And I'll get Jax to set up the arrangements for those haulers."

Sarah nodded, "Good. I'll let Pat know."

The ArcGeneral-President vanished, and Ursla let out a long breath. Freetown was being evacuated, at least for the time being.

Pat smiled as Sarah appeared on his screen again. It did him good to see her, even if she wasn't willing to smile back...

"We're getting ready to receive you. If you want to start preparing the people you have in the spaceport already, I think Andra's going to be sending down pinnaces for them soon."

"Good to hear... I won't be up for a while myself. Seem to be doing some good down here."

Sarah stared at him for a second, "At least one of us is. Get the civilians to safety, that's most important right now."

"Aye. I'll speak to you soon."

Sarah nodded and then the screen blanked, leaving Pat to turn back towards Plummer, "We've got pinnaces coming down to collect our wounded. I'll go tell the Earthers."

Brigadier Bengal closed his comm link to *Orion* just as Pat emerged onto the deck of the tower control room, and he waved to the Irishman, "I know, Pat. We're going to start evacuating people immediately."

Nodding, Pat still approached the cat Brigadier, "You think it might be an idea just to abandon the city and be done with it?"

Mustafa cocked an eyebrow, "I believe the human way of saying that is... it's above my pay scale."

Pat smiled and nodded, "Yeah, mine too. This is ridiculous, though. I mean, if he can infiltrate despite all our precautions, do all this damage... is this city really worth trying to hold?"

Bengal tilted his head, "I suppose you should put that question to Audrey. I just fight where I'm told to fight."

Pat laughed, "You *just* fight. Right. You saved my ass out there, by the way. Thanks."

Mustafa Bengal smiled, "We do what we can."

"Aye, and you do good. I'll go try to find Audrey and put that evacuation idea into her head, anyway. Haven't been able to track her down yet."

Mustafa frowned, "Indeed? Well let me know if you can't find her... it's been a confusing day, but I can't imagine that we've lost the Governor."

Pat laughed at the absurdity of the words, "You forgetful Guards, you."

Bengal bowed his head slightly, "Certainly. Let me know if you need anything, Pat."

"I will."

The Irishman left the control room.

•••

They were deep in the industrial sector now, moving fast and silent. Colin Brawn had the same squad with him, but fanned out on either flank, he also had the rest of the first battalion of the 49th marine regiment of foot. The battalion was extended in a long skirmishing line that, like a net, was hopefully going to catch Gillian and her Emergency Services truck...

But something was starting to itch in the back of Colin's mind.

Just *itch*.

The mobs were coming under control, so what could be bothering him?

Clenching his jaw, he forced his active mind away from that itch and to the matter at hand. He needed to catch Omega-Gillian. Then he could worry about the *itch*...

Presuming she wasn't causing it in the first place.

Something felt wrong...

Wrong...

Colin Brawn shook his head and tried to clear his mind, but for whatever reason he was having trouble with his thoughts.

Shifting his focus to his instincts, then, he tightened his grip on his saber and continued to move down the street.

She was out here somewhere...

CHAPTER 28

"So first we'll move up the mob casualties... that's about 13,000 you said?"

Jax Furgus' question from the comm screen drew a nod from Pat, and he continued, "Alright, so my pinnaces are coming down to get them now. Jim, could your regiments help with that?"

Plummer nodded, "Certainly, sir."

Pat looked from the screen to the Commandant for a moment, then his eyes turned back to Jax, "One thing I wanted to suggest was the total evacuation of the city. Pull everyone out, let Omega have it if he wants it. But I can't find Audrey to ask her."

Jax turned his head to look at Pat. Plummer's eyebrows went up and he looked at the Irishman, "Let him have it without a fight? Would that be good for morale?"

Pat shrugged, "Better for morale than having him take it from us despite having the Light Division on the ground. And I still don't believe this is over..."

Plummer frowned thoughtfully for a moment, then looked back to Jax, "Well, that's not for us to decide."

"No, it isn't," Jax agreed. "But if things take a turn for the worse down there, and you can't find Audrey, that'll be our fallback plan. Worst-case scenario we end up sending everyone back down... but I'll make the arrangements for the emergency evac, so we can do it if we have to."

Pat nodded to the wily old cat, "Thanks, Jax."

The lion shrugged, "All I'm doing is making calls, you have the hard job. But you might want to find Audrey."

A frown started to crease Pat's brow, "Yes. The Guards pulled us out, so I assumed she was with us, but it's been a chaotic day..."

For the first time Pat wondered seriously if Audrey had been left behind.

"I'll look into it again," the Irishman said quietly, and Jax nodded.

"I'll continue making calls."

With that, the conversation was ended.

Jax Furgus returned to his seat on *Aboukir's* bridge as the message to the command post closed, and as soon as that message ended, Ursla and Barty Stowt both glowed to life in the holo tank.

Standing again, Jax approached the plot, "Well, we're getting the pinnaces running. And we're setting up a contingency evacuation plan for the whole city, if it comes to that."

Barty nodded, "That's wise. Those haulers we're guarding could be filled right up, and if we take humans aboard our ships in addition to that, we could get everyone out. Did Audrey say when she'll make the decision?"

Jax shook his head, "Pat still can't find her. She might be in a coma somewhere, in which case I have no idea who makes the decision. Especially considering the amount of trouble there was just getting her into that Governor's job in the first place."

"Is it a call we could make? Because I might be inclined just to do it for safety's sake," Barty directed that question to Ursla, and the great bear Admiral frowned.

"In the absence of Audrey..." she let the words trail off, then picked them up again. "Let's go ahead and just put it in motion. I don't think Omega's done with the city... the people are safer up here under our guns than down there. I'll square it with Audrey, or she can countermand it when Pat finds her... but I think we have to take the initiative."

The amount of out-loud justification behind that decision revealed just how uncomfortable Ursla was with it. Of course *Admiral* Andra Ursla was no leader of Freetown, but under the military circumstances, her authority would be respected. Under *any* circumstances, the opinion of the great old war bear would have been respected.

Jax nodded, "Alright, I'll call Pat back. We're going to abandon Freetown."

The two bears in the plot nodded, and Ursla spoke, "Let's hope it's just temporary."

Jax's ear twitched and he nodded, "Yes. Well. We don't want to lose everyone from Freetown the way we lost everyone from Genesis."

The bears nodded again.

"We've got 13,000 wounded to take out of the spaceport right now — the ones Omega controlled for the first outbreak of mob violence. We'll be taking those aboard Earther ships in case there's any residual control to be broken," Jax recounted the information he'd already gotten from Pat and Plummer.

"Want me to start dropping pinnaces to individual sectors? That way we don't need to collect everyone at the spaceport first, save us some time," Barty was frowning thoughtfully as he offered the extra help.

"That's exactly what I'd suggest," Jax agreed. "You and me need to map a grid for quick evacuation, then hand it down to Mustafa so he can get marines deployed to look after the landing sites."

Ursla nodded, "Good. Let's get to it..."

They began to draw lines on maps.

•••

Colin Brawn slid to a stop in the middle of the street as he heard the report come through his earpiece, "I'm sorry, you said *what*, Mustafa?"

There was a pause, "We're abandoning Freetown. Admiral Ursla doesn't want to take any chances with the survival of the humans. Not against Omega, anyway."

Well that was probably sensible.

"Jax Furgus and Barty Stowt are working on a residential evacuation plan to take people up directly to space from their streets. I'm going to pull up all of the reserve to look after the landing sights."

Colin nodded slowly at Bengal's words, "Good. I'll be back in as soon as I can to give you a hand, I just want to make sure we get Gillian first. This wouldn't be a good time to have her running loose, I think."

"Indeed. Talk to you soon."

"Yep."

Colin keyed off his comm and took another breath. They were getting awfully close to the edge of town now — to the north edge, and to the sandy beaches that stretched along it. Once they got there Gillian would have no cover to hide behind.

She'd be theirs, very soon.

Sarah sat silently in her chair, wondering at the suddenness of the decision to evacuate. Perhaps if she'd had Ursla's good sense, she'd have done the same, and saved millions of lives on Genesis.

But she hadn't. She was a failure as a leader in that regard. All she could do now was hope that Ursla's decision, made in the absence of the Governor, was right. The broadcast for total evacuation and abandonment had just gone out over the Freetown comm net, voiced by Andra herself, and describing it as a military necessity.

Pickup sites would be set up by Earther marines in the residential district, announcements to follow... total evacuation was to begin in ninety minutes.

An hour and a half for every person on Freetown to pack one case of their most precious belongings and then to get to a pickup site... hopefully to return soon... but perhaps this would be the last time those people saw their world...

Sarah wished she'd been so smart about it at Genesis.

But now her people were dead...

"Ma'am... strange reading again."

Sarah blinked and looked towards the Sensor Chief, "Strange?"

"In the current north of the city."

Frowning, Sarah got to her feet and walked over to the sensor section of *Unity's* bridge.

Coming to a stop next to the chief's console, she frowned as a flashing red icon faded in and out of existence in the current north of the island that held the capital.

"Comm, get me Admiral Ursla please."

"We still can't see what it is... but it's close now. *Very* close..."

Ursla nodded to her Sensor Officer as she peered into the plot, and then the Signal Officer interrupted her thoughts, "Ma'am, *Unity* for you again."

"In the tank, please."

Shifting her eyes from the map of the island to Sarah's face as it appeared, Ursla frowned, "We see it too. Awfully close to the north shore."

Sarah nodded, "Best warn General Brawn that there could be company coming."

The 49th emerged from the last block of buildings on the edge of town in a line almost two kilometers long. They'd seen nothing of Gillian or her truck as they'd swept through the industrial sector, so surely she had to be on the beach here somewhere... that or they'd somehow missed her and they'd have to double back.

Colin Brawn was near the center of the long battalion skirmishing line as it hit the beach, and as his eyes swept around him he saw nothing... nothing...

Wait a minute.

Narrowing his eyes against the glare of the sunny day, he looked at the section of the city shield right in front of him.

The light blue shield wall should have been glowing.

It wasn't.

"Colin, Andra here. We're seeing increased Omega activity close to the north shore. Might want to keep an eye out there."

Colin stopped breathing.

The shield was open.

Omega was coming.

"Sir! The truck's down here! Looks like they ripped the shield-override out of it!"

That call came from a little ways down the beach.

"Colin?" Ursla's question came to his ear. "Is everything alright? Our sensors say the shield on the north coast is fine, but you might want to check... hello?"

Of course the sensors said it was fine. Because the gap was only fifty meters wide. Because that breach had been created not by a system failure but by an Emergency Medical Services override. The override that allowed, in theory, ambulances to carry wounded back through secondary defensive lines.

"Sir?"

"Colin?"

Colin was sure the blue waters beyond the shield were getting blacker as he watched them. He had to act. *Now*. If any were to be saved.

"Alright, I need every shield we have with us here *right now*. Close this gap with ours, see if you can get them to interface, and *hurry*," Colin tapped his comm twice to add Mustafa and the rest of the Light Division's personnel to the conversation. "We're about to have a major breakthrough in the north. Second Brigade, try to get into a position to contain it. Abandon the gates, Omega won't be using them. Everybody else, set up evacuation points for the residential population and hold them. We need to evacuate this planet *now*."

Colin had looked down for just a second as he gave the orders, now he looked up again.

And there was Gillian, standing in the water in her innocent surfer girl clothes, playfully flipping her wet hair over her shoulder. She locked eyes with him and waved and giggled.

Then from the sea all around her — all up and down the north coast — Omega minions rose.

Thousands of them.

They'd survived the shooting down of their transport, and rode the currents, swimming deep underwater to reach this beach.

By the Earth.

"*Forty-ninth!*" Colin called over his comm.

The marines were sprinting fast to join him, and he drew his sword again.

"Andra, they're coming. Save as many as you can. I'm not going to get away from here," Colin said softly into his headset.

There was a startled pause on the comm — everyone was still hearing the conversation, and none knew what to say.

"By the Earth, we have them on sensors..." Ursla barely rasped the words. "Hundreds of thousands and counting."

Colin heard their hiss, and then saw them — the mutated and Krogg-spliced humans that had once been of Genesis — running like animals out of the water.

He caught sight of Omega-Gillian again, and she was laughing.

"Mustafa," Colin's voice was even quieter now. "You look after the division. But everyone, listen to me, we have to save as many humans as we can. Even if that means we don't go home."

Colin ground his jaw.

"Battalion, *draw swords*. Let's stay in company order as long as we can!" the Colonel of 1/49th was running towards the breach in the shield, and the 500 marines of the battalion were still hurrying to get themselves into some sort of order before the Omega minions hit.

The monsters poured out of the waves.

"We'll take care of things, Colin," Mustafa Bengal's voice was smooth.

Brawn grunted and nodded, then looked to the Earthers forming a tight line around him. They'd be able to hold here for a while, hopefully. Buy time for Second Brigade to get deployed...

"It'll be an honor to fight my last fight with you all," Colin said softly as he raised his sword before him. "Let's charge them."

Then he ran forward, letting out a roar unlike anything heard since the Queen's plateau on Krogg 'A'.

The 49th followed him, to fight a sea of Omega.

CHAPTER 29

"Second Brigade is extending a line along the edge of the industrial sector, and Third Brigade is tying in on their right flank, but with their reserves scattered all over the city, their lines just aren't long enough. Omega's going to be able to break right around them..."

Mustafa Bengal's words over the comm captioned the situation that Ursla was seeing in her plot, and she nodded. Colin's last order had come five minutes earlier, and the fast moving Second Brigade was working hard to accomplish what he'd hoped for.

But there were at least a million Omega minions rising out of that sea. They must have been crammed to the deckheads in the ship that had been shot down. Or perhaps that ship had simply been a distraction which had allowed another to go unnoticed as it dropped more minions.

No 2,000 marines ever fielded would be able to stop such a tide of Omega.

"Alright, listen Mustafa. Tell your marines to pull back. Set up as many evac sites as you can, our pinnaces are on the way down now. Hold them back as long as you can where you can, but the priority needs to be to get civilians out."

"Yes ma'am. If you'll excuse me, I'll pass on those orders."

"Good luck, Mustafa," Ursla didn't get an answer as the Brigadier vanished from the plot.

An hour ago Ursla had been worried about mob control. Half an hour ago she'd thought things were under control but had decided to call for an evacuation as a precaution.

Now Omega had forced the pace. The people of Freetown would have to be fast runners.

And the pilots of Earther pinnaces would have to be faster still.

"Tom, keep your battalion here. I'm going out with the rest of the brigade to help hold them back. As soon as the last of those casualties get airborne, get Plummer's troops and your battalion up to the fleet."

Colonel Tom Katt heard all the words as Mustafa Bengal walked past him, but only processed them after a moment, "Excuse me sir, you don't want us with you?"

Bengal stopped, turned back to the tiger and shook his head, "By the time Plummer's troops are off the ground, we may not be alive out there. And you might not be alive here. If you are, go. I'd prefer that someone from the division survives this day."

Katt's ear twitched, "Yes sir."

Bengal offered another solemn nod to his old comrade in arms, then turned and walked past the Earthers of 1/First Guards. Then he waved the rapidly forming columns of 2/First Guards and both battalions of the Third Guards to follow him as he marched straight out through the shield.

Katt watched as the brigade, minus his own battalion, sprinted away from the spaceport.

"Landing in four seconds!"

Barty Stowt clutched the arms of his pinnace chair tightly, then gritted his teeth as the large craft landed with a hard thud in the middle of a field surrounded by bleachers. He was on his feet instantly, grabbing his sword out of the chair next to him and stepping quickly to the ramp as it lowered to the ground below.

There were sounds of panic all around him as he descended — humans of Freetown had just heard from Ursla that the evacuation had been expedited, and some had heard Colin Brawn's last words, and passed them on.

New mobs had risen very quickly — these ones fueled not by Omega's telepathy, but by a desperate will to survive.

And hopefully they would. Barty hadn't planned to come down himself for the evacuation, but given the short amount of time they had and the fact that the entire fleet had now committed its small craft to the operation, a senior Naval officer needed to be planetside to organize the lift.

Tapping his comm, he patched himself into the network of small craft frequencies, "Barty Stowt on the ground here. I've got about 1,100 people that need picking up. Home in on me..."

Barty rushed over to a nearby Earther marine officer as he spoke, "Pardon me Major, where are we?"

"Central stadium," the female wolf bobbed her head towards the sign. "My battalion's trying to secure the parking lot. We're right in the middle of the residential sector so we're getting a lot of people."

Barty nodded, "Alright, small craft listen up, everyone from a ship of the line, this stadium is your destination. Pinnaces from frigates, I want you scouring the streets looking for groups that can't get here. And one of you come pick me up to serve as a command ship!"

As he spoke, the atmosphere above him began to swerve into chaos. Ursla had ordered the landing gaps in the top of the city shield open to let pinnaces in, and now gunboats were dropping through the openings as well... and Barty's orders gave them all direction.

Almost a hundred pinnaces were over the stadium within the minute, and one of them collected him and took off again.

Pat slid to a halt inside the temporary command post and looked at Plummer, "The last of the casualties are being taken off now. Your transports are getting fired up to lift off, Commandant. You better get your marines moving."

Plummer looked from the screen to Pat and back, "There are about 30,000 minions coming right for us Pat, and there's only one battalion guarding the shield. I think we stay. Help those Guards..."

Pat blinked. Plummer was thinking he should stay and fight.

What the hell?

Pat closed his eyes for a minute, opened them, laid his rifle on a nearby table, walked over to Plummer, grabbed him by the collar, and dragged him to the nearby communications console. The Captains of 1st and 2nd Marine Regiment and Plummer's personal staff gaped as the big Irishman forced their leader down into a chair and pointed at the comm console.

"Give the godsdamned orders, please," Pat's tone was, perhaps unsurprisingly, all business.

Plummer didn't quite know what had just happened... but he realized as he stared into the determined eyes of the Irish veteran that it probably was in his best interests to obey.

Keying the comm tab, Plummer didn't stop staring at Pat as he spoke, "All units withdraw to space."

Plummer's finger came off the comm key and then the Commandant slowly stood, coming face-to-face with Pat. His anger at being humiliated was starting to rise...

"Open your mouth and I'll bloody shoot you, Plummer. Get your riot gear and get aboard a transport or I'll take you to one myself. *Move.*"

The Irishman's words weren't loud, but the menace in them couldn't be overlooked.

Plummer bridled for a moment, then his eyes narrowed, "Yes *sir.*"

He slid past Pat, took a riot gear helmet from one of his Captains, then led the way out of the temporary command center.

Techs began to break down the on-site equipment for withdrawal, and as they did Pat paused and realized he still didn't know where Audrey was. The wounded had been moved out... was she among them? Things were moving so quickly, he hadn't had a chance to find out.

Tapping his comm, he decided to voice his concern to a wider audience, "All personnel, this is Pat Conroy. Keep a look out for Governor DeBrooke. We haven't been able to confirm her location."

There wasn't anything more he could do right now, so he closed the comm and pulled on his helmet. He'd go and find Tom Katt. They'd stand together for now.

Mustafa Bengal and 1,500 Guards rushed into a public park just as a half dozen pinnaces landed in the middle of it. People too far from the stadium to reach that collection point had gravitated to this easily-accessed landing site, hoping that they'd be picked up.

Now they would be.

Mustafa tapped his comm, "We have about 2,000 people here needing a lift... Western Park. And looks like we've got more people coming this way."

There were acknowledgments from a couple of pinnaces, and then Barty Stowt's coarse voice repeated the location over the comm.

"Brigadier Bengal, I see Omega infantry... about six kilometers north and coming fast for you. I'll light them up, but you might want to go out and meet them."

That report came from one of the boats in the sky above, and just as Mustafa looked skyward a pair of deltas crossed overhead — about thirty gunboats now lining up to fire.

"Alright, First Guards, secure this location and oversee the evacuation. Third Guards, let's go. Fast."

The Genesis Marine dropships were lifting off all around as Pat rushed to Tom Katt's side, "Tom, you'll be clear to pull out soon."

The cat turned to Pat at the words, "I still don't feel right leaving."

Pat's unimpressed eyes settled on Katt's amber stare, "None of us do. But you 500 could make a damned great difference somewhere else. Here you'll die. And I've just had to beat that sentiment into Commandant Plummer. Please don't make me wrestle you, man!"

Katt's eyebrow went up, "Man?"

Pat shook his head impatiently, "You know what I meant!"

Looking back to the shield Tom Katt nodded, "Alright. First Guards, now's not our time. Let's get to the dropships."

Barty's pinnace cruised back over the stadium, and peering out the window as the small craft banked, the Vice Admiral could see almost 50,000 people in the parking lot, fighting to get in. There weren't enough marines down there to stop the panic... people were probably being trampled.

But, Barty realized as he ground his jaw, there was nothing he could do about that. If Omega got close enough, trampling wouldn't be the problem, wholesale death would be.

Many pinnaces were full and heading back to their ships now, so there was a backlog of people building up inside...

"I need more craft to the stadium... is there anything at the spaceport that can fly?"

There was no response for a moment, then Pat's voice came through, "The dropships for most of the Light Division. We'll send them to you."

That'd help.

Mustafa Bengal turned a corner at a full run, and then slid to a stop.

Both battalions of the Third Guards were sprinting behind him, but with the very same precision they stopped as they came around the corner. By instinct, then, they formed themselves into a veritable phalanx. None of them had bothered to carry their rifles from the park — those were being wielded now by Freetowners who were helping secure the landing site.

These Earthers were wielding swords only.

And Omega was standing there waiting for them — Omega in the form of thousands of minions. The street leading into the industrial part of town was a solid mass of them. They hissed and stopped advancing as they saw the Guards, and Mustafa stiffened. Here it was, then, the moment.

Gunboats roared overhead, and carronade shots lashed out suddenly, vaporizing hundreds in a cacophony of hisses, unleashing the searing smell of burned flesh.

The fire continued as the boats circled, but there were too many of Omega's soldiers.

This must have been what it had been like for the Guards of the Heavy Division at Krogg 'A'...

Except here, Mustafa knew the Earthers wouldn't carry the day.

Here, Omega knew the Earthers far too well.

Smoke from one of the buildings that had started burning under the aerial assault wafted between the two standing forces for a moment — they were split by about 400 meters.

It cleared quickly, thanks to the cool sea breeze, and when it did, there was Omega-Gillian at the front. Still dressed like a surfer girl, she was waving a white flag on a long staff.

Mustafa frowned at the flag for a moment — it was streaked in red...

Then he looked more carefully at the top of the pole.

Colin Brawn's head was mounted on it.

Every marine in the Third Guards seemed to see that at the same time. Omega had probably meant to demoralize them, showing them the head of their gallant General. Or perhaps the objective was to make them angry — to drive them into a rage.

But as Mustafa looked at the head of his old friend he simply let out a sigh. There was no hope of living. If Colin couldn't survive Omega, then Mustafa wouldn't.

He'd just have to buy time. Kill and delay.

Drawing his sword and raising it above him, Mustafa turned a final time to his marines, "Guards, advance. You know what we have to do."

Mustafa began to walk towards his enemy, and the Guards walked with him. Steadily, they began to cross the gap, blades drawn and ready. But not in rush, and with no roar.

Gunboats poured fire into the long column of Omega minions, and the acrid smell of death grew worse. Then the plague warriors hissed and threw themselves forward with abandon.

Mustafa Bengal leveled his sword at the charge, closed his eyes for a moment, then sprinted forward.

The Guards followed.

CHAPTER 30

Jax Furgus held up his hand, "Sarah, if you send down small craft he'll take over their pilots telepathically..."

"Only crews in riot gear!" Sarah protested in *Aboukir's* holo plot, and Jax opened his mouth, then closed it again.

"Alright. Send them fast then, and make sure you don't send anyone who can get infected."

Sarah vanished from the plot, and almost immediately the orbital map in one corner of the holo tank marked the launch of approximately 600 small craft from Sarah's fleet. More people could be saved.

Jax had ordered the Freetown haulers to maneuver close to the capital so pinnaces evacuating civilians could make more trips thanks to a shorter travel distance.

"*Savanna Felix* hailing, sir."

Jax blinked — Savanna was dead... but... shaking his head Jax cleared his mind. Of course old Savanna was dead, but *Savanna Felix* was still the advanced Battlecruiser that was the effective flagship of the Freetown fleet.

"Put him in the plot," Jax nodded, and Ed Jeffries appeared.

The dark-skinned human looked worn, fatigue and sadness clouding his eyes, "Jax, I'm putting my pinnaces into the mix. Has anyone found Audrey yet?"

Jax shook his head, "I haven't heard, but there are a lot of marines down there. We're not going to forget her. Just tell your small craft pilots to keep their riot gear on, and follow Barty's directions when they get down there."

Jeffries' face remained gaunt at the lack of news about his Governor, but he nodded, "Right. Talk to you later."

The man vanished, and Jax grimaced. The old lion had come out of retirement and cruised a long way to save these people.

It wasn't working out so well.

"Sir, this is Colonel Sarsaw, we're about to be overrun. It's me and twelve of my battalion now, we'll be dead in a minute... that's your left flank caving. The stadium is nine kilometers behind us, so I'd advise–"

The comm went dead, and Barty Stowt closed his eyes. Mustafa wasn't answering comms any longer either.

"Alright, marines, I don't know who's left but the stadium has to be our priority. If you're not holding down a landing site of your own, get between Omega and the stadium.

Tom Katt heard the words as he was boarding the last dropship at the spaceport. He glanced at Pat, then looked inside at the marines assembled there.

"I think that's our call."

Pat blinked, "No, someone needs to survive this…"

"You will," Katt turned to the Irishman.

"I'm not going to live if you land this thing in front of Omega, not now."

"You will," Katt turned away from Pat and climbed the rest of the way up the ramp, Pat following with more than a little anxiety.

The dropships of 1/First Guards took off and headed for the area of the stadium.

Sarah watched her pinnaces on the monitor as they dropped towards the stadium. They could pull at least 10,000 people out in one run…

"Admiral Jeffries signaling from *Savanna Felix*, ma'am."

Turning, Sarah nodded, folding her arms, "On the main screen."

Jeffries appeared, looking haggard, worn, beaten… much like Sarah looked and felt.

"Thanks for your craft, ma'am," he said quietly.

Sarah swallowed hard and nodded, "I learned before that speed is… critical…"

Ed Jeffries stiffened at the sadness of those words, and he got the sense he'd understand it even better before this day was done.

"I don't know if you're monitoring all the Earther frequencies, but I just heard that Pat's coming up with the Guards from the spaceport," he tried to move the discussion to more practical concerns. A long, long time ago, Ed had been in Sarah's Battlecruiser Squadron with Pat.

A lifetime ago.

Sarah hadn't heard about Pat. She wasn't monitoring those channels. Now she blinked.

"The Guards from the spaceport are going to defend the stadium," she knew that much, and she told Ed so.

The Freetown officer frowned, "Well, he's with them."

Sarah blinked again, and Ed realized the ArcGeneral-President suddenly had different priorities.

"I'll get off your comm," he rasped, and then he disappeared.

"Get me Pat!" Sarah turned to the Comm Chief.

Other concerns seemed to suddenly shift to the side… she hadn't worried about Pat at all until now, because she'd known he was in the only safe place in Freetown. He had the Guards Brigade with him...

But going out to fight?

"Not getting through, ma'am. Too much going on down there, our transmitters just aren't good enough to get through that much energy comm traffic."

Sarah ground her jaw, "Keep trying. Dammit keep trying."

The dropships of 1/First Guards landed in an intersection of some major streets in the commercial district, and the battalion rushed from their craft at high speed. All around, panicked Freetown civilians trying to reach the stadium slowed, then changed their direction, running for the landers with all the desperation they could muster.

Which was a lot.

"Load these things up!" Tom Katt ordered. "We won't need them!"

Fully packed, the landers could probably take 800 humans, maybe 1,000. And there were enough people nearby to fill each ship.

Pat wanted to be one of them... but then he *didn't*. For some reason he didn't even think of himself as he started waving people up ramps. One after another, the ramps of the first four dropships came up and they boosted, climbing sluggishly skywards with their overloaded marine bays slowing their ascent.

The last ship was actually only half full when Pat ran to it, the crowds having been absorbed by the other four. This was his chance to get aboard one...

So he gave the pilot a thumbs-up and watched the thing's ramp lift and the craft rise into the sky.

It was only when he watched it go that he realized he wasn't on it.

Terror tried to grab his spine, but he didn't let it. He felt strangely — ridiculously, insanely, even — disassociated from what he had just done. Certainty of death began to settle in, and as his gaze dropped from the sky he watched as the Guards set up a circular shield perimeter in the middle of the intersection.

"You were supposed to go," Tom Katt's sharp protest drew Pat to turn around, and he simply stared at the cat's eyes.

There was a pause as the veteran Colonel considered the Irishman, and then Katt nodded in reply to words Pat didn't actually say, "Yeah, me too."

Both knew this was their last stand.

They'd slow down Omega for as long as they could, and give more civilians a chance to get away.

Pulsars were set up facing the direction of Omega's approach — the battalion's heavy weapons might have some effect. The rest of the marines simply formed a firing line.

They wouldn't have to wait long.

Ursla looked up as Sarah appeared in the plot, "Sarah?"

The elder Manchester's eyes were wild, "Pat's down there with the First Guards. They're about to be overrun!"

Ursla froze, surprised both by the panic in Sarah's voice and what she was saying. Pat was *where?*

Dammit.

"I'll get gunboats there to help. And I'll let Barty know, he'll be able to sort it out," Ursla still managed to remain composed as she spoke, and Sarah nodded once and then vanished from the plot.

Shaking her head again to clear it, Ursla turned to Esther Arbear, "We'd better find Pat."

The Omega minions came out of almost nowhere, running like a stampede of monsters. The Guards opened fire as Pat watched, the pulsars incinerating some of the approaching foes, the rifles of the marines seemingly doing no good at all.

In seconds the minions were at the shield, *on* the sloping shield, *climbing.* The reverse-angle slant that made the shield useful against plunging artillery was working to Omega's advantage — his minions were climbing over it.

For creatures that felt any form of physical pain, such a feat would have been impossible.

But as Pat and Tom Katt stood together and watched with morbid fascination, the once-human creatures reached the top of the shield, and began to drop over its rim — right into the rear of the defensive perimeter.

The reserve line engaged them immediately, swords flashing in the sun as the minions launched themselves on to the attack. Tom Katt drew his own blade and stepped in front of Pat, and then Pat realized he didn't have his. He'd left it back on *Unity* — he hadn't thought he'd need it...

The marines at the edge of the perimeter stopped firing, dropped their rifles and turned back on the minions that now were beginning to rain in over the shield. The fifteen-meter drop to hard roadway didn't seem to faze them, but Guards' blades did.

Marines surged forward with roars, swinging fast and sometimes managing to catch limbs of minions... other times being swarmed by a half dozen and held down while their shields were beaten away and their flesh torn off.

Tom Katt and his personal squad held back as the entire battalion was overwhelmed, and Pat wondered why... until he realized they'd formed a semicircle around him.

"You might want to run for the stadium, Pat. Four clicks behind you..."

Katt's words were still smooth. "You might find a hover car or something to get you there faster..."

Pat blinked, then turned around and saw open road, and the stadium in the distance. Far, far away...

"Come with me, Tom. Let's go..."

The battalion was being consumed. Surely Katt didn't have a death wish...

But Pat knew immediately that the venerable old Katt couldn't leave his Guards to die alone...

A minion reached the squad surrounding Pat, grabbing one of the cat marines, knocking the sword from her hand, and dragging her away by her ankle. Her squadmates went after her, then their Sergeant looked at his Colonel, "Tom, get him out of here. We'll buy time."

Pat didn't know the Sergeant's name, but he very much wished he did.

Tom opened his mouth to protest, but the Sergeant put a hand on his Colonel's soldier, "One of us has to make it out of here. Go."

Pat watched Katt's eyes, and saw the pain flashing through them... so he grabbed the Colonel's arm and tugged, pointing with his rifle towards the stadium, "We'll need to move fast."

With a single nod, Tom Katt started to back away from his marines. Pat dropped his rifle, then crouched and grabbed the sword the marine had dropped. He followed Tom Katt out the rear shield at a dead run.

Barty Stowt frowned as the report on Pat's whereabouts came to him from Ursla, then he looked up and waved to the pilot, "Intersection about four kilometers north of the stadium. Get there fast."

Pat was short of breath, and though adrenalin was pushing him, he realized that his heavy gait wasn't going to allow him to escape the Hells' devil beasts running after him. Tom Katt had slowed to stay beside the Irishman, but now Pat came to a stop and looked at the Colonel, "You get out of here Tom. Go... tell Sarah I'm sorry."

"I'll carry you," Tom sheathed his sword.

"No no no, I'll slow you down and we'll both die. *Go*, man."

Tom blinked once, and considered the Irishman's words.

Then he was knocked onto his face and was being dragged away by a minion.

Pat screamed — an angry, brutal, horrid scream — and raised his sword. He looked all around him, holding the weapon before him without much style. It had just been a lone minion and it had come from nowhere to take Tom.

"*Gods damn you bastards!*" Pat roared as he caught sight of the Colonel being dragged towards a group of eight approaching minions. The Irishman charged towards them, but they were far away, and he was slow now. They started beating down Tom Katt's shield, and it must have failed, because blood was flung into the air with each blow.

Pat stumbled to a stop and let go his sword.

He dropped to his knees and let out a long breath.

They all died today. Gods dammit.

He hadn't seen this coming.

And he hadn't seen the pinnace dropping to the ground right in front of him either.

The ramp lowered before him, the pilot having come down on an angle that would give the Irishman easy access, but Pat wasn't in any condition to even see it, let alone stand and climb the ramp.

The pinnace had no marines aboard, but Barty Stowt and the copilot bounded down the ramp with swords in hand. The copilot grabbed Pat forcefully, and the Irishman's mind was forced brutally out of its tailspin as he found himself being dragged into the craft.

Barty followed quickly, using his mass and his blade to keep back a half-dozen minions that had come to take Pat.

The Irishman dropped to the pinnace's floor just inside the door, and the copilot ran forward to the cockpit. Barty stepped in and called over his comm, "Get off the ground!"

As the engines surged back up to full throttle, Barty looked to Pat, "You alright?"

Pat stared at the bear and didn't answer.

Barty nodded, "Alright, we'll get you back to... oh..." he looked down. "Damn..."

A minion found Barty's leg, and just as the pinnace rose off the street the minion pulled hard. Barty's legs were yanked out the door, and as the ramp finished retracting the computer halted the hatch closing sequence because it detected the Vice Admiral's hands on the bottom of the hatch frame. He was hanging on as six minions tried to pull him down.

Despite his shock, Pat somehow knew that he had to act. He scrambled forward, grabbed one of the big bear's burly arms in both of his hands, and heaved with all the might he could.

Barty's head popped up over the hatch frame and he smiled, "Thanks..."

Then there was another jerk and his hands slipped.

The hatch closed behind him as the computer discovered the way was clear, and the pinnace rose rapidly to high altitude.

Pat stared at the hatch. On the street below, Barty Stowt was murdered.

By Omega.

CHAPTER 31

"This is Lieutenant Gyle, piloting *Seraphim's* number three pinnace — we were Vice Admiral Stowt's C&C ship. We've lost the Admiral, but we have Pat Conroy aboard."

Sarah had opened her mouth to breathe, and it stayed open as the full weight of what the pilot had said struck home with her. Old Barty Stowt...

She closed her eyes for a second... a few seconds. Barty Stowt, Ami Dune's old Flag Captain from back during the Krogg War. The powerful, invincible old bear...

She opened her eyes.

"How long until the stadium is overrun?"

The question wasn't directed at anyone in particular, but since the comm was open a voice came over it, "This is Colonel Zar at the stadium, ma'am. We see them coming now, and I've got about 30,000 civilians left in here. We've got them all inside the building and shields up the whole way round... but I've only got about 500 marines to try to hold the place."

Ursla's voice came next, "We should have enough craft for everyone down to you in about ten minutes, Colonel. If you can hold that long, we can get them out."

"We'll hold, then. Hear that everybody? Let's get to the perimeter — 60th foot form skirmish line..." the Colonel switched comm frequencies to avoid clogging the airways with his orders.

"Let's get all boats to strafe in support," Sarah suggested immediately.

"I've got a different idea, actually."

Sarah frowned at Jax Furgus' comment over the comm, and took a couple of steps towards *Unity's* main screen to see if she could figure out what the old cat had in mind.

"Never tried this, have you Master?"

Aboukir's Master took a breath and shook her head, "But I like trying new things."

Jax nodded, then looked to his Flag Captain, "Ready Ron?"

Ronax Hobbes answered uneasily, "If I was trapped in the city, I'd rather be vaporized than tortured to death."

For a second Jax's eyes fell to the floor, and he took a deep breath. They'd protect the stadium with this attack, but anyone trapped away from the stadium and hiding from Omega would surely die…

“Chairs, everyone,” the Master interrupted the grim thoughts with her even tone, bracing herself on the backs of the chairs of her two Helm Officers.

Jax and Ron found their seats quickly as the great old 74 dove in on its target.

“Five, four, three, two, one…”

Aboukir began to rumble, the deck shivering as the ship’s hull pushed into the atmosphere of Freetown. Earther ships technically had the ability to do this, but it had never been attempted: no planet the Earthers had come across had warranted a devastating bombardment from space.

Until now.

“And… holding position directly over the city. Altitude 600 kilometers.” Under different circumstances, the Master would have sounded proud of this feat.

“Guns stand by. Master, starboard broadside to bear on the city, please. Let’s have canister, Ron,” Jax was giving the orders even though he was technically supposed to let Ron Hobbes command the ship… but neither of the cats cared who gave the directions.

They had to do this grim thing.

“Guns fire as you bear,” Jax finished. “Signals, broadcast a warning to the planet.”

Pat was poking his head into the cockpit compartment when the pinnace banked hard to port and shot upwards on a forty-five degree angle. Hanging on despite his surprise, Pat managed to turn to look out one of the windows behind him… and he watched a canister broadside level half the city of Freetown.

So the Earthers were taking the gloves off.

Usually Earthers didn’t believe in orbital bombardment because of the collateral damage such fire could cause to the surrounding terrain. But since this was a city, and since what Omega would do to any trapped people was much worse than an Earther broadside’s impact, the time had come to fling massive waves of energy shot.

“That killed almost 80,000 of the minions,” Esther Arbear looked up through the plot and Ursla nodded.

But then she stopped nodding as one of the gunboats went in closer to confirm the kills. It put a live video feed onto the leveled city… and it witnessed thousands of the fallen minions getting to their feet. Their engineered sub-dermal armor had resisted canister shot.

Were Ursla not seeing the holos herself, she wouldn’t have believed it…

“Alright, that didn’t work so well. They’re like roaches,” Jax said bitterly over the comm. "We probably just killed a lot of hiding Freetowners though."

"Better to die by energy shot than torture," Ursla's quiet affirmation of Jax's decision tasted bitter as she said it.

"How many left in that stadium?" Jax asked the most important question.

Ursla's eyes shifted to a different part of the battle tank, "About 22,000. Everything we've got is heading there now."

"Alright..."

Keying off the comm, Jax turned away from *Aboukir's* plot, "Master, take us as low as you can into the gravity well. See if we can get into carronade range."

Ron came to his feet, "Want to try a regular broadside?"

Jax shook his head, "Volcanic island, I don't want to accidentally blow it up by concentrating a full broadside on one point... yet. But if we carve a moat for that stadium..."

Cocking an eyebrow, Ron Hobbes nodded, "Alright. Signals, inform the boats with us to gently carve a moat for the stadium."

"I love how we're all medieval all of a sudden," Jax grunted.

That bastard Omega was reducing them to the tactics of castles.

Two carronade beams were cutting a trench outside the stadium when Pat's pinnace flew in. Pat stared at them for a moment, then moved through the cabin back to the hatch. Watching through the window as his small craft dropped over the rim of the stadium, he saw clearings and then throngs of people rushing towards the vessel.

He keyed the hatch open, then stood aside, waiting for the landing feet to get a grip on the ground as the pilots put the ship down. The copilot emerged from the cockpit immediately, and with Pat he descended the ramp and started waving people aboard.

The burning air stunk, and the sky roared. Those were sounds and smells Pat remembered from the last war, but now they were so much worse.

"We have to get up the ramp!" the copilot yelled at him, and Pat blinked and nodded, immediately pushing into the throng of people trying to get aboard. The copilot followed quickly, and as he got inside he keyed the ramp up, leaving hundreds hopeless on the field as he rushed to the cockpit.

Pat stood at the hatch and looked out as it closed, then felt the pinnace boost fast into the air. Another dropped right into the space it had been occupying.

Gunboats were making strafing runs on the parking lot just beyond the north edge of the stadium now, but Pat couldn't tell if they were cutting that trench or killing the enemy...

Then Pat saw a blackish minion leap over the north wall of the three-storey high stadium. A marine was on the minion instantly, and it was flung back over, but there was a new seed of panic sewn in the building.

Three gunboats settled over the north rim of the stadium and started using carronades to blast away any minions that tried to scale the sides of the building, but still 15,000 people waited for a lift out of there.

The Earther and Genesis pinnaces were managing an incredible feat in getting them off this quickly... but would they prove too slow in the final count?

Pat ground his jaw and watched as the stadium shrunk below him. As the pinnace banked around he could see black filling the parking lot outside, and pouring into the trench that had been cut to try to slow Omega down. Evidently there were enough minions to fill in the trench and to allow the rest to run over it.

For the first time — strangely only the first time — Pat started to feel sick.

The last pinnaces were coming off the field now — last because even from this altitude Pat could see black figures pouring over the wall into the stadium itself. The pinnaces waiting to land were waved off by the last three marines left standing.

They weren't standing for long.

Pat turned away from the window. He was off Freetown, with many other civilians. But not *that* many.

The pinnace accelerated into space.

Omega-Gillian stood at the center of the stadium and looked skyward. The Earthers had finally done something they'd always refused to do while in their do-gooding mode: they'd used their mighty (ha!) broadsides against the surface of a planet.

Well, they'd used sissy canister. The Earthers didn't have the guts to unleash their full firepower. They liked putting people into comas, or using canister... they didn't have the guts to kill with force.

But that suited her fine. She'd get off this island just in case one of them decided to crack its volcanic crust with a real broadside... but they wouldn't.

And there were other games left to be played with the ships in orbit...

And even more games to be played with the toy she'd kept.

Omega-Gillian didn't have to bark orders to tell her minions to bring forth the game, because Omega simply moved them to do it. As the stadium filled with a chorus of hisses and the screams of the last civilians who didn't escape, a group of Omega soldiers hauled a limp figure towards the avatar.

Omega-Gillian grinned as they came to a stop in front of her, then reached out and caressed the cheek of the victim.

"I always thought you were pretty," the plague avatar said with relish. "We're going to make some movies, you and me."

If Audrey DeBrooke had been conscious, she would have screamed.

CHAPTER 32

"Welcome to the new Admiralty House."

Setter looked around him as he walked into the foyer of the new building that held the rebuilt organizational mechanisms of the Earther Admiralty and Navy Board. Much had been lost with London.

It was tempting to remember all of that loss in great detail, but Setter resisted the urge, especially the urge to remember Elandra. He instead took a deep breath and examined the building. It was indeed a new construction, built to the same pre-fab blueprints that had been at the core of the previous Admiralty House, but instead of being situated in Britain, this house sat in Halifax, overlooking the city's harbor.

"Well, they did a good job getting it put up so quickly," Setter said quietly after a moment. "Not that I'm surprised."

Varnon Broadpaw came to a stop next to his friend, "Yes. It's almost like being home. But it's also an excruciating reminder of what we've lost."

The casual quality of that last statement gave Varnon's words a ring of sadness, and Setter nodded, unable to disagree. They'd both spent many long days working in the Admiralty House, both before and after the Krogg War. That the Earthers could build an almost-identical replacement so quickly was a testament to their engineering prowess…

But it wasn't the same. Replacements never, ever were.

"We're in the main briefing room. Ami and Dran are going to meet us there."

Lab Forepaw had led the two wolves into this building, and now he turned back to face his old friends. If Varnon and Setter were finding being in this new Admiralty House painful, the First Lord was finding it downright agonizing.

Though he knew he shouldn't dwell on it, he still believed his mistakes had left London wide open to destruction… No one blamed him for that; everyone had been certain Omega was going after Freetown. But Earth had been hit. And the Genesis civilians wiped out, while he and the fleet sat in defense of unmolested Freetown — a planet that had seen no trouble of significance since.

All that had happened on Lab's watch, and this building was a stark reminder of the painful reality.

Knowing he couldn't let that reality paralyze him now, Lab led two of his dear old friends down the corridor of Admiralty House to the briefing room, and refocused on the matters for today.

"So, she definitely has a way to eliminate it?" Varnon changed the subject as they started to move on, and Lab looked back as he walked.

"The old version, at least."

Varnon exchanged glances with Setter just before the trio entered the briefing room. Aside from the different view through the floor-to-ceiling windows on the wall opposite the door, this room seemed identical to the one in London's old installation.

Setter nodded to Dran Nightclaw, the panther sitting on the far side of the table, and Ami Dune, sitting next to the cat. He took a seat at the head of the table, with Varnon at his right hand and Lab at his left. Standing at the opposite end, with a holo glowing over the table in front of her, Doctor Celia Lazarus nodded to the new arrivals.

Celia had been working fast in Fengate Hospital's labs, using the Omega minion *Renown* had captured along with notes that had survived from the original project to try to reverse-engineer a cure.

The notes from Elandra's project.

Setter forced himself to think her name. There had been notes left behind by Elandra's work — the computers in the lab she'd been working at in London had regularly backed up their data to her facility at Fengate. The redundancy had been installed in case of something mundane — a data storage error or the like.

Now, that sensible backup policy had left Celia with threads to work with… though Setter knew a few research notes and test results couldn't compare to having Elandra on the project. They had some of the pieces to the puzzle, but they'd lost the one wolf who'd had a firm grasp of where to look for the rest. Celia would have to use all her skills to assemble something out of that faint background… but if anyone aside from Elandra could do it, it was Doctor Lazarus. Her career was long and remarkable, including time working with Elandra on the creation of regen, and memorably, saving Narosh's life after his crash aboard *Orion*.

"Alright," Celia nodded to Forepaw, "I'll get started. Basically, I've been comparing the notes that Elandra transferred to Fengate before the impact, and she had a couple of different things ongoing. One was a flux-cell system for getting past the Type 2 plague's defenses… that's interesting because in *Renown*, we found that Christine Schaeffer… that's Graham's aide, if some of you don't know about her… well, her cells seemed to be put in flux after a crash regen procedure. We're looking into that… there may be a way to get around Omega's Krogg-type cellular defenses, but I need more time before I can be certain."

That possibility — slim possibility though it may have been — made the ears of every Earther at the table perk up. A cure for Omega would be a veritable dream come true.

"In the meantime, we've been able to finish Elandra's other project... we *think*. We've developed a scrubber that can remove the Type 1 Omega from our own bloodstreams."

Each of the assembled officers began to frown slightly, and Ami Dune was the first to ask the clarification question, "As I understand it, Type 1 and Type 2 can't communicate... so Type 1 is just dormant in our blood, right?"

Celia nodded, "That's right."

"So..." Ami leaned forward slightly, "...what do we accomplish with this? Not that I don't like the idea of purging myself of any sort of Omega. But will we gain something?"

"Possibly," Celia stepped forward and changed the display in the holo plot at the center of the briefing table. The blue light presented what appeared to be various types of biological cells, though none of the Earthers sitting around it knew precisely what they were.

"Sorry, Celia, we're going to need an idiot's guide to these," Varnon frowned at what he was seeing. "I never did well with biology."

"No problem, of course," Celia nodded, stepping closer and then reaching her finger into the tank. "This is Type 1 Omega — the dormant version of the plague in our cells. Actually, it's what I'm calling Type 0, because this is the version that existed in us long before Type 1 infected the Larosians."

The Earthers around the table nodded, their eyes focusing on the innocuous-seeming cell.

"Hard to believe that little thing is... well..." Varnon shook his head, while Lab began nodding.

"Omega. We've been carrying him around all this time..."

Silence descended for a moment, and Celia moved her explanations forward by tapping the controls and adding another holo image: an Earther brain scan.

"We'd never thought anything of these cells — they were just another element common in our bloodstream, and they seemed inert enough. Since our immune systems destroyed their ability to infect anything with Earth-derived DNA, they never appeared hostile. *But*, knowing now that they're Omega's original form..." Celia hit another button and an area in the brain scan highlighted, "...we realized *this* might be significant."

The scan zoomed in, showing a section of the brain that appeared to be clogged with the Omega cells.

"We never bothered with this part of the brain before. The cells being presumed inert, we just thought it was a disused part of the brain that collected them by some fluke. But now we've compared the sector to the telepathic parts of Krogg and Larosian brains..."

Celia let her voice trail off, and let the assembled officers and consuls absorb the implications of what she was saying. Omega cells were choking a part of their brains that might have been the key to Earther *telepathy*.

"He's telepathic... if he was sitting right on top of our telepathic send-receive transmitter... he's the reason we're not telepathic?" Ami Dune came to her realization out loud, and Celia nodded.

"That's possible, indeed. I don't know why he wouldn't have released his blockage of our telepathic powers when his Type 2 self tried to attack us with them... it might be that he choked our transmitter and has no way of undoing it... but we need to be aware that if we scrub the cells from our bodies, we could become telepathic."

The doctor's words carried with them both a hope and a heaviness: telepathic Earthers could be a double-edged sword, being able to fight Omega on the battlefield of the mind, but also potentially being vulnerable to him.

"So... we'd be vulnerable to Omega's telepathy? I don't know if that'd be such a good thing..." Varnon's skepticism bled through into his words.

Celia bobbed her head, "It's possible. But I'm not sure we'd actually be *vulnerable*, so to speak... I think our *instinct* might already be a case of telepathy bleeding past the blockade. We've all experienced it — we've all read each others' minds. We do it all the time. I think harnessing full telepathy can't be much different. But of course, there's no way to prove such a thing."

Lab and Varnon exchanged somewhat taut glances, neither terribly comfortable with the idea of granting the plague that had so readily outwitted them access to their minds...

"Unless... unless his ability to predict everything we've been trying has been because Type 0 has been sending him intel," Ami leaned forward and planted her elbows on the table. "Maybe that explains how he always knows what we're doing. If we had full control of our own minds, maybe we could fight him off."

His eyebrow climbing, Lab looked at Celia, "Do you think that's possible?"

Doctor Lazarus frowned gently, "It's *possible*, but I don't think it's likely. Either way, I agree with Admiral Dune. I think we're all better off if we take control of our telepathic centers. I think we'll be able to put up better walls against Omega's incursion than those Type 0 has built."

Lab took a deep breath and sat back. Varnon scratched his chin absently. Ami's hands kneaded each other and Dran Nightclaw sat unmoving.

"I want to be able to see into *his* mind," Setter's sudden words were cold. "He's spent so much time pushing us off balance, I want to return the favor. Get into *his* mind."

The firm words came with a confidence that didn't sound manufactured. They weren't angry either... they were reassuringly powerful.

The Supreme Consul of the Earther people wanted to hit Omega with a dose of his own medicine — with some mental strife. And he believed he *could* hit the plague that way.

"How soon will the scrubber be ready for trial, Celia?" Setter leaned forward in his seat.

Lazarus quieted briefly before answering, perhaps feeling nervous now that the moment of truth was coming. She drew a vial out of her pocket and held it up, "I'll inject myself now, and head back to Fengate. If I'm vulnerable to being taken over, it'll be detected and he'll try to take control of me."

"Whoa, you're not going to be the first test subject," Varnon leaned forward again. "We can't afford to lose you if it goes wrong."

Celia opened her mouth, then paused. She didn't have a good, logical reason for being the first test subject, but she felt it was her duty to be.

"I have to do this. I'll be fine, I'm certain of that."

Varnon covered his eyes with his hand, "Somebody tell me she didn't just say that."

All he heard in reply was the sound of an injector gun, and as he opened a gap between his fingers to peer through he saw Celia pulling the hypo away from her arm.

"That was a bit abrupt," Ami managed, eyeing the doctor.

With a shrug, Celia deactivated the holo projection and slid the vial back into her pocket, "I know. But we have no evidence so far that Omega's telepathic powers are any greater than the Queen's... listen, I promise you all, this *will* work."

Setter sighed and looked down at the table. That sounded a lot like something Elandra might have said, long ago... actually it was exactly what she'd said, when she'd been growing him a new leg.

And she'd been right.

"Alright," he said slowly, "get back to–"

He froze. Everyone in the room froze.

There was something very, very wrong, and all their instincts — perhaps their repressed telepathy — caught it at once. All the eyes in the room turned towards the door just as a Lieutenant slid to a halt outside and stepped through, "Sirs, ma'ams, Freetown's been overrun."

Setter came to his feet at the same time as the other military veterans at the table, and led by Ami, they hurriedly left the room.

Celia Lazarus stood with her mouth open in surprise.

She hoped what she'd just done was right.

CHAPTER 33

Karl Kandam sat quietly in his cabin aboard *Namur*.

He was fleeing the system he'd commanded on-and-off for over forty years; Fox and Garvin had rightly decided that trying to hold the base against Omega would have been pointless. There'd be no Maginot Line out here — the Earthers had abandoned their mighty defensive position ahead of the plague's arrival...

Karl just hoped that *Conqueror* and any survey ships that returned to the system late received the warning to make a run for it before Omega got hold of them... and that they had the engine power left to escape.

After all that it'd been through in Genesis space, there was no telling whether *Conqueror* would be in any shape just to push on...

Karl closed his eyes and leaned back in his chair. There wasn't a whole lot he could do for *Conqueror*, one way or the other. So he just let thoughts of the ship glide to the back of his mind. For now he needed to focus on dealing with the situation at hand.

Specifically, he needed to figure out how to deploy the *Gibraltar* stations in Krogg space. It'd be most logical to put them directly over the planet as a last line of defense, but logic might not be the best guide for dealing with Omega at Krogg...

Garvin Jardaw was similarly thoughtful on *Medusa's* bridge. He was returning to Krogg space for literally the first time in forty years — he'd not been back to Krogg 'A' since the end of the Krogg War, having come only as far as Gibraltar to take up his post.

Now memories of the end of *Engadine*, the death of his old friend and mentor Draco Maximane, and the hard fighting of years past were stirring within him.

He was cruising to defend that place of such destruction, and he wasn't sure how he felt about that... he knew he couldn't let forty-year-old events manipulate the way he fought Omega... but he wasn't going to pretend they hadn't happened either.

So instead he scanned through a half-dozen reports on the state of the fleet he and Fox had to work with. Fox had come out with four squadrons of *Chimera*-class ships of the line — older warships, but still fairly powerful. Added to that were another six squadrons of frigates — four of the older *Pallas*-class and two newer *Cerberus* squadrons — and four squadrons of modern sloops. In addition to that were the 128 packed ships Fox had brought from Sol with him — nine squadrons of the line and seven squadrons of frigates and sloops from the Krogg War, which had been sent ahead and would be in Krogg space soon. Then there was Liz's Survey Service Provisional Battle Group... or whatever the official title for the Surveyors was right now. Because of the hasty departure, only fifty of those had been rearmed.

Finally, of course, Chronos Claw's Krogg station squadron would be waiting in Krogg space for them. A squadron of *Venerables*, a squadron of *Champions*, and a squadron each of modern frigates and sloops, all of them divided between the planet and the nearby hyperspace corridor.

Jardaw frowned as he did the math in his head. Officially that gave them six squadrons of modern ships of the line, totaling forty-eight. Plus fifty-six modern frigates, forty modern sloops, 128 recommissions and the fifty ships of Liz's group. A grand total of 322 warships... not a bad force in the numerical sense... save for the fact that according to the last pod from *Conqueror*, Omega was coming after them with at least 1,200 of those new black hybrid ships. And excusing the reality that most of the 322 Earther ships on hand were rather old.

Garvin tended to avoid pessimism, so he leaned back in his chair and drew a realistic conclusion: "We're not going to survive this."

Sitting quietly in his cabin — as seemed to be the vogue for fleet officers at this stage — Fox Magnus tried to figure out just how *not* to lose.

He really had no idea.

There was nothing his four squadrons of *Chimeras* could do, even in support of Chronos' *Venerables* and *Champions*, that would stop 1,200 ships — let alone 1,200 *Omega* ships. His 128 recommissions, once assembled, would be equally useful... or useless. They'd fight gallantly, but what could they really hope to accomplish?

Even if he'd taken more of those old ships from Sol with him, it wouldn't have mattered. Kylie Peregrine's force had been larger than his but of similar vintage... and many of those ships had been slaughtered alongside their Admiral, facing only Omega-modified Genesis ships.

Against these Krogg-spliced monstrosities...

Taking a deep breath, Fox leaned back in his seat. He wasn't the sort who tended to give up in the face of enormous adversity — his track record of defying the odds in gallant and dramatic fashion was long and colorful. Now he just needed to figure out something that would replicate past successes in the context of this new war.

How... that was the problem.

"I need some sort of... inspiration," he rubbed his eyes.

Walking over to her husband as he said the words, Thena Magnus rested her hands on his shoulders, "You looked at Garnan yet?"

Fox opened his eyes, "Oh, sorry that was a rhetorical question. Forgot you were here, hon."

Thena smiled, "You do that sometimes, don't you? Look at Garnan. Never know what you might find in there."

She stepped away from the back of his chair, walked over to one of their book shelves, yanked a copy of *Garnan's* volume on human Naval warfare from its place and tossed it to him. As the softcover book flew through the air it splayed open, then as Fox craned his neck around to see it coming it smacked him in the face.

"Ow!" the dapper fox yelped, rubbing his nose with his hand. Shifting his chair, he leaned down to grab the book as it landed on the floor.

He stopped in mid-movement. The book had opened on landing to the pages showing a particular battle.

"No way. There's *no way* that just worked like that."

Thena had returned to the kitchen, but now she stuck her head back through the door with a smile, "Opened to Leyte Gulf, right?"

Fox blinked and looked up, his mouth hanging open in surprise, "How... but... you... you *meant* for it to open to Leyte Gulf? But... why... you should've just told me..."

"Close your mouth dear. This way is much more entertaining!"

Smiling, Thena withdrew herself to the kitchen again.

Fox looked at the empty space where she'd been standing for a moment, then grabbed the book and pushed his chair back to his desk. After reading for two minutes, he reached to the table and smacked the comm key.

"Bridge."

"Order our four Battle Squadrons out of energy drive. All other ships to continue to Krogg 'A'. I need to meet with Garvin and Karl immediately."

"Yes sir."

It could be a mess... but it might help.

"Krag, we're getting ready to put our division on the ground to secure your biomatter pools," Chronos' words were matter of fact.

The Peacelord bowed slightly, "Very well. Your Fourth Division then, the one assigned to this system? It would only make sense."

Chronos nodded evenly, leaning back in the briefing room chair that didn't feel as comfortable as it should have, "Yes. We had the Third Division in the *Venerables* at Gibraltar, but most of that was lost with Lang at Genesis. So it's just 10,000 troops — all we've got."

Kragran nodded, himself leaning back, "I see. We could augment your defenses of course. We can supply approximately... three million warriors."

Chronos had been looking at the desk and trying to figure out how to bring up the subject of Freetown with the Peacelord when those words came out. The Vice Admiral nearly choked at the number — and he hadn't even been swallowing.

"Three *million*? What do you mean...?"

Kragran's mouth twitched into a smile, and Chronos stopped speaking for long enough to recognize it was a joke.

"Wish it were that easy, Krag. But I should show you what just came in on the pod from Ursla at Freetown. This is what Omega did to the city."

Tapping the controls on the desk, Chronos called up the holos of all that had happened when Omega decided to finish the job at Freetown.

Kragran's mouth closed and his eye narrowed as he watched the display. It took about five minutes to play through the accelerated account of the action, and Chronos found himself staring at the desk as it rolled.

He was a great friend of Freetown. From day one, the Freetowners had been good to Fox and him. Fox. Chronos didn't look forward to telling the First Space Lord about this when he arrived.

But to more immediate matters: the Freetown action proved that the Earthers might not be able to protect the Krogg biomatter pools.

"You believe your division can do nothing to stop his takeover of these pools if he lands?" Kragran asked after a moment.

Chronos looked at Kragran, "That'd be about the size of it. That was the Light Division there, Krag. Some of our very best... and it was a walkover."

It was rare to hear the cat so clearly discouraged, but Kragran's voice retained confidence, "You will not have to fear chaos from our citizens though, Chronos. Our Telepaths will scatter his attempts to control our warriors, we will not turn into mobs."

Chronos' ear twitched at the word 'warriors', but he assumed it was a slip of the tongue.

"You seem awfully confident," Chronos' eyes settled at last on his Krogg counterpart, and Krag nodded.

"We are ready for this circumstance. We will welcome General Wiskar and his troops as soon as you're ready to send them down."

Chronos tried to decide whether he was starting to get a bad feeling from Kragran or whether he was still just too stunned to think after what had happened to Freetown. It was probably the latter.

"Alright. Well, I'll call Garnet and get him down to you soon. Meantime, I've got to go have a look at our defensive disposition..."

Krag stood, "I won't keep you."

"Thanks."

The Peacelord left, and Chronos leaned back and huffed a deep sigh.

•••

The Krogg shuttle left *Formidable's* bay with Kragran aboard. He wasn't pleased he'd let slip that the Kroggs had warriors ready — it was foolish to reveal any hint of those troops' existence when the Earthers might still be in a position to restrain their use. He'd become over-eager, which was unfortunate. He'd have to redouble his efforts to hide his excitement at the impending rise of Krogg power.

Of course he had *not* revealed the full size of the new Krogg Army. That was something, at least. Three million, what a quaint number that would have been… and how unimpressive for a planet of Krogg 'A's size.

No, the Earthers would discover the full force once circumstance gave the Kroggs their chance. In the meantime, the new fleet and the Hyper Motherships needed to be moved away from the approaches to Gibraltar, so that arriving Earthers would not stumble upon them.

That would be his next priority.

In a short while the Earthers would see the full might of the Krogg people. And things would change forever.

CHAPTER 34

Christine Schaeffer shook her head and sat up in bed, her body tingling and her mind twirling. Her Earther-style calm was keeping her thoughts in check when it came to questions of where she was, why she was here, and so on... but her human side was still fretting over their diminishing significance. That said, the worries were becoming less and less pervasive... perhaps that meant she was becoming less human.

Releasing a sigh at that strange and grim possibility, Christine swung her legs over the side of her bed and got carefully to her feet. She wasn't wearing any clothing, which would have seemed racy or ridiculous to her before the regen. In this case, her nudity was neither — her cabin had been modified to include stasis field generators and airborne surface anesthetics which could dull the signals her skin was receiving, but only if she kept herself uncovered.

She couldn't even use bed sheets. The bed itself had a stasis generator in it so that her back wouldn't explode with pain when she lay down.

So she had a choice: she was either trapped in her skin suit, with its built-in field, or wore nothing at all. Months earlier, that prospect would have caused her no end of consternation — she knew some of her old friends had been very liberal about their bodies, but she never had been.

Now she genuinely didn't care... yet another sign that her old self was fading away.

I doubt Earthers have body issues or hang-ups... and now I don't either.

With that thought crossing her mind, she walked towards the washroom that the Earthers had installed for her, grabbing a stasis patch off her dresser as she went. She couldn't come into contact with cool water without wearing one of those patches to moderate the impact, so she applied it to the back of her neck and set it to mid-strength.

Arriving at her wash basin, she activated the faucet and splashed water on her face. Once upon a time, she had loved the feeling of cold water... now she couldn't feel it much at all. The pleasant reassurance was gone.

Well, at least this thing didn't go down my throat. If I couldn't taste *it I'd be so much worse off.*

The fact that her skin had been affected by the regen mishap was, in its own way, a blessing. Had the nerves in her mouth, for instance, become as sensitive, it would have been intolerable.

She had to count what blessings she had...

Which, she realized as she straightened up and stared at her face in the mirror, was another Earther trait. She couldn't *touch* anything or anyone... or more precisely, she couldn't really feel it if she did. That sort of sensory depravation was torture, but she was still looking on the bright side.

"Gods help me, who am I?" she muttered to herself.

Thankfully, she didn't get the chance to consider the answer to that question... or to have to admit to herself yet again that she really didn't have an answer. The comm chirped instead and Narosh's voice filled her cabin: "Christine, sorry to wake you but we've just arrived at the derelict fleet."

"Very good. I'll be up shortly," her reply was even, but she didn't stop staring into her own eyes as she gave it.

The comm closed, and she took a deep breath. Whoever she was, she had work to do. And that meant she had to go through the minor ordeal of donning her skin suit, and then the rest of her clothes for the day.

Her life right now was genuine hell. And she simply dealt with it.

Graham stood on the bridge of *Carnarvon* with his hands linked behind his back, his impassive stare locked onto the silver wall ahead, and his mind filling with images the Larosian bridge crew were kindly sending to him. He could count the thousands of derelict, Omega-riddled ships floating all around.

So many vessels, all victims of Type 1 Omega — a disease that could easily be neutralized. Surely, if the Larosians could bring all these ships back online, Omega could be beaten, no matter what forces he'd built up...

Chances are we won't be able to bring most of them online any time soon, if ever, Graham. And we only have crews with us for about fifty of them right now, anyway.

Graham nodded evenly towards Narosh, not fazed at all by the Larosian's telepathic answer to his mental assumption, "That's unfortunate. But given time your Empire will be able to put a mighty fleet to space again."

"Perhaps. But we've lost a lot. It'll take decades to rebuild the infrastructure that Omega robbed us of. Supporting a fleet of this size took us about sixty fully industrial worlds... though perhaps the Earthers can help our efficiency. Time will tell," switching to spoken words, Narosh came to stand alongside Graham. "Anyway, no sign of Omega yet. We may have beaten him here."

"Let's hope you're right about that," Christine emerged on the bridge just in time to reply to the remark. "We getting set to play possum?"

Graham turned and nodded to his aide, "Indeed. Thirty-six Warcruisers and six Battleships... we should get lost in here rather effectively."

The emotionless words of her boss rarely affected Christine. Her eyes settled on him as he looked back to the silver wall at the front of the bridge, and she felt for him for just a moment. Then she redirected her mind and looked at Narosh.

"So, no idea of when Omega might get here?"

The Admiral-of-a-Fleet shook his head, "None. As far as we know he may not even be coming..."

"He's coming," Graham's words were cool. "Count on that."

"We have him now..." Captain Mel Ramsay smiled through the plot at Rear Admiral Minnie Maximane, and the lioness nodded in reply to the fox's comment.

Omega's ships weren't moving as fast as Maximane's squadron, and they were headed just where Minnie expected them to head: they were going after the derelict infected ships of the old Larosian Fleet. But his plan wouldn't work.

The remnant of the Omega force that had devastated the New Halifax Squadron was on *Galahad's* scopes, meaning it was just a matter of time before battle was joined. Minnie could choose the moment to spring her twenty ships on the plague...

"So how do you want to do this? If we move to overtake in open space, he'll see us coming as we creep up behind him," Mel rounded the holo plot to stand next to her Admiral, and Minnie nodded.

"Yes, that wouldn't work so well... let's hang back. We know he's headed for the infected Larosian ships... once he stops we'll pounce on him. The full treatment. We'll start assigning specific ship targets now, so that when we get there we put at least two ships on each of his. We should be able to take him out with surprise on our side," Minnie's words were even as her eyes narrowed at the plot.

"Sounds good..." Mel's gaze shifted to the distance scale in the corner of the glowing star chart before her, "We've got about eleven hours until we get there. Time for you to get a bit of sleep, I think."

Minnie smiled, "Yeah, right."

Galahad thundered on through space.

Omega watched the Earther ships chasing him with some amusement. They had barely better than two-to-one odds... they were probably planning to jump him as soon as his old Genesis garbage ships dropped out of flux.

That was fine, let them think they had it under control. He'd infect Larosian ships and have them crushing the Earthers in no time.

It'd be poetic.

Bloody and poetic.

Omega *loved* that combination.

CHAPTER 35

Lieutenant Garth Badger, Lieutenant Ellen Arbear, and Captain Joyce Furgus each took their seats in one of *Carnarvon*'s briefing rooms as Graham paced before them. Already at the table, Narosh, Novash, and Tovarrin had all been telepathically conversing — and including Christine in their exchanges — but now they nodded in turn to the Earthers.

Badger, the commanding officer of the three squadrons of gunboats assigned to *Carnarvon*, and Joyce and Ellen, the senior marine officers from the detachment of $2/54^{th}$ that had been put aboard the Battleship, were the last of the personnel needed to begin the briefing, so with no care for niceties, Graham began speaking.

"Omega's been detected, eight hours out and closing quickly. He's heading directly for this fleet, so we're going to get ready for him."

There were nods from everyone in the room — Narosh, Novash and Tovarrin were all quite experienced with Earther-human mannerisms, so they were able to smoothly offer the gestures too.

"Our plan calls for us to lie in wait. We let Omega close to infect the fleet, then assault him when his guard is down. However, knowing that he likes to ram, I'm not comfortable with leaving our ships unpowered and in close proximity until the last moment."

Narosh and Novash's eyes narrowed almost simultaneously, the latter, junior officer leaning forward slightly, "You're concerned that he'll detect life signs and start hitting us before we're ready to respond?"

The veteran Larosian's words were right on the mark, and Graham nodded, "Precisely. We don't have sufficient forces to absorb those sorts of losses, particularly if he succeeds in infecting ships while we're scrambling to form up for an attack."

Christine frowned then — Graham hadn't given her so much as a clue as to what he was going to say in this meeting, he'd just made it clear (in his impassive way) that he wanted her present. Now she frowned thoughtfully and stared at the silver table before looking up again.

"You're going to try putting something out in front of him?"

Graham's eyes shifted to his young colleague and he nodded once, "My plan precisely."

Tabbing the key on an Earther mobile holo projector that he'd brought with him from *Renown*, Graham called up a map of the entire infected fleet's disposition. The ships hung together mostly in a cloud, but a few were scattered out beyond the perimeter of the main body of the infected force.

And as Graham tabbed another key on the projector, one of the silver icons started flashing, "I want us to take this one, and push it into position so that it's the first he sees. And the first he attempts to take over."

Narosh, Novash and Tovarrin had all pulled the plan out of Graham's mind the minute he'd walked into the room, but they looked somewhat surprised for the sake of politeness. Christine's mouth opened to speak, but nothing came out, so she simply sat in somewhat surprised silence.

Joyce, Ellen, and Garth raised their eyebrows, the Captain of marines speaking first, "So that's where we come in?"

Graham nodded, not skipping a beat, "Indeed Joyce. Your marines with some of Tovarrin's Stealth Guardsmen can lie in wait aboard this ship. Let Omega board it, then you can delay him as he tries to take it over. Garth, your boats can wait in its bay and launch as soon as the rest of the fleet reveals itself, thus keeping him occupied while we close range."

Christine finally found her voice, and everyone's eyes turned to her, "But he'll detect Earther life signs aboard the ship. He'll know they're there — destroy them from space..."

Graham's expression didn't change, "I'd suspect he'd sooner relish the chance to kill Earthers in person than destroy the ship."

Christine's mouth hung open, "You *suspect*... but that's risking every Earther on this mission for suspicion's sake..."

Her words halted as she realized what she was saying. According to everything she'd learned in her days at the Academy, she was certainly *not* supposed to question her superior's plan in public — it was bad for chain of command. But this sounded quite mad — why take such a risk?

Because Omega would never expect us to be so foolish. It seems that logic is a tactical tool that's past its prime, Narosh inserted the thought in her mind.

Well, there's still logic here, but indeed, this sort of baiting ploy is the last thing Omega would expect from an Earther operation, Novash put in.

They had that right. The newly-minted Earther side of her psyche got a very bad feeling about it. But again, it wasn't her place to bring up such concerns in so forthright a manner. Her eyes shifted back to Graham, nervous to see if there was any sign of anger at her little outburst.

But his eyes hadn't changed in the slightest, so she looked away, trying to decide whether that was a good or bad thing.

"So... we lie in wait, hope like hell they don't see us, and then hit him hard as soon as he boards the ship?" Joyce leaned forward now.

Graham nodded, "And as soon as his ships begin to pay attention to your presence, we'll use the distraction to power up and attack. At that moment,

Garth will launch his boats and strike with surprise. Hopefully Omega won't realize what hit him."

Lieutenant Badger nodded in response to that, "Indeed, it'll be confusing for him. And we know a similar tactic worked when we recovered *Carnarvon*... this time we'll just have a lot more firepower available to deal with his squadron."

Graham nodded again, his eyes sweeping over the assembled officers.

"Very well, then. Garth, Joyce, if you could inform me once you've arranged your forces with Tovarrin, we'll move into position to put you aboard the ship. Narosh, Novash, you're scattering the squadron appropriately?"

The Admiral-of-a-Fleet and the Admiral-of-a-Division each nodded in turn, silently thinking amusing things to each other about taking 'orders' from a human half their age. They accepted his leadership for now — so long as they thought his orders were conducive to victory. So far, they were.

"Good. Then we're finished here. Thank you."

The assembled officers stood and began to leave in ones and twos, Tovarrin catching up to the Earthers while Narosh and Novash left together, communicating silently about deployment.

Christine stood slowly and scratched the skin around the stasis patch under the ponytail on the back of her neck.

"I'm sorry, I shouldn't have let that slip..." her words were a bit more regretful than she'd meant them to be. Then, accidentally enough, she scratched a little too hard.

Inhaling sharply she bent at the middle and gritted her teeth, grunting as one of her hands slammed the table with an open palm to try to hold her up.

Graham was instantly beside her with his hand on her back, "You alright?"

She could have sworn she heard concern in his voice. Wishful thinking, obviously, but she straightened slowly and pulled her hand away from the back of her neck, "I'm okay. It's the skin right around the patch that gets the worst... was being stupid..."

"Hardly," Graham shook his head and took his hand away. "Never, in fact. You're right that I'm fighting on suspicions here... I simply trust that they're correct suspicions."

Christine closed her eyes and took a centering breath as the hot, stabbing pain began to fade.

"I shouldn't have said anything, though," she said as she opened her eyes. "You want me to go liaise between Tovarrin and Joyce on the ship?"

Graham shook his head with a slight smile, "Not a chance, you've had it rough enough. I'll see you later."

Christine let out a sigh and nodded to him as he passed behind her and left the room, then closed her eyes and slowly sat down in her chair again. Something about that conversation seemed strange, but she couldn't put her finger on what it had been.

Had Graham done something different? She couldn't tell, she was too muddled. So with a deep breath she slowly levered herself back out of the chair and decided to go to her cabin for a bit more sleep.

She'd need to be in fighting trim when Omega arrived... because there'd be plenty of fighting then.

She left the briefing room.

CHAPTER 36

"So the million dollar question, Fox, is why we're stopped right now."

Fox Magnus frowned at Karl Kandam's words, running back over the library of human expressions in his mind until he remembered what a 'million dollar question' was supposed to be. Right.

"I expect it is. We're forty hours ahead of Omega by all reckoning, right?" Fox leaned back in his chair in *Chimera's* briefing room, and Karl and Garvin Jardaw exchanged glances and nodded.

"Good. I was thinking it might be a good idea to give Chronos more time to get things set up at Krogg 'A' before Omega arrives. I mean, at this rate, the last *Gibraltar* stations are only going to be getting to the system forty hours ahead of the plague, and I don't know that that'd be time enough to get them ready to fight."

Kandam shook his head, "We'd need at least forty-eight. That's as fine as you can cut it these days."

Fox nodded, "Exactly. So we've got four squadrons of *Chimeras* to buy at least that much time."

Garvin and Karl frowned simultaneously, the polar bear speaking up first, "Not that I disagree with the sentiment, Fox, but how precisely do you plan to buy that time without getting us all killed?"

Fox's eyebrows bounced up and down and he shifted in his chair a bit uncomfortably, "Excellent question. I was grappling with it myself there for a while, and then my wife threw this at me. Hit me in the nose with it actually."

Fox patted his copy of Garnan's history, and Jardaw's frown deepened, "Alright, there's a couple of centuries of history in that book, so let's get to it then..."

With a smile, Fox nodded, "Ever hear of the Battle of Leyte Gulf? Second World War, a bunch of Escort Carriers from the United States Navy held off a huge Japanese Battle Fleet by fighting with as much gumption as if they were a Battle Fleet themselves. They confused the Japanese into thinking they were tougher than they really were, and thus bought enough time for the American Admiral with the real Battle Fleet to get into position... or scared the Japanese off themselves. Didn't read it *that* closely... but either way, it struck a cord with me, given our current situation."

Garvin's frown didn't go away, and instead he cast a slightly disbelieving glance across the table at Karl before looking back, "You want us to fight with thirty-two ships as though there's a whole fleet behind us?"

Fox half-shrugged and then nodded, "More or less. We have to make him think we've got something up our sleeve… to give Chronos time to actually find something and stuff it up our sleeve."

Garvin shook his head somewhat disbelievingly and sat back in his chair, "Alright. I suppose so. But he knew our entire pre-war disposition, how're we going to surprise him?"

Fox shrugged, "He doesn't know how many packed ships I brought out with me, for one."

That wasn't a terribly convincing advantage — 128 Krogg War vintage ships weren't going to terrify Omega and his hybrid horde... but then, Fox's point was that Omega didn't know it was only 128 ships.

Fox wanted to bluff that there were more. Many many more. Enough to slow him down, or stop him. That'd be a tough sell, but at least it was something to try to sell. Better than just running.

"Alright, so you think we puff up out here, act like we're just a skirmishing force testing his mettle, not the main body?" Karl took over on the questioning, and Fox nodded.

"So that he gets a bit more cautious, hopefully slows down. We want him to wonder how many of us are out here. Then when he shows up at Krogg we have a lot more ships than he thought we could have… might make him nervous and give us the edge."

Fox's words trailed off and the two bears in the room sat back in their chairs thoughtfully.

"But he'll still have a four-to-one advantage over us when he gets there, won't he?" Garvin's quiet question cut the silence, and Fox shrugged and nodded.

"Nothing we can do about that. If we get too ambitious trying to hurt him out here we'll lose a lot of ships, and I think we need to get this force to Krogg 'A' intact. When we get there we'll need every ship we've got… so for now we focus on slowing him down without losing our ships."

"And after we slow him down, we try to outrun him to Krogg?" Karl asked.

With a nod, Fox tapped his fingers on the table, "Indeed. Hopefully he'll go slower so we can get there ahead of him. And I've talked to engineering… remember Zed Dune's experiment with large-ship energy-hyper last war? Well… well we might have a desperate measure in our pocket if he gets ahead of us."

Both Garvin's eyes and Karl's widened slightly at that last point. Energy-hyper was not something anyone in a ship of the line generally wanted to mess with…

But then, Omega was not something anyone *anywhere* wanted to get caught behind.

"So. We'll need all the luck we can find," Garvin said quietly. "Been a bit of a rarer commodity these days."

There was nothing Fox could say to that: the polar bear was entirely correct. Instead, the dapper First Space Lord looked at his fellow Admirals, "Alright, we've got a plan."

A plan, at last.

Chronos Claw sat in his chair on *Formidable's* bridge and watched the red planet Krogg 'A' slowly turn in the bridge battle plot. Alongside the world were a half dozen orbiting Earther stations and the squadrons of his blockade force... other than that there was just the emptiness of space.

Forty years ago he'd seen this system alive with almost 20,000 warships. If only he had that many to call on today... if only the Earther Navy had somehow seen this coming and stayed up to pre-Quest strength...

But Omega had struck at just the right time — for him.

"Sir, we have signatures of ships coming in from Gibraltar. I'm getting transponders for the first wave of reinforcements: haulers with packed ships for recommission in our yards, and some transports."

Chronos blinked twice, having known those haulers were due in this afternoon, but not having paid enough attention to their expected arrival time.

"Have their commanding officer report to me when they get in-system. And let the yards know that they're about to get very busy."

His words were even but subdued. He was still seeing the images of Freetown's fall in his mind. If Freetown could fall to such a cheap ploy, what chance was there for Krogg 'A', with overwhelming odds and such a desirable objective in those biomatter pools...

Chronos stopped that line of thinking. They'd stop Omega somehow. They had to.

And the Kroggs? Well, Kragran had them under control, and if there was one Krogg who Chronos could trust, it was Kragran.

You must prepare the fleet for action within the week, my fellows, Kragran's thoughts were transmitted to all assembled in the great chamber of the Governing Palace, and the 100 Warlords — indeed, *Warlords* — and the more than 2,000 Telepaths assembled before him acknowledged the orders with a single word.

Indeed.

Peacelord Kragran smiled; Earther mannerisms and diction had, to a certain extent, come to impact the way the Kroggs communicated with each other now. Kragran did appreciate the niceties; in fact, from what he'd read of Omega, the plague made use of them himself. Of course, Omega was a perverse being, and would soon feel the sting of the Kroggs.

But not before the Earthers were shown that sidelining the Krogg people was not their wisest choice.

Chronos Claw would never see this coming, and that made Kragran quite happy.

Now, my good Warlords and Telepaths, go to your ships!

Chronos was standing beside *Formidable's* massive plot — watching the arrival of the first part of the Gibraltar convoy with some relief — when a black icon flashed onto the holo projection... and then vanished.

He'd seen it out of the corner of his eye, but now his gaze swept back to the planet of Krogg 'A', and it was gone.

Had he seen something? His instincts had been telling him there was something strange about Krag earlier. Could something sinister be going on?

"Sensors, give me a quick sweep of the planet. Could have sworn I saw something there," he turned and looked at the Sensor Lieutenant. She frowned, scanned the planet again and shook her head.

"Nothing sir... logs show a blip on the screen, but looks like it was just a glitch... or maybe a high-atmosphere transport. Not seeing anything anywhere near open space."

Chronos took a deep breath and nodded. He was seeing shadows everywhere. He had to get his head out of this space and just *trust* his allies again.

Yes, he'd focus on trust.

And Kragran was counting on that.

CHAPTER 37

Unity Genesis sat with what remained of the Genesis Fleet over Freetown, and aboard this ship Pat Conroy was being gripped by sadness.

"There's no record of her anywhere, Ed," the Irishman said quietly.

He was sitting in the cabin he shared with Sarah, and was on the comm with Ed Jeffries, now seemingly the leader of the Freetown people.

What remained of them.

The Commodore's expression tightened, making his evident exhaustion seem even more acute, "She didn't get out?"

Pat shook his head, "You're in charge now."

Ed's chin dipped and he let out a sigh, "Can... well. I..."

Nothing coherent came from the new leader of Freetown, and Pat understood precisely what he was feeling. He'd lost a world, with so much of its population sacrificed, and he'd lost his leader.

Audrey DeBrooke was nowhere to be found.

"Take some time with it, Ed," Pat said quietly. "Get yourself together. Your people are going to need you now."

"Yeah. I'll... get on that."

The link cut abruptly, and Pat sagged visibly and leaned back. His head and neck ached, either from some muscle strain that had come with his evacuation from Freetown, or from fatigue, or from stress... or from all of it.

At least that was all the physical discomfort he was feeling so far. But every time he closed his eyes, he saw his old comrade Tom Katt getting murdered, or Barty Stowt being pulled to his death... so far he was managing not to be overwhelmed by those images running through his mind.

So bloody far.

Well, if he could survive the annihilation of his planet, a few dead Earthers surely couldn't be more shocking...

But it was. Because *Earthers* were supposed to be immune to those sorts of defeats. They were supposed to be able to see the threat coming, and even if they died fighting it, they were supposed to win.

Many times Pat had heard Earthers explaining to humans that much of their success in the last war had been due to luck. Graham had spoken once of good old Savanna Felix, and a conversation that Pat had recorded in his *Renegade Equation* history book. As the junior Manchester recalled it, the great cat had said: "We're good fighters, Graham, and we know it. But we're riding a tide of luck, and we know that too. When the luck runs out, we'll keep fighting. We'll keep our word."

That was precisely what they'd done back then. On Krogg 'A', General Andros Grieve had said it best: Earthers do what they say they'll do, in a way that reflects them.

They hadn't killed the Kroggs wholesale, they'd fought and died to give the Kroggs a new chance at life. The Earthers were so good at fighting and had such strong moral fiber that they'd been able to save a species from annihilation — to give the carapaced aliens a new chance that, by all accounts, they were making the most of.

Even when they died, the Earthers died for *something*.

But no one had died for any good reason on Freetown — or at least that's how it felt to Pat. Precious few lives had been saved, and though this sort of thinking wasn't usually in his nature, Pat couldn't help but wonder if the fight against Omega would have been better served if the Light Division had saved itself, and let the people of Freetown die.

If the war against Omega would have been better served if Barty Stowt had just left him down there to die.

Because, Pat was realizing with a cold and irresistible bleakness, there was nothing the survivors of Freetown could do to help protect Earth. And there was nothing he could do to help, that Earthers like Barty Stowt and Tom Katt couldn't have done better.

He should have died. It wasn't just guilt, it was good sense.

But the Earthers were still fighting with that same old philosophy. They still did what they promised they'd do, and they still did it in a way that reflected their impossible goodness. While Omega was set on destroying them, they were determined to protect human lives, and even Krogg ones.

Pat could only hope that their willingness to trust and help didn't come back to haunt them.

They should have let us die. They should have killed all the Kroggs. All their good deeds are going to get them punished.

With that terrible thought, Pat got to his feet and went in search of a drink.

The Omega ship that the Earthers had thought they'd shot down over Freetown's oceans had not been destroyed. Specially augmented sections within its hull remained intact, and now, in one of these compartments, Omega-Gillian waited eagerly for her guest to arrive. While Omega's minions in the Larosian galaxy were dealing with their annoying Earther trackers, Omega-Gillian was going to have some fun.

Multi-tasking was just *great*.

Making sure all the cameras were operational, Omega-Gillian summoned her minions to bring in her toy for the day.

Audrey DeBrooke seemed resigned as the hissing minions deposited her on a couch in the cabin. The room was moderately lit and seemed comfortable — it appeared that it had once been a passenger cabin on a luxury liner. Though the floor wasn't quite level (it was a 'crashed' ship, after all) it was inviting and warm.

Audrey knew it was going to be the last place she ever saw. And she was relieved.

James had died, and then her people had been victimized by Omega... and as much as she knew she was supposed to struggle to survive, to lead what remained of the Freetown colony in its exile... she didn't want to. She was too weak. She wanted to be done with all this.

You sure have that right. You've always been weak...

Omega-Gillian penetrated Audrey's mind as she sat down next to the former-Governor. The avatar followed thoughts with words, "So weak."

As Omega-Gillian, still in the attire of a surfer girl, cuddled up next to Audrey, and wrapped her arms around the leader, all Audrey could do was shake her head, "I know."

Well, that wasn't a fun answer. Sometimes Omega did his work too well — he'd left Audrey so depressed by his successes that she'd already given up...

That didn't make for good vid, and Omega wanted something to show the Earthers.

Omega-Gillian caressed Audrey's cheek and leaned in close to her ear, whispering very softly as she probed deep into Audrey's mind, "Shaspa Charters. ArcMajor Sonya Fletcher... your first nemesis as a CO. And the woman who died because you were a bad CO who couldn't plan properly."

Audrey stiffened slightly, and Omega-Gillian smiled before nuzzling Audrey's neck in a farce of eroticism. Dredging up old demons — people who Audrey had killed and lost during the mutiny that ended the Quest for *Grendelsbane City* — gave her something else to feel horrible about.

Omega-Gillian massaged that bygone horror telepathically, and Audrey's battered mind slowly succumbed, tears beginning to flood from her.

"Good girl," Omega-Gillian purred. "No noble death for you."

Taking the last of the dignity from this supposed 'leader' would be a nice side-dish for the main course: taking those Larosian ships and crushing the Earthers in that distant galaxy.

Omega-Gillian would make it last for a while... but she'd start simple.

Putting her mouth on the soft skin exposed by Audrey's open collar, the avatar carefully bit down. Audrey wailed, and the first strip of skin started to come off.

More would follow, and Audrey DeBrooke would meet a death that no living being deserved — all on camera, so the Earthers could watch.

CHAPTER 38

Joyce Furgus was first into the airlock of the Larosian Battleship *Cuvarzon*, the dead ship that Graham had asked her and the marines of 2/54th to occupy. Her 150 marines — along with the thirty Stealth Guardsmen Tovarrin had committed to the operation — would have to secure this ship, and then make ready to receive an Omega invasion…

A Type 1 infected Larosian sprinted into the airlock just as Joyce got her footing, and before she could bring her rifle up to meet him, he slammed into her. Flung back into the bulkhead by the force of the impact, Joyce struggled to bring her rifle around with one hand and to shift herself off the deck with the other.

The Larosian lunged again, but this time he was caught in midair by the strong hands of Lieutenant Ellen Arbear. Daughter of *Orion's* current Flag Captain, Ellen was not a particularly small Earther, and she held the Larosian out in front of her as she walked into the Battleship corridors at a crouch.

The Larosian flailed, so Ellen pitched him down the deck, swung her rifle forward and opened fire, hitting him a few times before he went down. He probably wouldn't stay down for long, but that was fine…

"Sergeant, let's get the UDRC cylinder up here," Joyce picked herself up and waved the team of Earthers with the UDRC aerosol cylinder forward.

The marines came out of the lock at a run, having mapped their route to environmental control before they'd come aboard. Ten marines would head down to that chamber to tie the cylinder into the environmental systems while, from another lock, a team would head to engineering to activate the air exchangers.

This ship would be reclaimed, just as *Carnarvon* had been.

"Tovarrin to Furgus, come in please."

Joyce tapped her comm at the hail, "Joyce here. Your team headed to the engineering section?"

"We are just about to enter the section, there are no signs of uninfected crew at this stage."

Joyce nodded at the response, "Fair enough. I'm going to head down to the flight deck to get the doors open for Garth's boats. Meet you on the bridge in half an hour?"

There was a pause, then, "Certainly. See you there."

Stretching her sore neck gingerly, Joyce hefted her rifle and glanced at Ellen, "To the flight bay."

"Seems to be going smoothly," Narosh glanced at Graham, and the human nodded.

"Indeed."

They waited on *Carnarvon's* bridge, watching through the telepathic visuals that the crew poured into their minds. First the UDRC was detected entering *Cuvarzon's* environmental systems, then power came on to pump it through the ship. A few moments later the flight bay doors opened, and Garth Badger's two Pulsar and one Gun Squadrons began their landing approach to the ship's bay.

This all seemed a bit old hat now.

Old what?

Graham didn't even blink at the question piped into his thoughts by Narosh.

Old hat. As I understand it, it's an expression meaning 'not new'.

Ah. Interesting, Narosh offered the telepathic equivalent to a nod.

"Perhaps. ETA on the Omega force?"

Narosh paused and focused his mind on a different set of information as it was supplied to his consciousness, "Just over five hours."

Graham nodded.

Joyce emerged cautiously onto the bridge of the Larosian Battleship, checking her angles just in case an insane Larosian or two had been trapped on the deck. Instead of finding an infected alien, she found Tovarrin and two Guardsmen smiling at her.

"Seems to have gone to plan," the Captain-Elite said.

Stiffening slightly, Joyce glanced over her shoulder at Ellen Arbear, who grimaced.

Tovarrin was confused by the expressions, "Did I say something incorrect?"

Joyce let out an ironic chuckle worthy of her father and shook her head, "Nah, we're just raised not to say things like that out loud. Bad luck, they say."

Tovarrin tilted his head and glanced at his Guardsmen, "Really?"

Whatever telepathic chatter they exchanged was private, so Joyce didn't even bother to contemplate it.

They'd just taken the Battleship...

"So..." she paused and turned around to look in every direction, "How exactly do we want to set our trap?"

Tovarrin looked back to her and managed a shrug, "We're not experienced with ambushes."

Ellen Arbear shrugged back, "Neither are we. Maybe we should turn off all the lights and find a place to hide?"

Christine emerged onto *Carnarvon's* bridge with four hours remaining before the arrival of Omega's squadron. She'd decided to pull on her breastplate and wear her sword, just in case they proved useful, but as she came to stand alongside Graham she realized the Genesis ore in the armor was blocking the telepathic sensor images that would otherwise be fed to her mind.

Oh well, she preferred having the armor on. If Omega got aboard, she wouldn't mind the extra protection — both telepathically and physically.

Even without images to elaborate, the situation remained clear enough: Omega was still coming, and Novash and Narosh were spreading the ships of their squadron out amongst the infected vessels in their fleet.

They'd just have to wait for four hours, and then the show would start. Hopefully Omega wouldn't be ready for this... otherwise, Christine had a feeling she was going to do a lot of fighting.

"We'll overtake them just as they reach this outer ship right here."

Captain Mel Ramsay's finger stabbed into *Galahad's* battle plot, and Minnie Maximane nodded at the report. They'd catch Omega as he slowed down to deal with the battlewagon nearest his vector of approach, and then hopefully they'd finish his fleet in this galaxy.

After that, they'd figure out what to do next — go to Earth or go to Krogg 'A'...

"All ships beat to quarters in two hours, then. Make sure everyone's had a big lunch. We overtake in three hours."

Minnie's words drew nods from both Captain Ramsay and her Signal Officer, and the orders beamed out to the squadron.

Aboard one of the infected Genesis Destroyers out ahead of *Galahad*, one of Omega's avatars laughed. The rest of the crews of the infected squadron joined in.

On Freetown, Omega-Gillian stepped out of her cabin covered in blood, and laughed too.

This would be a joke. A great way to cap off an explosive, murderish day.

CHAPTER 39

Omega quickly jerked his eight ships out of flux drive, his minions handling the abrupt and painful deceleration with ease. The first Battleship of his newest fleet sat just before him, dead and crewed only by the mad Larosians who'd been infected by his older self.

Time for a reunion — at long last!

He'd always hoped that he'd be able to remain in control of his older self when he took on this new, Krogg-spliced version, but alas, some things were impossible, even for him. The older version simply wasn't compatible with the macro-consciousness he now enjoyed, so he'd abandoned its cells with plans to re-infect and reintegrate later.

Later meaning now. *Should have a welcome-home party!*

For the moment, though, he had work to attend to. He'd dock and infect, the way he always did...

He moved his smallest ship towards the Larosian battlewagon, then turned the other seven ships to face the chasing Earther squadron... ooh, so many old frigates to squish!

This'd be a nice bit of entertainment to fill the lull between Freetown and Krogg...

"Drop out of energy drive... *now*," Minnie Maximane's smooth orders were transmitted to the squadron, and the twenty Earther ships under her command returned to material state with their shields up and their guns running out.

They advanced towards Omega in two lines ahead, *Galahad* and *Hector* each leading one towards the enemy...

The enemy charged right at them.

"Missiles coming in, multiple vectors!"

Minnie nodded, "All ships, engage by division. Let's clean them up."

"Master, up angle twenty-four, ninety degrees starboard," Mel Ramsay was delivering her orders at the same time as Minnie, and *Galahad* followed the fox's commands into a fast turn that brought port guns to bear. "*Fire.*"

Shot lanced out at the first Omega ship as it dove towards the mighty ship of the line. A 74 following next in line replicated the maneuver, and as its broadside lashed out and it began to roll, the Omega ship crashed into it... and drove out the other side to fire a crippling salvo of missiles into a frigate before itself coming apart.

Minnie ground her jaw, and then watched two more 74s be destroyed by hails of missiles that had seemingly met them in mid-evasion. It was as though Omega knew just how the ships were trying to get out of the way, and was able to put missiles into the escape routes...

"Ships pull back and regroup, quickly!" she wasn't pleased to say the words, but this melee would get them all killed if they weren't careful. She had to pull back to win.

Her ships began to fall back; they'd killed two Omegas at the price of four of their own... no five, as another frigate went.

"Damn..."

"He's docking with the first Battleship," Mel pointed into the plot, and Minnie nodded. She needed to deal with this quickly, before the plague was able to augment his strength with these powerful derelicts.

"Ships reform and prepare to advance. Launch all boats."

"Did you say Earthers? Where the hell did *they* come from?"

Graham looked sideways at Christine's surprised question, "Does it really matter? Narosh, that'd be our cue, I suppose."

"Indeed," the Admiral-of-a-Fleet said evenly, then switched to telepathic communication: *All ships attack.*

Christine tapped her comm, "Garth, you've got fifteen Earther ships out there who need backup."

Minnie's thin line of gunboats formed up ahead of her fifteen remaining ships. She'd avoided deploying them at the beginning of the action because she didn't want them trapped if she'd been forced to withdraw... but who was she kidding, she couldn't withdraw now.

"We've got all boats up and accounted for... looks like about forty-five must have come off the decks of the ships we lost before they went down," Mel's finger moved in the plot again. "They're attacking the ship docked with that battlewagon."

Minnie nodded, "Good, all ships advance..."

Where the fuck did those extra boats come from?

Omega would have been wide-eyed if he'd only had one set of eyes to look through. As it was, he was in a minor state of shock. That Battleship had gunboats on it... what was going on...

He'd connected the locks of his smallest ship to that derelict, so now he sent through his minions — the seventy he had aboard his that vessel...

And...

How the Fuck?

• • •

Joyce Furgus was standing next to Tovarrin and Ellen Arbear when the hissing Omega minions rushed in.

"They've gotten nastier since *Genesis One*," Ellen observed coolly, and Joyce nodded in agreement. Omega clearly had been doing some more genetic manipulation on these warriors, making them even less human now than they'd been before.

But those changes wouldn't help the plague's cause. The marines of 2/54th had already faced these things once, and they now knew how to deal with the bastards.

"Let's push them back, everyone," Joyce's cool words rang out in the corridors, and the minions heard them... just before a roar deafened them. Marines and Stealth Guards with shining blades lunged from the dark.

"About thirty of the plague ships just came online and are closing... he must have found a way to get control of them..." Mel Ramsay glanced through the plot at her Admiral.

Minnie's mind raced as the new icons started moving in... the plague must have managed to get a ship out to these derelicts ahead of the squadron they'd been tracking. If those Larosian vessels were fully operational and enhanced by the plague, there wasn't much chance of her being able to stop them.

"Message coming in from one of the boats out there ma'am," the Signal Officer's interruption drew a glance from Minnie — what was a boat doing calling into the bridge at a time like this?

Must be important.

"In the plot," Minnie looked back into the holo tank as a boat officer appeared and nodded to her.

"Lieutenant Garth Badger, ma'am, of *Venerable* and more recently *Carnarvon*. Those ships coming out of the Larosian Fleet are of the friendly variety, under ArcGeneral Manchester and Admirals Narosh and Novash."

The words didn't actually process at first. Minnie had known Graham and the Larosians were out here, but she hadn't imagined that they'd be in just the right place, at just the right time, to help with this fight. That sort of Earther timing didn't work anymore.

"Excuse me?" was all Minnie could manage for an answer, but the report was instantly confirmed.

Novash appeared in the plot, his flagship *Lycrotar* being the only one in the Larosian group which still had working translators for energy comm, "Novash here, Admiral. You've chased Omega right into our trap, actually."

"Oh."

Minnie stared at Novash for a moment, and then looked through the plot at Mel Ramsay to discover that the Flag Captain was grinning with relief.

The lioness looked back down at the Larosian Admiral-of-a-Division, "Well, I suppose we have him right where we want him."

Novash smiled, "Damned correct we do."

Carnarvon was a mighty Battleship. As Graham stood on its bridge, Larosians piped visions into his mind that showed the tide of antimatter its guns sent forth, and the hail of missiles that followed. Narosh ordered the Battleships forward with elegant lethality, and Novash's Warcruisers danced as though they'd never spent a day away from action.

Graham almost smiled.

"Let's finish them off," Minnie Maximane addressed her Flag Captain, and Mel Ramsay grinned in reply.

"Don't have to tell me twice. Master, let's get guns to bear on their biggest ship!"

Omega had to admit that he was shocked by this one. He'd been caught in a trap by the Larosians and the Earthers… and he had no idea how they coordinated it.

Damn them…

He turned one of his larger ships towards the approaching Larosians and throttled it up to full speed, aiming to ram the first Battleship in line. A tide of antimatter forced him to veer away and switch targets to the third Battleship in formation. Coming from a high angle, his ram caught the lumbering vessel in the flanks, its bow crunching into the alloy of the Larosian hull and knocking both ships in opposite directions…

But the massive Battleship forced itself forward again, and the last two battlewagons in the Larosian line turned angrily and incinerated their attacker.

Simultaneously, the frigates of the Earther Navy came forward in a squadron line ahead, pouring fire at his most agile ships, while the Warcruisers dashed in from the other side. His smaller ships attacked both formations but were overwhelmed.

He tried to take control of the Larosian Battleship he'd boarded, but there were Earther marines and Larosian Stealth Guards aboard, and that damned Earther cure compound had been released into the atmosphere aboard the ship…

"Fuck."

Omega-Gillian was bathing away the gore of her time with Audrey, but she said that sharply — as did Omega-Natosh on Genesis, and Omega-Paine on Ecclesia.

So they'd got him. Once. That was fine. They wouldn't stop 1,200 black wave ships hitting Krogg, that was for damned sure. And he'd give the Earthers something else to think about soon.

Omega-Gillian ordered her minions on Freetown to start preparing a message for the Earthers, and to dump the remains of the planet's former Governor into the sea.

The plague could take solace after its little defeat: the Earthers would soon be horrified again. And once the Kroggs were in his arsenal, he'd wipe out the Larosians wholesale, and torture the Earthers before he finished them off. Fuckers.

The last Omega ship broke away from the Larosian Battleship it had been trying to capture, then attempted a run into flux.

Carnarvon clipped it first with a salvo of antimatter, then *Galahad* and *Hector* were in front of it, smashing it to pieces with broadsides. Its hull bubbled and then exploded, and the action was done.

Minnie Maximane let out a long, relieved breath as the ship came apart. Smiling at Mel Ramsay, she tapped her hands twice against the side of the battle plot, "Alright, let's assess damage, get the boats searching for survivors, and get me contact with Narosh... or Novash... or whoever's commanding those Larosian ships."

They'd won a decisive — if small — victory over Omega.

About time too.

CHAPTER 40

Lieutenant General Garnet Wiskar had been a part of the attack on Krogg 'A' at the end of the Krogg War, landing with the second battalion of the Second Guards and fighting that day from the firing line alongside his fine marines and gallant officers like Beckett Lupus.

Today marked the first time in years that he was back on the planet; he'd spent many years in orbit, but he hadn't landed on its surface for ages because Peacelord Kragran had clearly kept up the demilitarization that had been promised under the treaty that had ended the war.

Now Wiskar almost wished the Kroggs hadn't finished their warring ways.

Having fought them viciously through the last war, Wiskar could testify to their incredible military prowess. Too bad it had been left behind...

But alas, Garnet couldn't afford to think that way. Had the Earthers not demanded total demilitarization of mobile forces, the Kroggs might be menacing right alongside Omega now. They had needed time to learn new ways of interacting with the universe, and Setter's decision to have them lay down arms had been the right one. 'What ifs' were full of blind alleys, and Wiskar wasn't going to allow himself to be tempted by them.

Instead, he was busily walking the soon-to-be perimeter around the pools — which to Wiskar looked more like lakes, or even small seas — of Krogg biomatter that dominated the local red-soiled valley. Like tar-pits, these reservoirs were black and viscous, but they were far, far more lively than the oily formations found on Earth.

Raw biomatter had been a valuable tool for the Queen, who only fertilized and hatched some of her offspring — the most advanced, like Warlords and Telepaths. These pools could be used for great broods, churning out thousands of simpler Kroggs, like soldiers, at a time. At least, that's how it *had* been.

With the end of the Queen, all Kroggs were being bred in these pools, products of science and a mating process between Peacelords and a new caste of females. The process was still being perfected, but the Kroggs were making something where there once had been nothing. They didn't need their ambitious Queen anymore.

It was genuinely remarkable — Wiskar was greatly impressed by the Kroggs' ability to reengineer their means of reproduction in so short a time. But all that said, the vulnerability of these massive biomatter spawning pools was a massive problem for the Earthers, now that Omega was coming.

The Fourth Division, Garnet Wiskar's 10,000-marine force, had the task of protecting the biomatter. The problem was that these pools were huge and covered an area larger than the Freetown capital city.

And Wiskar, and every Earther in Krogg space, knew exactly what had happened when Colin Brawn's elite Light Division had tried to hold Freetown's perimeter. Wiskar had served alongside Brawn in the old days... for such a fate to have befallen the great Earther...

Again, Wiskar forced himself to stop thinking that way.

At least here the marines could trust that none of the people they were trying to protect would turn on them like a rabid mob. Garnet Wiskar may not have spent much time on Krogg 'A' itself, but he'd met with enough freed Kroggs since the end of the war to know that they weren't his enemy. Their modest, quasi-military security force was probably going to end up being his combat reserve...

"Good morning, General Wisssskar."

Slowing his stride for a moment, Wiskar looked back over his shoulder and nodded at the arrival of Peacelord Kragran and another Krogg. Though the Kroggs had lost much of their hiss over the years, Wiskar's name often caught them drifting back to their old brogue.

No matter — Garnet hardly minded the pronunciation, "Good day to you, Peacelord. Come to see the perimeter?"

The Peacelord nodded, then stood aside to indicate his companion, "Indeed, and to introduce you to Peacelord Kragthar of the security forces. He will be my liaison to your division."

Wiskar cocked an eyebrow, "Liaison? Will you be needing one of those, sir?"

Kragran tilted his head, "One can never be too prepared. Kragthar here is an excellent warrior, a veteran of the last war. He shall be able to anticipate any needs you might have and make sure our security forces meet them instantly."

A frown slowly formed on Wiskar's face and he turned completely around, linking his hands behind his back, "We'll appreciate having your security forces in position as our reserve, Peacelord, but as I understand it, things have changed since the war. I don't want you to put your security forces in if they're aren't... *ready*."

Kragran smiled, "Thank you for your concern, General. And you are right, we cannot mistake our current security forces for the army that fought the last war. Peacelord Kragthar will be most aware of the limitations of his current command."

Wiskar's ear twitched thoughtfully. This was very strange — his instincts were tingling, feeling that there was more to Kragran's words than he could recognize. The new security forces were not an army proper — their soldiers were smaller, less experienced, and far less numerous than the Krogg forces that had fought with such lethality in the last war. Wiskar had no interest in seeing them rush into battle, only to be shredded... the way the Queen's Guard had once shredded the human regiments that landed on this world.

But Wiskar's instincts sensed that neither of these Kroggs was worried about such a fate. Were they overconfident because of the past prowess of their soldiers... or did they know something he didn't?

A couple of marine engineers ran past the three commanders as Wiskar considered Kragran's words for a few more seconds. The first of the shield perimeter lines was going up as he stood there, and he realized that he had to get back to work. This instinctive worry was probably nothing — he wasn't getting a bad feeling from the Kroggs overall. So he buried his unsettled feeling.

"Well... any help is greatly appreciated. Let me know how many of your security force will be available, Peacelord Kragthar, and I'll be most honored to have their help when battle is joined. Now I'm terribly sorry, but I must return to my duties. Might I speak to you both later today, perhaps?"

Kragran's smile remained, "But of course. Good day!"

Wiskar clicked his boot heels together and saluted sharply in the same instant. Then he turned and continued on his walk.

Note the courtesy of General Wiskar — he is an exemplar of old-Earth charm, Kragran thought to his companion. *He has a great reputation for being reserved and thoughtful when under stress.*

Warlord Kragthar narrowed his eye and watched as the cat left them at great speed, giving the telepathic equivalent of a nod. *Did I not know better, m'lord, I'd say he was weak and vulnerable. But the Earthers do deceive well with their appearance; their courtesy is not a sign of weakness, but of power. They are so strong they can afford to be kind to all persons. Wiskar will not be easy to deceive.*

Kragran nodded physically once in response to those thoughts, then he turned slightly and looked up at the angled blue energy barrier that was rising over them.

Even though Omega's minions climbed over shield walls at Freetown, they are seeking to create a shield dome here, to cover these pools from above and all around. This will fail... I think your best opportunity will thus come from underground. No one will expect it.

Kragthar looked curiously at his superior, *Will Omega not be able to use the same route — burrow his way to our pools from below?*

Perhaps, but the pools are actually of no concern, Kragran turned and pointed to the great lakes of viscous black. *Even now our engineers are manipulating the pools to make them invulnerable to Omega, but we cannot let the Earthers realize that such a thing is possible — they might leave us before we reveal ourselves. They might try to draw Omega away and be destroyed by him, out of our immediate reach.*

Ah, I see, so these pools are to be the bait, for Omega, and Omega compels the Earthers to remain with us, Kragthar nodded and turned back to the shield perimeter. *The Queen herself could not have fashioned a better plan, m'lord.*

Kragran exposed his fangs in a smile, "Indeed not. The Earthers have taught us well."

Warlord Kragthar matched the expression, "And now they will see how their teaching has borne fruit."

The two Kroggs hiss-laughed.

Chronos Claw's brow furrowed as he stared down at the planet of Krogg 'A'. Every time he looked at that world now, he felt as though there was something he wasn't seeing... as though something under the surface was growing and changing and getting ready to... to...

To what? Seriously, you can't let Omega get you this panicked.

Letting out a sigh, Chronos tried to force his mind to give up its search for conspiracies. Instead, he turned back to his desk and tapped up the holo map of the system. The situation wasn't promising; his squadron of *Champions* and frigates from the Krogg corridor had arrived in system six hours earlier, but that only gave him sixteen capital ships and twenty-four frigates. The 128 recommissions were being unpacked and hastily brought online, and Liz's force escorting the Gibraltar installations was only five days out...

But none of it seemed enough.

Slowly lowering himself into his chair, Claw rubbed his tired eyes with the palms of both hands.

Almost as if some force knew he wasn't looking at that second, the black icons of four Krogg vessels flashed into existence on the plot, only to vanish again almost instantly.

All was normal when his eyes returned to the projection, so Chronos Claw began to plan for the worst Naval engagement he could think of.

His definition of 'worst', though, was not so informed as he thought it was.

The Kroggs were making ready for war.

CHAPTER 41

Fox Magnus leaned back in his command chair aboard *Chimera*. The clock on the plot was counting down, and the sensors were painting an unpleasant picture.

He breathed in deeply, then slowly exhaled and looked at his wife, who was sitting in the chair next to him. Thena Magnus smiled, and that did make him feel better... though he was far from comfortable.

What he and his ships were about to do verged on the insane... and that fact, he hoped, would make Omega think twice about just what he was facing on his run towards Krogg 'A'.

"We're under two minutes... now," Thena's eyes were again fixed on the chrono, and Fox nodded, gripping the arms of his chair and using them to propel himself to his feet.

"Alright, send tightbeam to *Namur* and *Medusa*, get ready."

Theoretically speaking, the maneuver they were about to undertake was pretty much textbook... the galling part was that they'd be trying it against Omega. This did seem like suicide.

Times sure change when a terrifying plague of doom hits...

Oh wise words. Stop thinking now before you get Thena killed.

Blinking his mind out of its state of chaos with surprising success, Fox got to his feet and stepped forward to the plot, "Squadron stand by to translate to material state. Port broadsides at the ready."

Thena came out of her chair and stepped up alongside him, "Stand by to translate. Lieutenant, let's have the port gunners ready to fire as they bear... Master, be ready for the order to roll."

The repetition of orders was almost calming, and the bridge sprang quietly to action as *Chimera* got ready to hand Omega a piece of hell.

Omega was still smarting from that sucker punch the Larosians had thrown him. He had to give the pasty grey samurai-wannabes some props for that one — they'd shown a little acumen in getting into the fight.

That was fine though, he'd get the fuckers in the end. He'd own them... but they were secondary to the glorified fucking teddy bears. He owed the Earthers plenty for the centuries of captivity — the cattle running the farm and destroying all the goals Omega had been bred to work for... of course they were going to pay.

And the Kroggs were going to be his. Leaderless without a Queen, the giant black bugs weren't all that impressive or capable... but with him controlling them, there wouldn't be much that could stop him.

Of course, by 'not much', he meant there'd be nothing at all.

And I'll have tons of fun... hmm, a bunch of school girls in a room with a couple of Krogg Soldiers? I'll have to make sure I set aside enough pretty little ladies for that delight...

The first sixty ships in Omega's Krogg-bound assault fleet vanished.

They'd been in flux drive — *improved* flux drive, but still only flux drive...

Oh shit, the Earthers were coming out to meet him. Stupid sons of...

Omega refocused his mind and tried to count what his sensors saw. There were at least a hundred capital ships, based on the amount of shot they were throwing. They must have moved a bunch of reinforcements through the Larosian galaxy without him realizing.

Clever fucks.

"Alright, game on..."

Garvin Jardaw turned to his battle plot just as Karl Kandam glowed to life in it, "We got the drop on them."

Nodding, Garvin let his eyes dart back and forth between the image of his friend and the sensor sweeps. Just about sixty of Omega's vessels had been wrecked by the shot from the first two passes by the squadrons of *Chimeras* — they were using the old in-and-out of energy drive trick that had served many Admirals and Captains well during the last war.

Hopefully Omega thought there were twice as many Earther ships out here than there were.

The next broadsides crushed another fifty Omega ships.

Fox Magnus now glowed to life in the plot next to Kandam, "We're doing well, but I'm going to pull us back after the next pass. If he finds a way to blow us out of energy drive we're done, so let's let him go past us, follow for about four hours, then punch him again."

Kandam frowned, "We're not going to keep constant pressure?"

Shaking his head slowly, Fox let his eyes narrow, "I want him thinking we're falling back through lines of prepared ambushes, and I don't want him knowing when we're going to show up next. Better on edge than under siege, I think."

Both bears nodded at the comment, and just as they did the four squadrons of ships of the line they commanded slid from energy drive, spewed another broadside, then rolled and fired the other before disappearing.

And as they did that, Karl Kandam's image in the plot quivered and was washed out by static for a moment.

The panda looked away and then looked back with wide eyes, "He just hit us with something from hyperspace!"

The link cut.

Most of his ships had been traveling in flux, but Omega liked to lead out his assault fleet with a hyperspace scout buried deep in the layers of subspace. This time the Earthers had managed to slip right past that ship's sensors, but he could still use it to get his hands on some of them.

Collecting some telepathic energy in the minds of the avatars and minions aboard the ship, he set off a blast in hyperspace, destroying the scout vessel as a matter of course, and triggering a hyperspace shockwave that thundered through the spatial layers.

Three Earther ships were swept up in the resulting hyper wake.

Omega smiled. At least the cattle weren't going to get away clean.

A hundred of his ships had died, but the rest came immediately out of flux, and as they did their missiles began spewing.

"By the Earth — incoming sir, seven *thousand* missiles."

Karl Kandam got out of his chair and nodded slowly, "Order the others to escape if they can. Those who can't, tie in point defense networks and get ready on canister."

"Only three of us got knocked out, sir..." the Sensor Lieutenant was frowning at her console, and Kandam nodded evenly.

"Then send to Fox... everyone else to leave the area immediately. We'll keep him busy. Captain, let's launch boats..."

The Signal Officer interrupted the Rear Admiral, "First Space Lord Magnus for you, sir."

Fox reappeared in the plot, "Karl, get out of there."

Shaking his head, Kandam locked eyes with Fox, "Afraid the shockwave scrambled our drives. Looks like the same thing that happened to Lang at Genesis. We're cooked."

Fox's eyes narrowed, "I don't take that kind of talk lightly. All ships, stand by to exit energy drive and offer assistance."

"No. Fox... seriously, get out of here. We have contact with missiles in..." he looked away from the First Space Lord for a moment to check the time, "...nineteen seconds."

For a second Fox was silent — a long second. Then the First Space Lord nodded slowly, "You're right, we can't risk the fleet."

Then he disappeared as Karl opened his mouth to say something of a goodbye.

Seconds later, *Namur* jerked sideways.

•••

"We're cutting it close..." Thena gripped the sides of the plot tightly as the force of the grav tractors pulling *Namur* towards *Chimera* shook both great ships.

"Tow range?" Fox rounded the plot to stand next to Cruising Master Gunth, and the veteran ship-handler ignored his presence entirely.

"Five... four... Tak, get the drive ready... two... one... *hit it...*" the Master's gruff words had the helm officers on the edges of their seats.

And then *Chimera* shuddered and dragged itself and *Namur* into energy drive.

Two other ships of the line collected the other victims of the hyperspace wake, and now the six ships dragged themselves out of Omega's grasp, taking an oblique course away from the rest of the force. There was no way they could keep up with the rest of the fleet while towing the wounded vessels.

"Tightbeam Garvin to head straight on for Krogg 'A'. We can't risk losing our squadrons this way..." Fox turned back to the Signal Officer. "Now, we need to find ourselves an out-of-the-way spot to stop and get these ships back up to spec."

Evidently Earther timing hadn't left them entirely... but it hadn't allowed them to slow down Omega appreciably.

So much for Leyte Gulf...

CHAPTER 42

Chronos Claw didn't like the feeling he got when he stood on the surface of Krogg 'A'. He'd spent countless months orbiting the planet over the past decades, but time on the surface had usually been short and intermittent. This visit would be short again, too. Chronos wasn't inclined to linger. There was still much to do, and he felt uneasy.

That feeling, of course, wasn't fair to the Kroggs who'd worked long and hard to get past their old, darker days... but no time to think about that now. Garnet Wiskar had come up in front of him.

Meeting the General's eyes, the Admiral gave a brief nod in greeting, "How's it going, Garnet?"

The General took a deep breath and managed a shrug, "Line seems to have gone up just fine. We have a dome shield now that I think should be able to hold back Omega... even after what he showed us at Freetown."

Chronos frowned slightly, "How sure of that are you?"

Garnet's ear twitched, "We'll do everything we possibly can, Chronos. Count on it."

Chronos paused thoughtfully and looked up at the alien sky.

"Days like this make me homesick, too," Garnet offered helpfully, detecting his Admiral's wish for a nice blue sky and a familiar wind.

Chronos replied with a slim smile, "Yes. Yes... well, as comforts go, I'll settle for beating Omega. I've got the stations up there unpacking ships like mad. About thirty are done now, and there are many more to come. But you're still going to have to do something special down here, Garnet." Claw looked down at the General again, "It's going to be one hell of a fight."

"That it certainly will be. We don't have enough marines to line the entire circumference of the perimeter, we'll just have to spread out and keep the fire hot if it comes to it. I'll be keeping First Brigade in reserve at the center, in case Omega pushes more strongly at one side than any of the rest," Wiskar's clipped, professional words were somewhat reassuring to Chronos.

But his uneasiness remained.

The dark feeling really had gotten worse when he'd landed on the surface of the planet...

It's as though my instincts are telling me something's wrong...

But what could be wrong?

Or more precisely, given the circumstances, what could be so much *more* wrong that it set off his alarm bells? Something here was trying to warn him that he was being *deceived*... but *what?*

"Have the Kroggs been cooperating?" Chronos frowned and looked towards the biomatter lakes as he asked the question, and Wiskar's ear twitched.

"Indeed, they've been rather excellent hosts. Offered to help several times, and they've not seemed to take my polite refusals badly. I doubt that we'll have any trouble remotely like what Colin faced on Freetown. Their Telepaths will jam Omega, their people will cooperate..." Wiskar followed Chronos' gaze to the biomatter pools as he spoke, and both cats watched as two caretaker Kroggs walked between the black seas, bending now and then to take samples.

Well, at least the Kroggs are on our side.

Still...

Shaking his head slowly, Chronos glanced back at Wiskar, "Good. Alright, I've seen the defenses. I have to meet Kragran once more to make sure all the preparations for hiding their population are in place, and then I'm back on *Formidable*."

Wiskar nodded, "I'll know where to find you."

For some reason, Chronos found himself trying to tread lightly as he walked through the round, pulsating halls of the Krogg Government Spire. The structure was a hybrid of concepts; it was an administrative building that served the same role as an Earther Government House, but its shape and composition were modeled after a Queen's spire.

And it was alive and pulsing... which was just plain unsettling.

Chronos found mixed messages in the hybrid design — he wasn't sure if bridging the influences from either side — Earther and Queen — was good or bad. But one thing was certain, feeling the fleshy floor squish under his feet didn't ease his discomfort.

Like wandering around inside someone's arteries. Give me a cold metal deck any day...

Chronos' guide, one of the security-force Kroggs that guarded the spire, at last stopped at an aperture in the wall, then stood at attention beside the doorway.

"The Peacelord is expecting you, Admiral," the guard said in close to perfect English, and Chronos' ear twitched.

"Thanks," he managed a smile which he hoped was understood by the junior soldier, then stepped through the portal.

Kragran and two other Peacelords were sitting quietly in the room, presumably lost in telepathic discussion, and at first none of them seemed to notice Chronos' arrival. Slowing to a halt, he stood and watched them for a moment, wondering what they must be going over — civil evacuation plans... or whatever the Kroggs called such things?

"Ah, Chronos, good to see you down here again," Kragran abruptly acknowledged him, and managing another weak smile, Claw nodded.

"Nice to see the planet again."

As bald-faced lies went, he sold that one well.

Kragran offered his own smile and approached the Earther at an even step, "And we are glad to welcome you. I trust you approve of the defenses? We are quite pleased by General Wiskar's deployment."

Chronos nodded evenly, then lied, "Yes, well, we think we'll be in a good position to make a stand against Omega."

He only realized it was probably a bad idea to think of that statement as a lie as he said it.

"Liz will be in-system with her force in four days, Fox's ships another day after that, and then none other than Omega himself," the Admiral went on. "That gives us ample time to finish our preparations."

Chronos felt like he was qualifying his words too much, but Krag merely smiled at that report and nodded, "Excellent. We look forward to watching your ships in action again — from the correct perspective, this time, of course."

That cryptic sort of comment didn't sit well with Claw just now.

"The way you're talking, I'm almost starting to get the sense that you're hiding something."

Without skipping a beat, Krag tilted his head, "We all hide things, don't we Chronos?"

Well, that wasn't the right way to diffuse Chronos' suspicions... it was more like waving a red flag.

"What do you mean by that?"

Krag's alien smile remained, "I mean... you're much more tired than you're trying to let on, my friend. And much less confident than you should be. Don't worry about us, our tunnels are dug. Omega minions will not get what they want from us. In the meantime, I advise you return to *Formidable* and rest for a time. We need you in top form."

Chronos realized the Krogg was seeing right through his façade. That meant he was either more exhausted than usual, or that Krag was more perceptive than most observers, or perhaps it was a combination of both. Either way, the Peacelord was right. Chronos was seeing shadows everywhere now, even in the presence of a Krogg who'd spent over three decades earning his trust and friendship.

He probably wouldn't be able to sleep if he went to bed now, but at the very least he should probably try.

"Yes Krag, yes you're right. Thank you. And thanks for helping Garnet as you have — we're very glad it's you we're defending, and not a mob of humans driven mad. At least we know you can't be manipulated, and where your loyalties lie."

With a friendly chuckle, Krag patted Chronos on the shoulder, "Yes, you do. And we are very glad of that."

Chronos smiled, then after nodding to the other two Peacelords, he turned and left the office.

Watching him go, Kragran released what humans and Earthers might term a relieved sigh. One of the other two Warlords in the room met his eye, *Does he suspect, do you think?*

Krag closed his mouth.

No, he has no idea. Now, Kardrath, you say the fleet is up to 1,300 ships? How many more will we have by the time Omega arrives in six days? And will our perimeter defense stations be operational?

Chronos Claw might not have been imagining the looming shadows.

CHAPTER 43

Varnon Broadpaw and Lab Forepaw stepped up onto the deck of the Caine house in silence, neither of them yet able to speak about what they'd seen. Leading the way wordlessly, Varnon knocked on the glass wall that went around the circular upper level of the house, then opened the door and stepped in. Lab followed closely.

Claire Schaeffer, Christine's sister and now a guest in the Caine house, sat up on the couch, "What do you want?"

Her a tone was both rude and obstinate, and Varnon simply stared at her, "You should find another room for now, Miss Schaeffer."

The girl narrowed her eyes, "Fuck you, I'll be where I like."

Varnon knew this girl was alone in the galaxy, her parents dead and her sister with Graham. He knew she was damaged and Setter and particularly Phealan were trying to help her heal.

But he was, at this moment, uncharacteristically unsympathetic.

With hard eyes, he walked over to the couch, reached around to the back of Claire's neck and clutched the collar of her shirt. Hauling her up off the couch and holding her in the air in front of him like a pup being held by the scruff of its neck, he met her string of curses with a stare so cold it actually shut her up.

"*Find another room.*"

He lowered her to the floor and with wide eyes, she staggered backward and stumbled up the stairs.

Phealan and Setter had emerged from the lower level as Varnon released the young human. Both Caines quickly read the darkness in the air, and neither asked whether Claire's treatment had been necessary.

It was clear to both of them that something horrific had happened... something worse, somehow, than the destruction of the Light Division on Freetown.

That news had been a dark shock, one that was still proving difficult to get past... but there was obviously a new layer of horror. Setter realized this as he led his son towards Varnon, and without speaking, Lab moved over to the console controlling the coffee table holo and activated it, feeding in the message that had caused the great torment.

"This came in with a pod from somewhere around Freetown. Andra didn't even see it leave, but its vector says Freetown. We don't think it was sent anywhere else... just here. It's addressed to you, but I think it was supposed to broadcast to all Earth receivers. Andra said someone was trying to beam a signal into her force's receivers, but she blocked it. Could be the same thing."

Forepaw's quietly mumbled explanation was uncharacteristic of him, and the significance of that was not lost on Setter or Phealan. Lab and Varnon had already seen the message contents.

"Play it," Phealan stepped past his father, his words cool.

The holo projection twitched and then Omega-Gillian appeared. On a couch next to Audrey DeBrooke.

Setter stood deathly still.

For the next ten minutes he, his son, Lab and Varnon watched. They stood immobile and stared as Omega-Gillian began the unspeakable process of destroying Audrey DeBrooke.

There were no words to describe the horrific nature of the destruction... It was complete... a total unraveling of Audrey's mind, her heart and, of course, her body.

When it had started, Audrey had seemed resigned to her fate, and ready simply to let go. But Omega-Gillian found ways to make the young ruler of Freetown care just enough about life again. Simple things.

Staring at an arm stripped of its skin... that seemed to have been the breaking point. From there Audrey's concerns for her people and for her dead husband had vanished. Her mind had been destroyed.

All she wanted was to die, quickly and without more torment.

Getting Audrey to that stage had taken Omega-Gillian ten minutes, and some cruel power kept Audrey conscious through the unthinkable, slow, and carefully-executed mutilations, her cries and screams cut forth like daggers.

"Stop it..." Setter breathed as Audrey's horror-filled eyes seemed to lock on his.

Her pleading eyes. As though she could see through the camera, and was begging for him to help her... to save her and fix her...

But there was nothing left for her. She wanted to die quickly... and Omega wouldn't let her.

Setter couldn't watch it.

"You lasted longer than we did," Varnon's words came out a whisper. "We're obviously going to stop this from getting around. I think... I think it was as much a personal message to you as it was anything else."

Setter looked away from the holo and nodded, "Yes."

He had to pause and force himself to think before he could say any more.

"It's good you stopped it."

Lab closed his eyes and took deep, calming breaths, "Audrey... she... well, we knew she didn't get away. We just..."

Setter, Lab and Varnon had all known Audrey DeBrooke for many years.

They'd helped her and James build Freetown... and now Freetown was gone. James was gone.

And Audrey was a victim of the most horrific of deaths. Another lost cause, another failure. Omega was piling those on now, making sure the Earthers knew that their efforts were for nothing.

"Turn it back on."

Setter, Lab and Varnon each halted for a few seconds before they looked at Phealan. The young Caine's words had lost none of their confidence, and now he stepped towards the holo, his gaze locked with Audrey's.

Lab shook his head, "We don't have to see more, Phealan."

"He wants us to watch it... he wants us demoralized. There's nothing in there that will help us beat him," Varnon added in soft, sad tones.

Setter simply frowned at his son, unsure why watching more would do any good.

"What Omega wants is what we're doing right now," Phealan turned back to the elder wolves. "He wants us to start watching it, and to stop because of how horrific it is. That's how he plans to demoralize us. He takes all the goodness away and drowns it in *this*. He does this to make us believe we can do no good. That it's hopeless."

The elder wolves each took a moment's pause at the young Caine's words, and then Phealan turned back to Audrey's pleading eyes.

"These were the last living moments of a person who I counted to be a friend. It's my duty, and all of ours, to watch them. Out of respect to her. No matter what he does, no matter what he takes away from her... she was our friend and we should do her the honor of watching her last moments. It's the only way we have to be there for her. And then when we get our hands on Omega... then he'll understand that it didn't demoralize us."

Turning once more, Phealan's voice was tinged with an aged timber that didn't naturally belong in one so young.

"It doesn't matter what he does to us, or to those we care about. He's trying to make us abandon the memory of our friends, and we can't let him. There's no unspeakable crime he can commit that will destroy our loyalty to Audrey. We're right here with her, to the very end. Do you understand?"

Silence was the only answer Setter, Lab and Varnon could manage. Phealan thus repeated his order, "Turn it on."

The First Lord of the Admiralty silently obeyed, and the holo began again.

Audrey was slowly and mercilessly robbed of everything that made her who she was. It went on for hours. Her screams made the Earthers twitch and sometimes tremble, her desperate eyes pierced like daggers.

Phealan stared at her.

I'm so sorry, Audrey.

The thought felt wholly inadequate as it went through Phealan's mind, but it was all he could offer. Earthers fought endlessly for what they believed was right. They'd saved the Kroggs, they'd helped the humans... and now Omega was trying to rob them of their beliefs by drowning their hopes in horror.

No Earther good deed, it seemed, could go unpunished.

That's what Omega wanted them to believe.

"Everything we did last war... everything we thought was good," Varnon rasped out quietly, "he's going to use it against us. Helping the humans. Saving the Kroggs. All of it."

Phealan nodded, "He's going to do his best. He's going to load you three with more guilt than you can bear, because you remember making the decisions. You remember saving the Kroggs. You remember helping Freetown begin. He's showing you this to make you believe your efforts have been for nothing."

Setter frowned at his son, reaching out with instincts and trying to understand where the words were coming from.

Phealan turned back to his father and elder friends, "Realize this, though. He's working hard to show you how you've failed. He's working *this hard* because he has a lot of convincing to do. It takes this much evil, this much *visceral* evil, to cast a shadow over the good you all did, and what you all fought for. The power of what you did in the war and since will *not* be eclipsed by this... not for long."

Lab shook his head, "You think we're going to be able to overshadow that?"

The young Caine bowed his head, "I think that everything you've done already overshadows this. And we'll see that soon enough."

He turned back to the holo.

"For now, we owe it to Audrey not to look away from her last moments. She was alone there... we can't let her memory fade just because we don't want to watch it."

Phealan didn't know why, but he was certain the good the Earthers had done throughout their history could not be undone by Omega. Even this couldn't change the fact that the Kroggs and Larosians owed much to the Earthers, or that humanity still existed explicitly because of Earther protection.

The Earthers were not going to stop fighting.

Phealan wouldn't let it happen.

Together, the leaders of the Earther people and Navy watched their dear friend Audrey robbed of her humanity, her mind, her heart and her life.

CHAPTER 44

A galaxy away, a combined fleet was forming.

"I figure we can make the Krogg corridor in five days, and be at Krogg 'A' in just about six," Rear Admiral Minnie Maximane looked up through *Galahad's* main briefing room holo plot at the officers of the newly amalgamated squadron, studying their faces.

Both Narosh and Novash were nodding in slow unison, while Graham sat with an impassive stare. Christine seemed to be paying closer attention, but even so, that left Minnie and Captain Mel Ramsay with precious little feedback to work from.

"So..." Minnie pushed on, "how many ships can you have ready to boost for the corridor in, say, three hours, Admiral Narosh?"

Narosh turned and glanced at Novash. It was a good question — recovery parties were taking control of more ships now that Omega had been eliminated as an immediate threat, but time remained finite, and even weakening the crews to their thinnest fighting numbers, he could only bring so many ships online.

"Perhaps sixty ships, Admiral Maximane. Some will obviously be in better fighting condition than others, but we can also send word to Laros now that the way is clear. More crews can be sent to reactivate additional ships, and within weeks we should have dozens more."

Graham looked sideways at his Larosian friend, though his expression didn't change, "I doubt if weeks will factor into this. If Omega gets control of Krogg 'A', your fleet and ours together still will be no match for him."

Minnie's eyebrows rose at that assessment, and she nodded slowly in agreement. After the fight at the New Halifax corridor, and the one here, she had a dreadful understanding of the power of Omega.

"Well, that was a bit of a negative, if accurate, assessment," Novash leaned forward and looked down the table at Graham.

The junior Manchester simply stared at the junior Larosian commander, then turned his gaze to the holo plot, "We'll need to move as quickly as possible. I'd suggest breaking into separate formations for the journey, but I fear that if we do we might get caught in another trap."

Christine agreed verbally, "Indeed. Best to keep us all together."

What she wanted to add to that comment, though she didn't, was that it'd be a great idea for Graham to transfer aboard one of the Earther ships... because

Earther ships didn't feel quite so alien.

She was surprised to find herself contemplating her own discomfort in a strategy briefing, but Christine was finding it difficult being back on an Earther ship — in the quieting and pleasant company of Earthers — when she knew she'd be returning to her unsettling alien bunk...

Stamping out those thoughts, Christine was abruptly glad she was wearing her armor today. She wouldn't have wanted Narosh to get the wrong impression — she was certainly glad of the Larosians' hospitality. It was just... alien.

And it hadn't struck home *how* alien until she'd gotten back amongst fellow Earthers. Her eyes darted up, and as they reached the fox Captain of *Galahad,* and then the Admiral, she realized that both Earthers were looking right at her, and in microseconds she was sensing broadcasts of general comfort from them.

It really isn't just in my head. Even Earthers who don't know me are connecting with me instinctively.

The discussion had actually gotten underway again while she'd been lost in her thoughts.

"...so my squadron will lead out," Minnie was saying. "If all goes to plan, we can get to Krogg 'A' in six days, and hopefully be there before Omega arrives. We'll just have to hope we don't turn up and find... well."

"You needn't say it, Admiral," Narosh interjected softly. "We know."

Minnie nodded once, then looked around at the assembled officers again, "Alright, we need to move soon, so I'd say everyone back to their ships."

"Indeed," Novash and Narosh simultaneously stood. The rest of the attendees got to their feet and began to leave with quick steps.

Graham rose as well, but before he could turn from the plot, Minnie interrupted his blank-faced musings, "ArcGeneral Manchester?"

With a single blink, he looked through the plot at the lion, "Something I can help you with, Admiral Maximane?"

Frowning slightly, Minnie's eyes shifted just for milliseconds to Christine, who stood next to her commanding officer.

"Was just wondering, sir, if you wanted to transfer your flag to one of our ships. *Hector* is attached to us and is in good condition."

Graham tilted his head very slightly, then shook it, "No, I do believe *Carnarvon* is the place for me, Admiral. Will you be collecting your marines and boats from *Carnarvon?*"

Minnie managed to keep her expression neutral, "If you need us to, certainly."

"Please do. We'll have a full Larosian crew aboard now, and Narosh assures me repairs will be complete by the time we get under weigh. Christine might join you as well."

Christine's eyes widened slightly and she looked from Graham to Minnie, her head shaking in sharp jerks to silently decline. Instinctively, Minnie picked up something else. Christine wanted to get back among *fellow* Earthers, or however that saying was supposed to go in her unique case.

But if Graham wasn't moving, she couldn't, and Minnie understood why. Even if Christine didn't understand it herself, being so young and genetically disheveled at the moment, the reason was clear to Minnie Maximane.

"I do believe she'll stay with you, ArcGeneral."

Graham glanced over his shoulder slowly enough for Christine to stop shaking her head and to start making affirmative eye contact. His eyes settled on hers for a moment, and began to fill with something she couldn't understand... then he looked abruptly back to Minnie.

"Very well. We'll be returning to *Carnarvon*," Graham turned and marched towards the door, and Christine sent an apologetic glance towards Minnie. The lioness smiled sympathetically, and with that, Christine turned and headed for the exit.

She walked right into Graham's back.

He'd stopped in mid-step, and didn't even react to her impact.

Instead he looked back at Minnie, "I should say, Admiral, that I had the privilege of serving with your father on his last day. You do him proud, and I'm honored to fight alongside you."

He walked out.

Christine stood still for a moment, and then looked at Minnie, who had a small, sad smile on her face.

"Well, thank him for me please..." the lioness said quietly.

Christine nodded, "I will."

Then she left, and hours later the Larosian and Earther contingent set out to reinforce Krogg 'A'. These seventy-odd ships would hopefully turn the tide.

CHAPTER 45

Setter Caine stepped through the front door of Fengate Hospital and repressed an instinctive chill. Part of him wanted to demand that the universe explain why Elandra hadn't just seen fit to stay here, to stay at her hospital, and to be safe... but he stood quietly for a second and forced that part to the back of his mind. Varnon Broadpaw barely even noticed that his friend had slowed as they entered the hospital, but now the First Consul looked back at the Supreme Consul.

"You alright, Setter?"

The question could almost have been considered comical, given all they were experiencing, but Setter understood Varnon's intent. Nodding just once, the Supreme Consul forced his mind to turn away from any sentiments of sorrow, and he put one foot firmly in front of the other.

As the two wolves moved farther into the hospital lobby, they sighted Lab Forepaw, and the First Lord waved at them both, "Hope this news brightens things."

Varnon nodded for both himself and Setter, "Yes. We could certainly use something... brightening."

The feed with Audrey's fate had not been widely circulated, though Ursla had apparently accepted a copy into *Orion's* receivers, so that she could see it... and so that others who knew Audrey could honor her memory and watch it.

Omega was making this fight so bitterly personal... Genesis gone, London gone, the Light Division gone, Freetown gone... those were huge losses, and tragic on their own scale. But there was something about the desperate stare of a dying friend that couldn't be forgotten.

Phealan's insistence remained, however, and rightly so. It was much less difficult for Audrey's friends to watch that recording than it had been for Audrey to make it.

It just made things difficult now. Hope that Krogg 'A' would stand against Omega was nearly impossible to maintain... but maintaining such hope was necessary.

And perhaps — just perhaps — hope would be bolstered a little today. Celia Lazarus had been through a battery of tests after injecting herself with the Type 0 Omega scrubber, and now she was ready to report.

As the three canine leaders stood in a cluster in the lobby, the good doctor emerged from one of the adjacent corridors and walked quickly towards them, holding up her hand in a wave.

"I have *good* news, I think."

Setter's eyebrows rose slowly and he contained a sigh, "We'll take any we can get right now, Celia."

She nodded as she came to a stop in front of them, "I heard about what happened to Governor DeBrooke..." she paused for a few seconds — she hadn't seen the vid, but she could read the mood of these leaders easily enough. She pushed on, "The news is that I've finished my blood tests and there's no Type 0 Omega left, and my brain scan is clear. Theoretically, I should be telepathically accessible now. Just don't have anyone to think to... except for..."

Her voice trailed off again, and she pointed towards the floor, indicating the basement of the facility where the captured Omega minion was being held. Based on what had been seen at Freetown, that minion had to be within thought range, and yet Celia was fine...

Varnon voiced the hopes that the findings created: "So the fact that you haven't been taken over by Omega's minion here is a good sign."

She nodded, "Exactly, a good sign. But there's more... if you'll join me in the lab downstairs."

The three old Navy veterans glanced at each other and then nodded. Celia Lazarus led them to the basement of Fengate Hospital.

The Omega minion was in an energy shielded cell in the center of one of the large labs in Fengate's basement, a squad of marines standing around with weapons at the ready in case it somehow escaped its energy containment.

As Celia led the way into the room, the almost-human thing turned in a jerky motion and smiled at her in an unsettling way, "Ah, Celia you're *back*. Lovely... ooh, you bring friends!"

Setter felt a chill as the words escaped what had once been the young Genesis spacer named Livia King. The voice wasn't hers, and he didn't have to guess who was actually talking...

"I see our friend decided to upgrade his presence. Not just a minion... an avatar now," Setter slowed to a stop and crossed his arms as he stared through the force field.

Celia glanced at him and nodded, her eyes traveling from Caine to Varnon and Lab and then back, "As soon as my blood was cleared of old Omega I came down here to see what'd happen. Nothing felt different to me, I must say, but when I used what I've always called my *instincts* to probe this minion here, I got something back... more than I'm used to."

Setter frowned, "So our instincts really are connected to telepathy?"

Celia's hands found their way into the pockets of her lab coat, "If they're not the exact same process, they're... how should I put this... they operate out of the same muscle group. Either way, knowing how to use one seems to be making the other one usable as well."

"My old self couldn't have you talking to the other telepaths around here. I've never been big on conversation with cattle," Omega's avatar... Omega-King, perhaps... chuckled from inside her energy cage, and Caine looked at the creature.

"We were wondering about your motives. Suppressing any telepathic ability so that we couldn't notice you, that makes sense. But you protected us from the Kroggs, and from your new self. I expect you couldn't be too selective about what you blocked and what you didn't."

Setter was almost surprised at his candor — not so much at the question he was asking, but at the fact that he was standing here, conversing with Omega directly. This was another avatar of the being that had butchered Audrey...

The avatar's grin stretched — past the point that it should have humanly been able to stretch, "Yeah, sometimes it's a double-edged sword. But I'm the one who killed the Queen, not you. Grieve was just the meatbox that pushed the button, *I* had to wrestle the little bitch."

Setter's eyes narrowed and he remained silent, but Varnon took the bait, "Well you have a creative memory, there, plague. We did the *hard* work, and if I recall, Larosians you *weren't* 'protecting' actually got to the Queen's chamber too," the wolf didn't sound impressed, and Omega's eyes shifted briefly across to the First Consul.

"Fuck off, underling."

Caine's eyebrows shot up, and Varnon looked disgusted as he shook his head, "You won't pull what you did with Audrey again."

That was unprompted by this conversation, but the visions of Audrey's horrible death were still seared into Varnon's mind. It wasn't quite the only thing he could think about, but it was close. And he needed to say that... to get his shot in at this plague, weak though the salvo felt.

Omega-King smiled and shrugged her shoulders delicately, "I love how I can kill whole planets, enslave humans and eat them from the inside out so you can never save them... but when it comes down to it, the most disturbing thing I do is good, old-fashioned torture. You fucking pussies... sorry, puppies. Just wait to see what I do to Krogg 'A'."

"You certainly like to talk," Setter took a couple of steps towards the containment field, folding his arms. "You also keep swearing as though it's going to bother us. And you're boasting, which I'll concede, you've earned the right to do..."

He paused and Omega-King bristled, the smile fading from her face.

"...but you're not as confident as you claim to be. You've been trying to get control of Celia, haven't you? You've been trying to take control of her the way you took over the people on Freetown... and you can't."

Omega-King's patience seemed to instantly wear thin, "I don't need to control you fucking cows. I'll just *eat* you. Literally, if you like, since it seems to make such an impression when I have fun with the torture."

Setter locked eyes with the avatar as she finished that spurt of threats, and he forced himself not to shrink from the gaze.

"We'll see what happens at Krogg 'A'," Setter said quietly, and the avatar's smile returned.

"Yes. I'll be sure to make plenty of movies so you can see what happens to all the people you lose contact with."

Setter smiled coolly, "Thanks. I'll watch them."

Turning away, he nodded towards the door. It didn't seem possible to get an advantage in a verbal sparring match with the plague, so for now it was time to leave. Omega-King heckled them as they departed, but the veteran Naval wolves and Doctor Lazarus all ignored the words.

They said nothing until they got back up to Celia's office — it felt right to put some physical space between them and the plague before they started discussing what to do next.

"The treatment is a success?" Lab Forepaw asked the confirming question as Celia waved her distinguished guests into chairs opposite her desk.

"Yes. There's no sign of mutation or short-term side-effects. And now that I've been around that avatar and haven't been taken over, I think we can confirm that becoming telepathic isn't going to be a danger for us."

As she said those words, the Earthers in the room all slowly looked towards Setter. For some reason, the Supreme Consul couldn't help but smile and shake his head.

"It's absurd," he said. "Five months ago, if we'd been offered telepathy, I don't think any one of us would have suggested it could be a bad idea. Omega really has turned us upside down."

Varnon tilted his head slightly, "So... think we should go forward with this?"

Setter's smile faded all too quickly, "I can't conceive of Omega being able to use his mind against us with any success. If we're all telepathic, that just gives us one more way to fight him. And we need as many of those as we can get."

Celia nodded, "I have to agree. We've made progress on a model for a cure for Type 2 — the flux cells — but we're probably going to need more samples from Christine to make it work... so that's another reason I hope she's alright. In the meantime, this could give us some sort of advantage."

"This may be the advantage that matters most, Celia," Setter's words quieted and his eyes fell to a place on the floor as a new idea came to his mind. Omega was a plague of an almost infinite number of individual cells, and he was able to survive where only one cell remained... *but*...

Interesting idea.

But he had to bury it carefully.

"Put this into production immediately," Setter's voice picked up again, and he looked back at Celia. "I want to get one of the first shots."

The telepathic walls were about to come down.

CHAPTER 46

Andra Ursla stared at the tabletop in *Orion's* main briefing room.

Sarah sat opposite her, and Pat had pulled his chair around from the side of the table to sit next to his wife. They stared at the table.

Jax Furgus stared at the table. Ed Jeffries returned to his seat looking as ill as when he'd had to leave it half an hour before, and then stared at the table too.

The Earthers had just finished showing the humans the bitter end of their friend Audrey.

"I..." Ursla tried to say that she was sorry she'd let Audrey be captured... but she knew as well as everyone else at this table that there was no blame to take.

The entire Light Division had been absorbed by Omega on Freetown. The capital city still sat below *Orion's* hull, appearing tantalizingly abandoned, but Omega had to be down there. Ursla hadn't ordered this force away from Freetown because the refugees from the planet were still being shuffled around between the ships of the Allied fleet...

And because she couldn't bear to abandon the place so easily. But the time was fast coming to leave. This recording sealed it.

Freetown could never be redeemed. They'd leave the planet as a standing monument to what once was, and then flee.

"You didn't need to show us that."

Sarah's icy words were merciless, and Ursla got a sharp twinge through her instincts. That just didn't seem like appropriate talk, and Ed Jeffries was in no mood to tolerate it.

"No, you *needed* to give us a goddamned hand down there so we could *get her out*," the man's emotions were running high as he turned on Sarah. He'd worked with both Audrey and James for many years, and Audrey had been a close friend of his.

Watching the butchery had been difficult for him, even though it had been a drastically edited and shortened version of the recording. The Earthers had expected the full feed would be too much for the humans... and based on this reaction, their assumption was correct. Now Ursla sympathized, but she couldn't afford to have the new leader of the survivors of Freetown coming to blows with Sarah.

Jax, thankfully, was thinking the same, and the hard old lion seemed much more immune to the horrors he'd just watched than Ursla had been, "Ed, sit back for a moment."

The normal gravel in Jax's voice seemed coarser as he spoke, and Ed looked at the cat and obeyed. Turning towards Sarah, Jax narrowed his eyes, "We *did* have to watch that, Sarah. Audrey being our friend, it's our duty to watch. It's the only way we have left to pay our respects."

Sarah didn't react at first, but then she shook her head, "Omega is trying to wrong-foot us. We're just helping him." Then pushing herself to her feet, she scowled, "I won't help him with–"

Pat's hand clamped onto Sarah's shoulder and he pulled her down again, "Audrey was at our wedding. She was our friend. And it was bloody harder for her to be in that feed than it was for us to watch it. It's the least we could do."

Sarah's eyes were wide in surprise at Pat's sharp words. Though they'd been sharing her cabin again since Freetown had fallen, they'd barely spoken. She refused to open up to him.

She snapped back harshly, "Just because you feel guilty about losing her down there–"

Ursla didn't even realize she was doing it, but she dropped her fist through the table with such force that it ripped her end wide open, tore the entire table off its moorings and made it hop off the floor, landing with a crash.

She then roared with frustration — simply *roared*, and the three humans in the room were reduced to small figures in their chairs.

Jax took his chance, then, to do the same — he spared the table, but his gravelly old roar came out too, and the room was drowned in those violent sounds for long, deafening seconds.

When the Earthers stopped, Ursla got to her feet, walked down the table to Sarah, grabbed her by the collar of her uniform and lifted her out of her chair, "*Stop this, Sarah.* Stop it now. We *need* you. None of us can lead your people, but at this rate neither can you. Listen to Pat, and stop this."

Sarah was too shocked to move as she hung from Ursla's grip.

Ursla had lost her patience.

Lowering her old friend back to the deck, Andra Ursla turned away, "I never *really* understood what Setter was feeling when he put his fist through the table in this room. Remember, he was meeting with Narosh about the fate of the Kroggs? I never understood what compelled him to do that."

She was addressing that to Jax while Sarah stared wide-eyed at her back.

Jax nodded slowly, "Sometimes a good roar comes in handy."

The old cat's amber eyes locked on Sarah's for a moment, then slid down to Pat's face. The Irishman didn't seem shocked or displeased… he almost looked relieved.

He knew, as Ursla and Jax both did, that the last time Sarah had been in this state aboard *Orion*, she'd nearly gotten Narosh killed. This time, Ursla's frustration would hopefully shake her out of her isolation.

Leadership couldn't only be about coldness and dispassion. Sarah needed to deal with pain instead of pretending it wasn't there, or the rest of the humans from Genesis and Freetown — the shattered remnants of a species — would die.

Pat took Sarah's dangling hand in his own, and gently pulled her down into her chair. She stared at Ursla as the great Admiral returned to her own chair.

The rest of this meeting will be awkward...

Actually, it wouldn't be.

At that instant, the collision alarm sounded — the warning chime that alerted the ship when impact with something large was imminent.

Orion hadn't even had time to beat to quarters — the collision alarm meant shields had to be raising, but weren't up yet...

There was nothing to stop the impact, and the explosion was considerable.

Captain Ron Hobbes came out of his chair on the bridge of *Aboukir* with his mouth hanging open.

"Omega ships... dozens of them!" the Sensor Officer barked as Hobbes took two steps towards the plot.

Where they'd come from he didn't know, but there were dozens of infected Genesis ships suddenly appearing all around the fleets, making kamikaze runs on big ships... *Orion* taking the first hit.

"Beat to quarters!" Ron Hobbes whirled back to his First Lieutenant, then turned immediately to the Signal Officer, "All ships scatter and engage. Signal Alix to join us, we have to get *Orion* out of there."

Captain Esther Arbear struggled to her feet on *Orion's* bridge, "Report!'

"Major hull breach in our forward section, power grid is failing!"

Orion, perhaps the greatest Earther warship in history, had gone through countless battles with little or no damage. Now, for the second time, Omega had carved into the great ship's hull.

"Communications are down, I can't get orders to fleet!" the Signal Officer was rushing between his techs' panels, and Esther nodded, turning quickly to the plot... just in time to watch it wink out of existence as the power failed.

Aboukir, in company with Alix Tarkham's 74-gun *Bismarck*, leapt through the suddenly unraveling formations of Earther and human ships in the space over Freetown, making directly for *Orion*.

Ron Hobbes, a longtime Flag Captain but never an Admiral himself, now realized that no orders were being given in the human fleet — aside from those he'd issued. Barty Stowt was dead, and the Admirals were meeting aboard *Orion*.

The Earther Commodores of the First Fleet were looking to their own devices as they took fire... but the Genesis ships were sitting stunned.

"Order the transports with refugees into energy drive and flux drive, on my authority," Ron looked to his Signal Officer. "And tell the humans to get out of here — they're floating targets!"

Organization of refugees be damned — they'd all be dead in a minute at this rate. A Genesis Superdreadnought blossomed in silent flame in the plot as Ron gave the orders, and he ground his jaw.

"Time to *Orion*?"

Another two Genesis ships — they looked like *tugs* — were lining up to ram the First Rate, and its shields failed almost as if on cue. Ron didn't even bother wondering how Omega had managed to pull off this surprise... it was the plague's hallmark at this stage...

"Nine seconds to *Orion*..."

Ron gritted his teeth and turned to this First Lieutenant, "*Deal* with those tugs."

Scant seconds later, *Aboukir's* chase guns spat their shot, and *Bismarck's* guns similarly fired their salvo. The tugs were, in one of the minor victories of this moment, battered away.

"See if you can get Esther Arbear on comms. Tell her we're going to tow her out. And order all ships to cut and run, there's no reason to stay here."

It was a big decision for a Flag Captain to take upon himself, particularly when there were so many Commodores around, but Ron Hobbes was one of those Flag Captains — like Lab Forepaw before him — who was trusted and listened to.

As the Genesis Fleet slowly broke orbit and accelerated away from the planet, Earther ships slid into position behind them, keeping hordes of small Omega ships from chasing their most vulnerable targets.

"Where did he come from?" Ron let himself ask the question under his breath, and then he gripped the sides of the plot as the Master executed a rather violent maneuver to get *Aboukir* over *Orion's* torn bows.

Bismarck went beneath the flagship, and as Earther vessels all around them began translating to energy drive and marking course for Earth, these two 74s locked the great First Rate into their grav tractors and pulled themselves close.

"We're patching into *Bismarck's* nav computers now," the Master looked over his shoulder to deliver the report, "Ready on your mark."

Ron Hobbes took a deep breath and nodded, looking through the plot at the sudden and ill-defined chaos that had literally come from nowhere.

"Get us out of here."

Cooperating carefully, *Aboukir* and *Bismarck* pulled themselves — and *Orion* — into a single energy drive field, and the amalgamated vessel pushed its way out of the system at a modest speed. Behind it, the rest of the Allied fleets took their turns to escape as well.

Hopefully they hadn't lost too much.

Watching the Earthers and humans run from a couple of squadrons of tugs, Omega grinned. Sure, the Earthers had fucked him in the Larosian galaxy and slapped him on the way to Krogg, but he was still the king of showing up unannounced.

And now Freetown was all his.

He laughed.

CHAPTER 47

Grimbold was the first ship out of energy drive, leading the long line of rearmed Survey Service ships that made up Liz Hastings' new command. The aged 64 still seemed to be moving with its old military precision as Chronos Claw watched it slow in *Formidable's* main battle tank. Now, as his gaze settled on it, Liz's pennant on the icon flashed once — a traditional greeting from her to the officers already in-system.

A small, tired smile came to Chronos' face, so he glanced at his Flag Captain, "Dip our pennant to *Grimbold*, please."

Formidable's pennant flashed, and greeted the fifty ships of the Surveyors Battle Group, and the many disassembled stations they'd escorted from Gibraltar. More of the defense force had finally arrived… much of it was already here and being put together.

Chronos let his eyes traverse the tank and settle on the 128 Krogg War ships that were in various states of unpacking and reconstruction. The yards were bringing those vessels online in record time, so hopefully all of them would be ready for the fight when it came…

And it was definitely coming.

With Liz's force and these recommissions, Chronos now had just about 300 ships in Krogg 'A' space. That wasn't bad, and Fox was bringing another thirty-two *Chimeras* along as well… but there were 1,100 Omega ships coming. It was exceedingly difficult not to dwell on that fact.

"Signal coming in from *Grimbold*," the Signal Officer interrupted Chronos' thoughts at an apt enough time.

Nodding, Chronos looked to the Lieutenant, "In the plot, please."

Liz Hastings appeared as Chronos turned back to the holographic display, smiling in a friendly fashion as she sighted the cat Admiral, "Good to see you again, Chronos."

He smiled in kind, "And good to see you too, Liz. Last pod I got from Fox said he hadn't been able to slow Omega down much… so we've got about a day and a half... probably not enough time to assemble the Gibraltar stations."

Liz's smile sobered and she nodded, "I'd wondered if Fox would try to slow the bastard down. I suppose we'll just have to make do without the stations' guns. Did Fox take any losses?"

Shaking his head slowly, Chronos let his eyes descend slightly, "Nothing serious, from what I know. Though Fox got separated from his squadron, so he's *tailing* Omega now, with Karl Kandam and four other ships. Garvin's out ahead."

Liz nodded, "Alright. As long as he's still coming. How go the preparations here? Looks to me like you've got things well in hand."

Chronos' ear twitched slightly — *prepared* wasn't how he felt, not at all. His instincts were pounding on his consciousness every day now, telling him over and over that he was missing something... that he didn't understand the fight that was coming... that something huge was happening right under his nose.

His eyes drifted to the red ball of Krogg 'A' in the bottom of the plot, but nothing came to him, so he bit back minor frustration at his instincts failing him. Bad time to lose those things, that was for sure...

"That bad, eh?"

Blinking, Claw looked up with a start and realized he'd let himself trail off in mid conversation, "Sorry. Just... it's not a good feeling. My instincts are nearly rebelling and I can't tell why. But yes, our preparation goes well. We'll only be facing four-to-one odds by the time Omega gets here... and we'll just have to hope that's enough."

Liz's eyes widened slightly at the bleak numbers — how Chronos could hope such numbers were positive was beyond her, but the Earther did seem to be certain that he was doing everything possible.

"The Kroggs are in line?" she asked after a moment. "Last time I fought a battle here, they tried to blow me up with their sun."

Some certainty returned to Chronos' voice, "If there's one part of my instincts I trust right now, it's the part about them. Kragran is looking after things below for us... we'll have no problems like Freetown did."

Slightly surprised by the assured words, Liz nodded, "Okay, good. I'll get formed up, and then we can start looking at final defense plans."

"Excellent... oh, some bad news for you: I might need to steal some of your veteran officers for my recommissions. We have enough regular crews, but I wouldn't mind having some veteran squadron skippers with them," Chronos tried to force energy back into his voice.

Nodding slowly, Liz narrowed her eyes thoughtfully, "I'll see who's interested. I don't imagine you'll have a shortage of volunteers."

"Glad to hear it..." Chronos released a long sigh, "Alright, until later then."

Liz smiled, nodded and disappeared.

Chronos Claw closed his eyes and wondered at his own, uncharacteristic state of mind. He had to stop worrying about his rampaging instincts. Everything was as it was supposed to be.

Yes, everything is exactly as it should be under the circumstances: all bad.

•••

Warlord Kardrath stood on the bridge of his Hyper Mothership, a marvel of Krogg bio-engineering that was all the more impressive because of its great secrecy. More massive than any Mothership before it, this vessel had been designed and grown to make best use of all the lessons of the Queen's War, and of Earther energy technology.

It was a true sight to behold, and Kardrath enjoyed doing just that — beholding it — in his mind's eye as it and its seven sisters swum amongst the thousands of Destroyers, Dreadnoughts and Superdreadnoughts that made up the new Krogg Navy.

This ship even had a name, something Krogg ships of the old armada had never had. It was known as *Death*, and its sisters were each known by similar names: *Chaos, Anguish, Brutality, Pestilence, War, Pain* and ironically enough, *Plague.* The names were very fulfilling to recite — Kardrath looked forward to the day when all Krogg ships bore names, but alas, there wasn't time enough to assign names to the thousands of other vessels now at his disposal.

After their victory, perhaps, they could be named. Perhaps the Earthers would even help.

Kardrath spared an eager laugh at that last thought. He had more than 2,000 ships at his disposal: the Krogg Fleet was once again assembled.

Signal coming from Krogg 'A', it is from Warlord Kragran.

Kardrath nodded at the telepathic report from *Death's* Captain, *Very well, direct to my mind please.*

The Earther niceties of command really did seem to smoothen the process of ship operation. One of the inadvertent gifts the Earthers had given their former foe was an understanding of the chain of command, and how it improved redundancy and speeded action, even when compared to the efficiency of a single Telepath operating a ship.

During the Queen's War against the Earthers, only one Telepath would control each vessel, and though very powerful in mind, each could only focus on so much at one time. The 'chain of command' was much better. Thanks to the Earthers, the new Krogg Navy was truly much more formidable than the old armada.

Kragran now appeared in Kardrath's mind, the leader of the Krogg people smiling as he did, *The fleet is assembled?*

Indeed, Lord Kragran. 2,017 ships of war, over half being Dreadnoughts and Superdreadnoughts, and eight being our new Hyper Motherships. I have to admit that I am quite confident of our pending success.

Kragran's smile broadened, *Excellent news. Lord Kragthar has our legions ready for the ground operations as well. About twelve million warriors. And Liz Hastings just arrived, meaning Omega is a mere thirty-six hours away.*

Kardrath matched his leader's smile, *Am I to assume, m'lord, that they still haven't noticed us? I've been keeping us clear of the approaches from Gibraltar.*

Indeed, we're thought to be passive and uninvolved, according to the intercepts I just received. They will have no idea what we are up to. But remember to wait for my signal, Lord Kardrath. We must wait until Omega has shown us everything he has brought before we can spring our trap.

Kardrath bow-nodded in an almost Larosian style, *Of course, m'lord. I'll move our ships into position near the approaches just beyond the system, so we will be ready to flank him when he arrives.*

Good, thank you, Kardrath. Remain out of sight there, and I'll be in touch soon.

With that, the Warlord leader of the Krogg race vanished from Kardrath's mind.

Turning back to the Captain Telepath who commanded *Death*, Kardrath smiled, *We must move to position one. Lowest possible emissions — the Earthers will not be looking through hyperspace layers for Omega, but if we make ourselves obvious we will be seen.*

The Telepath bow-nodded, then broadcast those basic instructions out from *Death* to the Krogg Fleet. Kardrath watched the magnificent sight in his mind's eye — 2,017 ships sitting in Earther-style ranks cruising through hyperspace, silently waiting as their old foe prepared to face a new enemy.

Both the Earthers and Omega would be very, very surprised to meet the new Krogg Navy.

CHAPTER 48

Fox Magnus grimaced and kept his eyes fixed on the plot.

Chimera, *Namur*, and four of their classmates were still trailing the Omega black wave ships, and there was no sign that getting past that force was going to be possible. The Omega vessels were moving *very* quickly, and the drives on the *Chimera*-class ships simply couldn't push them fast enough to overtake.

That was not good.

"I *genuinely* hate this. I mean it. *Genuinely*," Fox said after a long moment, glancing across at his wife in the seat next to him.

She raised an eyebrow, "Well, I'm glad you don't just fake hating it."

"Hmph," Fox folded his arms and let his eyes settle back on the plot. He was a sloop officer by trade... it may have been decades since he'd skippered plucky little *Flame*, but all the same, he still believed most in speed and maneuverability.

It felt right now as though he had neither... though in absolute terms, *Chimera* was in fact both faster and more maneuverable than *Flame* had ever been, absurd as that sounded given the much greater mass of the new ship.

Technology has made even these ships of the line handy... but not handy enough to get around Omega...

Unless.

Fox took a deep breath as he started to contemplate his wild idea again. He *had* threatened to use energy-hyper if it came to this... but what a terrible idea it would be.

Chronos Claw had masterminded energy-hyper back in the Krogg War, and while it still worked now for pods and for the occasional sloop, it was usually quite deadly for big ships. It was as though there was something about hyperspace that took offense to the Earthers' attempts to travel too fast, and thus tore them mercilessly apart when they tried it.

Such explanations seemed fanciful, but they were all the scientists could come up with while large ship experiments with energy-hyper continued to fail.

Sometimes, though, the ships got through. And Fox wanted to get around this Omega fleet, and reach Krogg 'A', so he could help with the defense. He couldn't stand to arrive late.

He thus took a centering breath and looked at his wife, "Think... we should try?"

She nodded slowly, "I don't like to be late."

Fox smiled nervously in acknowledgment of the words, then looked back at the plot, "Signal Officer, send to Karl to drop back with us and get him on the line."

There was a very brief pause before Karl Kandam turned up in the plot, and Fox shook his head as the panda appeared, "Don't think we can outrun them this way, Karl. They're flying."

"Aye," the bear let out a disappointed sigh. "You're going to do that thing you said you might do, aren't you?"

Fox shrugged, "Yes. You don't have to come along with us if you don't want, but I have to try."

"Even if trying gets you blown up? Won't be much good to the defense if you never reintegrate into a material state," the panda pointed out in a sober tone, and Fox scratched his forehead with his thumb.

"I've always been bad at the 'responsible CO' thing, Karl, you know that. I'm too much of a sloop skipper at heart. I have to try it... but you should stay back with the other four. Follow Omega the whole way in, make sure he doesn't try something crazy."

Kandam took a deep breath, "If you're going... I should... no... no I suppose you're right. We'll chase him in and jump him from behind. You go ahead. We'll send all our luck with you."

Fox smiled again, "Hopefully the exchange rate on luck today is better than it's been lately."

With a frown, Karl tilted his head, "Exchange rate?"

"Sorry, currency joke. Human thing," his smile then faded. "I'll get my engineer on the preparations here. Call you before we go."

Karl nodded, "Good luck."

"Thanks..." Fox nodded a last time, then Karl disappeared.

Straightening up, the First Space Lord looked at his wife, then tugged on his collar. Thena smiled reassuringly and called for *Chimera's* engineer to start the preparations. The ship of the line was going to attempt an energy-hyper jump.

"Call it twenty-four hours from... *now*."

Chronos Claw nodded at Liz Hastings' words. The pair sat in *Formidable's* briefing room, with Garnet Wiskar, Farley Karr, Jessica Forbes, Rodney Evan-Thomas, and a handful of other officers assembled around them. They had one more day in which to get everything ready.

"So," Chronos leaned back in his chair and made sure to hide his uncertainty from the humans present, "We need to figure out the best way to use what we have. Thoughts on how this is going to play out?"

In the old days there'd have been no shortage of thoughts — against the

Kroggs, it had been fairly easy to predict how the fight would unfold. Winning the fight was never a sure thing, but the enemy was at least a known quantity.

But now no hands went up, no one leaned forward and no one spoke. No one had so much as a clue as to what Omega was going to pull when he got here. No one even knew what abilities to expect from those new, black ships.

"We probably need to talk this through," Chronos said. "We know he wants the biomatter that's down there. Garnet, you're on the ground looking after that, but the question is how he's going to get his ships over Krogg so he can drop a landing force. And where we can stop him. He's had a lot of success appearing out of nowhere, and since we won't have the Gibraltar stations ready in time to help, we need more options."

"Keep in mind that some of the pickets at Freetown were Genesis ships, with bad sensors," Liz took over for a moment, then tapped a couple of keys in front of her to activate the table holo map of the system. The pools of biomatter were marked as black blobs on the glowing red surface of the planet, and all eyes turned to them.

"At Freetown he dropped in close and infiltrated… though there aren't any oceans here for him to use as secret landing zones. Anything he puts down will be on solid ground," Jessica Forbes offered quietly, and there were nods.

"I'd say he doesn't even try to sneak in. Against Genesis ships he probably had a sensor advantage, but here he's facing Earther sensors all the way around. And he'll probably want to show off his new ships… by massacring us…" Evan-Thomas's frank turn of phrase probably sounded a bit too abrupt, but none could deny the truth in his words.

Omega wants to win morale victories as much as tactical ones, and one will come when his new, black ships overwhelm the defenses here.

Chronos stopped himself. He hadn't just thought *if* the new black ships crushed the defending fleet, but *when* they did.

He couldn't tolerate that sort of thinking from himself.

"True. So… let's assume he fights us wherever he sees us. Where can we go that gives us the tactical edge?"

Calis Landry, one of the Captains who'd fought the last war alongside Ami Dune, leaned forward, "We could pull in close to the star, force him to fight in a heavy grav well…"

Chronos frowned thoughtfully and then shook his head, "No, that'd make it too easy for him to drop an overwhelming force on Garnet."

"The station line? We could make him think we've reactivated them somehow…" Liz's eyes fixed on the sphere of Krogg stations that had, in the final battle of Krogg 'A', been so destructive. The globe of floating fortresses surrounding the system had been nearly impenetrable in the old days, thanks to each one's massive auto-spine batteries. If only they could reactivate those beastly stations…

But even if they could only make the stations *look* dangerous, perhaps that would work to their advantage. If Omega thought the stations might be active, he couldn't risk his new fleet in attacking them — their spine batteries had been devastating in the last assault on this system.

"If we attack him beyond the stations, then fall back through Draco's breach and look like we're going to try to *hold* that breach, we might just get him stacked up and take away his maneuverability. Force him into a bottleneck," Chronos started thinking out loud.

Draco's breach, of course, was the colloquial name for the breach in the station perimeter that Draco Maximane had created with his dying carrier *Engadine* during the last battle of the Krogg War. It remained, thanks to insufficient grazing by freed Krogg ships, the only gap in the perimeter of stations.

So it would be a logical place to hold back an Omega assault — if the stations were indeed active.

"We pull him into that gap... then hit him with what?" Farley Karr's question was an apt one, and Chronos frowned.

Stacking up the enemy was great — it had been working in military history since Thermopylae and before — but it wouldn't do much good if the Allied ships didn't have a way to defeat the plague fleet once they had it where they wanted it.

But what could they do...

Aha.

Chronos' mind latched onto the name — Draco's breach — and to his memory of watching that breach being created. It had been a gallant *ram*.

"Some of the recommissioned sloops. We configure their nav computers for remote piloting and then we slam them into his heavy ships in *energy drive*. Big explosions... that should shake him up," Chronos' eyes darted from the plot to the faces of the officers around him. "Then the rest of us just need to fight like we've never fought before."

There were a few nods around the table — the idea seemed plausible, if desperate, enough. They could take a page from Omega's own book and use good (albeit uncrewed) warships as self-sacrificing rams. That was their only chance to force him back...

"But this whole thing requires us to make those stations look alive. And there's no way I can think of to do that," Jessica Forbes leaned forward with a frown.

Right. The small complication in this whole idea was the need for the stations to seem active. Chronos should have recognized that immediately... and he should have thought of those stations long ago. They'd always been sitting out there, dormant... and unnoticed...

But now he needed them... and... *of course*. There was one person in this system he could turn to who'd be more than happy to help with them, even on such short notice.

"Kragran will be happy to help, I'm sure," Chronos smiled, feeling as though his instincts were suddenly sated.

Eyebrows went up around the table, but slowly everyone began to nod. It had come to that: they were asking the Kroggs for help. The old nemesis against the new...

"You sure we can trust the Kroggs to rearm?" Liz asked suspiciously.

"Well, we're not talking about giving them back a fleet, but if they can get the stations to just look like they're online, we're in business," Chronos replied. "I'm sure Krag is on our side. We don't have anything to worry about with him."

Liz studied Chronos' expression for a moment, then nodded, "If you say so."

He did say so. Kragran was his friend and ally, and Chronos trusted him implicitly.

CHAPTER 49

Chimera was bucking under Fox's feet, so he was holding the plot with one hand, and his wife's hand with the other.

This had been an incredibly bad idea.

Karl had been right to warn him that it was going to be a risk… this was not the way dapper First Space Lord Fox Magnus had envisioned his death, but evidently, he didn't have much choice.

"Reactors are going to lose it — we have to get out of this!" Cruising Master Gunth was remarkably sure-footed as he moved around the helm consoles, the ship's pitching and tumbling having no effect on him.

Fox didn't waste any time agreeing, "Back to material state, Master!"

Perhaps they had leapt past the black ships of the Omega fleet, and now could continue on to Krogg 'A' under regular drives… get there ahead of the plague…

"Killing the drive *now!*" the Master roared.

Fox gritted his teeth and looked straight at Thena. For obvious reasons, he feared this would be his last opportunity to see her face…

Chimera returned to its material state, but in many pieces. The vessel had passed the Omega fleet by many, many hours, but the strain had been too much.

Chunks of the once-proud ship of the line tumbled through hyperspace, emergency atmospheric shields keeping them from decompressing as they scattered into the great unknown.

But conveniently, there was an entire Krogg Navy on hand and ready to collect what remained of the Earther ship.

Warlord Kardrath's eye widened as the energy output of that failed attempt at energy-hyper entered his mind. There were still twenty-two hours to wait before the Omega ships arrived… this must have been an Earther vessel which had attempted to pass the plague ships. While the new Hyper Motherships had perfected energy-hyper technology, the Earthers were clearly still wanting.

But Kardrath had no time to feel pride at the Krogg Navy's superior technology. This Earther ship's failed attempt to return to material state might have caused a hyperspace disturbance, and drawn attention to the sector of subspace in which the Krogg ships were hiding.

Fleet to redeploy to alternate positions, but move Death *towards the wreckage. What ship was that, can we tell?* Kardrath put the question to his Sensors Officer, and the Telepath reached out with his mind and found a transponder.

Chimera, *flagship of the Earther First Space Lord Magnus. Each section of the ship is intact and pressurized, there are undoubtedly many survivors.*

Kardrath nodded, *Very good. Order our escorts to collect those parts and bring them into* Death. *As soon as recovery is complete, we will move to our secondary position.*

Yes, Warlord!

The ships of the Navy scattered, some of them collecting chunks of *Chimera* as they went.

"That was a hell of a spike... my guess is a pod that came apart on its exit attempt..."

Chronos Claw nodded as his Flag Captain reported on the abrupt energy signature in subspace.

"Send two sloops out to have a quick look around, but don't let them go too far. It could be bait for an Omega trap," Chronos said quietly, then turned to his Signal Officer. "Got Kragran yet?"

The Lieutenant was just looking up as the question came, "On the line now, sir."

"In the plot," Chronos turned his attention to the holo display.

After a few seconds, Kragran appeared, and Chronos could almost have sworn the Krogg looked disheveled... which would be a remarkable feat for a creature that wore no clothes and had no hair.

"Chronos... that was rather a large energy spike, are you aware of what caused it?"

Chronos probably should have read more into the question than he did, but instead he just shook his head, "No idea. A couple of sloops are going out to have a look, but my guess would be either a failed pod translation or some sort of taunt from Omega."

Krag nearly released a relieved sigh, but caught himself in time.

"That's not why I wanted to talk to you, though, Krag. We need to make it look like all the stations in the system have been reactivated — we want to try to force Omega into a bottleneck where Draco broke the line in the last battle here. You think it'd be possible to give the appearance that the stations are online?"

Krag's mouth opened, and then hung open, seemingly in surprise.

Chronos smiled, "No rush, Krag, but we only have twenty-two hours."

Krag closed his mouth, then glanced away, presumably thinking something to one of his junior Peacelords. Then he looked back, "I've just sent a signal to my chief Telepaths. They... uh... it should just be a matter of waking the brains of the stations. And once those are active, they have systems that when powered will... give the appearance of a crew and of full effectiveness."

Chronos' eyebrows went up and he grinned, "Excellent. I knew you wouldn't let us down. You may just have saved us all, Krag — thank you."

Kragran's look of disbelief was genuine, and he managed to work his mouth, "If you like, I'm sure we could use the stations'... emitters... to project a hyperspace echo of a Krogg *fleet* into the space around them. It might help with your fiction?"

A crafty idea, but if they were only projections from stations... no, Omega would see right through them.

Chronos shook his head, "No thanks, Krag... they'd look strange tied to the space around the stations, and I doubt Omega would believe you'd rearmed a whole fleet in the meantime anyway. This should be enough — I don't want to tap out your Telepaths when you might need them to help stave off his attacks on the ground."

Krag nodded ponderously, "Very well. That all now, Chronos?"

Chronos smiled, "Yes, thank you."

He felt better as Krag vanished from the plot. When Omega arrived, the aliens would play their part in the defense of their home system, and that seemed only right. The last time they'd protected this place, it had cost a hell of a lot to take it from them. Hopefully it would be the same for Omega.

Chronos Claw returned to his chair.

Kragran left the Earther transmitter array in the Chamber of Lords and began to laugh.

The stations are activating now, m'lord. This will save us having to start them up after the fight begins.

Kragran nodded to the Warlord who made the report, *Indeed. It seems the Earthers' trust in us grows. Can't imagine more helpful timing! Has the fleet broken up to avoid those sloops?*

Kardrath appeared in Kragran's mind, as if on cue, and made his report: *We are scattered, m'lord. It seems only two sloops have come to investigate the explosion. They will not see us.*

Excellent, Kragran smiled in approval. *Can you tell me about that blast?*

There was a pause as Kardrath began sending mental images, *Many survivors. It was the flagship of First Space Lord Magnus' reinforcement force...* ENS Chimera. *My guess is the First Space Lord was trying to reach our system in advance of Omega, attempted energy-hyper in a ship of the line, and the vessel couldn't handle the strain. Likely the same problem that our researchers have documented with artificial hulls in hyperspace transit.*

But there are many survivors? Kragran sobered now, his laughter fading in the chamber.

There are — Earthers do build their ships with many redundancies. I would say that, remarkably, over ninety percent of the ship's crew survived. Including First Space Lord Magnus and his wife.

Kragran grinned — the toothy, almost sinister way Kroggs grin — and nodded, *Make them your* honored *guests on your flagship, Lord Kardrath. I want them to witness our ascent — there could be no better witnesses to it. Fortune has smiled on us today.*

Kardrath nodded, *Yes m'lord. And the plan remains the same?*

It does. Just tell the Earthers with you that… that Chronos and I have coordinated your presence there as a secret trap. That Chronos decided to tell no one so Omega wouldn't find out.

Yes, m'lord.

Kardrath vanished.

Omega was fast approaching, and Kragran's optimism grew as he turned to his fellow Warlords. Everything was coming together perfectly for them; after their long wait, at last, they would be able to restore their power and glory.

CHAPTER 50

Fox Magnus had to keep his hand on Thena's shoulder to stay upright as he walked.

The words 'what the hell were you thinking' were pouring through his mind at sluggish intervals, but he didn't have an answer. What he'd done with *Chimera* was what he always did: the daring and dapper thing, the thing that had the odds stacked against it, but which would work because he was the one trying.

This time, though, it hadn't, and he'd killed some of his crew.

Preoccupied by that thought, he kept pushing one foot in front of the next, and as Thena helped him through the black corridors of the ship that had rescued the chunk of *Chimera* they'd been in, he began to realize just what was going on. The numb ringing in his ears was fading... the effect of the blow he'd taken to the head was wearing off.

And he was on a *Krogg warship...*

He'd only been aboard a Krogg ship once before — he'd boarded one back during his days on *Atlas*, and that had been a nightmarish fight.

What the hell was one doing active now? More than one, because another one had towed his chunk of *Chimera* to *this* one...

"How... how long since we translated?" he asked in a groggy rasp.

Thena looked back with a concerned frown, "Just about five hours..."

She probably wanted to find medical attention for his head injury, but they were seemingly captives right now.

The Krogg leading them took a turn and suddenly the party stepped through a portal onto the Krogg ship's bridge, where Cruising Master Gunth already stood — not shackled or restrained in any way — with a Warlord. Er... Peacelord.

Fox tried to straighten himself up as he saw his longtime Cruising Master, but he wasn't able to correct his posture. His eyes settled on the Krogg, "Forgive my speaking, Peacelord, because I was hit on the head, but, um, what's all this?"

"I am Kardrath," the Peacelord bow-nodded, Larosian style, "and this is... part of Admiral Claw's trap for Omega. He didn't wish to alert you to our presence here, as he did not want Omega to intercept the intelligence."

Fox eyed the Krogg, then staggered forward slightly and put a hand up on the surprised alien's shoulder, "Now let me look you in the eye. Oh dear, I must be seeing double because I'm seeing two of them. So much for the head injury wearing off... there, let me look."

Settling on the real eye with his two, Fox winced slightly and stared with the intensity unique to a fox who'd recently taken a head injury.

"So you're on our side?" he asked with some unintentional swagger.

Surprised by the proximity, and fearing that the First Space Lord had seen through his deception, Kardrath nodded, "Yes, Lord Magnus. Of course we are... how could we not be?"

With a grin, Fox patted the Warlord on his shoulder and sighed, "Omega tries to make us believe the whole universe is against us. Good to have you lot back in the shooting, though. On the correct side, of course!"

He turned away from Kardrath and stumbled back to Thena and Master Gunth, both of whom helped steady him.

"Well, that's good, anyway..." he let out a relieved sigh.

His instincts were satisfied: the Kroggs weren't up to no good. The fact that they had warships was just a strange sort of thing about something or whatever...

Fox's mind drifted out of making sense.

Now he could rest...

Thena poked him, but his mind had already spiraled too far away. Frowning, she looked at Mister Gunth and shook her head. The pair traded feelings of distinct discomfort — there was *no way* this Krogg ship was part of Chronos' plan. The cat would have warned them, or at least Fox, no matter the risk.

This wasn't what it seemed. The Kroggs were up to something and that was the last thing the Earthers needed under the circumstances. But what could a few marooned officers do about it?

"Can we get some chairs, Peacelord? Fox took a heavy blow with the destruction of our ship," Thena was careful to ask cordially, and Kardrath smiled in an unsettlingly broad way.

"Of *course*, we want you to be as comfortable as possible to witness this."

The words sent a chill up Thena's spine, but as Fox started to tip towards her she had to focus on holding him upright. After the chairs grew out of the floor and she sat her husband down, she moved closer to Gunth.

The Master leaned in next to her, and waiting for the Krogg Warlord to look away, they traded whispers about what they could do.

"We take the bridge and order the Krogg ships to attack Omega?" was Gunth's question.

"We probably won't get away with it, but it's our best option," Thena agreed.

It was a long shot, but if it worked, setting the Kroggs against Omega — even for a brief moment before the old foe realized its orders were coming from imposters — could help Chronos.

If they could seize this bridge, and defeat the fourteen Kroggs on it.

Thena took a deep breath and leaned back towards Fox. She'd have to wake him up... better three Earthers than two for this mission...

Not that the odds were good. Not by a long shot.

"We're about eighteen hours from Krogg 'A'."

Graham looked up from his sword as Christine stepped into his cabin without knocking.

"Good time," he said in a monotone, looking back down at his blade as he gently rubbed a new coat of oil over it.

"You know, you don't actually need to oil Earther swords... they've been treated to be immune to corrosion..." Christine took a couple of steps forward, her eyes sizing up her ArcGeneral and his Larosian blade-cleaning kit.

Graham shook his head, "I know... just helps. Feels right to do, you understand."

Christine smiled sadly, "Of course."

She actually found an interesting word in that sentence: oiling his sword *felt* right. It might be reading too much into the choice of words to suggest that Graham was having some sort of emotional response, however mild, to the comfort of a simple activity like blade maintenance... but perhaps he was. Perhaps it was progress.

She hoped so. Either way, she was glad to be back in her own galaxy... even if she was running towards Krogg 'A'.

She had never had any interest in visiting the seat of power of the most evil foe the galaxy had seen... before Omega. Now that Omega would probably be going after it, she was even less enthusiastic about the prospect of going there... and yet she knew she had to. They'd done a great thing in keeping Omega from taking the derelict Larosian Fleet, but it'd be a worthless victory if Omega turned the Kroggs against them.

Christine had spoken to Narosh and Novash about the situation a couple of times — those Larosians had the most experience with the Kroggs, and both were wary of the possibility of seeing their great old nemesis being merged with such evil as Omega.

Christine refused to even contemplate the potential horror of such a blending. Even her new Earther-grounded calm might not withstand that sort of horror. To merge the most vicious qualities of the two greatest enemies of humanity would just be cruel... could the universe be that cruel?

The universe isn't *cruel, humans just interpret it to be so because they don't like the way events transpire. The universe isn't partial one way or the other... oh boy, listen to me... I sound like an Earther...*

And Graham is staring at me.

Indeed, Graham was standing in front of her, staring.

She blinked as she realized she'd zoned out, and she smiled and shook her head with a short wave, "Don't worry about me — I'm just... dwelling."

With a smile, Graham put his hands on her shoulders, "You're in the best condition of either of us. I'm not worried at all."

He turned back to his sword, picked it up off the table, sheathed it, and passed her as he headed out of the cabin, "I must talk to Narosh."

With a deep breath, she turned and followed, still preoccupied by her thoughts.

Narosh was on *Carnarvon's* bridge when Graham arrived, and as the alien turned and welcomed the two humans to the command deck, he ran a very quick scan of both. Christine was holding herself in check with Earther-worthy resolve, Graham seemed empty. Still.

Perhaps as they grew closer to battle, the younger Manchester's anger would bubble forth, but for the moment he remained icy. Maybe that would work to his advantage.

"We've never pushed Larosian engines this fast," the Admiral-of-a-Fleet spoke in greeting, "but we're keeping up with Admiral Maximane's squadron thanks to the speed we're managing."

"Good news," Graham observed. "We shall be there in time for any fight that breaks out."

Narosh nodded, "I do hope so. We may only be seventy ships, but my understanding is that every ship will count when battle is joined. And to be honest, I do not trust the Kroggs. I want to keep an eye on them myself."

Graham concurred, "That would seem prudent. I can't say I have confidence in them either, whatever Chronos Claw's recent opinions of them."

Narosh nodded evenly, and Christine added her own single nod as well... though she had to admit to herself that the Kroggs would probably be the least of their problems in the hours to come.

"Omega remains the priority," Graham's tone didn't waver. "We've taught him now that he isn't all-powerful and superior, we just have to reinforce that lesson."

"We will," Christine said quickly, letting her mind wrap around some of the pictures that one of the helpful Larosians on the bridge was sending to both her and Graham, showing the disposition of the seventy-ship force as it advanced. "Admiral Maximane has alerted Krogg 'A' that we're coming?"

Narosh nodded, "One of her frigates stopped and sent the pod just after we passed through the corridor. Should be there by now."

Christine nodded again. Good.

They were on their way...

CHAPTER 51

Liz Hastings glowed to life in *Formidable's* tank just as Chronos Claw turned towards it. The former ArcGeneral and President was grinning, "Did I get that right? Graham and Minnie Maximane and Narosh and Novash are coming in with seventy ships?"

Chronos smiled and nodded in return, "Indeed, and they cleaned Omega's clocks in the Larosian galaxy. Good news."

Liz nodded eagerly, "Indeed it is. Alright, I'll get back to preparations over here. We've got what... seventeen hours?"

"Just over sixteen now," Chronos replied.

"Talk to you later then," Liz vanished.

Taking a deep breath, Chronos turned back to his chair. Things weren't going all that badly. The Krogg stations appeared to be online, the various squadrons and battle groups were assembled... the defense of this system was prepared.

All he could really do now was sit and wait.

Lieutenant General Garnet Wiskar stepped into the mobile command building the engineers had set up for him on the soil of Krogg 'A', feeling more than a little apprehensive. Wiskar had known Colin Brawn quite well, and everyone knew the reputation of the Light Division — the *well-earned* reputation. Their loss at Freetown was looming larger and larger in Wiskar's mind.

His troops were good, that he knew... but he still had to be anxious.

Omega was coming in ten hours.

"Sir, Peacelord Kragthar is at one of the pickets asking for you," one of the Captains called from a nearby console, and Wiskar nodded.

Kragthar... not the head Peacelord, the liaison to the security force. Right. Garnet departed the command building almost as quickly as he'd stepped in, immediately sighting the Krogg in the distance to his right. He was surprised he hadn't noticed the Peacelord's presence on the way in, but then he was rather more preoccupied than he'd have liked.

Turning in the direction of the picket, Garnet Wiskar fell into a quick, crisp march, his rifle slung behind him as he walked across the red ground. Seeing him coming, Kragthar turned and offered a deep bow-nod.

"I have come to ask if there's anything more you need, General Wiskar.

We're quite happy to provide any further assistance at this juncture," the Krogg's manners were as impeccable as Wiskar's own.

The General delivered a smile and a curt nod as he came to a stop, "Terribly good of you to offer, Peacelord, but I do believe we're alright for the time being."

"Splendid news," the Krogg replied, selling the words as if they were natural to him.

Then something occurred to Garnet Wiskar, and he managed to keep his thoughts from changing his expression, "Perhaps you'd like to join me in the command post. I'd be honored for the company, and if we do need your help, it'd be rather handy to have you there."

Peacelord Kragthar paused for a minute — he managed to avoid looking as though he was surprised at the offer, but he was clearly not able to decide immediately. That made Wiskar wonder just why such a friendly and helpful chap *wouldn't* want to stay in the building.

Was he hiding something?

"I'd be overjoyed!" Kragthar's words were eager, and the cat sized up his liaison.

Well, it didn't *seem* like the alien had ulterior motives...

Garnet Wiskar offered a polite smile, and then gestured to Kragthar to join him in a walk back to the command building.

Admiral Garvin Jardaw came to his feet as *Medusa* returned to material state. Linking his hands behind his back, he stepped towards his new flagship's battle plot and looked over the situation before him. They had at last arrived in the Krogg system, with no sign of Fox coming up behind them... but with 1,100 plague vessels approximately two hours in their wake.

"Signals coming in, sir. Admiral Claw and Admiral Hastings," the Signal Officer's report was smooth, reflecting none of the tension of their flight from Omega.

"In the tank," Jardaw didn't look away from the holo display, and now his eyes settled on the two figures that glowed to life in the three-dimensional plot. "Good to see you both."

Chronos smiled first, "And you, Garvin. Any word on Fox?"

The polar bear shook his head, "I'm afraid not. I have to assume he's behind the Omega fleet with no way to get around."

Chronos nodded slowly, and Liz moved immediately to business — they had just two hours, after all, "We've got all the Krogg stations looking alive but not actually battle-ready, so the plan is to engage near the hyper limit first, then fall back to Draco's breach and try to trick them into a bottleneck."

Garvin blinked at the mention of the breach. It was the closest thing to a sore spot the bear had: Draco Maximane had been his friend and mentor.

Perhaps it was fitting that the site of the old lion's death would be the place Garvin made his last stand against the greatest foe in Earther history.

"Sounds fair. How many ships total now?" Garvin's eyes shifted to the tactical display floating next to his fellow Admirals in the plot and counted a few before Chronos answered.

"With you here, about 330, and Graham, Narosh and Minnie Maximane are coming in from the Larosian galaxy with seventy more. They creamed Omega out there, Garvin, and they're hoping to be here in time."

Garvin Jardaw blinked again, "Really? I'll take that good news. So three-to-one odds?"

Liz took her turn to nod, "And we're going to try using some of our unpacked sloops as energy drive rams. If we can ram the bastard's ships, that might wrong-foot him and give us a better chance to get gun-to-gun kills. Garnet Wiskar is on the ground protecting against any landings at Krogg... You know the latest about Freetown?"

Garvin looked hopeful, "Good news?"

Chronos' smile faded, "Rather the opposite. We'll send you the intel... but what matters now is that we're here, and we're ready."

A slow nod was the polar bear's reply, "Very well. I'll get my ships into position with your battle line and we can chat a bit more. But we have less than two hours before Omega arrives... and those ships of his aren't lightweights. They seem to be more Krogg than anything else... I don't even want to know what he'd be able to do if he got his hands on a planet full of biomatter."

"Let's not find out," Chronos said solemnly. "Talk to you soon."

Liz bobbed her head in agreement and then both disappeared, leaving Garvin to stare at his plot. His eyes zeroed in on the breach — Draco's breach.

I hope you're with us today my friend...

Omega was hungry for this. He wanted Krogg 'A', not just for the biomatter but also for the symbolic value. He was the biggest, baddest monster in this galaxy. The Queen had nothing on him, even though the bitch had mysteriously appeared at the same time he had. That coincidence still made him wonder, but wondering wasn't for now. She was dead, and there were Earthers to slaughter.

Conveniently, he had 1,200 (well, 1,100 since those Earther attacks, but still) of the most advanced hybrid ships in his arsenal just an hour away from Krogg, ready to do said slaughtering.

After butchering Audrey, this would be the crowning glory. And when he was finished here, the survivors of his attack force could move on through the Larosian galaxy and take or destroy everything there while he built an even *newer* black fleet from the Krogg biomatter pools.

Newer not only than the 1,100-ship force about to hit that system, but newer too than the 5,000-strong fleet of almost purely Krogg ships that was already nearing completion in Genesis space.

That's the great thing about being a fucking disease... I know how to multiply...

Omega-Natosh, standing in the now-corpse-filled Krogg War memorial on Genesis, smiled at the thought. The fleet that was about to hit Krogg didn't have a full avatar, so Omega-Natosh was handling the operation... as much as any one part of Omega's massive consciousness could 'handle' other parts.

Sometimes it even confuses me... ha!

It didn't matter. He was coming for Krogg 'A'. The Krogg Telepaths were already jamming him, which he supposed was a testament to their strength... but no matter. He was coming.

And as usual, the Earthers would have no sweet fucking clue what was happening until it was too late.

Omega is about ten minutes away now, m'lord, with five Earther ships pursuing him. We've collected the fleet at the breach coordinates as you requested. Holding formation is difficult as we're within the hyper limit, but I do believe we'll be an unpleasant surprise, Kardrath reported smoothly into Kragran's mind, and the chief Krogg Warlord nodded back.

Excellent. How are your guests?

Kardrath cast his mind's eye to the three Earthers sitting in chairs on the bridge of *Death,* allowing Krag to see them, *They are suspicious of our intentions — except for Fox Magnus, who appears to approve. But he's suffered a head injury.*

Kragran grinned, *Fox Magnus was daring enough to order his capital ship into energy-hyper, it would be typical of him to ask for help from an old enemy I think. Thank you Kardrath, I'll try not to send many orders when battle is joined. I wish you good killing, my friend.*

Thank you, m'lord. We will strike like death itself.

Krag smiled as that transmission ended, then he patched into his other leading Warlord, *Kragthar, you remain in the command centre of the Earther Marines?*

Indeed, m'lord, Lieutenant General Wiskar is an excellent host. I almost feel badly for not informing him of his... how should I put it... his irrelevance to our fate.

Krag's smile continued, *Indeed, best keep that to yourself until your legions appear, and then be most polite. Discourtesy is not tolerable.*

Kragthar telepathically chuckled, *He will be rather shocked, I think. I'll report once the action is joined.*

Excellent, think to you shortly then.

Krag let that link close as well, and then he stood alone in his command chamber, smiling as he looked out at the red soil of his world. Omega's hubris would soon be ended, and the Kroggs would rise again, thanks to all the advice and help of the Earthers.

In just about nine minutes.

•••

"...one minute."

Chronos Claw returned to his chair and sat silently, settling himself in and watching the plot.

"Still no sign of Graham's force?" he glanced at the Sensor Officer, and that cat shook her head.

His ear twitched, but he nodded. That was fine. He had 330 ships drawn up in a battle line on the edge of the Krogg system. They'd give hell to Omega at this position, then fall back to the station perimeter and Draco's breach, where they'd fight to the bitter end.

Funny, that was so very similar to how the Kroggs had handled the defense of this system the first time... but hopefully Omega didn't have energy drive, which the Earthers used to great effect in breaking the defenses.

"Have the Omega ships on short-range sensors now, sir."

Chronos nodded and took a deep breath. Someone needed to say something to the fleet. Garvin hadn't broadcast any wise words, so it was up to the longtime master of the Krogg station...

"Fleetcomm, please," Chronos came to his feet and waited for the telltale Fleetcomm chime. As all Earther ears in the system twitched and turned to speakers, Chronos took a few steps forward and closed his eyes.

"This is where we proved forty years ago that we do what we say we'll do, and that we do it in a way that reflects us. We saved Krogg 'A' because we believed that to be the right thing. Now we have to do it again. We're all probably going to die. Omega is powerful. But if we do die, we'll die throwing everything we've got at him. And for me, that'll be enough. These Kroggs we saved forty years ago have earned our trust and our loyalty. I say they're worth fighting for. So we fight for them, we fight for ourselves, we fight against Omega. And if we win, then we'll have written something into history — ours *and* his — that declares in a loud voice that we are as powerful as we say we are. We don't regret helping the Kroggs, we don't regret being out here. It makes us strong."

Chronos opened his eyes.

"All ships present starboard broadsides and prepare to roll. Time to fight."

Earthers and humans all through Krogg space roared their desperate determination.

And Omega began to decelerate.

CHAPTER 52

Omega's ships came out of flux drive and the plague surveyed the situation before him with some satisfaction. He had a hard time figuring out the Earther plan for the first few seconds, but then he noticed power emanations coming from the massive Krogg perimeter stations. They must have reactivated those old things.

Interesting... Omega pushed outward with his mind, fighting the resistance of the Krogg Telepaths in the system. The aliens were hiding something... *from the Earthers*.

"Well this will just be poetic," Omega-Natosh verbalized that thought with a smile, and light years away, his fleet formed up for the attack.

Trusting the Kroggs with pointy things and stations. How stupid of Chronos...

The Earthers were lined up out here to meet him at the edge of the system with about 330 ships... they'd probably fight for a while and then pull back to the perimeter, hoping to draw him in... or maybe hoping to force him into that breach Draco Maximane had gallantly cut with his suicidal run in *Engadine,* four decades prior.

Yes, force him in there and throw all they had at him...

Well, that meant the first thing he had to do was outrun them to the breach. If he got there first, they'd have troubles... better yet, he could send his landing force ahead...

That's what he'd do, yes.

Omega forced his nine massive minion-carrying transports back into flux drive in the blink of an eye, and they ran in-system at nearly 500 pls, diving straight through Draco's breach before the Earthers so much as realized ships had gotten behind them.

As Omega-Natosh smiled and watched in his mind's eye, his transports closed range with Krogg 'A', and his black wave warfleet moved forward much more slowly, focusing its attention on the Earther ships that sat so dumbly on the system edge.

This'd be a nice, playful fight.

He fired thousands of spines with a mental twitch, and the battle was joined.

"All ships fire canister and roll!" Garvin Jardaw, as the senior Admiral on scene, was officially in command, but the reality was that he, Liz and Chronos would all do their part.

Garvin was still hoping Fox would arrive — the dynamic little First Space Lord could always be relied on at times like this...

The Master on *Medusa's* bridge was barking orders and the *Chimera*-class ship went into a fast roll quite smoothly, spraying its port broadside load of canister to follow its starboard shot.

"All ships get moving, break by squadron and try to keep out of ramming range!" Chronos' voice came over the speakers, and Garvin simply nodded to himself.

The chain of command wasn't too relevant at this moment, but that didn't matter to the bear.

Medusa's Captain ordered the ship forward, and Garvin turned to the Signal Officer, "Let's have the *Chimeras* stick with us. Standoff range, parallel lines ahead as we engage."

Liz Hastings held onto the side of her plot as *Grimbold* surged forward with the ships of the Survey Service. The Surveyors were probably the weakest force in the fight from a technical standpoint, but she was determined that they'd make themselves felt.

Jessica Forbes was beside her at the plot, and the human Captain looked through the holo at her former ArcGeneral and smiled, "Guess we finally get to fight a battle on an Earther ship."

Liz grinned despite herself and nodded. After a whole war of watching these ships do their invincible dance, they'd finally be part of one.

"My squadron to port, kick it up to 95 pls and target the nearest formation!" Liz looked back over her shoulder, and the Signal Officer transmitted the orders.

Farley Karr had been put in command of the recommissioned ships at Chronos Claw's request, and now from the bridge of his own Survey Service 64 *Hammer*, he ordered his 113 unpacked Krogg War veterans forward.

"Follow Liz in," he turned to his Signal Officer, "Let's break by squadron and try to get around them. All ships stand by to jump in and out of energy drive."

Karl Kandam and the five ships that had been left behind the Omega formation leapt from energy drive, and on the bridge of *Namur* the panda roared his orders.

"Get us into the attack, in-and-out jumps from energy drive. We'll operate as a squadron for now!"

Those ships of the line began blazing away, joining the fight.

•••

Chronos Claw had the newest ships in the fleet at his disposal — including his eight *Venerables* and eight *Champions*.

"My frigates to join the rest of the fleet on squadron harassing action," he said in an even tone, listening as the orders were repeated. "All boats from all ships, launch and attack. My capital ships are going right down their throats."

It was an uncharacteristic plan of attack for a former sloop commander, but Chronos' blood was pumping hard.

Formidable leapt ahead and turned straight for the Omega fleet, two squadrons of mighty Earther capital ships — one of *Venerables*, the other of *Champions* — following. All around the Omega armada, ships were shifting into energy drive and popping out, avoiding counter-fire from spines and spraying their own broadsides with angry intensity.

Boats fountained from all ships now, thousands upon thousands lunging into the fray and using their guns to cut into the new Omega ships. In their traditional claw formations, they sliced their way into the black formations, and Chronos watched with narrowed eyes.

"We'll be closing to a ramming distance, sir," his Flag Captain pointed out in quiet tones, and Chronos nodded.

"I know... I know."

Omega watched and couldn't contain his laughter. The Earthers went to work the way they always had, dancing and flitting their way out of direct contact with his weapons — using energy drive to appear and disappear and not stand to receive fire.

But they weren't doing so well when it came to actually *hitting* his highly maneuverable ships, and when they did manage to land their fire, his newly-designed armor was working well. Shot was glancing off much of the time — for all their broadsides, he'd lost only six small ships so far.

It was time to make them feel the burn.

So Omega launched his hyperspace charges.

"By the Earth — *hold on*!"

Garvin Jardaw's Sensor Officer delivered the order with force, and everyone grabbed something on *Medusa's* bridge just in time for the big ship of the line to be pitched sideways by a massive hyperspace blast.

The shockwaves reverberated through the higher levels of subspace — not the layers of subspace used for travel but shallower ones — and the incredible wakes that surged from the blast sites bounced every Earther ship sideways. Those in energy drive were catapulted back into a material state by the intensity.

Garvin gritted his teeth, "Reform the lines, quickly!"

Spines were hurtling from the Omega fleet now — the plague armada was still all together in a single, strong formation, and it was coordinating fire very well...

Numerous Earther ships exploded into fireballs, less able to protect themselves from the onslaught without the benefit of a larger formation's mutual point defense.

"Pull us back into line! Return fire!" he roared.

Karl Kandam had an iron grip on the sides of his plot, and as *Namur* tried to out-maneuver the spines flying at it, he managed to stay upright. Until the moment his gallant ship vaporized all around him.

He died at his plot, the first Earther Admiral to be lost in the Krogg system since Draco Maximane. Sixteen other *Chimeras* were obliterated in the same moment.

Jessica Forbes managed to catch hold of Liz with one hand and the edge of the plot table with the other as *Grimbold* lurched sideways.

"Thirty-one of our ships got torn apart by that blast!"

Liz didn't quite register the report as she tried to get her feet under her and pull herself back to the plot. The deck stabilized enough for her to get a look at the situation... and then the words processed.

She'd lost more than half her force just like that. The old hulls, long in space and not reinforced for this new war, had been no match for the sort of shockwaves and volleys that had come at them.

"Reform," her tone was cool, detached even. "Reform and engage..."

"Admiral Kandam's ship is gone. And Captain Karr's gone, ma'am. No one's commanding the recommissions."

Just like that. Goodbye Karl, Farley...

Liz spared little time for those thoughts, "Tell the recommissions they're under my orders, all ships break by squadrons and go straight in. If he's lobbing shot like this we can't afford to try to stand off!"

The ships of the Survey Service and the recommissioned ships of the Krogg War turned fast and dove into the echelons of black vessels.

Chronos Claw stood still and watched the mayhem. He was down to 250 ships already, and they'd only killed fourteen. The gunboats were being swallowed by hails of spines like nothing he'd ever seen before. And Omega wasn't even moving.

The plague ships just stood there and waited. Taunting him.

Well that suited Chronos fine. The *Venerables* were about to prove they deserved their names. When Lang had been blindsided at Genesis, his ships hadn't been ready for action. This squadron was. Now Omega would learn the power of Earther engineering...

"Point-blank range *now*," *Formidable's* Captain looked at Chronos as he spoke.

Claw nodded immediately, "All ships, transfer secondary power to your shields."

The orders were sent out, and Chronos watched in his plot as the *Venerables* and then the *Champions* cruised single-file into the center of the mayhem. Spines started to come at them viciously as they entered the ranks of the Omega fleet, but the massive shields of these new-generation warships held firm, as they had been designed to.

The *Champions* took the hits harder, but they held for the moment too. And no Omega ships came forward to ram. Perhaps Omega didn't want to waste his precious new vessels in such a crude manner. That'd be a mistake.

Chronos ground his jaw, "All ships, open fire, maximum yield."

Instantly, the *Venerables* began to fire. With 250 quick-recharging guns on each ship, and eight ships in the formation, the weight of fire was epic. To anyone looking from the outside, the Earther ships must have appeared as though they were giving birth to *suns*. So much energy, so much blue light was pulsing from that one line...

And no matter how maneuverable, the Omega ships were being washed away by the firepower.

But not in great enough numbers.

Beyond this corner of the battle, recommissioned ships died hopeless deaths, while *Chimeras* were worn away. The *Champions* fought on, but were bludgeoned methodically, and Chronos saw it.

As the first of those ships blew up, he issued his order, "Tell the *Champions* to change vectors and get out. My squadron, all stop, we'll draw heat."

The orders were coming from Chronos Claw with blinding speed, and with that same sort of velocity the *Champions* hurried to make their escape. Six of them survived to exit the melee and regroup.

Led by *Formidable*, the *Venerables* came to a stop in space.

This was completely against combat doctrine, but it was necessary — if for no other reason than to show Omega what he'd get when Earthers knew he was coming.

"Shields at full, weapons at full. Squadron forming full diamond."

Chronos nodded once.

His squadron was now forming a three-dimensional diamond in space, with six ships on the points and two at its center. The shot seemed to fly out faster as each ship rolled and fired and rolled and fired and rolled and fired *endlessly*. The squadron's output totaled 2,250 guns, all of which recharged faster than any guns before them, and that onslaught was augmented by the vicious beams of nearly 1,000 long carronades. Omega's spines flew at this diamond in great clouds — veritable walls — but none of them struck home.

The *Venerables* made their stand.

•••

Alright, that was actually pretty impressive, Omega had to admit it. When you put the new Earther ships in a situation like this they were tough to crack. But they were firing everything they had just to keep his spines from swamping them, so he wasn't worried — no eight ships could stop him now.

He smiled. If those *Venerables* wanted to live up to their name, that was fine. The rest of the Earthers would die more easily.

And his transports were almost over Krogg now too.

This would be a good day.

CHAPTER 53

Garnet Wiskar watched the holo plot as the 250 boats protecting Krogg 'A' orbital space tried to stop the transports that seemed to appear out of nowhere. They had no luck — the boats lost half their number in a minute of action and then did the smart thing: they ran.

"Send to the orbital yards: try to stay alive and save your boats for ground support. We'll need them."

Kragthar looked at Wiskar with a serious gaze as the order was given, and the Lieutenant General frowned, "Problem, old fellow?"

"Hardly, my dear General. Just observing the situation."

Garnet actually managed a polite smile, then looked back at the plot, "They're coming down here, I'm sorry to say. And we're going to have to fight them."

Kragthar nodded, "Something like that, indeed."

Wiskar ignored the comment as the sky above began to roar.

Grimbold was smacked sideways again, this time by about seventy spines, and the ship's shields ceased to exist.

"We have to fall back!" Jessica Forbes didn't ask for permission so much as she yelled that order to the ship's Master, and just as more spines closed to point-blank range the 64 vanished into energy drive and got out of their way.

Some of the squadron followed as Liz latched onto the plot table and held herself upright, "We need to recall the recommissions. We have to get everyone to Draco's breach right now... in open space we don't stand a chance."

Under other circumstances, she might have been horrified with herself for sounding so negative before her crew... but who could deny the truth of her words today?

Their boats were all dead or dying, and only four Survey Service ships remained, along with a couple of dozen of the recommissions. For all that gallant determination, Calis Landry, Rayn Felner, Farley Karr and even Karl Kandam were gone. So was Rodney Evan-Thomas and every other officer she could think to name...

"Signal all my ships to run, and tell Garvin and Chronos to do the same!"

Garvin Jardaw watched two more of his *Chimeras* vanish and he gritted his teeth. He was down to eleven — Omega was too much for the older ships... and

Liz was running. She was right to.

"Order everyone out," Garvin's words were cold. "Get to the breach. Draw him there."

Omega watched as the Earthers fell back abruptly — all but the *Venerables* ran for that breach, clearly begging him to fall into their trap. But theirs was not a trap that could contain the black wave fleet. Sure, the spine guns on the reactivated stations could be a problem, but that breach was held only by weak Earther ships. And he could deal with those, even if they did get desperate.

So he pushed almost all his remaining ships forward… save for fifty, who stayed in a sphere around the *Venerables.*

Chronos' eyes narrowed as he watched Omega's fleet move out from around him. Not so much as a single ship in his squadron had been badly damaged, and now Omega was begging off, leaving only — *only* — fifty to contain him?

Chronos didn't know where the sheer hunger and determination that was flowing into him now came from, but it was strong. He was going to *reward* the plague's arrogance…

"Destroy this token he left us," the cat's words were sharp and low.

Fire patterns began to shift.

Omega actually turned in surprise as the first of the ships he'd left to contain the *Venerables* burst in a pyre of blood and steel. Then nine more went in the blink of an eye.

Well, that was a bit testier that he'd expected the Earthers to be, but no matter. As long as they were sitting back there, the *Venerables* meant nothing to him.

He pushed the rest of his fleet forward slowly, and he set his sights on the breach, lining his formations up into a huge column in space. They'd punch through that hole like a piston — no little stopper of 100 Earther ships would halt the advance.

"We've got 100 ships, counting the survivors from Chronos' force. That means half of what we have are new frigates and *Champions*… the rest are your *Chimeras* and my recoms. He's coming with well over 900 now," Liz was glowing before Garvin Jardaw's eyes in *Medusa's* plot, but her image was flickering in and out as *Grimbold's* transmitter array began to fail.

Jardaw nodded at the report and took a deep breath. He felt as though his spine was tingling — there was something about being here, in this breach. Where Draco had died.

"They're in column now, Garvin. Let's send our rams…" Liz was talking quickly, just in case her comm failed.

Turning to his Signal Officer, Garvin nodded once, "Order the rams to attack."

"Here goes nothing," Liz said quietly.

Omega didn't quite *see* it happen at first, but suddenly fifteen energy balls were colliding with the front end of his column.

Sloops, in energy drive...

He realized he'd failed to consider the possibility that the Earthers would dare ram *him* on his jaunt inward, and now his column seemed to scatter in the shockwave as over 100 ships at its front were incinerated in a single fell swoop.

Clever fuckers... Omega had to admit it, the Earthers weren't *bad* at this. But then they were *his* creations, after all.

And that just made it a bit more fun.

He pulled his ships back slightly and reformed the column, paying more attention now.

Did the Earthers have more rams?

There was a cheer on every Earther bridge as their plots cleared after the immense blasts. More than 100 Omega ships gone!

"That hit him!" Liz grinned over *Medusa's* plot, "Maybe we should take it to the next level, Garvin. If we hit that formation with the rest of our ships, it can't possibly stand..."

Garvin opened his mouth to say something... but closed it again. It was a tempting thought — it was how Draco had saved the battle here last time, perhaps it could be done again.

"They're pulling back, sir. Looks like we've got a minute to breathe," *Medusa's* Sensor Chief delivered the report.

Garvin nodded once, opened his mouth, and closed it again. A fleet *ram*?

Garnet Wiskar stepped outside the command dome to see if what the sensors were telling him was true. And it was.

Minions were raining from the sky. Millions of them.

"Counting four million signatures from those transports, sir. They're all dropping from about 400 meters up... no energy cushion or anything, they're just *dropping*."

That report came into Wiskar's ear through his headset. He didn't bother to reply; he just watched the spectacle, holding his mouth shut in a hollow attempt to maintain his poise.

They were landing on the shield above him and sliding down to the ground outside the perimeter. They were landing in the plains outside the perimeter. They were *falling* on his position, and hissing and thrashing as they did.

He watched them and couldn't quite believe what he was seeing.

He didn't have enough troops. Not nearly enough.

There was just no way, with so long a shield to defend...

Without really thinking about it, Wiskar began to pace toward the outer perimeter, where the marines were stretched out in their thin line. Each Earther was twenty meters from the next one in the battalion — there was no shoulder-to-shoulder formation like there had been during the landing against the Queen. There was no way to mass fire against that many Omega minions...

But he had to try. He had to do something. And if the shield held, then with time perhaps even his 10,000 marines could slowly wear down these invaders.

"Shield's beginning to drop. Down one percent... one point one percent... one point four..."

Wiskar's gait didn't change as the words came into his ear. What could he say? The shield, even with the massive reactors they had powering it, was a finite barrier — it could only take so much.

He heard some energy shot overhead — the deafening roar of energy bolts searing through the air as gunboats hurled their fire through the Omega rain. Thousands of minions were probably killed... but clearly not enough.

Then a gunboat, covered by minions, appeared in the distance, a trail of smoke coming out of its port side.

It was going down... and it was coming right at Garnet.

The shield emitter won't survive an impact from a crashing gunboat...

"I need three battalions of reserve troops to my position now, if you please," his words were calm and clipped, and there were 'yes sirs' in his ear as Earther marines, despite the spectacle above them, sprinted forward from the inner perimeter and began to form up near the command dome.

They moved quickly. By the time that gunboat — now reduced to a flaming wreck — slammed into the shield that Garnet had been walking towards, they were in a three battalion shoulder-to-shoulder line, ready to advance.

The explosion was, by ground warfare standards, enormous, and it blasted Omega minions back from around the perimeter with its power. Inside the shield dome, the Earthers felt nothing; the powerful barrier had absorbed all the shock.

But now the emitter that had taken the brunt of the blast gave out, having endured far more punishment than it should have.

"We need to restore that shield, my friends," Garnet turned and waved to the reserve battalions as he spoke into his headset. "Forward at the double quick!"

The five marines that had been assigned to that section of the shield were at the breach immediately, standing firm as if they alone could stem the tide of Omega. Fortunately for them, the minions had been blasted back by the power of the explosion; the defenders had breathing room, and they took advantage of it. One of them — luckily enough an engineer — rushed to the shield emitter's location and pulled a fresh one out of his backpack.

As he knelt to place the new one, though, nine minions were suddenly upon him, and he was dragged out into the cloud of dust that had been kicked up by the impact.

And then with great hissing, the waves began to push through the breach.

Garnet Wiskar stopped in his tracks and opened fire, and the 1,500 marines behind him did the same.

Omega came on.

CHAPTER 54

"New ships coming in! Pennant of Rear Admiral Maximane and Admiral-of-a-Fleet Narosh!"

The abrupt and plainly excited report stopped Garvin Jardaw from having to say anything about ordering his fleet to ram. The words 'Rear Admiral Maximane' sent a chill through him, and then he realized — just as Minnie Maximane appeared in the plot before him — that they didn't refer to his old friend Draco.

"Minnie," he managed to say as the lioness appeared. He'd known this fine officer since she'd been a cub and he'd been her father's First Lieutenant.

"Good to see you, Garvin. My ships are coming in under energy drive to your position, and the Larosians are riding in from the hyper limit."

Still in the plot, Liz managed a smile, "That's seventy more... got anything else for us Minnie?"

The lioness smiled, "Good luck, I hope."

"I'll take it," Garvin nodded.

"Is that *Formidable* and Chronos' squadron back there?" Narosh frowned at the mental pictures he was seeing, and Graham nodded.

"It appears to be. He's doing some very fine killing."

Christine had shed her breastplate to be sure she got clear telepathic images while on the bridge, and she nodded now, "Good work... but look at the holding force in the gap there. Doesn't look like they'll last long against Omega's column."

Narosh nodded, "Indeed."

Switching to telepathy, he broadcast his order, *All ships, best speed to that breach. Battle configuration — we're just in time.* Once again, then, he used his voice, "We'll be there in moments."

Led by *Carnarvon*, the Larosian ships surged in-system.

"Sir, report that the minions have broken through the shield on the surface of Krogg 'A'!"

The Signal Officer on *Formidable's* bridge didn't bother to hide the urgency of the report, and Chronos frowned. Damn, so much for their stand in space.

"Order squadron to energy drive. Give me 600 pls, put us over that shield dome in lowest possible orbit. Stand by for ground support fire."

The *Venerables* left the fight in a flash.

"Omega's coming forward again," Liz said in *Medusa's* plot, and Garvin's eyes darted to the tactical section of the display. Like a slow battering ram, the plague was advancing.

"Some of us ram?" Liz asked then, quietly. "*Grimbold's* not in condition to do anything else."

The Omega ships accelerated, and Garvin didn't know what to say to Liz. The reinforcements had just arrived... all seventy of them, in two separate groups...

They weren't enough, though. Not to fight conventionally.

"Garvin," Liz's voice came over the plot again, and the polar bear locked eyes with her.

"Liz... it's up to you."

Liz Hastings had fought many battles, dating right back to the days when the Larosians — part of the cavalry now trying to rescue this situation — were her foes.

As Garvin's sad eyes met hers in *Grimbold's* battle plot, she swallowed, and then looked up through the plot at Jessica Forbes, "All hands abandon ship. I'll do this myself."

Jessica Forbes met her Admiral-ArcGeneral-President's gaze, and then shook her head, "I don't think the crew would stand for that, ma'am."

Those simple words brought a smile to Liz's face, and she nodded, "Target a ship at the front of the column. And give me a link to *Carnarvon.* I need to talk to Graham immediately."

She looked back down at Garvin's image in the plot, "It's been a real honor to fight alongside Earthers today, Garvin. It's... it's the way I'd have chosen to go..."

Standing on his bridge, Garvin opened his mouth to say something, but somehow he couldn't find any words. For the second time in this breach, he'd be losing a comrade in a ram. For the second time he was hearing a last message that carried so much significance with it.

"They're surging ahead now, sir!"

He heard that report distantly, and it took him a second to shake his mind back into tactical thought. His eye flicked to the plot, expecting to see *Grimbold* surging ahead.

Instead he saw an Omega destroyer racing at *Medusa*, and in that same second he felt the ship twist under his feet in an attempt to evade.

The attempt failed, and Garvin Jardaw's eyes darted back to Liz's, "They're ramming — you have to move now or—"

Medusa was obliterated under his feet. Garvin Jardaw, the great polar bear Admiral, died in almost the same spot that had claimed his old friend Draco Maximane.

"They're coming in fast — ramming now!"

Liz's eyes went wide as Garvin evaporated from her plot. Her head whipped around to look at the Sensor Officer as he made that report, and then *Grimbold* hurled itself sideways to avoid the first charging Omega ship.

"I guess he decided ramming was fair game..." Jessica said, and then a glancing impact from one of Omega's ships blew out the power relays on *Grimbold's* bridge. A piece of shrapnel wedged itself in the chest of the veteran Captain, and she dropped with eyes wide in surprise, clutching the end of the shrapnel as it stuck out through the front of her uniform.

Another piece of shrapnel sliced off Liz's leg — the leg Elandra Caine had once grown for her. She toppled to the deck with a wail of pain, then somehow hauled herself up as *Grimbold* went into a fatal spin.

Her plot was dead, there was no one to talk to, and there was no way she was going to manage a ram.

"Abandon ship!" she barked, and some of the Earthers from nearby consoles rushed to help her and Jessica. She tried to shoo them away but they were insistent... not that it'd make a difference. Liz knew Omega was right on them.

Another blast rocked *Grimbold*, and more shrapnel flew. Liz didn't even seen the piece that knocked her out. Her ship came apart shortly thereafter.

CHAPTER 55

"Back to the secondary line — we can't hold them here!" Lieutenant General Garnet Wiskar's orders were shouted over a din of hissing. There was no way his reserve of 1,500 could close the breach in the shield.

"Evacuate the forward command post, stand by to transfer all power to the secondary line shields as soon as we're through..."

The reserve battalions that had come forward and formed a line at the breach now turned and sprinted, and Garnet meant to follow. As Earthers all across the perimeter fell back to a smaller, secondary shield ring, he too turned and began to run.

In his haste, he didn't see Kragthar, and so he ran right into the Peacelord.

Stopping in surprise, he looked up at the Krogg, "Kragthar, we have to move *now*."

Smiling in his unsettling alien way, the Krogg both thought and spoke his reply, *"Now's the moment, m'lord Kragran."*

Over Krogg 'A', *Formidable* and its squadron came out of energy drive in a burst of speed, and their shot smashed the Omega transports that hung over the planet

"Get us into close bombardment range. We have to force them back," Chronos' words were cool.

"Omega's fleet just punched through the breach, sir... I don't see any pennants from our flag officers. Only about twenty of our ships are left..." the report from the Sensor Officer drew Chronos to look at a different part of the plot, and his breath caught.

Liz, Garvin, Karl... gone.

He'd known they probably wouldn't live... but knowing... they...

Locking out those losses, Chronos forced himself to think. Narosh was here, as was Minnie Maximane... they could try to hold the breach. They were moving towards it...

But 700 Omega ships were already *through* it, and inside the perimeter of stations. The plague could come straight for Krogg 'A', and with that many ships dominating the space over the planet...

Well the Allies had to try, "Signal to Admiral Narosh and Maximane to do everything they can to hurt that bastard... all ships left over from the original blockade force to regroup, as quickly as possible."

The orders went out.

Standing in his command chamber, which had been designed to emulate the massive telepathic-enhancing abilities of the Queen's chamber, Warlord Kragran smiled at the mental picture forming in his mind.

Omega had come through the perimeter. At last.

And at the same time, Kragthar reported that the minions had breached the Earther shield. Perfect. Omega was totally committed, and the Kroggs held all the power.

Now was his time to reveal the might of the Krogg people. Omega, the Earthers and now even the Larosians would be present to see this ascent.

Begin saturation broadcast. Everyone must hear this!

"Huge power broadcast coming from *Krogg,* sir!"

Chronos was gripping the sides of his plot, but that report drew his stare away from the icons of his ships, "Excuse me?"

Kragran's voice was suddenly everywhere.

It boomed through massive speakers grown out of the biomatter pools on the planet. It boomed over every comm in the fleet. And it roared in Omega's mind.

Omega stopped — he froze everything in place and smirked, waiting with amused curiosity to see what the Kroggs had to say. This would be a hoot.

Kragran looked up at the black, pulsing walls and ceiling of his chamber, and he smiled, "Omega, welcome to Krogg space. I suggest you enjoy the time you have here, because you will never return. And soon all your ships and minions will be dead."

Omega-Natosh, standing back in the war memorial on Genesis, grinned. Ooh melodrama was good. His reply boomed back — he sent it over comms, over accessible minds, and on the surface of Krogg 'A', he had a million minions hiss it back together in stereo.

"You know, I doubt that. How about this? You let me kill the Earthers and I'll let some of you live free. I don't want you spoiling my fun right now."

Chronos' mouth fell open — what the *hell* was going on now?

Standing on the bridge of *Death,* Kardrath smiled as he looked back at Fox, Thena and Master Gunth, "I must say, I was lying earlier. Your Earther friends had no idea that we had *2,000 ships of war* ready to fight today. And twelve million warriors. Please enjoy the show while it lasts."

Fox was still out of it — he just looked up and smiled, "It'll be a good one."

Thena looked at Gunth, they nodded to each other, and launched themselves out of their seats, trying to reach the Peacelord.

They hit him full force… and a personal shield — an *Earther-style personal shield* hummed as they bounced off.

Dropping to a heap on the floor, they glared up at a chuckling Kardrath.

"Really, that wasn't necessary," he smiled. *All ships, exit hyperspace.*

"By Praaxus' soul…"

Narosh's mouth dropped open and he started to feel slightly light-headed as the hyperpoints opened. From here — from *within* the hyper limit — Krogg ships began to pour. Hundreds… thousands…

The Larosian Empire was in no condition to fight this war again. No. No…

In an instant he cursed himself, and cursed Setter Caine, and wished he'd done his duty the last time he'd been in this system — that he'd destroyed these monsters forever.

But he hadn't… and now… the old nemesis was pouring ships out of hyperspace. Those ships filled the space all around Draco's breach.

And they kept coming.

Garnet Wiskar stepped back from Kragthar and his instincts flared. No longer thinking of Omega, he dropped his rifle and instantly drew his sword, "What's going on?"

The Warlord before him smiled, "Wanted to tell you earlier my friend, really did. But had to wait until there was no opportunity for escape."

As he said the words, the Krogg tapped a black band on his wrist, and the unmistakable blue glow of a shield formed around his body.

Garnet managed not to look startled — a testament to his poise, "Rather surprised to see you have one of those."

Kragthar managed a shrug, "We've had forty years to learn why we lost the Queen's War, and your people have been very obliging about sharing knowledge."

Garnet Wiskar didn't know what to say.

"But that's a conversation for another time," Kragthar said comfortably, then looked down at the ground and his eye narrowed. "You'll want to move about six meters to your right."

Wiskar opened his mouth to say something — to question or object — but realized there would be no point. So he turned to his right, walked six meters, and stopped.

"Perfect," Kragthar smiled. *Emerge now, my legions!*

The ground where Wiskar had been standing suddenly fell in… the mouth of a tunnel being collapsed in a flash. All around the perimeter, tunnels were opened.

And out poured Krogg warriors.

Real Krogg *warriors*.

Thousands. Hundreds of thousands. Millions.

Chronos Claw stood on *Formidable's* bridge and was certain he felt his heart stop.

Thousands of Krogg ships. Millions of Krogg warriors.

How… how had he missed it? Why hadn't he looked closer? His instincts… he should have trusted them!

There was no hope now. No hope at all.

His knees felt weak, so he held himself upright with his hands welded to the plot. His head spun. He didn't know what to do.

Omega stopped grinning.

"Well… that's a bigger military than I figured you had. Guess the Earthers were even more incompetent than I thought when it came to keeping an eye you."

Kragran looked down from the ceiling and glanced out a window at the red soil of his beloved homeworld, "We've learned a great deal from them, including some breeds of subtlety."

Omega was impressed.

"Clearly. Well at least I know you'll kill them all for me. Then when *I'm* done with Earth, I'll be coming for you. Don't forget it."

Krag's eye narrowed.

Chronos took a deep breath and closed his eyes.

Narosh felt all the anger of the old days bubble though him anew.

Fox Magnus straightened up in his chair, "Wait, he thinks you're trying to *kill us?*"

Kardrath glanced at the First Space Lord and replied with a shrug, "I can understand how he'd make the mistake. We did spend a lot of time trying to kill each other."

Snorting a laugh, Fox nodded, then leaned back in his chair and closed his eyes.

•••

"You think that we wish ill on the Earthers?" Kragran actually started to laugh as he asked the question. "Good grief, I expected more from you."

Omega paused, "Clearly. You've built that fleet… what other reason…?"

Kragran laughed louder, "We want to restore our power. To be friends and allies to those who saved us from the Queen's ambitions. To show the Earthers that they were mistaken in thinking we could not be trusted to stand beside them in a fight against you. To demonstrate our power. Sounding good so far?"

Then the laughter faded, and Krag's words became serious, "You've spent a lot of time trying to convince the Earthers that all their good efforts of the past four decades have been for naught. That their deeds… like saving my people… have been futile, or worse. Well we, the Krogg people, disapprove of your petty attempts. And while you are clearly very, very strong, we are strong too. And we mean to fight you, and to *reward* our friends for their kindnesses. We are not your food, Omega. We are your enemy's ally. We are *your* enemy."

Omega froze.

"Oh. Shit."

Krag smiled viciously.

"You really might want to consider improving your language. The Earthers taught us about that too. But don't mistake me, Omega. We're still *Kroggs*. We still *love* to *kill*. We just need a good reason… and you, my dear plague… you qualify as a very good reason."

Omega-Natosh's smirk was gone, and reaching across space he tried to figure out how to extricate his ships… but they were within the perimeter of Krogg defense stations… and now a Krogg fleet three times the size of his own was blocking the only clear way out.

He'd have to scatter the black wave, try to slip its ships between stations…

But the Kroggs… the bastard Kroggs… they'd trapped him.

How did they do this to me?

Krag's next orders went out both telepathically and verbally, and they lost all relationship to the carefully machined English that the Peacelord… Warlord… had worked on for forty years. They emerged as a feral hiss — the Krogg sound that had once tormented the galaxy.

Omega minions mimicked this hiss, but theirs was a pale imitation of the genuine article.

Looking skyward again, and with a smile that hungered for carnage, Kragran did not spare the melodrama: "*Dessstrooy him!*"

The Krogg armada leapt into action.

The Krogg legions surged upward from their tunnels.

Every Earther, human, and Larosian left alive in local space stood still, completely disbelieving.

CHAPTER 56

For the first time since he'd been victimized by the Earthers' immune systems seven centuries prior, Omega didn't know quite what was happening. Indeed, it seemed the only people in the Krogg system with an inkling of what was going on were Kragran, his Warlords, and for some reason, Fox Magnus.

As Thena tried to peel herself off the floor of *Death's* bridge, Kardrath extended a hand and helped her up, "Sorry I had to be cryptic with you earlier. With Omega this close, we've been a little paranoid about thinking our plans too loudly. Now we have him trapped."

Thena's mouth was hanging open, and Cruising Master Gunth sidled over to her with a frown, "You've been secretly rearming and used Omega's arrival as a chance to reveal that... while proving you're on our side?"

Kardrath managed a pretty good shrug, and Thena and Gunth exchanged surprised — and not quite convinced — glances.

"If you'll excuse me," Kardrath nodded to them both, then turned back to the front of his bridge. He'd actually begun delivering telepathic orders to his fleet while he'd been talking to the Earthers, but now he had to focus. Thanks to the losses the Earthers had already inflicted on the plague, the Krogg Fleet benefited from a nearly three-to-one advantage, but Kardrath knew he couldn't afford to be distracted when challenging Omega.

The two Earthers backed towards their chairs, clearly still not believing what they'd been told.

Thena glanced back at Fox, "Can you believe this?"

Fox opened his eyes and blinked a few times, "Believe what? Oh, that they're on our side? Well why not? They do owe us one. And I think we're pretty likable."

Frowning, Thena glanced back up at Gunth.

Then *Death* rolled.

Garnet Wiskar watched Kroggs pour from the ground, and each one that saw him nodded to him with due respect to his rank, and telepathically saluted Kragthar.

"Think we surprised them, General Wissskar?"

Garnet blinked twice, "Rather think you surprised all of us, Peacelord Kragthar."

Kragthar smiled and looked down at the cat, "It's actually Warlord, officially, General. Peacelord sounds... well, rather awkward, I think."

Garnet Wiskar only managed to nod — this was completely surreal.

The Kroggs hissed and a chill went down his spine — it was a hiss louder and stronger than the one that had crossed the Queen's plateau during the landings there...

And it was charging away from him.

Not quite realizing what he was doing, Garnet sheathed his sword and just stood still, hands at his sides.

"Sir, are they... friendly?" the question came into his ear from one of Fourth Division's Colonels, still waiting at secondary shield line.

Wiskar didn't answer at once. Instead he was watching the Krogg legions roam forward, each soldier with its customary four arms, as tall as a mid-sized bear, and as fast as lightning. But they were moving with a precision that Garnet Wiskar had never before seen in Krogg infantry.

The Omega minions watched them come, and Omega-Natosh inexplicably kept his ground forces frozen in place as he watched them charge... then he launched them into action. Mutated minions crouched a little lower, countered Krogg hisses with their own, and began to surge forward again.

"Sir?" the question repeated.

"Hold your ground, all divisions... don't attack the Kroggs. Unless they attack you..." he glanced up at Kragthar, and the Peace... er... Warlord flashed what looked like an evil smile, then nodded.

"I... think they're with us."

"Understood. Cautious allies..."

Garnet wasn't listening anymore. His eyes were locked on a spectacle that was quite unlike anything he had ever seen.

The Kroggs were going to war with Omega.

As Kragthar's troops advanced, Garnet realized they were shaking themselves into rough assault columns, with as much coordination as Earthers might have had under the circumstances.

"Hope you don't mind, General, but we borrowed some unit tactics from you as well. We expect they'll serve us well," Kragthar crossed all of his arms as he said that, his smile remaining.

"Help yourself," Wiskar's answer was barely audible. The Kroggs were certainly doing just that.

Their columns slammed forward, moving with blinding speed, closing the gap to the minions... and the Omega minions launched themselves against the columns like beasts.

That visual caused something in Wiskar's mind to click. Omega against the Kroggs... it put the real enemy into clear contrast with the former one. For decades Krogg warriors had been remembered as the greatest enemy of the

Earthers. Even up until now, as Omega used Krogg biomatter to augment his minions, *Krogg* had been a word that in so many ways implied 'adversary'.

But watching Krogg warriors colliding with Omega minions made the distinction rather clear. Kroggs were friends. They were fighting Omega... and Omega wasn't pulling any punches. As Wiskar watched those monstrous plague soldiers piling onto the Krogg columns, his eyes widened at the spectacle. The Krogg formations looked as though they'd be absorbed...

Please, please. Good luck, please...

Kragthar's smile broadened.

The minions exploded away from the columns, powerful blows from the Kroggs tossing them aside like toys. With hisses growing louder, the warriors threw themselves into the fray, their columns shattering into thousands of sections — not just groups, but small organized fighting units.

The Omega minions tried to overwhelm these squads.

Garnet found his hand on the hilt of his sword again. He watched in the distance as the minions pounced on Kroggs and pounded on the warriors' personal shields, and he was sure he saw some of those shields drop... but it didn't matter. Krogg carapaces were just as tough as ever, it seemed. Even when the shields went down, they were well protected against the minions' assault...

And the Kroggs still had their bone blades. Those weapons, the old enemy of the Earther marines, went to work against the minions.

For all their Krogg-type enhancements, Omega's soldiers were still modified Genesis humans underneath. While the carapaces they'd grown were enough to defend against energy weapons, they lacked the rigidity to withstand the brute force of a warrior bent on breaking them.

"We've come a ways since the Queen's War. Genetic upgrades have made our carapaces tougher than theirs," Kragthar explained helpfully. "That and we still train in the carapace-breaking traditions of our ancestors. Remember, before the Queen unified us, we used to fight each other. We know the weaknesses of the exoskeleton."

Garnet nodded very slowly as he watched the Krogg soldiers in action. Their blades, instead of trying to slash, were piercing — like pickaxes driving into stone, or the beaks of seagulls lancing into crabs.

The minions were falling in heaps.

Drawing his sword again, Garnet found himself tapping his comm, "Fourth Division, charge."

"Sir?"

The fact that the order was questioned was evidence enough of the shock that gripped every Earther on the ground.

"If the Kroggs are going to turn on us, it won't matter if we're next to them, or standing back here. So let's trust them," Garnet's tone was unusually frank. He looked up at Kragthar again, "Care to join me, Warlord?"

A slim column of Earther marines sprinted forward past the two infantry commanders, and Kragthar nodded, "My pleasure!"

They raced off to do some killing.

CHAPTER 57

Chronos Claw wasn't sure what he thought or felt. Too much was happening right now. Liz, Garvin and Karl were gone. There was no sign of Fox Magnus at all. And the Kroggs had a fleet of more that 2,000 ships and were fighting against Omega as allies of the Earthers? It was pretty much inconceivable...

"All ships hold position for a minute," Chronos' earlier fury had faded away. He really didn't know what to do except watch.

We have them trapped within the station perimeter. They'll probably try to scatter, so we must fall on them now, while they're concentrated. Remember they are vicious fighters: close and engage by squadron.

Kardrath's orders to his fleet reflected some prudent caution: the Kroggs had numbers here, but one of the greatest lessons they'd learned from their war against the Earthers was that sending more ships wasn't always the formula for victory. Tactics and good sense counted for so much more.

Krogg squadrons advanced in line ahead, and Omega's ships unfroze and began to attempt to scatter. In small groups they might be hoping to penetrate the station perimeter — a foolish and vain hope, but one the plague was evidently entertaining.

It wouldn't matter, though.

Coordinated with Earther-style precision, the Dreadnoughts and Superdreadnoughts of the new fleet tore into the Omega black wave, and in their first taste of battle in forty years, the Kroggs gave as good as they got.

Spines lanced back and forth through space, and neuro pulses cackled silently through the blackness. Krogg warships, organic to the core, tensed, sprinted, sometimes writhed, and then some began to die.

But they fought hard.

Omega-Natosh scrambled... he needed options. Telepaths controlled those vessels... perhaps he could jam their controls...

Reaching out to Krogg ships, Omega felt his attempts blocked. Those ships now had multiple Telepaths aboard... dammit.

If he took his time and focused, he could break through their defenses... but he didn't have time to focus. The Kroggs were coming too damned fast...

These bastards...

•••

Death and the other seven Hyper Motherships joined the fight with a furor. Each of those ships was like an old Mothership, but many times the size. They mounted numerous spine batteries as well — batteries very similar to those on the defense stations. The result was mobile firepower to rival that of the *Venerable*-class ship of the line.

Bring us in close to the core concentration, all batteries into rapid fire, Kardrath gave that order to his squadron's Captains, and they obeyed.

The Hyper Motherships sprayed their spines, and the machine-gun-like bursts of those projectiles shattered any Omega ship they caught.

The audience aboard *Death* heartily approved, "Top notch shooting!"

Blinking his single eye, Kardrath looked sideways and down, and found dapper little Fox Magnus standing next to him with a grin, watching crude displays projected on the front wall of the bridge for the Earthers' benefit.

With his smile broadening at the approval, Kardrath persisted in his orders, *Destroy the plague. Savor his death!*

All ships full stop!

Narosh didn't know how to react. These were his enemies... a race he'd fought for centuries, and which had effectively shattered his Empire, indirectly or directly. He should attack them... but he shouldn't...

The answer wasn't clear to him. What... who was he to...

Graham put a hand on Narosh's forearm, snapping the Admiral-of-a-Fleet out of his thoughts. The Larosian's eyes shifted immediately to the human, and then something else was suddenly wrong. A hungry smile was spread across Graham's face, and the junior Manchester's thoughts almost seemed to reach into Narosh's mind.

This is the other shoe dropping. Let Omega learn the price of hubris.

Narosh stared at Graham for a moment.

All ships... reprioritize to Omega ships. And advance. The Kroggs... share our foe.

If the Kroggs turned on the Larosians next, then cruising into the midst of this fight would be certain death... and yet Narosh gave the order anyway...

Begging your pardon, Admiral-of-a-Fleet, but we are indeed on your side.

Narosh frowned, wondering which of his crew had thought that.

Not one of your crew, in fact. Warlord Kardrath, of the Krogg Navy. I am pleased we're meeting under different circumstances this time... when last you were here, we were enemies. That is no longer the case.

Narosh's mind froze. He'd been infiltrated. The command and control of his force was at risk — if a Krogg was in his mind...

Probe deeply into my mind, Admiral-of-a-Fleet, and you will find my claims to be true. You don't have to worry about us.

No. Surely not. But... no. No...

But perhaps...

Narosh peered into the suddenly-accessible mind of the Krogg, marveling at the creature's much-enhanced telepathic discipline. In the old wars, the Kroggs had lacked the mental strength and focus to pierce Larosian thoughts over great distances.

We've worked on communications — it was one of the problem areas we identified when we audited our performance against the Earthers.

Narosh dove deeper. And deeper. As Krogg ships spat spines and dodged counter-fire, he threw himself unopposed into the very core of the Krogg Warlord commanding them.

And what he saw startled him. The Earthers had imprinted upon the Kroggs, as surely as a new Queen would have. The menacing beast aliens had adopted many Earther-like characteristics... but the hunger for death and killing remained.

Could that be compatible with the Earther way? At this moment, did that even matter?

Narosh decided it did not, because one thing was clear as he went deeper: the Kroggs no longer saw him as an enemy. Or the Earthers as an enemy.

They wanted to join the Allies. To be a strong power among others...

They wanted to change sides.

No, they *had* changed sides.

It was quite an about face... and was too complicated to study carefully at the moment. But it felt valid. The Earther blood in Narosh's veins seemed to flare approvingly as it met some Krogg instincts, and his mind found nothing but truth in Kardrath's.

The Kroggs are with us, Narosh thought simply to his ships. *Cooperate with them, and destroy the plague ships.*

The Larosians were rightly stupefied, but they pressed forward to the attack all the same.

"Narosh is going right in," Chronos Claw stared at his plot. *Formidable* was still standing in Krogg 'A' orbit, but the Krogg legions below the great ship's hull made it clear the guns of his squadron weren't needed there.

And while it appeared the Krogg Navy didn't need assistance either, the remaining Earther ships left here could do more good helping against Omega's fleet than against Omega's soldiers.

"Send orders to all ships, attack Omega. Destroy Omega. Squadron, let's get back there, 500 pls."

Thena Magnus came to stand next to her husband as *Death* hurtled through the fray, and she watched the slightly haphazard mishmash of images that were projected onto the front wall of the ship's bridge for the Earthers' benefit.

It was stunning.

Not since the last battle here had so many ships fought so neatly in squadron order… but back then it had been Earther ships with the organization, and the Kroggs being caught in disorganized hordes.

The firepower of *Death* itself was… like death itself.

Thena allowed herself that bad pun, because it was so accurate.

Standing beside the shocked Earthers, Kardrath watched the unfolding engagement in his mind.

Omega's remaining ships were writhing, trying to twist away from his grasp, and they were certainly causing the Krogg Fleet harm — Kardrath's new Navy was losing at least one ship for every one it destroyed.

But those were ratios the Krogg Navy could afford here. And the satisfaction of destroying Omega was worth the losses. For decades the Kroggs had enjoyed no killing: now they were making up for lost time.

Continue to maneuver carefully — and beware of rams!

Spines continued to spit from his ships in fast volleys, and neuro pulses shattered the blackness at point-blank range. Omega's spines and lasers shot back.

And then the Larosians dove into the fight, Narosh and his crews convinced — at least for the moment — that the Kroggs were no longer their nemesis. And the Earthers appeared back in Draco's breach, led by *Formidable.*

Omega must have seen the vice closing around him, because in a single great motion, half his formation scattered, many ships running in ones and twos for the perimeter of stations that trapped them, while others remained as a sacrificial diversion at the center of the Krogg Fleet's fire.

That was fine, he could try to run, but his attempt would fail.

Stand by on station batteries.

The stations had been silent so far, their threat having the desired effect of controlling where Omega moved his ships… but now the Kroggs would be able to remind the plague of just why Draco's breach was so significant. The spine guns on those stations were vicious and devastating.

Fire at will.

Machine-gun bursts of huge spines began to stream from the globe of stations, tracking quickly and accurately and managing to catch all the ships — *all* the ships — that Omega had sent to escape. The Telepaths commanding those stations had worked long and hard on their coordination, and it was paying off.

It helped, of course, that Omega's black wave ships were no match for the spines those batteries fired. No vessels were a match for them.

Kardrath smiled as the fleeing plague was shattered — a very satisfying kill. No matter how the Kroggs evolved, that primal joy of inflicting death could never be taken from them.

CHAPTER 58

Garnet Wiskar cut and slashed a few more minions, and then his progress slowed as he realized the ground around him was no longer swimming with Omega soldiers.

There were two Earther bears with him — they'd instinctively attached themselves to him as the division had charged. Kragthar was about ten meters off to the left, with three of his warriors... and there were no more Omega minions nearby. The hissing had moved off into the distance, as the Kroggs drove their new adversaries back, and tore them apart.

As Garnet watched, Omega minions threw themselves at the Krogg warriors... it was almost like watching wolves trying to tackle moose — the minions lacked size and strength compared to their targets. But unlike moose, the Kroggs could fight back with deadly blades, blinding speed, and a hunger for killing that rivaled Omega's own.

That hunger was definitely there — Garnet's instincts were distinctly recognizing it, even from the distance at which he was watching the fight. The Kroggs were *enjoying* this, which was somewhat unsettling...

But his instincts weren't telling him that they were a threat, just that they liked killing. Could they like killing and yet somehow not be a threat?

Kragthar and his escorting warriors arrived alongside Wiskar, and the two bears flanking their General eyed the Kroggs warily as they approached. Old habits could take a few minutes to die, even among Earthers: the Kroggs *might* still be the enemy.

"Good killing, General!" Kragthar called happily, examining his carapace as he did. "I do find killing while wearing a shield to be quite antiseptic, though. It's doesn't feel the same as being covered in the blood and gore of one's enemy. Less personal."

"Cuts down our laundry bills," Wiskar's reply was smooth and surprised even him with its casualness. "I must ask, Kragthar... you do seem to be quite enjoying the carnage..."

The Krogg laughed, "We've learned much from you, my dear fellow. But we still do hunger to kill. I'm afraid that's a desire buried deep in us, as I suspect it may be in you. But like you, we've chosen to control that urge. You see, we cannot find a kill satisfying unless we believe the victim deserves to die."

Wiskar's eyebrow went up slowly and he looked squarely at his Krogg counterpart, "So what happens if there isn't any killing to be done? Do you get frustrated?"

Kragthar shrugged, "It's been forty years since our last kills... we've held out quite well, I think."

"Fair point," Garnet Wiskar's reply was cautious.

Perhaps it was alright to have a deep-seated desire to kill in one's nature, if it was controlled. Very different from the Earthers... despite what the Kroggs might assume about the influence of the Earthers' animal ancestry.

"I should probably get back to the command post, see what the overall situation is," Wiskar looked back toward the abandoned Earther building. "Since your warriors have things in hand, Kragthar. Do you mind?"

The Warlord smiled and bow-nodded, Larosian style, "Not at all. If you don't mind, though, I want to get more killing in while I can."

Garnet managed an awkward smile, "Suit yourself, of course."

With a curt nod, the Krogg led his soldiers after the fight, which was being driven further and further away.

Wiskar and his two escorts watched the Kroggs run off, then headed for the command post.

Chronos Claw stood at his plot with his hands linked behind his back, and he smiled.

Kroggs, Larosians and Earthers were pouring all manner of hell into the scattered remnants of Omega's black wave fleet, and while the plague was certainly getting his shots in, there was no way he could win now.

"We're closing in," *Formidable's* Captain drew Chronos' attention to a corner of the plot, and the Admiral's eyes darted over to that section.

With his smile broadening, he nodded, "Bring us alongside those Motherships, let's add to that considerable firepower."

"Would you look at that... er... in your mind," Christine couldn't help but be impressed.

Carnarvon was pushing in close to Omega ships now, taking advantage of the disorder created by the Krogg attack to get into point-blank range unscathed. The great Larosian battlewagon was spraying forth massive amounts of antimatter and missiles.

But nothing the Larosians had could match the mighty firepower coming from the new Motherships and the *Venerables* alongside them. It was almost impossible to tell which ships were reaping more destruction, but it was quite clear that both squadrons were proving to be devastating.

"The Krogg *Hyper* Motherships," Narosh nodded in agreement at Christine's words, then he spared her a glance and a smile. "I am certainly quite *glad* they're on our side."

Christine matched his smile, and followed it with a friendly pat on the arm.

Then she glanced in the opposite direction, to discover that Graham was smiling... coldly smiling. He wasn't saying anything, he was just enjoying the sight of Omega dying. Perhaps this was what he needed to shake himself loose...

But as the last of the Omega ships were destroyed, and the carnage ebbed away, the junior Manchester's smile began to fade, and his chill returned.

Christine's smile faded too, and she just managed to contain a sigh as she closed her eyes again. Hopefully that had been progress. Hopefully.

Omega-Natosh tore a child in half to vent some his anger. The satisfaction of that kill did little to reduce the sting of what had just happened, though: he'd gotten too arrogant, and he'd lost a small fleet to these fuckers.

Seriously, who the fuck did the Kroggs think they were playing with? Sure, they killed his first black wave fleet, but they did it at one-to-one ratio. What did they think they'd be able to do against 5,000?

They'd just have to learn the hard way, the bastards.

Meantime, he had to reprioritize. He had to acknowledge his own fuckups, and move on. Stupid bastards. Shit.

As the last of his ships died, Omega-Natosh stomped around in the Krogg War memorial on Genesis. It would take a while longer for all his minions to be killed on the surface of the world... but not that much longer. There were plenty of Krogg soldiers there.

And then they'd probably be thorough, and burn all the bodies, so he didn't have anything left there to work with...

Omega's frustration bubbled now through every one of his major avatars. Omega-Gillian wandered into a cell with a family of Freetowners and started mutilating. Omega-Paine cut off his own arm on Ecclesia.

None of it really helped.

So *frustrating*.

So mad at himself. He'd vowed to himself not to get overconfident when he had his chance to come back, but now he was facing a two-front war and a long campaign against Kroggs who clearly still loved killing. The Earthers might be do-gooder cattle, but he had to respect the Kroggs.

Even without their Queen, they'd be a headache.

So he needed to reprioritize fast. If he wanted the Earthers dead, he was going to have to do it quickly, before the Kroggs could regroup and get their ships to Earth.

The next attack would be against Earth, then, and Omega would have to take it more seriously.

Well, that he could do: 5,000 ships, all slightly better than those he'd just lost at Krogg, and nine *billion* minions, the army he'd grown and cloned out of segments of the Genesis and Ecclesia populations... that would seal the Earthers.

He'd take back Earth, and deal with the rest of the galaxy afterwards.

No more fucking playing.

"Signal coming in from the planet," *Formidable's* Signal Officer drew Chronos' attention, and the cat nodded.

"In the tank."

He didn't ask who was calling — it would either be Wiskar or Krag... and it was the latter. The Krogg appeared in the plot with a broad grin, and he nodded to his Earther friend.

"I'm so happy to see you well, Chronos. I feared we'd left it too late."

Chronos stared at Krag for a moment, and realized he didn't know how to reply.

"I'm sorry we had to wait so long... I see that *Grimbold, Namur* and *Medusa* have been lost. I can only hope that some of the Admirals were saved... but we had to leave it late, you see. We couldn't reveal ourselves until Omega was trapped within the perimeter."

The elation Chronos had felt earlier unraveled as Kragran mentioned the lost Admirals, and he nodded, "I... I can understand it. But Krag... you could have told us, you know. Told us so we could plan for this..."

Krag's smile seemed to sadden, and the Warlord shook his head, "If I'd told you we had this fleet ready, I don't think you'd have trusted us. You'd have been rightly suspicious of us rearming under your nose. Better this way. Better that we debut with proof of our friendship. My dear friend."

Shaking his head briefly, Chronos started to object, "I'm sure we... we..."

But he wasn't sure. He didn't know what he'd have thought if 2,000 Krogg ships had appeared around his tiny squadron and offered assistance. Perhaps they would have gotten along well, and integrated... perhaps there would have been suspicion.

It didn't matter. Omega had been *beaten* today, thanks to the *Kroggs*.

Karl Kandam, Garvin Jardaw, Liz Hastings and Fox Magnus were all gone, though. It wasn't a one-sided win by any reckoning...

"Call from *Death* coming in..." the Signal Officer managed not to sound surprised by the unsubtle name of the hailing vessel, and Krag perked up.

"I'll join that conversation with you, if you don't mind," the Warlord said eagerly.

Chronos could only shrug, "Sure."

Kardrath appeared next to Kragran, smiling as widely as his leader, "Admiral Claw, it has been a glorious day of killing! It is our honor to have fought alongside you."

Beginning to nod politely in reply, Chronos stopped when another figure glowed to life next to the Krogg.

"Good shooting, Chronos. It's *great* to see you buddy... sorry if I sound stunned, got hit on my head when I tried to energy-hyper *Chimera*, but Kardrath picked us up you see..."

Fox Magnus.

Having written his old friend off for dead when *Chimera* didn't turn up for the fight, Chronos now couldn't help but smile again. And then to laugh.

"Fox..." he said as his chin dropped with a sudden onrush of fatigue. "Dammit Fox. Dammit I'm so happy to see you."

The relief was spelled all over Chronos Claw's face, and as Fox Magnus laughed and nodded in agreement, some of the shroud of darkness seemed to lift from the shoulders of the cat.

Omega was beaten here, and they weren't *all* dead.

A good day.

CHAPTER 59

"Well, that's something you don't see every day."

Setter Caine somberly looked sideways at Lab Forepaw. The pair were sitting in the cockpit of their pinnace, slowly circling the darkened hull of a ship they'd called their home for many years. Many particularly dark years...

ENS Orion was floating quietly over Earth, its forward hull splayed open and charred from the impact of what everyone presumed was a mutant Genesis tug. After weathering all those battles, in all those places far from home, *Orion* had at last accepted damage — severe damage — at the hands of Omega.

And worse, neither Lab Forepaw nor Setter Caine had been aboard for it.

Sure, there had been many Captains and flag officers on that great ship over the years, but these two canines had been aboard *Orion* for the most dangerous days. It almost felt wrong for the ship to accept injury without them being with it.

But such was the war with Omega.

So the two old friends quietly circled their former ship in a pinnace, watching and pointing, taking deep breaths, wincing, and wondering at how the old First Rate had even *survived* that sort of hit.

"Bay two says they can take us aboard... if we're careful..." the pilot of the pinnace, who'd remained silent as the senior wolves aboard took stock, now looked up over her shoulder. "Shall we go aboard?"

Lab nodded, "Definitely."

The pinnace began angling towards bay two, one of the few unscorched sectors of the ship. Repair crews had already arrived around the massive First Rate to begin checking the damage, but from experience, Caine knew too well that it would take a couple of weeks in dock for that much destruction to be repaired... the same length of time it would have taken one shipyard to build two *Venerable*-class ships of the line.

The question now was whether *Orion* should have priority going in for repairs. The ship was a great symbol of Earther might, but at the same time, the yards were working hard on their first order of *Venerable*-class ships of the lines in six years — they'd promised to deliver over fifty within another ten days if uninterrupted...

Well, that question would be dealt with presently.

"Here we go," Lab pointed towards the edges of the flight bay doors as the pinnace slid through, and Setter nodded slowly.

He found it surprisingly tough to let out a breath as the pinnace cruised over the deck and carefully lowered itself. The small craft's feet settled ponderously on the alloy hull, and the sounds of the engines began to fade as the drives wound down.

"Standing by the hatch, sir," the pilot looked back and nodded to the two wolves, and they both came to their feet at the same time, Lab leading the way back out of the cockpit.

The hatch slid open as they reached it, and Lab maintained his lead on the descent, though his pace slowed considerably as he stared at all the scorch marks and ruptures along the internal hull.

"Looks like a *bomb* went off in here," he said in a rasp, and Setter stopped outright and nodded.

"You don't want to see Bay One, sir. We had two boats collide in there, and it went downhill after that."

Setter and Lab both blinked simultaneously, their eyes shifting from the dismal surroundings to one of two bears standing at the bottom of the ramp.

Lab continued down after that pause, coming to a stop before Esther Arbear and taking her hand slowly as his eyes looked up past her. He could see through a hole in the ceiling right into the gym, "How many casualties?"

"Eighty-one dead, over 300 seriously injured," she said quietly, then looked over Lab's shoulder at Setter as he finished descending the ramp. "I'm sorry sir, I promised I wouldn't get a scratch on it."

Setter slowly shook his head before extending his hand to her, "Not your fault at all. You kept old *Orion* alive despite the odds, as I see it."

"Exactly what I've been saying."

Setter felt the wash of relief through his instincts before he even recognized Ursla's voice properly. He wasn't sure how, but she'd masked her presence behind Esther's, and now she stepped around her Flag Captain with a sad smile.

"We were driven out, Setter. He has Freetown, now," Ursla's tone was dark — it sent a shiver through Setter, reminding him for a moment of the day Savanna Felix had died…

He put that thought down quickly.

"Jax, Sarah and Pat were aboard?"

Ursla nodded, "We were in the briefing room. I nearly got cut in half by shrapnel but Jax got me down in time. They're already heading back to their ships, to get some order restored."

Setter looked around again as he nodded, and darkness seemed to descend upon him. His old champion of a ship had been victim of a surprise attack. Taken completely off guard. And not because of a poor crew, or bad conditions, but because Omega was that good.

"Esther, would you mind showing me around? I'd... I'd like to see my old ship," Lab looked to the new Flag Captain of the great First Rate, and she nodded once.

"Gladly. Any advice you have, too..."

She gestured towards one of the hatches out of the compartment — one now propped open by a cargo container — and the two set off with quick nods from Ursla and Setter.

For a moment Setter just gazed at their backs. He watched Lab step out of the bay into a ship that had once been the invincible home to both of them.

He'd faced his nemesis aboard this ship, and now Omega had reduced it to a wounded wreck...

As if listening to his thoughts, *Orion* blew two overhead relays in protest. Caine looked up as sparks showered down to the deck and took the hint.

Alright, my old friend, you're wounded, but you're still alive.

"It was bad?" Setter's question was quiet, and Ursla's sad smile stretched slightly.

"As bad as the recordings, and worse I think. We got off lightly in orbit, all things considered. It looks like Genesis ships have a big blind spot we need to close. But everyone's doing as well as can be expected."

Setter's ears twitched and his eyes drifted down to the deck, "And you, old friend?"

"I'm home. How are you holding? Without Elandra, I mean."

Setter blinked. That's right, Andra had been guarding Freetown when London had been annihilated.

"I'm here," he said quietly. "And Phealan is helping with the weight."

He stared at the deck.

"That's about it for now."

Ursla nodded, knowing well that nothing else needed to be said for the moment. Her instincts and Setter's interlocked and they traded pain and despair, and neither said a thing about those sentiments.

Omega was killing them, but they weren't going to let it show...

"We'll have to find a way to stop him," Setter interrupted what probably should have been a long silence with that comment.

"Seems everything we do, he expects," Ursla answered as she scanned the blackened walls of the bay. "It's funny, I think I was standing just about right here when I met Liz that day. Remember that day?"

Setter's ears twitched and he nodded, "I thought then that it was a long one. If I'd known then what I know now..."

Ursla smiled more heartily at that, "Just as well you didn't. You'd have gone into a cave and not come out, if you'd had any sense."

A short laugh escaped the old grey wolf, "Indeed. Every good deed it seems, is coming back to punish us."

"Now that's just too much pessimism. What word from Krogg?" Ursla frowned down at Setter, and he shook his head.

"None yet..."

That was the cosmic cue, and in the fullest tradition of Earther timing, the comm chirped — or in this case hissed, since the speakers were bent out of shape.

"Bridge to Admiral Ursla, energy-hyper pod just arrived in local space, broadcasting broadband."

Ursla took a deep breath and nodded — to herself, since no one on the other side of the speaker could have seen her anyway — then waved her hand towards the door.

"Best place to get bad news, the bridge of this ship," Ursla's smile remained.

With a weary nod, Setter led the way to the door.

CHAPTER 60

Narosh stood now in a place where only one Larosian had ever stood before — inside the command chamber of the Krogg people. Technically, of course, Torallis, the Captain-Elite who had joined Andros Grieve in the mission against Krogg 'A', had stood in a different version of this chamber... but to Narosh the distinction was immaterial.

This was the seat of the enemy, home to the Krogg's military leader. The telepathic amplification abilities of this room let a mind reach across the galaxy to give orders... it was a mighty place.

I still feel awkward being here, Novash was standing next to Narosh, and the more senior Larosian nodded in agreement. These two, escorted by Captain-Elite Tovarrin, had been invited to meet with Kragran, Kragthar and Kardrath, the leading Krogg Warlords.

And despite having looked into Kardrath's mind — and having probed it deeply — Narosh still felt unsettled. After centuries of fighting these Kroggs, and after the death of Praaxus and the Son of Praaxus, this was a difficult place to come to meet friends.

I think it will take... "...some getting used to," Kragran started his greeting with a thought, but decided to finish it with words.

The Warlord and his two deputies entered the chamber behind the Larosians, and now hurried forward to greet them with Earther-style handshakes.

"Admiral-of-a-Fleet, Admiral-of-a-Division, and Captain-Elite... I am very pleased to be able to meet you under these circumstances," Krag extended hands to each of them at the same time — one of the benefits of extra arms — and then stepped back to allow his junior Warlords to do the same.

"I'm speaking because I think it might be easiest for us both to communicate that way, at least for now. For so many centuries, our only telepathic contact was for war... speech is the communications medium of the race that brought us together here, so perhaps that's best," Kragran rounded the Larosians now, to stand opposite them for parley. "Of course, probe my mind deeply whenever you wish to... I don't want you to worry that we're hiding anything."

"You do understand why we might think that, Warlord Kragran?" Novash asked politely.

Krag smiled, "Ours was a long, bitter war. I remember most of it. I was lucky to survive it."

"As were we all, I think," Narosh agreed.

The Larosian's silver eyes locked onto Krag's single one, and for a moment the two old leaders simply studied each other. Within his veins, Narosh's Earther-influenced blood seemed to tingle a little, as if he could sense a connection with the Warlord that was new, and different.

"Old nemeses, standing together in this place... it's momentous, in a way, isn't it?" Krag spoke after that silence. "The beginning of a new era."

Narosh continued to study the Krogg, and then he decided to take the next step, *It is a momentous occasion. And I'll admit, Kragran, that we Larosians are not comfortable with it. Not yet. We don't doubt your deeds today, and... and I do trust you. But centuries of pain cannot be easily washed away. With time, perhaps...*

With time, Krag agreed, honored that Narosh was willing to communicate telepathically, *we will be friends. I believe that, and I look forward to it. That we can help right some of the wrongs our Queen, and indeed,* we *committed against your Empire. But for the moment, I think we agree on our mission.*

"The Earthers," Novash had of course 'heard' their telepathic conversation, and now he joined it, verbally at first, but then opening his mind. *Omega wants to destroy them. Omega used them to get to both of us, but now he wants them dead.*

Our friends and allies, Krag concurred. *Without them, you and I would both be dead... we would have died annihilating each other at the end of the last war. Omega is trying to use those good deeds against our friends, but I mean to prove him wrong. I mean to kill him.*

You still enjoy the kill? Narosh asked, and Krag frowned.

"When the cause is just, it is the most savory thing to kill. That hasn't changed," Krag confirmed with words. "And Omega is a just kill to make. We two, you and I, must join together with the Earthers against the plague. They have stood on their own for too long."

Narosh studied Krag's face as he said that. This friendship the Krogg was speaking of — this hurried alliance, in support of the Earthers, did feel right. What the Warlord had said was truth: the Earthers had been struggling, alone but for the humans, to stop Omega. Now it was time for old enemies who both owed much to the Earthers, to put aside their differences, and join the fight with all the force they could manage.

That thought drew a smile to Narosh's face, and he bow-nodded, "You used to be my enemy, Kragran. Today you are my ally. One day... one day, we'll see about friendship."

With a smile Krag bow-nodded in reply, "Yes, we will. Old nemeses, off to war together!"

Chronos Claw couldn't help but hug Fox Magnus as soon as he came down the ramp of his pinnace, and Fox hugged his old friend right back.

"Glad someone made it," Chronos said quietly as he pulled away. "There don't seem to be many of us left."

Thena Venus had descended behind her husband, and now she hugged Chronos too.

"Search and rescue teams finding anyone?" Fox asked softly, rubbing his sore head as he did.

"Not so far. Minnie Maximane is coordinating that right now, then she'll be over to see us. But other than you and me, the only flag officers we have left came from the other galaxy. We lost *everyone*."

Fox's ear twitched, and he sighed, "Well. At least Krag's on side with us."

A small smile came to Chronos' face, "I knew the old Lord had it in him."

Minnie Maximane had left *Galahad's* bridge in the hands of Captain Mel Ramsay, and was on the flight deck as escape pods from Earther ships were being pulled in. She couldn't really do anything to improve the efficiency of the process — the crew knew what they were doing, and didn't need more hands — but at least she could see with her own eyes how many were being saved.

Not as many as she'd have liked, that much was certain.

"Another one coming in — clear the deck!" *Galahad's* deck chief barked the warning, and the Earthers working to clear the last pod that had been brought aboard scrambled out of the way.

Minnie watched as the next lifeboat came in — a battered one from a Survey Service 64. Boats pulled it into the flight bay, then cruised right out the opposite side to continue with their recovery operations. As the deck grav tractors lowered the pod to rest, a team of technicians and medics hurried over to it, and cracked open its hatches.

There was the usual bustle of motion, and then several Earthers climbed out of the pod, haggard, bloody, but quite active. A couple of hover gurneys were summoned, and then two humans were laid out on them, and pulled away.

Minnie took a deep breath as she watched the efficient process. It was comforting, she found, to see people saved. Particularly when so many had been lost. Like her uncle Garvin, dear friend to her father...

As the gurneys passed Minnie, her thoughts halted with surprise. Missing one leg, Liz Hastings was floated past her. Jessica Forbes was on the next gurney, in stasis so that she wouldn't die from the piece of shrapnel sticking out of her chest.

That was... that was two people Minnie had counted as dead. Important people.

A smile crept onto the lioness' face, and she decided to go call Chronos Claw. He'd be happy.

Graham ignored the knocking on his cabin door. He sat silently staring at the bulkhead, the elation of watching Omega writhe having long since ebbed away. There was no lasting pleasure from that, he'd just wait until the next time he could hurt Omega, and then feel the pleasure again.

For now, his emotions were buried, and he would wait. Omega was not finished. Help from the Kroggs would make him easier to kill, but he was still powerful, and still dangerous. This fight was not over. Far from it.

Graham didn't notice at first when Christine opened his hatch uninvited, and sat down next to him on his bed.

He only noticed when her hand covered one of his, and then he blinked and looked at his young aide, whose eyes were growing older and older as the days passed. She was becoming part Earther, and it was serving her well.

She smiled sadly at him, "Your smile's gone."

He nodded, "It was a smile derived from the desire to kill. That hasn't passed, but the opportunity has. So the smile is gone for now."

Christine's eyebrows played upwards at the honesty of Graham's words, and then she looked away, "Well, there'll be more opportunity soon."

"There will be," he agreed.

They just sat there for a while, until Christine left him to his peace.

"Not all of us," Chronos couldn't help but smile. "Liz lost the same leg the Crusaders took off her years ago, but she's still alive. She might be able to get back in this fight."

He was standing in the Krogg command chamber, having landed an hour after Narosh's party left.

Kragran's hands clapped together in happiness, "I'm so glad!"

His words were genuine. Now he turned and shook his head, "Chronos, I am so happy we are finally able to be allies like this. It was distressing not to tell you for all of those years."

Chronos' smile tightened a little. He felt awkward about discussing the deception, but he nodded, "It's worked out. Now if Omega will just give us enough time we can get some of your ships through the Larosian galaxy down to Earth... because you know that's where he's going next."

Krag shook his head instantly, "No my friend, we're not sending any ships to Earth through the Larosian galaxy."

The smile on Chronos' face faded, and he feared the other shoe was about to drop, "Well.. we can't make it safely or quickly through our own galaxy. It took Fox weeks just to get to Gibraltar. Unless... you're not sending anyone..."

Kragran laughed, "No my friend, we're going through this galaxy. We'll go by way of energy-hyper."

Chronos' expression neutralized. Energy-hyper? Fox had just proved rather dramatically that energy-hyper wasn't the most user-friendly drive system. His response reflected his confusion, "I... don't get it."

Krag held up a couple of hands, "I'll have to get someone better qualified than myself to explain the technical details, but suffice it to say, those new Hyper Motherships you saw… the ones without any corvettes aboard them. You know the ones?"

"Yes, *Death* and its siblings," Chronos confirmed.

Krag smiled, "Those ones, yes! They were grown so that between them, they could carry a fleet of warships through energy-hyper. They'll get us all to Earth in less than a day, when the time comes."

Chronos' eyebrows shot up, "Really?"

Krag grinned and nodded emphatically, "Really."

As seemed to be the norm now, Chronos didn't know what to say. He'd have to look at the science, see if it made sense… but somehow he doubted Krag would have made this promise if the Kroggs hadn't already confirmed it was possible.

"Well… thanks, my friend," Chronos finally managed to smile, and Krag beamed in his alien, Krogg manner.

"You're more than welcome."

CHAPTER 61

Phealan Caine found his father sitting on the beach of their estate, staring out to sea again. But unlike the last time the two wolves had been on this rocky shore, a feeling of relief — not loss — dominated the air.

Kragran's words seemed to be stuck on repeat in Phealan's mind — great words, that had come along with great images. The black wave had been destroyed, and the Kroggs had destroyed it.

"This plague seeks to tell you Earthers that all the good you have done has been foolish and useless. We Kroggs have benefited more than any race from your kindness, and now it is our privilege to call you our allies, and our friends..."

Chills had run up Phealan's spine when that message had been broadcast through his holo tank. Everywhere across Earth, the news from Krogg 'A' had been spread.

"We will fight to the very last if we must, to protect our friends, as they protected us."

Earthers across the planet, and in the space around it, had smiled and felt such relief at Krag's words. It didn't make Omega go away — not at all — but it gave the Earthers a new, better chance.

They had lost so much, fighting for what they believed in. If they'd been selfish, they would have let Freetown burn and Krogg stand alone, and just concentrated their defenses at Earth. They might have made their home system an impenetrable fortress... but as Earthers always did, they went out and fought for what they believed.

Each time they fought against Omega, they seemed to lose. Omega knew them too well, had set this whole plan in motion just to kill the Earthers, and the humans along with them.

But the good deeds of the Earthers' past were coming back to *help* them. The Larosians and the Kroggs between them had contributed to two real victories over the plague. With those former rivals at their side, the Earthers had a chance.

Maybe — just *maybe* — they could beat the plague that had created them.

That feeling of hope filled the air over this beach, and as Phealan felt it run through his veins, he smiled to himself. This was what they'd needed... now they could go on.

"You were right."

Setter's words shook Phealan out of his thoughts, and jogging the rest of the way down to the beach, he came to stand next to the rock the elder Caine was sitting on, "About?"

"The recording of Audrey. You knew exactly what Omega was trying to do to us... how he was trying to take away our hope by making it feel as though the good we'd done was for nothing," Setter was actually smiling as he said it.

Phealan's ear twitched, "I suppose I was."

Chuckling at his son's modesty, Setter pulled an injector from his pocket, "You aren't tainted by the last war, but you're still wiser because of it. You're exactly what Omega doesn't want to face. Take this."

Pulling the injector from his father's hand, Phealan frowned at it, then looked back up, "The cure for Type 0?"

Setter nodded, "Take it and you'll be telepathic within hours. I had mine about an hour ago, so I'm still waiting."

Without hesitation, the young Caine put the injector against his wrist and triggered it. The scrubber that would remove Omega from his veins went to work.

"We're not guaranteed to win after this, are we?" Phealan found a nearby rock and hopped onto it.

"No. The Kroggs give us a better chance than we had, but they also caught Omega off guard. He's going to be much more cautious and much less brash now."

Phealan smiled, "So after all he's done to wrong-foot us, we'll finally be doing something to get him off balance."

Setter blinked at the remark — he hadn't actually thought of it that way. He'd basked in the good news with Ursla while on *Orion's* bridge, and he'd gone to Admiralty House where bright smiles and reaffirmed confidence had greeted him.

Everywhere he went, Earthers had been happy to have a new ally in the fight, and to know that the sacrifices of the last war, and the decision to give the Kroggs a chance, had not been for nothing. No matter what Omega said, the Earthers had done right...

But no one had viewed the question from the other side, and again Setter realized how lucky he was to have Phealan's fresh mind considering this situation. Omega *had* to be uncomfortable now. The plague had prided himself on his omnipotence... his ability to out-wit the venerable Earthers.

Now, though, he himself had been outwitted, and he faced enemies he didn't know as well as he knew the Earthers. Certainly, he'd witnessed both the Kroggs and the Larosians in action during the last war, but his connection to them was nowhere near as intimate as the one he had with the Earthers.

He hadn't created them. He hadn't lived in their blood for centuries.

They were new enemies for him — friends the Earthers had earned through blood and honor.

So while Setter didn't doubt that the plague would come again, and that this time it would be a massive strike at Earth with a mind to end the Earthers once and for all, Phealan was right. The plague was off balance. His hubris had been rewarded with a significant loss, the way the Earthers' own confidence had been.

The advantage hadn't turned to the Earthers, then, but perhaps the playing field had been leveled.

"I think we need to work on him now, dad," Phealan's eyes had narrowed as he too looked out to sea, the cold wind brushing through his fur. "We need to make it real personal for him, so that we get him focused on smaller issues. We have a chance here to really steal the initiative."

Setter looked over at his son with a smile, "You're getting the hang of this pretty quickly."

Chuckling, Phealan shrugged, "I have the advantage of not having already won a war. I'm an unknown quantity to him, so he hasn't been after me. I just... I just know what I'm seeing as I sit back and observe. But now I think it's time we go after him."

With a nod, Setter looked back to the sea, "He's going to come here, one way or the other. So it's better for us if we make sure he's agitated and off his game when he arrives."

"It'll be a big fight when he does come," Phealan concurred.

The wolves sat in silence for a moment, and Setter suddenly felt a difference in his mind. His thoughts were the same, but they felt a little freer than before.

Mind is clearing, he thought to himself.

Can he see us?

Setter frowned at that thought, which seemed unusual, but he ignored it and looked back to the ocean. Soon he'd be able to get into the room with that Omega avatar... and there, with a fully telepathic mind, he could start rattling the plague's cage.

And perhaps his idea could turn into a plan... time would tell.

A couple of wolves from the pack were on the beach, one coming to a stop next to Setter, the other near Phealan.

"Hi guys," the junior Caine smiled and petted the new arrival in a friendly fashion.

Reaching out with his instincts, he sensed the wolf's intention, and then looked over to his father.

"They're moving on for a while."

Setter nodded, scratching the wolf next to him behind the ears, "They've been around for weeks, I figured they'd leave soon."

The wolves did as the Earthers' instincts suggested, and trotted away moments later.

Watching them go only reinforced the truth in Setter's mind: Omega had to be stopped, before he could victimize this planet again.

Good luck…

EPILOGUE

Setter Caine stepped into the dark chamber below Fengate Hospital, and his eyes settled on the plague avatar in the cage. Omega-King grinned back at him, and then clawed briefly at his mind.

Aha, you had that shot. So we can play...

Feeling a tug, Setter let Omega move their thoughts to a new playing field. His eyes closed, then opened, and instead of white and amber they were swirling with blue light. That was what anyone looking at the Supreme Consul from the outside saw. From within, Setter found himself standing in a white space — all white, but for himself... and Omega-Natosh standing opposite him.

"Telepathic plane, this. The Kroggs and the Larosians used to use them a lot. I think they're good for heckling," Omega-Natosh grinned.

Setter's eyebrows raised and he looked around him. It was nothing but whiteness.

"Well, it's austere enough," the wolf smiled, and then looked back at his adversary. "Why is it Natosh I'm seeing, and not that poor spacer King?"

The avatar shrugged and morphed its appearance to that of Omega-King, "It doesn't matter how I appear, just that I can squish you like a bug."

Setter frowned unsympathetically, "Like a bug? You can't think of a better description?"

Omega-King snorted a laugh and shook her head, "You think you're going to win an argument with me on semantics?"

"I'm not even arguing with you, my dear foe. Just came in to have a little look around, see what it was like to be a telepath."

"Your first day with telepathic powers and you come to the big kids' sandbox. Bright," Omega-King shook her head.

Setter's smile broadened a little, "You've stopped swearing. Nervous?"

"Fuck off, fucker."

A genuine laugh escaped Setter, and then he turned his back on the plague avatar — not something he'd normally have done, but now it felt right.

"You're getting a taste of what it feels like to be wrong-footed the way you've been wrong-footing us," Setter said in a cool tone. "How's it sitting with you?"

"Fine. Because I know I'm still going to win. I have *5,000* ships getting ready to come here to crush you. And nine billion soldiers," Omega-King spat those numbers with the petulance of a child in an argument, and as the plague made the claims, the white all around seemed to flash for brief seconds, showing images of the mighty force.

"That's impressive," Setter turned back to the plague, his hands linking behind his back. "Don't mistake me, I don't think we're going to win easily. But I'm not convinced you can beat us, even with all that."

Omega-King lunged forward two steps and locked eyes with Setter, "You're like the first Caine, you know. Did you know your great-great-great... however the fuck many greats... did you know he was the first Earther to come out of his mother? He was the one who caught me the first time. You're like him."

Setter's eyebrows bounced in surprise, "I'm like the last Earther to defeat you? Isn't that something you should keep to yourself?"

Omega-King leaned close to Setter's face, "He didn't defeat me, did he? Here I am, having just wiped out most of humanity *again*, and the Larosians too. You're not going to do any better than he did."

Setter's smile faded, and he leaned even closer to the face of the avatar, "Maybe I won't. Maybe a mind as big as yours can't be defeated. But I'm not going to die without trying to beat you."

"Then this *will* be fun," Omega-King smiled viciously. "I am one mind, it's good you recognize that. One consciousness in a mind bound by telepathy, that spans billions of billions to the power of billions of cells, scattered across two galaxies. You'll never destroy all of me."

Setter's eyes narrowed as he studied the avatar's face, and Omega-King predicted his thoughts, "Try a cure on me. Go ahead. My Krogg defenses will stop your drugs from ever getting to me. Try it."

Setter continued to stare, wordlessly, and Omega-King's expression flinched slightly, revealing the question that seemed to cross the plague's mind... Setter was calm and unmoving... did the fucker have something up his sleeve?

"You're worried that I have something up my sleeve," a grin spread back across Setter's face, and Omega-King's expression twisted into a snarl even as the body morphed back to Omega-Natosh's. Damned Earther was pulling thoughts out of his mind.

"Yes, I am pulling thoughts out of your mind you bastard," Setter took a step forward, and his grin disappeared again. "You and I will fight soon. We'll finish this soon."

"My old nemesis, finally willing to stand up and face me," Omega-Natosh spat, and Setter simply studied the avatar's face.

"Today I've seen old nemeses become new friends. I've seen enemies learn from their foes... and change. Maybe that's what we're supposed to do, we Earthers. You know us so well, Omega, maybe it's time we learn from the Kroggs and Larosians, and evolve our ways."

Omega-Natosh wore a look of disgust, and that brought Setter's smile back.

"You know what I'd call that?" the wolf asked pleasantly, and the avatar shook his head.

The white world went away, and Setter's eyes returned to their white-and-amber, the blue light draining from them.

As the real world surrounded him, the wolf was still smiling, and now he turned for the door.

"Don't you say it, you fucker. That's so lame when you fucking say it."

Setter laughed as he walked, "So you do know what I'd call that, don't you?"

The avatar in the energy cage hissed at Setter as he reached the door. Then the wolf turned and his smile grew.

"We'll see how it works, very soon."

The Supreme Consul left the avatar spitting with anger, but as he went, he said the infuriating words:

"The *nemesis* equation."

APPENDIX A: CHARACTERS

Omega's onslaught continues. Here's a reminder of who stands against the plague, and who's become *part* of it.

Arbear, Ellen – Lieutenant
A marine with Cadmus Howler's elite 2/54th who was stationed aboard *Renown*, Ellen is the daughter of venerable Krogg War Captain Esther Arbear. Ellen now serves in *Carnarvon*, stationed in Larosian space, helping command the marine company of Joyce Furgus.

Arbear, Esther – Captain
During the Krogg War, Esther Arbear was one of the Earther Navy's finest Captains. Having retired after the end of that conflict, she has rejoined the service in order to help battle Omega. She has been posted as Flag Captain aboard *ENS Orion.*

Bengal, Mustafa – Brigadier
A veteran marine and the Brigadier commanding the Guards Brigade of the Light Division, Bengal has been assigned to protect Freetown.

Brawn, Colin – Lieutenant General
Colin Brawn commanded the marines aboard Fox Magnus' *Atlas* during the Krogg War, and has since moved up through the ranks to command the elite Light Division. Tasked with the protection of Freetown, he will lend his exceptional experience to the defense of the colony.

Broadpaw, Varnon – First Consul
Varnon Broadpaw is the First Consul of the Earther people. One of the most respected veterans of the Krogg War, he has a keen military mind and a bad sense of humor — though the latter quality has been considerably dampened by Omega's grizzly successes.

Caine, Elandra – Doctor
Elandra Caine was the wife of Setter and mother of Phealan, and the greatest genetic scientist the Earther people had ever known. Her efforts to cure the

plague were halted when she was killed during Omega's destruction of London.

Caine, Phealan – Deputy Supreme Consul of Earth
Phealan has assumed the role of deputy to his father, and seeks now to help Setter carry the burden of leadership in the battle against Omega. Unscarred by the Krogg War, he brings a fresh perspective to the battle with the plague.

Caine, Setter – Supreme Consul of Earth
Setter Caine is the patriarch of the Earther people, and commands them now in the battle against Omega. Reeling from the death of his wife, but benefiting from the support of his son, he is the Earthers' greatest hope for victory in the battle against the plague.

Claw, Chronos – Vice Admiral
A veteran (and subsequent Commander) of Fox Magnus' *Flame*, Chronos Claw finished the Krogg War as one of the Earther Navy's most distinguished sloop officers. Electing to stay out at Krogg 'A' after the war, he moved up through the ranks and now commands the Earther force protecting Krogg space.

Clyde, Jason – Commissioner
A former marine, Jason Clyde is the Commissioner of the Freetown Constabulary police force. His men and women will make up a significant part of their colony's ground defense in the case of an attack by Omega.

Conroy, Pat – Historian
Pat Conroy finds himself with no formal role. With Genesis taken by Omega, his life as a historian is either on hold or over, and with his wife Sarah isolating herself in order to focus on her duties, he cannot even serve to comfort or advise. He has thus seconded himself to Freetown, to help the colony prepare for any assault by Omega's landing forces.

Cuttar, Ernile – Sergeant Major
Ernile Cuttar is the Sergeant Major commanding the elite Recon Squad attached to 2/54th and General Beckett Lupus. Having fought alongside both Beckett and Colonel Cadmus Howler in the Krogg War, he is acknowledged as one of the most elite marines in the Earther service.

DeBrooke, Audrey – Governor
Now a widow, Audrey DeBrooke finds herself Governing Freetown in what might be its darkest hour. The threat of Omega looms large, and the people of the colony will rely on her leadership to see them through.

Dune, Ami – Rear Admiral
Ami (Cairn) Dune was one of the Krogg War's best-known officers, her exploits having been covered extensively by Will Rust and the Genesis Free Press. After the war she married Zed Dune, her fellow wartime Commodore, and joined the Earther Consulate.

Dune, Zed – Rear Admiral
One of the most innovative thinkers in the history of the Earther Navy Engineering Corps, Zed's fingerprints can be found on the first versions of Earther hyper charges and energy-hyper cutters. He is also an experienced frigate officer.

Forbes, Jessica – Captain
Formerly Pat Conroy's Flag ArcColonel, Jessica Forbes joined the Earther Survey Service after the war, seeking to escape the politics and return to her love: space travel. She has worked with Liz Hastings for a decade in this capacity.

Forepaw, Labrador – First Lord of the Admiralty
Lab Forepaw is probably the best officer ever to serve in the Earther Navy, though his confidence was shaken by Omega's misdirection during his attack on Earth. He remains determined to battle the plague, but he will have to continue to adapt if he hopes to see victory.

Furgus, Jax – Admiral
During the Krogg War, Jax Furgus had many ships shot out from him. Now he commands the recommissioned 74-gun *Aboukir*, and is attached to Ursla's command at Freetown.

Furgus, Joyce – Captain
Commanding a company of Cadmus Howler's elite 2/54th based aboard *Carnarvon*, Jax Furgus' daughter remains in the Larosian galaxy, assisting the Earthers' allies and Graham Manchester in their efforts to restore a working Larosian fleet.

Gunth, Wilbur Percival III – Cruising Master
Mister Gunth was Fox Magnus' Cruising Master in *Atlas* during the Krogg War, and has taken up that post again aboard *Chimera*. He is one of the First Space Lord's most invaluable veterans.

Hastings, Elizabeth – Group Captain
Liz Hastings spent decades as the matriarch of the Genesis Navy, and then twenty years as president of that world. Seeking to escape Genesis after the end

of her term, she joined the Earther Survey Service, and is now skippering the exploration-configured 64 *Grimbold.*

Hobbes, Ronax – Captain
A carrier skipper during the Krogg War, Ron Hobbes returned to the service when Lab Forepaw asked him to serve as Flag Captain of *Aboukir* on a run to Freetown. He now serves with Jax Furgus aboard that ship, and sits at Freetown preparing to counter whatever moves Omega attempts to make.

Hodge, Gillian – Avatar
Gillian Hodge isn't herself anymore: her body belongs to Omega. The plague was able to infect her (despite the protection of Earther regen treatments) by infesting her unborn fetus, and now she is one of his favorite avatars. Omega-Gillian has killed many innocent humans in unspeakable ways.

Howler, Cadmus – Colonel
Cadmus Howler had commanded Beckett Lupus' old recon squad on Krogg 'A', and since then he's remained at Beckett's side, turning the recon squad into a special escort unit for its former Sergeant, and eventually taking over command of 2/54th. He has returned to Earth space with *Renown*, and remains ready for action.

Jardaw, Garvin – Admiral
Formerly the commander of Draco Maximane's escort force, Garvin commands the Earther forces on the far side of Genesis, including the fleet at Gibraltar and the ships at Krogg 'A'. He remained in the service partly in honor of his fallen friend Maximane, and now must face a possible Omega onslaught against his side of the galaxy.

Jeffries, Ed – Commodore
A veteran of Pat's Pirates, Ed went to Freetown after the Krogg War, and rose to command of *Savanna Felix*, one of the colony's new Earther-hybrid warships. He remains one of the senior officers in the Freetown service, and with Audrey having been named Governor, he has taken control of what Freetown ships remain.

Kandam, Karl – Vice Admiral
Karl Kandam has been the commanding officer at Gibraltar intermittently over the years since the Krogg War. Having assumed that post shortly after the base's activation, he is the leading expert in its operation. During the evacuation of Gibraltar, he will return to mobile ship command.

Kardrath – Peacelord
Kardrath is the Krogg assigned to command the massive new Krogg Navy. He looks forward to revealing it, and its Earther-inspired enhancements.

Karr, Farley – Captain
Formerly the skipper of the carrier *Diadem*, Karr joined the Earther Survey Service after the war. He now operates in a survey group with Jessica Forbes and Liz Hastings.

Katt, Tom – Colonel
Colonel Tom Katt commands one of the battalions of the First Guards regiment, attached to the Light Division. A veteran of the Krogg War, he spent time after that conflict on Genesis, assisting the Genesis Marine Corps establish its Special Ops teams. His name is clearly awesome.

Kragran – Peacelord
The leader of the new Krogg people, Kragran committed to developing his race in a new direction unaffected by the evil of their Queen. He works closely with Chronos Claw — so closely that Claw has come to trust him. Kragran intends to take advantage of this trust, and to show the Earthers precisely what the Kroggs have learned during the Earther trusteeship.

Kragthar – Peacelord
The new legions of the Krogg army are commanded by Kardrath. A generally agreeable Krogg, he hungers for the chance to kill again.

Kudlee, Karyn – General
A distinguished veteran of the Krogg War campaigns at Avalon and Amaratsu, Karyn has steadily worked her way up to her current post, General commanding the defenses at Earth. Karyn is decidedly aware of how her last name is pronounced, and she uses her considerable body size to make sure no humans give her grief for being a 'cuddly' bear.

Lazarus, Celia – Doctor
During the siege of Krogg 'A', Celia Lazarus was a medic aboard *Orion*, and it was she who stabilized Narosh after his crash landing on that ship's deck. Her actions saved his life then, and the injections of Earther drugs she gave him spared him from infection by Omega forty years later. Having returned to Earth with *Renown*, Celia takes over the research for a cure to the plague.

Locke, Tom – Commodore
Having skippered carriers during the Krogg War, Tom Locke is an experienced Earther officer. When the first call for reserve officers went out during the Church coup crisis, he was quick to answer, and as such took over the frigate squadron attached to Jax Furgus' command. He remains with Jax at Freetown, preparing to meet Omega.

Lupus, Beckett – General
Beckett Lupus has risen to the top of the Earther Marine Corps in the forty years since the end of the Krogg War, and is thus the overall commander of the service. He is at Earth with his wife in *Renown*.

Lupus, Varnia – Rear Admiral
Varnia (Broadpaw) Lupus is the wife of Beckett Lupus and the daughter of Varnon Broadpaw, and up until the Church coup was the Earthers' senior ambassador to Genesis. She now commands *Renown*, and that ship lies in Earth space.

Magnus, Fox – First Space Lord
First Space Lord Fox Magnus is the commander of the Earther mobile forces — he commands ships away from Earth space while Lab Forepaw controls the Navy from Earth. He is now the overall commander of all forces on the Krogg side of the galaxy. He will be Omega's ultimate opposition in any moves towards the Krogg homeworld.

Magnus, Thena – Vice Admiral
Wife of Fox Magnus, Thena is an elite Admiral in the Earther service. She met Fox while commanding *Vulcan*, one of the 74s in his Batron 186 during the Krogg War. Now she is with him aboard *Chimera*.

Manchester, Graham – ArcGeneral
Having chosen to remain outside his own galaxy aboard the Larosian ship *Carnarvon*, and with his wife under the sway of Omega, Graham has suppressed all emotion. The junior Manchester sibling has taken a page from his elder sister's book: he intends to deny his humanity until his objective is reached. He means to hurt Omega, and he doesn't care what it costs him.

Manchester, Sarah – President, ArcGeneral
As President of Genesis, Sarah witnessed the destruction of her planet and of billions of her people, and then went on to lose the survivors in an Omega ambush. Her guilt is enormous, and it has virtually destroyed her.

Maximane, Minnie – Rear Admiral
Daughter of Draco Maximane, Minnie followed in her father's footsteps and joined the Earther Navy. She now commands a chase force that seeks to destroy Omega's ships in the Larosian galaxy, flying her flag from *ENS Galahad*.

Narosh – Admiral-of-a-Fleet
Narosh was rescued from the clutches of Omega by *Renown*, and was returned to Laros. He now commands the restored ships of the Larosian Navy, and is determined to lead the counterattack against the plague.

Natosh – Avatar
Natosh is no longer himself, but is instead the chief avatar of Omega. He was the vehicle through which Omega captured Genesis, and his physical and telepathic prowess is considerable. He is one of the plague's preferred vehicles for torture and mutilation.

Novash – Admiral-of-a-Division
The first Larosian to ever meet an Earther, Novash has spent the past decades commanding the defensive blockade of Laros. With the move to offensive operations, he joins Admiral-of-a-Fleet Narosh in his counterattack against the plague.

Nightclaw, Dran – Comptroller of the Navy Board
Acknowledged by one and all as the greatest frigate officer who ever lived, Dran is the Comptroller of the Navy Board.

Omega
The creator of the Earthers, Omega is coming for his revenge. The Earther immune system that he created in the twenty-first century was so powerful it defeated him, but now that he has been spliced with Krogg DNA, he's ready to show the Earthers just how nasty he can be. Having already destroyed London, he has a mind to do even more harm...

Paine, Gregory – Grand Chancellor
Once the leader of the Commonwealth of the Faithful, Paine has become an avatar of Omega.

Plummer, James – Commandant
Since the loss of Gillian Hodge to the clutches of Omega, James Plummer has taken over command of the Genesis Marine Corps. He is a young officer, but is seemingly equal to the responsibility. His troops will participate in the defense of Freetown against any landings by the plague.

Ramsay, Mel – Captain
Mel Ramsay's parents served with Draco Maximane over their careers in the Earther Navy, though both survived the destruction of *Engadine* at Krogg 'A'. Forty years later, Mel serves as Flag Captain for Draco's daughter, Minnie. She commands the *Champion*-class *Galahad*.

Sandpelt, Lang – Rear Admiral
Lang Sandpelt was one of the intrepid officers aboard diminutive little *Flame* during the Krogg War, and he has remained with the fleet over the interceding forty years. Stationed now at Gibraltar, he commands two squadrons of *Venerable*-class ships of the line, and he's eager to use them against Omega.

Schaeffer, Christine – ArcLieutenant
Christine Schaeffer is Graham Manchester's aide. In a freak accident on *Genesis One*, she was critically injured, forcing Doctor Celia Lazarus to give her a rapid regen treatment. Unexpected side-effects from that treatment have left all the nerves in her skin hyper-sensitive, confining her to a specially-designed skinsuit that uses stasis fields to create a constant state of sensory deprivation. Despite this torture, she remains loyally at Graham's side aboard *Carnarvon* in the Larosian galaxy.

Schaeffer, Claire – Citizen
With her parents dead and her sister lost, Claire Schaeffer is under the care of the Caines. They hope to help her heal, though they realize she may be a lost cause.

Stowt, Bartemius – Vice Admiral
Barty Stowt was Ami (Cairn) Dune's Flag Captain through the Krogg War, and continued on in the Navy for some years during the peace before retiring. With the rise of Omega, he returned to the fleet, and joined Ursla's command at Freetown.

Tarkham, Alix – Captain
Alix Tarkham developed a reputation as one of the fleet's best hand-to-hand combatants before the Krogg War, and then served with distinction as a fleet officer during that conflict. He commands one of the 74s attached to Jax Furgus' force at Freetown.

Tigar, Artemis – Vice Admiral
Artie Tigar was Andra Ursla's Flag Captain through the entirety of the Krogg War, serving with her aboard *Agamemnon*. He flew his flag from that ship when Omega attacked the New Halifax corridor, and in the battle that followed he lost

both arms and legs. He is thus at Fengate Hospital, awaiting replacements.

Ursla, Andra – Admiral
Andra has taken command of the Allied forces at Freetown, lending her massive experience to the defense of that human colony.

Wiskar, Garnet – Lieutenant General
Garnet Wiskar is a veteran of the assault on Krogg 'A' during the Krogg War, and has since moved on to command the Fourth Division of the Earther Marine Corps. A dapper cat, Wiskar will be responsible for protecting the planet he once assaulted. He finds the task quite agreeable.

THE ENTIRE SERIES FROM ICEBERG PUBLISHING

THE EQUATIONS NOVELS

The Earthers evolved after humans were driven from the Earth by an intelligent bio-weapon dubbed 'Omega'. They are faster, stronger, smarter, wiser, *better* than humans, and they are the only hope for the survivors of the human race as an interstellar war between two great alien powers absorbs the galaxy. But all is not as it seems, and the humans and the Earthers face challenges that overshadow the wars of alien empires and threaten to destroy their civilizations...

The Equations Novels by Kenneth Tam

Book One: THE HUMAN EQUATION (Oct 2003)

Book Two: THE ALIEN EQUATION (May 2004)

Book Three: THE RENEGADE EQUATION (Dec 2004)

Book Four: THE EARTHER EQUATION (July 2005)

Book Five: THE GENESIS EQUATION (July 2006)

Book Six: THE VENGEANCE EQUATION (July 2007)

Book Seven: THE NEMESIS EQUATION (July 2008)

Book Eight: THE DESTINY EQUATION (July 2009)

The Equations Novels are complete, but there are spinoff series and new stories in the Earther universe still to come!

For more information, please visit

www.earther.net

ABOUT THE AUTHOR

Born in 1984 in St. John's, Newfoundland, Kenneth Tam holds both a Bachelor's and Master's degree in history from Wilfrid Laurier University in Waterloo, Canada. His MA thesis examined the creation and operation of the Caribou Hut, a hostel for Allied servicemen in St. John's during the Second World War.

In 2006, Kenneth received a prestigious Canada Graduate Scholarship from the Social Sciences and Humanities Council of Canada. He was also awarded a Balsillie Fellowship at the Centre for International Governance Innovation during 2006-07. In that capacity, he worked for Mr. Paul Heinbecker, Canada's former ambassador and permanent representative to the United Nations. He presently serves as a Communications Consultant for Kitchener–Waterloo's federal Member of Parliament, Peter Braid.

Since releasing the first *Equations* novel in 2003, Tam has promoted his books across Canada, speaking with junior and high school students, delivering writing workshops, and doing book signings at bookstores and Iceberg-organized events. He frequently appears as a guest author at science fiction events across the country.

Kenneth is a partner in Iceberg Publishing, the company he and his family started in 2002. He has authored many of the company's existing titles, and is also responsible for graphic design, including the company logo, website, banners, advertisements, and other marketing materials. He acts as a primary contact with printers and suppliers, and is also key in new author development and recruitment.

He remains very lazy about writing his author bios. When they told him to make this one longer, he mostly copied and pasted it together from the Iceberg website, www.icebergpublishing.com.

www.ingramcontent.com/pod-product-compliance
Lightning Source LLC
LaVergne TN
LVHW091031080826
845145LV00002B/443

* 9 7 8 0 9 8 6 5 0 1 7 7 7 *